Please return items on or before the Due Date printed on your receipt.
Register your email address and you will receive a reminder before your books are due back.
You can register your email address, check the Due Date and renew your loans online at
www.dublincitypubliclibraries.ie
Have your Library Card Number and PIN to hand.
You can also renew your loans in person or by phone.

Leabharlanna Poiblí Chathair Bhaile Átha Cliath
Dublin City Public Libraries

 Comhairle Cathrach
Bhaile Átha Cliath
Dublin City Council

KU-489-986

Discover more at millsandboon.co.uk.

PREGNANT WITH HER BEST FRIEND'S BABY

ALISON ROBERTS

THE SURGEON'S SURPRISE BABY

TINA BECKETT

MILLS & BOON

First Published in Great Britain 2019
by Mills & Boon, an imprint of HarperCollins*Publishers*
1 London Bridge Street, London, SE1 9GF

ISBN: 978-0-263-26976-5

MIX
Paper from
responsible sources
FSC® C007454

This book is produced from independently certified FSC™ paper
to ensure responsible forest management.
For more information visit www.harpercollins.co.uk/green.

Printed and bound in Spain
by CPI, Barcelona

PREGNANT WITH HER BEST FRIEND'S BABY

ALISON ROBERTS

MILLS & BOON

CHAPTER ONE

'Do you know what the French word for a midwife is, Joe?' Maggie Lewis jammed her helmet over her blonde curls but let the ends of her chinstrap dangle as they strode swiftly out to the helipad.

'What's that got to do with anything?' Maggie's crew partner, Joe Wallace, pulled open the side door of the helicopter, briefly obscuring the logo of Wellington's Aratika Rescue Service emblazoned on the side of the aircraft.

'We're going to a woman in labour.'

'Ah…is that what it is? Hasn't come through on my pager yet.'

'Prolonged first stage,' Maggie added. 'And the midwife has called for assistance because she's now caught up with another patient who's having a miscarriage and she can't get back to check on this woman anytime soon.'

Joe stood back to let Maggie climb on board first. Their pilot, Andy, was already in the cockpit, well into an automatic pre-flight routine with the crewman and co-pilot Nick sitting beside him. The rotors were gathering speed and the downdraught was enough to make Joe push his sun-streaked brown hair back off his forehead and out of his eyes before he pulled his helmet on. How was it that he always managed to look as if he was overdue for a haircut?

Maggie fastened her chinstrap as she sat down and then pulled her harness over her shoulders. 'Anyway… I'm sure you don't know what a midwife is in French, so I'll tell you. It's a *sage-femme*. Direct translation is actually "wise woman".'

'Ah…' Joe was grinning as he pulled the door shut behind him. 'I see where this is going. You want to take the lead on this one, don't you, even though it's my turn? And even though you had all the fun of the post-cardiac arrest case we just finished?'

'It was a good case, wasn't it?' Maggie smiled back as she pulled down her microphone, responding affirmatively to Andy's query about whether they were good to go and then watching the ground recede as they lifted into the air. She was still thinking about their last mission, however. 'It's not often you get to bring someone back to life enough to have them cracking jokes with the ED staff when we get there.'

'But you want this one, too.'

'I was a midwife, once upon a time, you know. One of those wise women.'

'Last century, you mean?'

'Hey…you're older than me, mate. I wouldn't go making ageist jokes if I were you.'

'At least I knew I wanted to be a paramedic from the get-go. You had to be a nurse and then a midwife before you saw the light and found your true calling.'

'I must have been crazy,' Maggie muttered. 'I could be working in a nice, fully equipped maternity unit with colleagues who appreciate me and...*whoa*...watch out for those potholes, Andy.'

'Sorry.' But their pilot chuckled. 'It might be a bit of a bumpy ride today. That's Windy Wellington for you.'

'I *do* appreciate you, Maggie,' Joe said a few seconds later. He sounded perfectly sincere but Maggie could still hear a grin in his voice. 'You know that, don't you?'

She shrugged. Joe had been one of the first people she had worked with on the base when she'd joined the crew five years ago. 'You've put up with me long enough, I guess.'

'And there I was thinking it was you who was putting up with me.'

For a second, they caught each other's gaze, with the ease and familiarity that only came after a friendship had had years to gather strength along with the kind of depth that could only come from shared experiences that often involved a life or death struggle. Their banter might push the limits occasionally but the trust and respect between Maggie and Joe was rock solid.

'Actually...' Andy's voice coming through the in-built headphones in their helmets broke that moment of connection. 'It's me who's had to put up with both of you for years now. Years and years of listening to you bicker about who gets to lead which job.'

'We're the dream team,' Joe informed him. 'As well you know.'

'Yeah, yeah... I'm going to toss a coin when we land. Whoever gets heads gets to lead, okay?'

Maggie and Joe shared another swift glance. They both knew it wouldn't actually make any difference. Neither of them had the kind of ego that interfered with clear communication or with deferring to someone who was more skilled in a particular area. They really were a 'dream team' and, while there were many medics on the Aratika Rescue Base that Maggie loved to work with, Joe was definitely her favourite.

'It's not as though we're likely to have to deal with a delivery, anyway,' Joe added. 'If the mother's had a prolonged first stage she'll be exhausted and may not be anywhere near fully dilated. She might end up having a Caesarean. It's the midwife's call to get her into hospital instead of continuing with a home birth. I guess she's requested a chopper because it's an isolated property.'

'Long, unsealed road to the nearest highway, too,' the crewman, Nick, put in. 'I don't imagine a bumpy road like that would be very good for a woman in labour.'

Another pocket of turbulence made Maggie reach for a handhold. 'At this rate, the ride with us into hospital might speed things up as much as a road trip could.'

'We should be out of the worst of it when we get up north a bit,' Andy told them. 'ETA's twenty minutes.'

Maggie peered down at the rugged, forest-covered hills and nearby coastline beneath them.

'Isn't that the Castle Cliffs resort down there?'

'Where Cooper and Fizz are having their wedding?' Joe leaned sideways to see where Maggie was pointing to a group of buildings half-hidden by forest on the edge of a cliff top. Cooper had started working at the base six months ago after emigrating from Scotland and Fizz was one of the emergency medicine specialists who were part of Aratika's elite staff.

'I think it must be.' Joe nodded. 'Certainly looks like the only way to get to it is by four-wheel drive or chopper.'

'I might take my bike.'

'What—you're not going to wear a dress?' Joe sounded shocked.

Maggie sighed. 'I suppose I'd better. I hadn't thought about it yet.'

'The wedding's next weekend. You'd better get on with it.'

'I know. It's just happened in a bit of a rush, you know? I really wasn't expecting Fizz to suddenly get so formal. She told me not so long ago that she was never going to get married again.'

'I guess finding out they're going to have a baby changed things. Not that that's the best reason to decide to tie the knot.' There was an odd note in Joe's voice.

'It's as good a reason as any,' Maggie responded. 'And I've never seen either of them looking so happy.'

Joe's grunt was reluctant agreement. 'Yeah... I would have thought Fizz would have been more upset having to give up her shifts at Aratika but I've not seen the smile drop from her face once.'

'Mmm...' Maggie closed her eyes for a moment. She could imagine how happy Fizz was feeling. Not just because she'd won that life lottery of finding the person she wanted to be with for ever—something Maggie had failed to find yet—but with the anticipation of holding their first baby in her arms in the near future. Maggie's own arms were loosely folded in front of her and she could actually feel an emptiness there. An ache of longing...

It was getting stronger, that longing. The ticking of a biological clock. One of Mother Nature's tricks to persuade women to reproduce before it became too late and, at nearly thirty-six, Maggie knew that her window of opportunity to become a mother easily was starting to close. She'd been envious of Fizz when she'd heard the news. Dead jealous, if she was really honest with herself.

'That's the road we're looking for down there.' Andy's voice broke into Maggie's thoughts a few minutes later. 'We'll follow it but keep an eye out for a farmhouse with a red ute parked in front of it. Apparently there's an empty paddock by the road that we can land in.'

'I'm getting an update.' Joe was reading his pager. 'Our patient is a thirty-one-year-old first-time mum. No problems with pregnancy and she's full term. Name's Kathy Price.'

It wasn't Kathy who met them at the door of the house a few minutes later but her husband, Darren, who looked like he'd just come in from working on the farm. He had a checked shirt on over a pair of shorts and he dropped a pair of boots onto the veranda of the farmhouse before inviting the paramedic crew to come inside.

'Dunno what all this fuss is about,' he said, as he led them through to a bedroom. 'I could have driven Kath in to the hospital. We don't need all these bells and whistles.'

'I think Kathy's midwife was a bit concerned about how tired your wife was sounding,' Joe said calmly. 'And it is quite a drive.'

Maggie was slipping her arms out of her backpack straps. She crouched down beside the bed.

'Hi, Kathy. My name's Maggie and that's Joe. We've come to take you into hospital to have your baby on your midwife's advice. Are you happy with that decision?'

The exhausted-looking young woman nodded. 'I'm

just so tired,' she whispered. 'It's been going on since the middle of last night.'

'Your midwife checked you this morning, yes?'

'Yeah…and I was two centimetres dilated at ten o'clock. She came back after lunch at one o'clock and I'd only got to four centimetres by then.'

'So…' Maggie checked her watch. 'That's about four hours ago now. How often are you having contractions?'

Kathy rolled her head from side to side. 'I'm not sure. It feels like every couple of minutes and…and it hurts. I know I said I didn't want any pain relief in my birth plan but I didn't know it was going to hurt this much.'

'We can give you something for the pain.' Maggie glanced at where Joe was opening their packs and readying the equipment that they might need. A birthing pack that included neonatal resuscitation items like the miniature airways and bag mask. IV gear. Their small tanks of oxygen and Entonox. 'We'll start with some Entonox but we'll put a line in your hand, if you're happy with that, so we can give you something stronger if you need it.'

'He's a big baby.' Darren sounded proud. 'They said that at the last scan.'

'Oh?' An alarm bell sounded a warning for Maggie. 'How big?'

'Not too big,' Kathy said. 'My midwife said it was below the limit for it being a problem for a home birth and we both wanted that.'

'Birth's a natural process.' Darren nodded. 'Why go near a hospital if you don't have to?'

'You can't just tie a rope around a hoof and pull it out,' Kathy snapped at her husband. 'I'm not one of your sheep. Ow…it's starting again.' She dropped her

head back against the pillows and groaned. 'It *hurts*…
and…and I feel *sick*…'

Joe was right beside Maggie now. He raised an eyebrow. 'Transition?' he suggested quietly.

Kathy was shaking as the contraction subsided. 'I
need to go to the toilet,' she moaned.

'It's okay, Kathy,' Maggie said reassuringly. 'I think
that perhaps you're a bit closer to having your baby than
we thought. I'm going to get your clothes off and see
what's happening, okay? Joe's going to take your blood
pressure and things and…' She caught Joe's gaze. 'Let's
get some oxygen on, shall we? And it would be great to
get a foetal heart rate.'

'What's going on?' Darren asked as they worked
over Kathy. 'I thought you were just going to take us
in to the hospital.'

'That was the initial plan,' Maggie replied as she cut
clothing clear. 'But we can't transport Kathy if a birth
is imminent. We can manage things a lot better here
than in the back of a helicopter.'

'Crikey…' Darren's face became noticeably paler.
'It's happening now?' He moved to the head of the bed
to lean over his wife. 'You okay, hon?'

'No…' Kathy grabbed at his hand. 'Where's that gas?
I can't do this… I need to *push*…'

'Wow…you're crowning, Kathy.' Maggie could see
the dark whorls of damp hair on the baby's head. 'Your
baby's almost here… Keep pushing—you're doing
great.'

Joe had the blood-pressure cuff wrapped around
Kathy's arm and the bulb in his hand but gave up trying to take a reading as he leaned to see what Maggie
was watching.

They both saw the moment that it happened. The baby's head was almost born and then it pulled back like a turtle retreating into its shell.

'Turtle sign,' Maggie said very quietly. She glanced up to catch Joe's gaze. They both knew that this had the potential to become an obstetric emergency in a very short space of time.

'Don't push any more for the moment, Kathy,' Maggie said calmly. 'Try and pant for the rest of this contraction. Darren? Can you take Kathy's pillows away? We need to get her lying as flat as possible.'

Maggie was going to hold the baby's head and apply some gentle traction with the next contraction. Kathy was red-faced and gasping as she pushed. This time the baby's head came a little further but then it stopped.

'What's going on?' Darren looked fearful as he looked up from the baby to meet Maggie's gaze. 'Why isn't it coming out?'

It was an effort to keep her voice this calm, especially as Kathy started sobbing. 'Baby's shoulders are just a bit caught behind the bones at the bottom of Kathy's pelvis.'

Darren put his arms around his wife. 'It'll be okay, hon. These guys know what they're doing.'

'*Why* is this happening?' Kathy cried. 'After all this time and it's been so hard…it's not *fair*…'

'It could be a positional thing,' Maggie said. 'Or maybe your baby's a bit bigger than the scan suggested. Don't worry, we have several ways we can help.'

And less than five minutes in which to do so.

Joe was right beside her and they were able to talk quietly for a few moments as Darren tried to comfort and reassure Kathy as she sobbed.

'We can only spend about thirty seconds on each manoeuvre to deal with shoulder dystocia,' Maggie said. 'I know the protocol but I'd like to get some expert obstetric backup on the radio.' She lowered her voice even further. 'We need to be prepared for a neonatal resuscitation, too.'

Joe reached for the radio clipped to his belt but he was still listening to Maggie. 'We'll try the McRoberts manoeuvre first. If that doesn't work, I'll need you to provide traction while I put on some suprapubic pressure.'

Maggie turned to Darren. 'Help me move Kathy down towards the end of the bed,' she told him. 'And, Kathy? I want you to pull your knees up to your chest and then push as hard as you can with your next contraction.'

Even as she was encouraging Kathy to push and telling her how well she was doing, Maggie's brain was racing through the next steps, which would mean applying pressure to try and move the baby's shoulders both externally and then internally. If that didn't work she would have to follow guidance from one of the consultants in the maternity wing of Wellington's Royal Hospital. She didn't want to have to think about the more drastic measures that might need to be taken or the risks to both baby and mother.

Joe caught Maggie's gaze as the sounds of the effort Kathy was putting into pushing began to fade into exhausted groans. Maggie nodded and they shifted positions, with Joe gently taking hold of the baby's head and Maggie moving to the side of the bed where she could feel for the position of the baby's shoulders.

'You're going to feel me pushing this time as well,'

she told Kathy. 'We need the biggest push you've got this time.'

'I can't,' Kathy moaned. 'I can't do it...'

'Yes, you can.' Darren was lying across the top of the bed, holding both of Kathy's hands. 'Hang on tight... you've got this...'

Maggie could feel the curve of the baby's back beneath her fingers and then the lump of the tiny shoulder. She locked her hands by weaving her fingers together and then put the heel of one hand just above the shoulder. As Kathy's next contraction gathered strength and she started to push, Maggie pressed down on the baby's shoulder. Joe was applying traction. At one point during the tense thirty seconds of effort, Maggie and Joe held eye contact with each other. They co-ordinated a rocking motion as Kathy's contraction began to recede and, finally, Maggie could feel the movement beneath her hands as one shoulder and then the other was freed.

'Keep it going,' she urged Kathy. 'Just a little bit more... Baby's coming... *Push*, Kathy...*push*...you can do it...'

And there was the baby, in Joe's hands. Looking... alarmingly limp. Maggie reached for the clamps and sterile scissors from the birthing pack roll. They needed to cut the cord fast if resuscitation was needed.

'Is he okay?' Kathy was trying to push herself up onto her elbows. 'What's happening...?'

'He's breathing,' Joe told her. 'And starting to move. I'm just going to check his heart rate.'

The baby was moving and screwing up his little face as though he wanted to cry but couldn't find the energy yet. They were both good signs but his colour wasn't great, with his extremities a dark shade of blue, and

Maggie wasn't sure that his breathing was adequate. Joe wasn't looking too worried, however. He was smiling down at the baby as he dried it off with a soft towel.

'Hey there, little guy. You going to tell us what you think about all this?'

Maggie had the cord clamped and the scissors in her hand but, if an urgent resuscitation wasn't needed, she didn't have to rush.

'Darren? Do you want to cut the cord?'

'Apgar six at one minute,' Joe told her. 'Heart rate is over a hundred but the resp rate is on the slow side and he's pretty blue.'

By the time Darren had cut through the cord, the baby was starting to make sounds. The first warbling cry came a few seconds later and Kathy burst into tears and held out her arms.

'Can I hold him? Please?'

Again, Maggie and Joe shared a glance. And a smile this time. This situation was under control now with the emergency delivery successfully managed. Kathy still needed careful monitoring because she was at more risk of a postpartum haemorrhage after the complication with her baby's delivery, and she needed to transfer to an obstetric unit as quickly as possible. But keeping the baby warm was also a priority and the best way to do that was to have him skin to skin with his mother and to cover them both with warm blankets.

It was Maggie who scooped up the infant to place him in Kathy's arms and, as she felt the weight of the newborn in her own arms and against her own breast, she felt oddly close to tears. Because it was a reminder of that ache of emptiness she'd been so aware of earlier when she'd been thinking of the baby her friend Fizz was going to have?

No. These were more like tears of joy. How precious was this new life? Especially this one, after giving them all a fright on his way into the world, but all babies were just amazing and the joy of being part of a delivery was something that would never grow old.

This was more than a purely professional satisfaction, however. Maybe there was an echo of that ache of longing. Of the emptiness. Not in her arms that were still full of this new life but somewhere further down in Maggie's body—in the space where a baby of her own might grow one day.

Her smile was definitely a bit wobbly as she helped Kathy move her clothing and gather her baby onto her chest.

'He's just gorgeous,' Maggie murmured, stepping back to let Darren get close to his wife and baby for a few precious minutes of family bonding time as she and Joe got packed up and ready for the transfer to hospital.

Darren sounded a lot closer to tears than Maggie was. 'Looks just like his daddy, I reckon,' he said. 'How 'bout that?'

Maggie checked her watch as she rapidly assessed the baby again before turning away to give this brand-new family just a moment of relative privacy. 'Apgar score eight at five minutes,' she told Joe.

He nodded, grinning, and then stripped off his gloves and unclipped his radio. 'Andy? We'll be ready to go inside ten minutes. Crank up the central heating in the cabin, we've got a baby to keep warm on the way home.'

Darren overheard him. 'Will there be room for a dad in the helicopter as well?'

'Sorry, mate.' Joe shook his head. 'It's going to be a bit crowded. You'll need to follow us by road.'

'Don't worry,' Maggie added, to soften the blow. 'We're going to take very good care of both Kathy and the baby.'

A medical team, including Fizz Wilson, was waiting on one side of the Royal's rooftop helipad to take over Kathy's care as soon as they landed and lifted out the stretcher.

'Third stage happened en route,' Maggie told Fizz. 'Oxytocin was administered on scene after the birth but I would estimate blood loss with the delivery of the placenta was still around three hundred mils with ongoing but slower loss now. She's on her second litre of normal saline. Blood pressure's one hundred and five over fifty.'

'I feel fine,' Kathy said. 'Just a bit tired, that's all.'

But Fizz took note of the low blood pressure and the urgent need to control any ongoing bleeding.

'Let's get moving,' she instructed the ED staff with her. 'Maggie, can you bring the baby, please? We've got a paediatric team waiting for him downstairs.'

Maggie followed Kathy's stretcher with Joe walking beside her. 'I could get used to this,' she said.

'What? Having full-on cases with successful outcomes? That's two today.' Joe was smiling. 'I could get used to it, too.'

'No… I mean *this*…' Maggie looked down at the tiny sleeping face visible amongst the folds of blanket in her arms. 'Carrying a baby around. I think I want one.'

Joe made a shuddering sound. 'Rather you than me, mate. Hey…' He increased his pace as the stretcher was slotted into the rooftop elevator. 'Is there room for us in there, too?'

They squeezed in.

Fizz was right beside Maggie. She had her gaze fixed on monitor screen of the life pack, taking in as much information about Kathy's condition as she could, but she slid a quick sideways glance at the baby a moment later.

'Any problems?'

'Not at all. He was a bit flat to start with but he picked up quickly. Apgar score was ten at ten minutes.'

Fizz was smiling as she turned back to her patient. 'He's so cute,' she told Kathy. 'Have you decided on a name yet?'

'I like Aiden,' Kathy said. 'But Darren wants him to be Patrick, after his dad. We decided we'd wait and see what suited him more.' She twisted her head, trying to see her baby's face. 'I think he looks like an Aiden, don't you?'

Maggie smiled. 'Aiden's a great name.' But so was Patrick, she thought. One of her favourite boy's names, in fact. She wondered if Fizz and Cooper had already started discussing possible names for their baby or if they knew whether it was a girl or a boy.

The elevator doors opened again as they reached the ground floor and Fizz stayed by the head of the stretcher as it was swiftly rolled towards a resuscitation area in the emergency department. Kathy would have no idea that her doctor was pregnant, Maggie thought. And here she was, with baby Aiden or Patrick still in her arms. It was baby overload today, that was for sure.

Her head was still full of it when she and Joe finally got to take a break and sat down in the staffroom of the Aratika Rescue Base.

'I haven't finished the paperwork for the post-cardiac arrest case yet, let alone for the birth,' Maggie sighed.

'It won't take too long,' Joe said. 'I'll do the cardiac one.'

'Because it's half-done already?'

'No. Because you're the one who wants a baby. This way, you get to enjoy the case all over again.'

'Hmm…' Maggie shook her head. 'It could have turned out to be not very enjoyable at all. I was so relieved the moment I felt that shoulder start to move.'

'I'll bet.' Joe pulled the folder of paperwork towards him and took a pen from the pocket of his overalls. 'Keep it in mind when you choose the father of your baby. You're so short, it might be wise not to marry a solid, over six foot tall farmer like Kathy did.'

'Five foot four is not short. I'm average,' Maggie countered. 'And I don't even know any farmers. Or any potential baby daddies at all, in fact.'

'They're out there. In droves. You just haven't been looking.'

'That's because I got fed up with relationships that were going nowhere fast.'

Including the one she'd been in with Richard, years ago, when Maggie had first started working at the rescue base. One that had had a promising start but had ebbed into being nothing more than flatmates. Friends. And it hadn't been enough for either of them.

'Maybe that's because you go into them expecting them to *be* going somewhere. That can scare guys off, you know. It would scare the hell out of me, that's for sure. In fact, it's precisely why I'm currently single again.'

Maggie snorted. 'It's a baby I want. A partner would

be a bonus, of course, but I'm running out of time to jump through all those hoops.' She was only half joking. It really did feel like she was running out of time, given how many dead ends she had already come up against in the search to find someone to share her life with. 'And who says you have to *marry* someone to have a baby, anyway? You might marry someone and end up being a single mother anyway—like Laura.' Her flatmate had escaped what she suspected might have been an abusive relationship years ago when her son, Harrison, was only a tiny baby.

'So you're going to do the independent professional woman thing and go to a sperm bank or something?'

Maggie blinked. 'D'you know, I hadn't actually thought of that.'

'Why not? You read about people doing it all the time. Especially older, professional women who choose not to get married or realise they're running out of time. People just like you. And it seems like a great way to get a designer baby. You could practically choose its hair colour and how smart it'll be.' But Joe was frowning now. 'Of course, you're going to provide the other half of the genes so it might just come out with blonde hair and blue eyes and to be not very...' His lips twitched.

Maggie threw her pen at him. 'Are you trying to tell me that I'm not very smart?'

Joe had already caught the pen. 'I was only going to say you're not very tall.'

Maggie narrowed her eyes. 'Not sure I believe that. And what did you mean by "something"?'

'Huh?'

'You said a sperm bank "or something".'

'Oh...' Joe picked up his coffee cup and took a swallow. 'You could just pick someone you liked the look of, I guess, lay on the charm and lure them home and hope that he's not too careful about birth control.'

'*Joe*… How irresponsible would that be?'

'Irresponsible on the part of the guy, that's true.' Joe shook his head. 'I'd never relinquish that responsibility.'

'I couldn't get pregnant and not tell someone that they were going to be a father. That's just not right.'

'I guess.' Joe was focussing on the paperwork in front of him now. 'Do what I read about a gay couple doing recently, then. The women asked one of their good friends and he agreed to be the donor. He said he wanted them to have their family and he was happy to be a kind of uncle but never wanted to be a father.'

They both concentrated on the paperwork for a while but, even as Maggie filled in the precise details relating to the obstetric case that was clearly going to be the last job for their shift today, another line of thought was ticking along somewhere in the background of her brain.

Thoughts about sperm banks. How easy was it to get accepted for treatment and how expensive it might be. And how it worked. Did you have a wish list of things to tick off, like physical characteristics of height and hair colour or evidence of intelligence such as a university qualification? What about more important attributes like whether someone could make you laugh or how kind he was?

Thoughts about the other things Joe had suggested circled in her mind, too. Randomly picking some guy with the intention of seducing him and possibly lying about being on birth control was not an acceptable option but…but the idea of using a co-operative friend, now that *was* interesting…

So interesting that it was the only thing Maggie was thinking about as she kicked her bike into life and threaded her way through the city traffic not long after her conversation with Joe.

By the time she was getting into bed that night, it had started to feel like it was her own idea.

And, out of all the men she knew, there was only one that stood out as a perfect possibility.

Joe Wallace.

The thought of broaching the subject was a bit nerve-racking. Enough so to keep Maggie awake for quite some time. On the positive side, he'd had a half-smile on his face when he'd said 'rather you than me' when she'd been holding Kathy's baby, and had said she wanted one as well, so maybe he was on the same page as that co-operative friend he'd told her about—who didn't want to become a father but was happy to be a kind of uncle.

On the other side of that coin, however, was the fact that she'd be stepping into a realm that had never been there with Joe and that was why their friendship was so solid. They'd both been in long-term relationships when they'd first met as colleagues. By the time they were single, they were already good friends and Maggie had learned the hard way that friendship was not enough to base a long-term relationship on. Joe was off limits and he clearly felt exactly the same way and that had never been a problem. But baby-making, no matter how you ended up actually doing it, had everything to do with sex and even the thought of opening that conversation with Joe was enough to make Maggie blush.

But it wasn't enough to make her dismiss what seemed to be a perfect plan. As she drifted off to sleep Maggie's thoughts were tumbling, interwoven with memories that went back so far they were no more than misty glimpses. She'd had an old-fashioned child-sized pram when she was very little and she would cram every doll and teddy bear she owned into that pram and wheel it everywhere.

My babies, she would tell everyone.

When she was older she had her fashion dolls that gave her a mother and father figure and she would add smaller dolls as their children. Lots and lots of children because that was what made a 'real' family. It wasn't that she hadn't been happy and loved as an only child, it was just that she knew it was a case of the more the merrier. Her parents had desperately wanted more children and had been sad that it hadn't happened but it hadn't dented the rock-solid love they shared. They would be the best grandparents ever.

That was something else that Maggie wanted, of course. A relationship that was as perfect a match as her parents' one was. The 'love at first sight' whirlwind romance like the one they'd told her about so many times and starting a life together that would get better and better as they got older. It wasn't that Maggie hadn't found the 'love at first sight' type of thing, it was just that any whirlwind romance eventually crashed and burned and she'd been let down so many times that, for the moment at least, she was giving up.

That desire for a family of her own had never vanished, though. In the last moments before sleep claimed Maggie, she could feel the intensity of that longing that morphed from a pram full of beloved toys to the feeling of holding a real, live baby in her arms, as she'd done today.

There was something a bit weird happening.

Joe couldn't put his finger on it but, as the day wore on, he wondered if it was because Maggie seemed even bouncier than normal. More enthusiastic. More…smiley…

Several times, he caught her opening her mouth as if she was about to say something and then snapping it shut and throwing herself into whatever task she was doing on their downtime, like reading a journal article or washing up some dishes. It wasn't until they were in the locker room, when their shift had finished, that Joe finally gave up. The way Maggie was looking at him felt like the heat of a laser in the middle of his back as he pulled what he needed from his locker.

He turned his head. 'You've been staring at me all day. What's going on?'

'Sorry…' Maggie smiled brightly at him. 'There's something I wanted to ask you, that's all. I was…um… waiting for the best moment.'

'Now's good.' Joe smiled back. If Maggie wanted a favour, then he was her man. Always. 'Shoot.'

'Um…' She was fishing in her locker, putting things into a shoulder bag. Her voice sounded as if she was trying hard to keep it casual. 'It's about what you said. Yesterday. When I was talking about wanting a baby?'

'What did I say?' Joe tried to think back. 'Oh…you mean about sperm banks?'

'No…' Maggie's hands stilled. 'About asking a friend.'

'Oh…' He liked that she'd liked his idea. It was always great to find a solution to a mate's problem. 'Glad

I could help.' He unhooked his jacket from the back of his locker. 'So who's the lucky guy, then?' He raised an eyebrow in Maggie's direction when she didn't answer. 'Your potential baby daddy? Is it Jack?'

'Jack's my flatmate. How awkward would that be?'

'Don?'

'Shh…' Maggie threw a glance over her shoulder, checking that they were still alone in the locker room. Her cheeks had reddened even at the idea of their boss being involved.

'Who, then?'

He could see the way Maggie swallowed hard, as if what she was about to say was terribly important. He could see how wide her eyes were as well. Shining with something that looked very like hope. The hairs on the back of his neck prickled as they rose.

'You, Joe,' she whispered. 'You're the person I'd choose out of everybody I've ever known.'

He should have seen it coming, perhaps, but he hadn't and it hit him like a steam train. The blast of remembering what it was like to be a child that hadn't been wanted. The absolute determination to never, ever be on the other side of that coin—the father who hadn't wanted that child.

Joe could feel the colour draining out of his face. He could see the reflection of his own horror in Maggie's eyes. She knew she'd made a terrible mistake but she had no idea how to go about fixing it. He could solve this problem. Just make a joke and brush it off.

Except he couldn't. The words had been said and couldn't be unsaid and they had touched such a very deep chord within him. The idea of him casually— *deliberately*—fathering a child was hanging in the air

between them. Totally abhorrent. Totally unaccept-
able. Joe couldn't begin to find any words to let Maggie know just how shocked he was but maybe he didn't
need to. She was looking rather pale herself.

Embarrassed. Mortified, even.

For once, Joe had no inclination to make her feel any
better. He shook his head, slammed his locker door shut
and was walking out as if it was simply an ordinary end
to their run of days working together.

'See ya,' he muttered, without meeting her gaze.
'Enjoy your days off.'

CHAPTER TWO

'Wow…CHECK YOU OUT, Maggie. You're wearing a *dress*…'

'Hi, Jack… Yeah, I know… I'm just trying to decide if I want to keep it.'

Maggie had spent half her afternoon off today shopping for something suitable to wear to a wedding but it felt very odd having all this loose fabric brushing against her lower legs. Just how long had it been since she'd tapped into her feminine side and worn a dress instead of her uniform or jeans or the leather pants she wore for protection when she rode her beloved Harley-Davidson sportster motorbike with its sky-blue fuel tank and mudguards?

She turned back to where their other flatmate, Laura, was sitting on the couch, Harrison snuggled up beside her. They were both staring at her thoughtfully so she did a bit of a twirl, one way and then the other. That was enough to make her wonder how long it had been since she'd been anywhere near a dance floor. At least a year, she decided. About when her last relationship had faded into oblivion after a few months had made it obvious it should never have got going in the first place. That 'love at first sight' wasn't to be trusted. Maggie stifled a sigh.

'So...what do you think?'

'It's perfect,' Laura pronounced. 'That blue is exactly the same colour as your eyes and I love the little daisy print. Very summery.' She ruffled her son's hair. 'What do you think, Harry? Doesn't Maggie look pretty? Isn't it fun that we're all going to get dressed up for the wedding tomorrow?'

Harry wrinkled his nose. 'I don't want to get dressed up.'

'You don't have to get *really* dressed up. It's not a fancy wedding where you might have to wear a suit, but you have got an important job to do. You get to carry the rings.'

'I'd get dressed up,' Jack told him, 'if I could go. I'd wear my very best jeans and a shirt.'

'A T-shirt?'

'No, a real shirt. With buttons. Maybe even a tie.'

'Why can't you go?'

'I wish I could but I have to work, buddy. Someone has to be ready to go up in a helicopter or off on a bike and look after the people who get sick or injured.'

And Jack probably hadn't even tried to juggle his roster to take time off. He'd only recently succeeded in winning one of the hotly contested paramedic jobs on the rescue base and his excitement was still palpable.

'Who were you crewed with today?' Laura asked. 'I didn't see anyone from Aratika come into Emergency during my shift.'

'It was a really quiet day. Joe and I got a bit bored, to be honest. And we ate far too many of Shirley's cookies. I'm meeting him at the gym as soon as I've collected my gear to try and burn some that sugar load off.'

'How come Joe was working?' Maggie asked. 'He's on the same roster as me.'

'He was covering for Adam, who called in sick. Food poisoning or some kind of gastro bug. I hope he's back on deck tomorrow. Joe said he could come in again but he wouldn't want to miss the wedding.'

'No...' But Maggie could hear the doubtful note in her own voice.

Maybe Joe had a reason that meant he wouldn't be too upset to miss the wedding. Or rather, to miss having to spend any time with Maggie.

She hadn't seen him since the last shift they had worked together. Since that awful moment when she'd made the cringeworthy mistake of telling him that she wanted him to father a baby for her.

'I reckon if Cooper had decided to have a best man, it would have been Joe,' Jack added.

'Yes,' Laura agreed. 'And then Maggie would have been a bridesmaid for Fizz.'

Thank goodness their friends weren't going down such a traditional format for their wedding. How awkward could that have been, with everyone they worked with watching them? Someone would have picked up on the odd vibe between the best man and the bridesmaid and maybe asked what the problem was, which would have only ramped up this odd tension.

There hadn't been any chance to try and convince Joe that the notion of him being a sperm donor had only been a joke because the night shift crew had been outside chatting to their pilot as Maggie had followed behind Joe, who had got into his car and simply driven past, with a casual wave. Maggie had texted him later with what seemed a slightly awkward attempt to tell him he had nothing to worry about but the response had been a terse 'Forget about it, I already have', which didn't quite ring true.

It was probably unfortunate that their days off had meant they hadn't had to work together the following day. It would have been so much easier to brush off and genuinely forget about it if they hadn't both had a couple of days to think about it.

Because Maggie was quite sure that Joe *would* have been thinking about it, even if it wasn't filling his mind to quite the same extent as it was hers. Who wouldn't have to give it some thought, when confronted by something you would never have expected your friend to come out with? Something that had clearly shocked him. She couldn't text him again, either, because that would be making it into a bigger thing than it actually was. All they needed was to be in the same space, an opportunity to make a joke about it and then they could go back to the way things had always been—a friendship that made it possible to work and socialise together and to always feel perfectly safe.

'Anyway...' Maggie pasted a bright smile on her face. 'Even though I'm not a bridesmaid, I think I will wear a dress. *This* dress.'

'Good choice.' Laura encouraged Harrison to slide off the couch but kept hold of his hand as she got up. 'Want to help Mummy decide what she's going to wear?'

'I'm tired...' Harrison was climbing back onto the couch. 'Can I watch TV?'

'I'll help Mummy choose,' Maggie offered. 'Let's both go girly with pretty dresses. How often do we get the chance to do that?'

'Almost never,' Laura said. She was smiling now, too. 'It's going to be a great day,' she added. 'I can't wait.'

Maggie had to stop herself crossing her fingers, the way she used to when she was a kid and believed that the gesture excused you if you were about to tell an outright lie.

'Me, too.'

'You're a brave man, Cooper Sinclair.'

'Why is that, Joe?' His colleague was grinning. 'Because I'm taking the plunge and getting married?'

'Nah… You're on a hilltop in famously windy Wellington and you're wearing a skirt.'

It was more than a hilltop. They were actually standing on the top of a cliff, with a spectacular view of the sea and islands through the archway that would frame the ceremony due to begin shortly. And, yes, while it was a gloriously sunny day, the currents of air were enough to be stirring the hemline of the kilt Cooper was wearing.

Cooper snorted. 'What else would a Scotsman wear for the happiest day of his life?' He wasn't looking at Joe, however. His gaze was fixed on the Castle Cliff resort buildings and he obviously couldn't wait to catch the first glimpse of his bride coming to meet him. He glanced at his watch then—a nervous gesture that was completely out of character.

'It's time…'

'I'd better find a seat, then.' Joe left his friend standing alone and headed for the far side of the last row of white seats that had been arranged in a semi-circle facing the archway. He wasn't at all bothered that the first rows were already full of settled guests. He was happy to be attending this celebration but he didn't want to be too close to the action. Weddings made him a little nervous, too. Didn't Cooper and Fizz realise what a huge risk they were taking? How high the chances were that it wasn't going to turn out to be happy-ever-after? And they had decided to get married because there was a baby on the way. Not that he was going to say anything but it felt a bit close to a death knell to Joe.

Just before he turned to sit down, he noticed another kilt-clad figure appear on an upper balcony of the resort building, a set of bagpipes cradled in his arms. At the same time, three figures were hurrying down the steps from the lower veranda, two of them wearing dresses. The other was a small boy and Joe knew that it must be Laura's son, Harrison, who was apparently in charge of the wedding rings. Laura had to be watching over her son, as she always did, and that meant that the other woman was most likely her flatmate and close friend. He didn't really need the glimpse of sunlight catching blonde curls to light them up like a halo to confirm his guess.

Maggie...

Joe sat down with a thump and fixed his gaze on the scene ahead of him, where the celebrant had joined Cooper.

The level of discomfort Joe was aware of now was far greater than anything weddings normally engendered. He hadn't seen Maggie for days. Hadn't *wanted* to see her after that shocking conversation at the end of their last shift together, and as the time apart was increasing, so was the level of...what...awkwardness? Certainly tension, anyway.

It wasn't something he'd ever been aware of with

Maggie. She was, in fact, probably the only woman he ever felt completely at ease with. Other than Shirley, of course, but the self-appointed housekeeper of the Aratika Rescue Base was a mother figure for everyone there, with zero risk of her wanting anything inappropriate from her relationship with Joe. He'd thought his friendship with Maggie was just as sacrosanct. That they were real friends who trusted each other and that there was no threat of the usual sexual tension that inevitably seemed to develop when he tried to be simply friends with a woman.

The other seats in this back row were filling up quickly from the aisle side as people realised the ceremony was about to start. Joe noticed Don, the base manager, take a seat and then Tom, one of the emergency department consultants at the Royal, took the next seat, leaving only two spaces. Tom was becoming more involved with the base, having taken over the shifts Fizz had had to relinquish when she'd discovered she was pregnant. Laura went past Joe on the other side, holding Harrison's hand, leading him to where a seat had been saved in the front row, and then there was a swish of blue fabric right in front of Joe.

'Excuse me.'

He pulled his feet closer as Maggie edged past his knees. Seeing Laura and Harrison had been a reminder of the example of successful single parenthood that Maggie was inspired by and that was yet another sharp reminder of the awkwardness that now lay between them. The fact that she was choosing to sit beside him came as something of a relief. Perhaps they could get past what was threatening to be an elephant in the room when they next had the opportunity to talk to each other, let alone the next time they had to work together.

Except that a quick glance showed that the empty seats beside Joe were the only ones available and Maggie chose the one next to Tom, leaving an empty seat between herself and Joe. She flicked him a quick smile of greeting but then turned to say hello to Tom and the slightly nervous way she had avoided more than a split second of eye contact gave Joe an odd jolt of something that he couldn't define but which he definitely didn't like.

Wow…how could a simple, white chair that wasn't even solid suddenly feel like an impenetrable barrier?

The mournful wail of the bagpipe music starting in the background only added to the sensation that something had changed. Or been lost? Something potentially huge?

Like everyone else, Joe turned his head to watch Fizz come out onto the veranda and then walk down the steps towards the central aisle that led to the archway where Cooper was waiting. It was no surprise that she wasn't wearing a white dress. Joe knew that she'd been there and done that once already and that her first husband had been tragically killed in an accident on their honeymoon. Maybe it wasn't even surprising that she'd chosen to wear a bright red dress because that was Fizz all over, wasn't it? Daring as well as confident enough to pull off something so different. Her long, dark hair was hanging loose down her back and she looked gorgeous, Joe decided.

And *so* happy…

No wonder there was a collective sound like people

were catching their breath around him. He thought he heard a happy sigh coming from Maggie, too.

Was *she* a believer as well? If she was, why hadn't she already conducted a successful husband hunt? She could have done it years ago and then she wouldn't have had to worry about the clock running out on her reproductive years. She wouldn't have had to even think about alternative routes to motherhood and she wouldn't have tried to involve *him* when bringing a child into the world was, without doubt, the last thing he would ever contemplate doing.

The celebrant welcomed everybody as the wail of the bagpipes finally faded.

'You have all been invited to attend today,' she told the gathering, 'because you are the family, friends and colleagues of Cooper and Fizz and they want you to witness their commitment to each other and share the joy of that promise.'

Joe sucked in a deep breath. He wasn't feeling particularly joyful right now. It was more than awkwardness filling that space between him and Maggie.

He was angry, that's what it was.

Or maybe it was more that he was sad. He let out that breath in a long sigh. He knew that Maggie had heard that sigh because he could feel the sideways glance he received. Turning his head just a fraction, he could catch a reflection of what he was feeling in her own eyes.

That hint of sadness.

There weren't that many things in life that you could be certain of and a true friendship was one of the most precious things there was. Maggie Lewis had been his favourite person to crew with ever since he'd joined the Aratika Rescue Base and the foundations of that trust between them had been rocked the other day. Possibly even damaged beyond repair judging by the aftershocks. All by a few words. There had been more than sadness in that swift glance they had just shared, however. An impression of something else was lingering. Regret? Along with a desire to put things right?

A flash of guilt threw itself into the confusing mix of emotions that was unsettling Joe right now. It wasn't as if Maggie had done anything wrong. After all, he'd been the one who'd thrown that anecdote of people using a friend as a sperm donor into the conversation. He just hadn't expected it to come back and bite him and it had only bitten that hard because it had touched a raw spot.

He'd overreacted, hadn't he?

Cooper and Fizz had written their own vows for this ceremony and the message that was coming through loud and clear was the deep friendship that was the basis of their relationship. The trust. How rare and special it was to find someone who felt the same way about you.

That was so true.

Not that Joe wanted to marry Maggie, of course. He had no desire to marry anybody. And he'd never been sexually attracted to her. He could acknowledge that she was a very attractive woman—she just wasn't his type. They had started out as colleagues and had become friends. Just because Cooper and Fizz had added benefits into their friendship that had taken them to a very different level didn't mean that his relationship with Maggie was any less valid.

All too often, in Joe's experience, friendships could outlast marriages.

As their friends exchanged a rather passionate kiss to seal their vows and the congregation clapped and cheered, Joe turned his head to find that Maggie was doing exactly the same thing and turning her head towards him.

This time, the smile they shared felt genuine.

The friendship was still there and there was an astonishing relief to be found in that knowledge. All they needed to do now was clear the air and sweep away the remnants of that disturbing suggestion of him helping her to achieve her dream of motherhood, and what better place to do that than during a party?

There were photographs against the dramatic backdrop of the cliffs and islands and a spectacular sunset. A live band was setting up for when they were going to provide the music for dancing later on and, in the meantime, there was a great range of wine and beer at the bar and delicious food that wasn't offered in any traditional kind of wedding breakfast. A spit roast was happening in the courtyard garden with an amazing range of vegetables or salads to accompany it and inside one of the reception rooms of the resort a taco station had been set up on a long trestle table.

'It's because we loved the taco nights at your place when Cooper was still living with you,' Fizz told Maggie.

'Yum…' Maggie had opened the lid of a huge container. 'That's proper pulled beef…'

'The taco shells are keeping warm as well.'

Harrison was already holding a shell and Laura was helping him to add shredded lettuce and grated cheese from the bowls further along the table.

'No tomatoes,' he told his mum. 'I hate tomatoes.'

'Sauce?'

'Only tomato sauce, not that hot stuff.'

Maggie laughed. 'But you just said you hated toma-toes, Harry.'

The deep voice right behind her after she spoke made her jump. It also made her heart skip a beat. Good grief…when had she ever been nervous to be in Joe's company before? But the way he'd looked at her when the ceremony had been getting underway—as if she'd done something completely unforgiveable—had made that tension between them feel like it was rapidly es-calating. Mind you, the way he'd smiled at the end of the ceremony, when Fizz and Cooper were having their first kiss as husband and wife, had been a glimmer of hope. So was the amusement coating his words when he spoke now.

'Tomato sauce is different, Maggie. Everybody knows that.'

'Yeah.' Harrison nodded, although he'd edged closer to his mother. 'It doesn't even taste like tomatoes.'

'You can have whatever you want on your taco,' Fizz told him. 'They're the rules today.'

'And I get to stay up late, right?'

'Let's see how tired you get,' Laura cautioned. 'I don't want you feeling sick tomorrow.'

'I'm not going to get tired.' Harrison was looking de-termined. 'Because I know a secret about what's going to happen later and I have to be awake.'

'Oh?' Everybody turned to look at Fizz.

'Can't say.' She grinned. 'It's a secret. Harry only knows because he did so well with his special job today.' She glanced down at the wedding ring on her hand. 'And now I'm going to find a beer and make sure my husband has one, too. Enjoy the tacos, you lot.'

Joe was right behind Maggie as she loaded salad and cheese onto the meat in the crisp taco shell. They both added sliced jalapeño peppers and chilli sauce.

Drizzling the super-spicy sauce made Maggie smile. Instead of putting the bottle down again with the other condiments, she handed it to Joe.

'D'you remember the first time we ever worked together all those years ago?'

'When we knocked over the chilli sauce bottle on the table because we were both reaching for it at the same time?'

'And we discovered that there was someone else in the world who like putting hot sauce on scrambled eggs?'

The softening of Joe's features told Maggie that he was remembering more than those scrambled eggs. That it had been more than a moment of bonding as new colleagues. *The hotter the better* had become a private catchphrase and had ended up becoming a kind of code of encouragement. How many times had they been dispatched to what promised to be a challenging situation and they'd used that code?

This could get hot.

That's okay. That's the way we like it, remember?

Yeah...the hotter the better...

She could see the way Joe stilled for a moment, the sauce bottle still in his hands. Then he caught her gaze with the most direct look they'd shared since before that awkward conversation.

'It was the start of a great friendship,' he said quietly.

'One that I hope we still have,' Maggie said, just as softly. It was more than a great friendship, it was the best kind of friendship it was possible to have. She loved

Joe and she knew that he felt the same way about her. It was a bond that nothing could break.

'I'm really sorry, Joe,' she added. 'I just wish I could wind the clock back and that I never talked to you about any of that baby stuff.'

'It wasn't entirely your fault. It was me who put the idea into your head.'

'It's not there now. Can we pretend it never happened?'

It seemed that Joe was thinking along the same lines.

'Consider it forgotten,' he said. 'Never to be discussed again.'

'What were we talking about?' Maggie tilted her head. 'I've forgotten.'

They both laughed, reaching for paper towels for what looked likely to be a messy meal, and virtually all of the tension that had been there between them seemed to evaporate with the sound of that laughter.

Normal service had been resumed and thank goodness for that. Maggie could finally relax enough to really enjoy this party to celebrate the wedding of two of her closest friends.

They couldn't really forget about it. Maggie knew that. Some things just couldn't be unheard in the same way that images from things seen could never be erased from your memory cells. But they could pretend to pretend, couldn't they? And maybe that would be enough to make everything all right again.

If nothing else, it was a good start.

CHAPTER THREE

THE SECRET THAT Harrison knew about was a fireworks display that happened later in the evening against the inky black sky over the cliff edge. Maggie used her phone camera to capture the excitement on the small boy's face as he watched the display from within the safe circle of his mother's arms. Then she turned to catch some of the amazing explosions of light and colour in the sky and, by chance, caught the moment when Fizz and Cooper—standing a little way in front of her—turned towards each other to steal a kiss.

They were only a silhouette against the bright display of exploding light in front of them but nobody could mistake the long hair being gently blown back from Fizz's head or the ruffled hem of Cooper's kilt. Maggie knew the instant she'd taken that photo that it was something special. The guests had all been firmly told that no wedding gifts other than their company were desired but Maggie now had the makings of the most perfect memento—just as good, if not possibly better than any of the formal photographs that had been taken today. She just needed to print this picture and find a pretty frame and she could present this captured moment of quintessential celebration when Cooper and Fizz came back from their honeymoon in Scotland.

Anticipating the pleasure of their reaction made her feel almost as good as it did to have her friendship with Joe back on track. It certainly made her feel confident enough to seek him out a little while later, after the fireworks had finished and the resort's four-wheel-drive taxis had taken the guests who needed to leave early back to the city.

She wanted to show someone the photo she was so proud of. Cooper and Fizz were out of the question, of course, and Laura had taken Harrison home because it was well past his bedtime already. There were plenty of people here who would love to see the romantic shot of the newly wed couple but there was only one person that Maggie really wanted to show it to and that was Joe.

Except that he was standing with Cooper, talking to the members of the band who were gearing up to try to get everybody on the dance floor for the rest of the evening.

'Bit of rock and roll, I reckon,' Cooper was saying as Maggie joined them. 'Nobody can resist that.'

'Like this?' The lead singer nodded to the others and they launched into Elvis Presley's 'Jailhouse Rock'.

The introductory notes were enough to bring a whoop from Fizz on the other side of the dance floor and Cooper had a huge grin on his face as he went to meet her in the middle of the space. Maggie's body was responding to the music without her even thinking about it, so when Joe grabbed her hand and pulled her onto the floor, she was only too happy to follow. She'd known that this new dress would be just perfect for a bit of rock and roll dancing with the way the skirts billowed as she was twirled and spun and even had her feet off the floor in a lift, but what she hadn't known was that Joe would be this good at it. One song led into another, the best music from the sixties and seventies that was far too good not to dance to, and it wasn't until quite some time later that Maggie was breathless and tired enough to head off the dance floor for a rest. Joe seemed happy to follow her.

'Where on earth did you learn to dance like that?'

Joe shrugged. 'Got dragged along to lessons once with a girlfriend.'

'Takes more than a few lessons to learn that many moves.'

He grinned. 'Guess she lasted a bit longer than most. In fact, she was the one I was with when we first met and she lasted almost as long as you and Richard, from what I remember. Maybe that was because she was more interested in dancing than anything off-putting like getting married or having babies.'

Maggie froze for a moment at the reminder of what she'd managed to forget about completely while they'd been dancing. But Joe was still smiling.

'Want a drink?'

'I need about a gallon of water, I think.'

'I need a very cold lager. And a bit of fresh air, maybe? Don't know about you but I'm cooking after all that exercise.'

'It was great fun, though.' Maggie followed Joe outside when they both had a drink in their hands. 'I really should get back into doing some dancing on a regular basis. It was always my exercise of choice.'

Joe shook his head. 'Not for me. You can't beat windsurfing. And Wellington's perfect for it.'

'Mmm… I was going to say that there's always some wind here but…look at this…' Maggie held her palm up above her head. 'There's not even a puff right now. What a perfect evening.'

There were bench seats built into the outside of the low stone wall surrounding the courtyard that provided the same view of the cliff edge that the wedding guests had been treated to earlier and, by tacit consent, Maggie and Joe headed for one of them and sat down. The white chairs had all been cleared away but the pretty archway was still in place and, above it, a crescent moon hung in the night sky.

'I've got to get a photo of that.' Maggie put her glass down on the bench beside her and fished in her pocket for her phone. As soon as she'd caught the image, she remembered the earlier shot and held her phone out to Joe.

'Look at this.'

'Wow…that's very cool. Looks like a cover for a romance novel.'

'They'll love it, won't they? I thought I'd get it framed while they're away on honeymoon.'

'They're not calling it a honeymoon, remember? It's been a huge thing for Fizz to even get married again and Cooper said he was careful to call this holiday a "babymoon". He wants to show her his home country before she's too pregnant to be allowed to fly long-haul.'

Maggie sighed. 'I'd almost forgotten the tragedy of her last honeymoon. Maybe because she's looked so incredibly happy today.'

'They both have, haven't they? Good luck to them, too. I hope they stay that way for ever.'

They sat in silence for a long moment, staring up at the moon.

Maggie took a sip of her champagne, a kaleidoscope of images from today's ceremony flashing through her mind. She loved weddings but the aftermath did tend to make her feel a bit lonely these days. Kind of like the way dealing with babies or even talking about them could make her arms feel empty. She slid a sideways glance at Joe.

'Have you ever got close to getting married, Joe?' she asked. 'You've never been short of female company in the time I've known you. Except for now, mind you. What happened to the last one…what's her name? That redheaded nurse?'

'Amanda.' Joe took a swig of his beer. 'I was a re-bound. She went back to her ex and got engaged to him.' He wiped his mouth with the back of his hand and returned the curious glance. 'What about you? Why are you still single? Especially given that you like the idea of having kids so much.'

Maggie shrugged, aware that he'd avoided answering her question by turning the tables, but she wasn't going to force him to talk about something he preferred to keep private.

'Just haven't found the right person, I guess,' she said. 'And I'm not about to settle for anything less than the "real thing".'

Joe's breath came out in a dismissive huff. 'You don't really believe in that, do you?'

'In love? Of course I do. How can you even ask that when you can see how happy Cooper and Fizz are?'

'I mean that idea that there's one perfect person out there and when you find them you're destined to live happily-ever-after. That whole romantic myth of the "real thing".' He took another swig of his drink. 'Yes, it can work. Sometimes. If you're really lucky but, all too often, it turns into a disaster. That's the real reason I'm still single,' he added. 'It's because I don't believe in it. In any of it.'

Maggie's jaw dropped as she caught a note of something like bitterness in his tone. 'Don't let anyone else hear you say that tonight. Man…talk about raining on someone's parade.'

Joe made an apologetic face. 'You're right. Okay… I won't say anything else. And, for the record, I think that Cooper and Fizz make a great couple. If anyone can make it work, those two can.'

Maggie couldn't help trying to score another point. 'Maybe that's because they've found the "real thing".'

The sound Joe made now sounded resigned. 'Which is what, exactly?'

Maggie considered the question. She'd asked herself often enough when past relationships had failed for one reason or another.

'It's got friendship in there,' she answered. 'It needs a solid foundation of genuine friendship. Just being able to enjoy each other's company and respect each other's opinions.'

'We're friends,' Joe said. 'But it's never going to be anything more than that.'

'God, no,' Maggie agreed. 'That's because there's no chemistry. Just being friends is never going to be enough. I found that out with Richard. You've got to be attracted to someone to fall in love with them. Really, really attracted. And it happens instantly, if it's real.'

'That's just hormones. It wears off.'

'Probably. But if it lasts long enough for a friendship to develop as well it can create something that *will* last.

For some people it lasts their whole lives. My parents are like that and that's what I want to find. They fell in love at first sight and it's still there. They're in their sixties and they still hold hands when they're walking down the street. They still look at each other sometimes in a way that makes me want to tell them to get a room.'

'Good luck with that,' Joe muttered. 'At least you won't be getting married just because you're having a baby. Much better to do that by yourself if that's what you really want. Better for everybody but especially better for the kid.'

This time, something in his tone struck a note that made Maggie think there was more to his words than what was on the surface. It took her back to that look of horror on his face when he'd realised she was thinking of him as a potential baby daddy and she knew, instinctively, that it was the cause of how awkward it had felt between them afterwards. Maybe it also had something to do with that bitterness that had crept into his voice when he'd said he didn't believe in true love.

As Joe had reminded her, they were good friends. And friends cared, didn't they, when they learned about things that could affect their quality of life?

'What makes you say that?' she asked gently.

'Kids get caught in the flak,' Joe said quietly. 'They can grow up thinking that it's their fault. That, no matter how hard they try, they can never fix things.'

Maggie blinked. Yep…there was something deep and dark beneath those words. She'd never thought of her tall, confident, outgoing crew partner as a small child who might have had a less than happy upbringing but right now she wanted to find that little boy and give him a cuddle. To tell him that things were going to be okay one day.

The best she could do, however, was to simply sit there beside him and offer a sympathetic ear and encouragement to talk about it if that was what he wanted.

'You're talking from personal experience?'

Joe drained his glass. 'Yep. I was that kid.'

Maggie swallowed hard. 'I'm so sorry, Joe... Didn't anybody try and help you?'

The slow shake of his head was heartbreaking. 'From the outside, I doubt that anybody even guessed. My mother got pregnant, so my father did "the decent thing" and married her. Maybe they believed it might work out okay in the end but it didn't. He walked out when I was about five and my mother never stopped telling me that it was my fault. That I was an accident. That he hadn't wanted a kid and she was far too young and hadn't had the chance to get a good job or meet someone special. Bottom line was that I'd ruined her life.'

'She *told* you that? When you were so little? That's...' Maggie shook her head with disbelief. 'That's just awful...'

'She apologised for it later. She met someone else eventually and I think she's happy enough but it was more than enough to put me off the whole business of marriage and kids.'

Maggie was almost cringing. 'And then I go and start talking about sperm donors and baby daddies. I'm really sorry, Joe.'

'It's me that should apologise. You're right. I'm raining on the parade here. I don't know why I even told you any of that crap.'

Maggie did. There was an apology of some kind hidden in there, for how he'd reacted the other day.

'If I'd known,' she told him, 'I would never have started that conversation. Not in a million years.'

'What conversation?' Joe flashed her a grin and the glimpse of that unhappy little boy faded away. 'I can't remember any of it.' He got to his feet. 'They're playing my song in there. You coming in or do I have to go and find a new dance partner?'

Maggie felt a sudden need to shake off anything negative to do with weddings and babies. She wanted to be happy for her friends and she did, genuinely, believe that Cooper and Fizz were perfect for each other and that they were going to be happy together.

And maybe it hadn't been the best time for Joe to tell her about his unhappy history but there'd been a reason for that, hadn't there? He was offering her an explanation of why she had shocked him so badly and it was enough of an apology for her to believe that they could really put that conversation behind them. By the time they were working together again, it would all be forgiven and forgotten.

'Wait for me...' Maggie jumped to her feet to follow Joe. 'That's actually *my* song, not yours...'

Why on earth had he told Maggie so much about his childhood?

Joe closed his locker door and headed upstairs.

'You're an early bird.' Shirley was busy in the kitchen area of the staffroom. 'There's been a couple of late calls so the night shift crews aren't back yet.'

Joe glanced at his watch. He was very early. He'd woken up feeling an echo of the tension that had been between himself and Maggie when he'd arrived at the wedding two days ago and he couldn't just lie there and think about it. He'd needed to get up and get moving but even a run hadn't quite dealt with that note of tension.

He had ended the night of the wedding feeling like he and Maggie had not only mended any crack in their friendship but had strengthened its foundations considerably, but that had been flavoured by a party atmosphere of music and fun and a few beers. How different was it going to be when they were working together again? Now that Maggie knew something about him that nobody else did?

'I could smell those sausages,' Joe told Shirley. 'It was irresistible.'

Shirley smile was delighted. 'We've got bacon as well. And I'm going to grill tomatoes. Want a piece of toast while you're waiting?'

'No, thanks, Shirley. I won't spoil my appetite for one of your awesome breakfasts. I'll have a coffee and read the paper.'

He sat down at the table but he was reading headlines without taking much notice because he was still wondering whether his working relationship with Maggie might have changed after telling her something so personal.

Joe had never told anyone about how unhappy his childhood had been. He didn't even think about it, if he could help it. It was past history. Okay, it had shaped the way he lived his life now but why he might not want to get married was his own business. He was quite happy for other people to see him as being so committed to his career he didn't have the time or inclination to complicate his personal life by having his own family. He knew that some people considered him to be self-centred by making his life all about himself—his career, his hobbies, his parade of female companions—but he'd never cared about that, either.

Until Maggie had asked him to father a baby for her.

Until—for a split second—he'd actually imagined the reality of that. Of Maggie becoming pregnant. Of him feeling the pressure of being forced to do the 'decent' thing, even if that meant being involved in a child's life rather than marrying the mother. Of another child in the world who could end up without a father or feeling like his existence was some kind of horrible mistake.

'And here's another early bird.' Shirley's voice cut through his thoughts. 'Don't tell me you could smell the sausages halfway across town, too, Maggie?'

Joe's gaze flicked up and caught Maggie's instantly. Was she arriving at work early due to the same hint of nerves that had been bothering him? If so, it didn't show. Maggie looked just the same as ever, with that ready smile and palpable eagerness for whatever challenges lay ahead that day. She was one of those people who could brighten a room simply by walking into it.

'Morning, Shirley.' Maggie went to give their volunteer housekeeper a hug. 'How are your feet after all the dancing the other evening?'

Shirley sighed happily. 'Wasn't it just the best wedding ever?'

'It was. I haven't had so much fun in a very long time.'

'You and Joe were the stars of the dance floor,' Shirley said. 'Everybody knew that you could dance, Maggie, but Joe surprised us all.'

'I know. Talk about hidden talents… Who knows what else he's hiding? Maybe he's good at knitting?'

Both women laughed and then Maggie's smile was being directed at Joe and he found himself releasing a breath he hadn't known he was holding.

That was why he'd told her something so private the other night. Because he wanted her to understand why he could never do something like casually fathering a baby. Because he didn't want her to think he was being selfish or that he didn't value their friendship. Because he didn't want the 'dream team' to break apart.

Now he could relax. It was all good. Neither confessing something so personal about his childhood nor the step Maggie had taken onto totally unwelcome territory with the sperm donor conversation mattered any longer. Nothing had changed.

'Just wait till Christmas,' he warned them. 'You'll be first on the list for my homemade knitted slippers.'

Nothing had changed.

So why did it still feel like something *had* changed?

Responding swiftly to their first helicopter callout that day, getting airborne and getting as much information as possible about the scenario they were heading into was the same as it always was.

'Twenty-six-year-old male. Fall from height.' Joe read his pager message aloud as he got himself into the kind of head space he needed to be in when heading towards a potentially major trauma.

'What height?' Nick, the crewman, sounded curious.

'Not clear,' Maggie put in. 'He was putting up scaf-folding on a high level of an industrial building but nobody actually saw that he was falling until he bounced off a platform about three metres off the ground.'

'Landed on concrete?'

'Yep.'

'Ouch…'

'You said it.' Joe was thinking of just how serious this could be. A major head injury, serious fractures, chest trauma. Would their patient still be alive by the time they got on site?

He was not only alive, he was conscious.

Maggie got to the man's side first, although they hadn't had any discussion about who was going to lead this case. Not that it mattered and that was something that hadn't changed, either.

'Hey, Sean… I'm Maggie and this is my partner, Joe. We heard you had a bit of a fall…'

The young man groaned. 'It hurts really bad,' he told Maggie.

'Where does it hurt the most?'

'Legs…belly…'

'Were you knocked out?'

'Dunno…'

'He was out of it for a few minutes.' One of the group of builders clustered around the injured man was keen to help Maggie get the answers she needed. 'But he was breathing okay. We knew he wasn't dead.'

'And we didn't move him,' another man told her. 'We knew he might have hurt his back.'

'Good work.' Maggie nodded.

Joe glanced up from where he was getting a set of vital signs. Sean's airway was clear and his breathing was rapid but not shallow enough to suggest a serious chest injury. His heart rate was up and his skin was pale and clammy, which made it more likely that he was losing blood from somewhere and going into shock. Joe was reaching for the IV roll to get a line in and some fluids started when he glanced up at the circle of men around them and noticed that every set of male eyes here was focussed on Maggie.

Because she was leading the assessment of their workmate?

Or was it because she was blonde and cute?

And there it was. *Bang.* The 'something' that had changed. Not that he was going to spend more than a split second to take the information on board right now but he was aware of it.

He was thinking of Maggie as more than his paramedic partner. A part of his brain had stepped back to give him a bigger picture and he was observing her as a woman. As a potential mother. Or wife, perhaps, if she got over being so picky about trying to find the non-existent perfect man. For heaven's sake, she clearly had no trouble attracting male attention.

'I'll get some fluids up,' he muttered.

Maggie nodded. She was into her secondary survey now, having checked that there was no visible major bleeding going on.

'No external sign of head injury.'

'He had his hard hat on,' someone told them. 'But he pulled it off as soon as he woke up.'

'Ow...' Sean's cry was almost a scream as Maggie's hands reached his lower abdomen.

'Is that pain in your tummy? Here?'

'No...it's in my back...my legs... *Ow...*'

'He's got outward rotation of his left foot.' Joe finished securing the IV line he'd just put in. 'Hip or pelvic fracture?'

'And/or femoral. He's in a lot of pain.'

'Fentanyl and ketamine?' As usual, the lines of who was the lead medic in this case were blurring. They were well into their 'dream team' zone, where they could work as a single unit that had the advantage of two brains and two pairs of skilled hands.

'Please. I'll get a collar on. And a SAM?'

Joe nodded his agreement.

The SAM was a pelvic splint, a wide belt that Maggie slid beneath the hollow in Sean's lower back so that Joe could catch the strap on the end and help her position it low on Sean's hips.

'Hang on a tick... I haven't checked his pockets for anything like keys.'

Maggie double-checked the pockets on the other side. 'Clear.'

'Same.' Joe fed the long strap through the buckle on the belt and then applied tension on his side as Maggie pulled on a loop on the other side of the buckle. The belt tightened until it clicked into a locked position.

They had pain relief on board for their patient, oxygen and fluids running, and a neck collar as well as the pelvic splint. They still needed to get him securely onto their stretcher with his neck further protected by the cushions and straps that would prevent his head moving and then get him into an emergency department as quickly as possible where he could get the scans that would reveal any injuries and the surgery that was highly likely to be needed.

It wasn't until a long time later that they had the opportunity to do what they always tried to do after a scene like that, which was to think about the job as a whole, tick off the things they had done well and to discuss anything that they thought could have been managed better.

Except that when Joe took that mental step back to look at the job as a whole, he found he was still looking at Maggie in that different way.

'Ooh, look...' Maggie had opened the fridge in the staffroom kitchen. 'There's some left-over sausages from breakfast. Fancy one rolled up in a slice of bread with some tomato sauce?'

'Make that chilli sauce and I'm in.'

'Oh, *great* idea...' Maggie's grin was as good as applause. 'You're not just a pretty face, are you, Joe?' Her grin widened as she straightened, a container of sausages in her hands. 'Oh, that's right...you're actually not a pretty face at all.'

Maggie was, though. From this new and speculative viewpoint, as he watched her ferry the supplies they needed to the big table, Joe was rating his colleague as if he were a man who was seeing her for the first time—like those men on the building site this morning. Petite in height but a bit curvy in all the right places, blonde curls that refused to be restrained in any meaningful manner and big, blue eyes. Joe had never actually realised quite how blue they were until he'd seen her wearing that dress at the wedding the other day.

What was wrong with him that he'd never been attracted to his partner? Or *had* he been attracted when he'd first met Maggie and simply put it into the 'off limits' basket because they had both been in long-term relationships at the time? No, it had to be a chemistry thing, like Maggie had suggested, because from this viewpoint he'd give her a ten out of ten on an average male's attractiveness ratings chart. He also had the advantage of knowing how smart she was. How skilled. How kind she was to animals and small children. She'd be the perfect wife—for someone who wanted to be part of a big family.

Joe picked up a slice of bread, buttered it, put a sausage in the middle and slathered it with chilli sauce before rolling it up and taking a big bite.

'Mmm...'

Maggie made the same full-mouth mumbling noise of pleasure and Joe caught her gaze.

And then it really hit him...

He wasn't just thinking about Maggie in general terms of her attractiveness and why she was still single.

A very deep part of his brain was thinking about her in a much more specific way. Joe dragged his gaze free of Maggie's so fast it had to be impossible for her to have guessed what was going through his head. He certainly hoped that was the case, anyway, because he couldn't quite believe what it was he was thinking about.

If he'd been open to her crazy idea about finding a baby daddy, how would it have played out?

With an impersonal sample bottle and a turkey baster? Or would Maggie have thought a more natural form of conception might have been preferable? Maybe it had been the sound she'd made expressing her pleasure in the food she had in her mouth that had been the catalyst for going down this particular track. Joe could hear an echo of it again. It was just the kind of sound he could imagine her making in bed, if she was really enjoying some company...

Oh...*man*... He suddenly found it too much of a challenge to swallow the mouthful of food he had finished chewing. Maybe it wasn't a part of his brain that was responsible for what had changed between Maggie and himself.

At this precise moment, it felt like it was a deep part of his body that had been shocked into life by the whole episode of having to think about Maggie and baby-making. And it was putting two and two together and coming up with a total that was as unexpected as it was inappropriate. It felt like some sort of chemical reaction was taking place and it was...appalling...

Forcing himself to swallow was actually painful. Slamming both mental and physical doors to what was going on in his head and his body was also almost painful but it had to be done. Quickly and conclusively. And it could never be allowed to happen again.

Ever.

'I think you used too much sauce,' Maggie told him. 'You look like you're breaking out in a sweat.'

'Doubt it.' Joe didn't dare look up to catch her gaze again. Instead, he took another bite of his sausage and, this time, it was much easier to swallow.

Maggie wasn't to know that anything had changed between them so all he had to do was pretend things were normal and they would be again. Hopefully very soon.

He could do this.

No sweat.

CHAPTER FOUR

'HE'S GOING TO make a great dad, one day, isn't he?'

For a moment, Maggie couldn't think of anything to say in response to Laura's comment, so she turned her head to see what had prompted it.

Harrison was a little way away from where she and Laura were unpacking the barbecue supplies onto one of the picnic tables at this beach, watching Joe set up his windsurfing board and sail.

'What's that?' she heard Harrison ask.

'It's called an up-haul. It's a rope for pulling the sail up out of the water.'

'And what's that?'

'That's called a dagger board. It's like a big fin. If I pull on this lever here, it makes the board go down, see?'

'Why?'

'You can use it to stop the board being so wobbly sometimes. To stabilise it.'

'Can I try?'

'To pull the lever? Sure.'

'No…' Harrison looked up at Joe. 'Can I try in the water—like Jack's going to do?'

'Sorry, buddy…you'd need a wetsuit in this cold

water. And you're a bit little to try windsurfing just yet. The sail's quite heavy to pull up.'

Jack was zipping up the back of his wetsuit as he joined Joe and Harrison. 'I don't know if *I'm* going to be able to do it, Harry,' he said. 'This is the first time I've ever tried windsurfing. You just wait. I bet I fall into the water with a big splash.'

Harrison laughed and Joe ruffled his hair, which made the small boy duck his head shyly. 'You can help me,' he told Harry. 'I'm going to stand here and tell Jack what to do. You can watch and tell me if you think he's doing a good job, okay?'

'Okay.' Harrison's nod was solemn. He was going to take this responsibility seriously.

Maggie was smiling as she turned back to Laura. 'He's so cute.'

'Which one? Jack, Joe or Harry?'

'Harry, of course.'

'Yeah…' Laura's smile was misty. 'He is pretty cute, isn't he?'

She seemed to have forgotten the comment she'd made about Joe's future as a father and Maggie certainly wasn't going to remind her. She'd never reveal the private information that Joe had shared with her about not wanting to be a husband or father and she would never, ever break that confidence and tell anyone about why he felt like that. It felt good to know that he'd trusted her enough to tell her and even better that she could protect his privacy. Their friendship was back on track. Better than ever, even, judging by the last few shifts they had worked together.

'It's a treat to get out like this to a beach,' Laura added. 'How often do we get a day like this on a weekend?'

'About as often as we all get a day off at the same time.'

'I know, right? When Jack said that Joe was going to give him a windsurfing lesson, I knew we had to gate-crash the party. That's why I offered to do the barbecue.'

'And I wasn't going to miss out on the fun.' Maggie nodded. She lifted the lid of a cooler. 'Did we remember to put bacon in here? It's not a proper barbecue without bacon.'

'We've got hamburgers, bacon and some steak. There's wine and beer in the other cooler. Ooh…why don't we take a break and have a glass of wine while we watch the boys?'

'Sounds like a plan.'

By the time Joe had shown Jack how to carry the board and sail into water that was deep enough for him to try getting on, Laura and Maggie were set up on the sand, sipping their drinks and waiting for the entertainment.

'Okay, Jack…' Joe called. 'Make sure the dagger board is down and that you're standing in line with the sail on the other side with the wind at your back.'

'Yep. All good,' Jack called back.

'Now put your hands on the centre line, shoulder-width apart and climb onto the board.'

'He's making it wobble,' Harrison said.

'He is,' Joe agreed. 'Stay on your knees, Jack. And hold onto the up-haul before you try standing up.'

'Doesn't look that easy,' Laura said to Maggie.

'No… Uh-oh…'

Trying to lift the sail, Jack was leaning too far back. He lost his balance and crashed back into the water with a huge splash that make Harrison shriek with laughter. Laura's chuckle was an echo of her son's enjoyment.

'It's so good to see him out like this. He used to be so scared of men.'

'I know. I remember when Jack moved in with us and Harry burst into tears every time he came into the room.'

'He never had a problem with Cooper, though, which surprised me because Cooper's so big.'

'He likes Joe now, too.' Maggie was looking at the backs of the two figures in front of them. Tall Joe and short Harry. Their postures were almost identical, standing there with their feet apart and their arms folded. It gave her a beat of something rather poignant because it looked as though they could be a father and son. Because Laura had been right in that Joe would make a great father. He was always so kind and gentle in dealing with children but he could be firm if he needed to be—to keep them safe or provide essential medical treatment.

It was completely a personal choice whether or not to be a parent but it was sad to think that no child would get to have Joe as a father. And that he might miss out on learning that a family could be so much better than the one he'd experienced as a child himself.

'We're lucky,' Laura said. 'It was the best decision I ever made to move into a big house and find people to share it with rather than to stay by myself with Harry in that small apartment. He'd never have had any male role models if I'd done that.'

That was probably true, Maggie thought. She'd never known Laura to show the slightest interest in dating anybody and she never talked about Harrison's father.

'It can't be easy, being a single mum.'

'No.' Laura took another sip of her wine. 'But it's much better than being in a bad situation with a partner.'

Maggie made a sympathetic sound. She'd always had the impression that Laura had escaped from an abusive relationship but she'd never tried asking questions that her flatmate might not want to answer. Given her own recent thoughts about choosing to be a single mother, though, she was curious.

'How old was Harry when you split up with his father?'

'About three months. Just when I was due to go back to work after maternity leave.'

'Oh, no…what did you do?'

'What could I do? I just did my best and got on with it. I'd already arranged childcare so that I could go back to work.'

'So you were working all day and then looking after a tiny baby by yourself all night…'

'It wasn't easy,' Laura agreed. 'Leaving him in day care when he was so little was the hardest thing I'd ever done but we muddled through somehow. And life's good now. I love my job and Harry's happy. What more could I want?'

Again, Maggie responded with no more than a sound of agreement. She was answering that question silently, however. Maybe Laura could want a partner to share the parenting. Or to make part of her life about herself as someone special and not about her being a mother or a nurse. Even with a child as company constantly out of work hours and adult flatmates around a lot of the time, there had to be moments when Laura felt lonely or that there was something missing in her life.

The way Maggie did at weddings?

Or when she was holding other people's babies?

How much worse could that be, though, if she was struggling to hold down her job and look after a baby alone, the way Laura had done?

'I don't think I could do it,' she murmured aloud.

'What—windsurfing?' Laura was watching Jack again.

'Keep your hands on the boom,' Joe was telling him. 'You lean the sail towards the back of the board to turn into the wind and to the nose of the board to turn away from the wind.'

'He's wobbling again,' Harrison shouted.

'He's okay. Look at that. Well done, Jack…'

'You could do that with your hands tied behind your back,' Laura told Maggie. 'You can ride a motorbike, for heaven's sake. And dangle out of helicopters when you need to. You could do anything you put your mind to.'

'I was talking about being a single mother. I was actually thinking of trying it, seeing as I can't seem to find anyone remotely suitable to partner up with.'

'Really?' Laura sounded shocked. 'How was that going to work? Get pregnant and not let the guy know?'

'No, I'd never do that. But you know…there are sperm banks available.'

Laura shook her head. 'Don't rush into anything. I mean… I love Harry to bits and I wouldn't be without him but it's not what I would have deliberately chosen for my life. No way… You've still got lots of time to find someone.'

The sound Maggie made this time was less than convinced.

'It does happen. Look at Cooper and Fizz.'

'They're due back from their honeymoon soon, aren't they?'

'Next week. I'm looking forward to having Fizz back working in Emergency.' Laura scrambled to her feet. 'Looks like Jack's had enough of his first lesson. Might be time to get that barbecue started.'

But Maggie stayed where she was for the moment. Joe had taken the board from Jack and was heading further out to sea, making it look easy as he manoeuvred the sail to catch the wind and began to pick up speed.

Jack and Harrison came past where Maggie was sitting on the sand.

'That's a lot harder than it looks,' he told her. 'The way my shoulders feel right now, I might have trouble lifting a beer.'

'You wobbled a lot,' Harrison agreed. 'But Joe said you did a good job.' He skipped ahead of Jack. 'Mum? I'm *starving...*'

Maggie was still watching Joe, who was skimming across the relatively flat water at an impressive speed now. He was making the board jump from the surface, catching a short ride in the air before landing again and doing turns that changed his direction so swiftly and smoothly it looked like a kind of dance. She knew how much muscle strength that would take. Like other forms of dancing, being able to make it look that effortless and elegant actually took enormous strength and skill.

And that made Maggie remember all the dancing they'd done at Cooper and Fizz's wedding and how much fun it had been. She could almost feel his arms around her and the strength she had felt in his muscles as he'd lifted her feet off the ground and spun her around. And then, somehow, her memories and what

she was watching right now and even that conversation
with Laura somehow coalesced in Maggie's brain, and
she was simultaneously thinking about Joe not wanting
to be a father and what he'd looked like standing beside
Harrison and about his muscles and his arms around her
and even the disappointment of knowing that he would
never agree to be a sperm donor crept into the mix, and
the alchemy of it all became very weird.

Because Maggie suddenly thought about what might
have happened if Joe had been open to the idea of fathering a baby for her and how they might have achieved
her goal. For the first time ever, she was thinking of
Joe…and sex…and it was doing something very pecu-
liar deep inside her body. She knew what that spear of
sensation was all about, too.

Physical attraction.

Pure, unadulterated lust, that's what it was.

Her body liked the idea of having sex with Joe. A lot.
So much so that Maggie could feel the flush of colour
heating her cheeks and she had to scramble to her feet
and turn her back on Joe before he carried his board and
sail from the water and got close enough to see what
might be a very odd expression on her face.

She had to get her head straight and make sure she
never tapped into that line of thought again. Not that it
had anything to do with any plan of becoming a single
mother that had been fading away even before she'd
taken Laura's warning on board. No…it was bad enough
feeling any kind of attraction to a good friend. Not only
a good friend but the person she loved working with so
much. The other half of the 'dream team'.

If Joe knew that she had entertained any thoughts
of sexual attraction to him, he'd either be horrified and

back off to a safe space or he might be curious enough to make something happen. Either way, it would not only change and potentially destroy the friendship they had, it could do exactly the same thing to their working relationship.

No matter how good that sex would probably be, it wouldn't be worth it. Maggie was going to make absolutely sure that nobody knew what she'd been thinking. She wasn't even going to allow herself to think about it again.

Ever...

Thoughts could be like unwanted seeds. Weeds that insisted on growing no matter how diligently you tried to pull them out.

Despite Joe's best efforts, it was proving impossible to stop having inappropriate thoughts about Maggie. Even in a moment like this, when he should have been revelling in what was a different kind of adventure at work. Getting a callout to assist the coastguard in responding to a medical event on a ship was the kind of variety that made their job so exciting and Maggie was clearly loving every minute of this wild ride out to the entrance of Wellington Harbour. Daylight was fading and the winds were strong enough to have made the prospect of winching a paramedic onto a boat too dangerous so here they were cresting huge swells and crashing into troughs in this powerful and well-equipped rescue vessel. Maggie was small and light enough to be bounced right out of her seat and she was hanging on tightly as a splash of spray caught her face, but she was laughing as she shook the sea water from her skin.

And, okay, the rigid-hulled inflatable boat was unsinkable with the fat air cushions surrounding it but most people would be terrified by being thrown around in waves this big. Nothing really scared Maggie, did it? Or, if it did, she kept it well hidden.

Who knew how sexy that kind of courage in a woman could be?

Just how physically attractive his colleague was had been right under his nose for so long but it was only now that the genie had been released from the bottle that it was becoming apparent that there had been a lot of other stuff bottled up as well.

Like the way Maggie looked when she was in her leather gear for riding her bike.

Or the way she'd looked on the beach that night, when they had been toasting marshmallows on a drift-wood fire after he'd given Jack his first windsurfing lesson. The way her face had glowed in the firelight. The sound of her laughter. Although focussing on Maggie had perhaps been a way to distract himself from the poignant feeling of loss that having Harrison standing beside him and 'helping' as he'd watched Jack's progress. He'd felt an odd bond with the little boy who didn't have a father around but at least Laura would never make Harry feel like he'd ruined her life. He was clearly the centre of his mother's universe and deeply loved. A little boy as lucky as all children deserved to be.

'Whoa...'

They hit the bottom of the next swell with a thump that sent Maggie toppling sideways. Both Joe and one of the coastguard crew reached to help her catch her balance but Joe got there first. For a moment, as he helped her upright, his face was within inches of hers.

'You okay?'

'I'm good.' Maggie was smiling and nodding but then her gaze caught Joe's as she settled back into her seat and he saw the flare of...*something*...

Oh, no... Had she guessed what had just gone through his head? When their faces had been so close? That they had been almost close enough to kiss...?

He knew exactly how horrified she would be if that was the case. He could still hear the echoes of that conversation they'd had at Cooper and Fizz's wedding about what Maggie thought the 'real thing' was all about and he'd said that he and Maggie were friends but it would never be anything more than that and Maggie's response had been vehement.

God, no...because there's no chemistry.

What he was feeling right now felt a lot like rather powerful chemistry but he knew it was one-sided.

He had to try harder, that was all there was to it.

Good grief...

Had she really thought that she could simply order herself to stop thinking about something and have it magically disappear from her head?

Ever since that trip to the beach, Maggie had found it impossible to stop those inappropriate thoughts about Joe from sneaking into her head. Or sometimes into her body *before* her head. Like the way they just had when she'd felt his hands grabbing onto her body to stop her falling. Catching his gaze had been a big mistake because that had only made it worse. Hazel brown eyes had always been her favourite colour so how come she'd never noticed that Joe had eyes that looked like there was sunshine making the brown so golden and warm.

It had felt like it took far too much time to drag her

gaze clear of his and, for a horrible micro-second, Maggie wondered if he'd guessed what she'd been feeling and thinking. She clung onto the handles on the edge of her seat even more tightly as they rode the next swell. Falling into Joe's arms again would not be a good idea.

Catching his gaze like that again was a no-no, too. Imagine if he knew what she was thinking? He'd spelled out his lack of interest in anything more than friendship the night they'd been talking at the wedding when he'd said that they would never be more than friends. And she'd been so quick and definite in her agreement, hadn't she?

How could things have changed so much?

It was a puzzle that Maggie didn't even want to think about and it was more than easy enough to forget thanks to the adrenaline rush of this job. The ride on the rough sea was awesome but the challenge of getting alongside the larger fishing vessel, catching the ladder that swung against the hull and getting themselves and their equipment in through the narrow door needed absolute concentration. That they completed that part of this challenge successfully was enough to have Maggie grinning from ear to ear as Joe and some of the ship's crew helped to pull her inside and out of the wind.

'Well done. That wasn't easy.'

The fishermen were grinning back at her but Joe wasn't. He almost looked irritated as he picked up one end of the stretcher that had their pack strapped onto it.

'Let's go. Where's our patient?'

'Follow us. He's going to be happy to see you guys. He's in a hell of a lot of pain.'

'He's had a fall, yes?'

'Yeah. He lost his footing on a ladder and he was

hanging on with one arm but then he fell when we hit another wave. Looks like he's broken something. His arm, or his shoulder, maybe.'

There was a strong smell of fish on this lower deck of the ship and it was rolling enough to make the combination a little nauseating. Maggie breathed through her mouth to lessen the impact.

'Did he get knocked out?' she asked.

'Don't think so. Not judging by the amount of noise he was making as soon as it happened, anyway. Listen… that's him you can hear now.'

Fishermen were tough but a complete dislocation and possible fracture of an elbow joint was a very painful injury. It was also urgent that it be relocated as quickly as possible because of the danger of damage to the brachial artery and nerves.

'Hang in there, mate,' Joe told him, as soon as he'd introduced himself and Maggie. 'We're going to get some pain relief on board for you asap and try and sort that elbow out for you. Are you allergic to anything that you know of?'

The injured man, who had turned out to be the ship's chef, shook his head. Even that movement made him cry out in pain as he tried to hold his arm still.

Maggie busied herself getting an IV line established as Joe quickly checked the man for any other major injuries and then looked at his limb baselines on the injured arm.

'Sharp scratch,' she warned, when she was about to slide the cannula into their patient's skin. 'Don't move…'

With the level of pain the chef was already in, he didn't even notice the needle going into his arm.

'Can you wiggle your fingers for me?' Joe asked.

'If you close your eyes, can you feel me touching your hand here? And here?'

'Limb baselines are down,' Joe told Maggie moments later as she was drawing up the drugs she knew they were going to need. 'Skin's cold, capillary refill is slow and I can only get a faint radial pulse.'

'I'll get set up for oxygen and SpO2 monitoring.' Maggie reached for the ECG dots for the life pack and a mask for the oxygen cylinder.

Joe administered the drugs that would sedate their patient deeply enough to make it possible to try and relocate his elbow and then he and Maggie positioned themselves, with Maggie wrapping her hands around his forearm and Joe preparing to provide counter-traction on the upper arm.

'Ready?'

Maggie caught his gaze. 'Ready.'

How often had they done this? she mused as they gently began to apply pressure in opposite directions. Worked like this, so closely together, knowing that each of them completely trusted the other. If she was ever sick or injured, Maggie thought, it would be Joe she would want to turn up and look after her. She would trust him with her life, if it ever came to that.

Joe held her gaze for a moment longer.

'Even if this doesn't work,' Joe said, 'it should re-store circulation enough to be helpful.'

His crew stood in the background, watching.

'It's still hurting him, isn't it?' one of them muttered.

'He won't remember it,' Joe told them. 'And…there we go. I think we've got it in the right place now. We're going to splint the arm and get him secured onto our stretcher there. We might need a bit of help from you guys to get him onto the coastguard boat.'

'Wind's dropping,' someone told them. 'It won't be quite as bad as it was when you got here.'

It was still a mission. Climbing down that ladder, after the stretcher had been lowered and taken on board, was the scariest thing Maggie had done in a very long time. It didn't help that a wave broke and soaked her as she reached the lower rungs. With salt water in her eyes and a boat that was a moving target, she was extremely grateful to feel several hands grabbing her arms to pull her safely on board.

It was no surprise to blink the stinging water from her eyes to find that one set of those hands belonged to Joe. But she'd known that already, hadn't she? She had felt it...

It was only a skeleton staff that stayed on the Aratika Rescue Base for night shifts. By the time Maggie and Joe got back there, having transferred their patient to a road crew at the coastguard base, the crew on duty were out on a job and they knew the night manager would be manning the radio and probably catching up on paperwork in his office.

They needed to fill him in with any extra details he needed about their mission but there were more important things to do before they went upstairs from the locker room level. Despite the protective clothing that allowed them to get wet and work outside, delaying the development of hypothermia, at a certain point conditions could defeat the fabric technology.

'You're frozen,' Joe told Maggie. 'Look at how hard you're shivering. And you smell kind of like a dead fish.'

Maggie beamed at him. 'I know,' she said, through chattering teeth. 'It was great, wasn't it?'

He had to smile back. 'It was a hot one, all right. And what we both need right now is a shower that's just as hot. You can go first.' He took the depleted pack of medical supplies to the far corner of the locker room. It would need to be sorted and restocked but that could wait until morning.

'J-Joe?'

Turning back, he could see Maggie's head poking out from the door that led to the showers and toilets.

'What's up?'

'Um…'

She sounded embarrassed, Joe decided. Or worried? He was closing the gap between them rapidly.

He saw what the problem was as soon as he stepped through the door to the shower room. Maggie was still shivering and her fingers were obviously too cold to be functioning as well as was needed to cope with all the Velcro fastenings and zips on her flight suit and boots.

She was colder than he'd realised. The need to look after her and treat the problem took over and Joe flipped the handle to get the shower running and warming up. Then he turned back to Maggie.

'Sit down,' he ordered. 'Let's get those boots off first.'

Maggie sat obediently on the bench seat facing the open shower. Joe's fingers felt clumsy but were co-operating well enough to unzip the boots and pull them off and then peel off her socks.

'Okay. Stand up again and we'll get this flight suit off. You should be able to manage the rest.'

He started undoing all the fastenings as soon as Maggie was on her feet again. This small room was getting warmer by the minute thanks to the steam from the running shower behind them. Joe realised he must have pushed the door shut without noticing when he'd come in to assist Maggie.

He peeled back the top of the flight suit and she grabbed onto his arm to keep her balance as she stepped out of the legs.

'All good?'

'Um…' Maggie held her hands out in front of her. They were still shaking. She tried to hook her fingers under the hem of the thermal top and then pull it up but she was laughing at the same time. 'I've gone a bit wobbly,' she said. 'I had no idea how cold I'd been getting.'

'Fine.' Joe was still in professional mode. This was no problem. He took hold of the hem of the long-sleeved shirt and pulled it up over Maggie's head.

Oh…*man*… His jaw dropped. How could she not have been wearing a bra under that shirt? The shock made it hard to raise his gaze from somewhere it should not be resting. Every instance of realising how attracted he was to Maggie coalesced in this moment into a desire like nothing he'd ever felt in his life. When he did manage to drag his gaze upwards, he saw something in Maggie's eyes that was even more of a shock.

Desire…

And it looked as fierce as what was threatening to produce the greatest test his self-control would ever have to deal with.

For a long, long moment, with the steam of the shower billowing gently around them, they held each other's gaze.

And then, before he'd started trying to analyse whatever was going on here, and without the slightest idea of who had made the first move, Joe was kissing Maggie.

Or Maggie was kissing him...

It didn't matter. It was rapidly becoming the wildest, most exciting kiss he'd ever had in his life. The moment Maggie's tongue first touched his, inviting him to deepen that kiss, drove any rational thought behind a door in his brain that he had no immediate incentive to open.

Maggie wanted this. As much as he did.

How astonishing was that?

Oh...

If being in a steamy environment after getting too cold had made Maggie feel a bit wobbly, it was nothing to how weak this kiss was making her legs feel. She'd thought she'd known how good sex with Joe might be but she'd had *no* idea...

Maybe it was being enhanced by the adrenaline rush of the sea rescue job they'd both been challenged by. Or maybe her brain wasn't functioning perfectly thanks to the early stages of hypothermia. Whatever it was, this was an experience like nothing Maggie had ever had and she just knew that whatever alchemy had come together in this moment was never going to happen again.

This was a once-in-a-lifetime thing.

Normal rules could not be applied. This was a case of *carpe diem* if ever there was. Seize the day. Or seize the moment, anyway...

Her fingers seemed to be working a whole lot better now. Enough to be getting past the fastenings of Joe's flight suit and trying to find some actual skin to touch. The tight fabric of her thermal leggings made it feel as though Joe's hands were inside them as he cupped her buttocks and pulled her closer. Close enough for her to realise that he was just as into this as she was.

Her groan of need against his lips seemed a signal to finish that blissful meeting of their mouths.

'*Maggie*...' Joe's voice was raw. 'We can't do this...'

She couldn't pull away. 'Why not? I... I want this, Joe...'

'Oh, *God*...so do I but...'

He pulled back far enough for Maggie to see his eyes. To see that desire had darkened them enough to appear black. How sexy was that?

'But it's not a good idea,' he ground out.

'Skin-to-skin contact is supposed to be a great way to treat hypothermia.'

Joe closed his eyes. He was clearly struggling. 'We work together, Maggie. We're *friends*...'

She had her hands on his back, beneath his thermal shirt. She could push her fingertips against his bare skin as she pressed herself closer. She didn't want to think about consequences right now. Whatever they were, they could deal with them later. This was a one-off. They would lose this moment very soon.

'Stop talking,' she whispered. 'Start kissing.'

His lips were on hers again almost instantly. Joe was just as carried away by whatever had ignited between them as Maggie was and that made this only more ir-resistible.

'Not safe...' she heard Joe groan against her lips.

Maggie managed to engage one small, rational part of her brain and extracted what she needed to know to give her a wash of relief. That was one normal rule that did need to be applied but it took only a heartbeat to be quite sure she was right. Her cycles were as regular as clockwork and she was close enough to the end to make any risk so small it was insignificant.

'It's safe,' she told Joe. 'I promise…'

CHAPTER FIVE

STUNNED.

That was the only word for it.

Joe had seen his own bewilderment reflected in Maggie's eyes in the immediate aftermath of that explosion of passion in the shower room of the Aratika Rescue Base.

He'd even articulated it, although admittedly it wasn't a particularly eloquent comment.

'What the hell was that?' he'd murmured as they were both trying to catch their breath.

Maggie had blinked back at him. She looked as if she was trying to smile but couldn't quite manage it. 'So… I guess your other hidden talent isn't knitting, after all?'

That had defused the sudden, alarmingly awkward tension between them as the reality of their nakedness and the intense lovemaking they had just shared sank in. Joe's breath had been expelled in a bark of laughter. Shaking his head, he'd dropped a quick kiss on Maggie's lips, gathered his discarded clothes and left her alone in the room that had been so steamy on far more than a literal level.

He was still bemused, if not shocked, by what had happened by the time he was dressed in a clean uniform and was nursing a cup of coffee in the upstairs staffroom. He had to wait for Maggie to appear. Not that he had any idea of what he was going to say to her but he couldn't just head home after that extraordinary encounter, could he?

It wasn't just the fact that what he'd considered for years as being a close friendship with no sexual agenda had just been proven so wrong in such an explosive manner. It was...the *sex*...

The most exciting—*satisfying*—sex he'd ever experienced in his life.

Was that due to the unexpectedness of it? he wondered. Or the risk that they could have been discovered by the crew returning to the base? Or perhaps it was the fact that it was the first time he'd ever had unprotected sex?

Oh...*help*... A bubble of panic rose in Joe's throat but he took a deep breath and swallowed it away. Maggie had assured him that it was safe and there was no one in the world he trusted more than Maggie.

But...what now?

They were colleagues. They had been friends for years. Neither of them had ever been attracted to each other before and they were the opposite of suitable candidates for anything more than a friendship because they wanted very different things from life. And Joe didn't want a relationship with Maggie because his relationships always fizzled out in the end and that was the last thing he wanted to happen with a friendship he valued so highly.

Maggie had made a joke about it so maybe it had been no big deal for her. Perhaps they could put it down to a moment of madness and pretend it had never happened. But that would mean it could never happen again. While Joe's head was telling him that was the sensible way forward here, his body was registering something like rebellion. How could you experience something like that and not want it to happen again—if nothing else, just to find out if it actually *had* been that good? A knot formed in his gut as he heard the clatter of boots on the stairs because he knew that just seeing Maggie again could be enough to reawaken the flames of the astonishing desire that had blindsided him.

Except it wasn't Maggie. Or it was, but she was following Cooper and his night shift partner, Jack, who were both carrying take-out containers of food. Maggie swerved without looking at Joe, heading to the kitchen counter to make herself a cup of coffee.

'Look at you,' Jack said to Joe. 'You look like you've been out windsurfing.' He sat down at the table. 'You should have paged us to let us know you were back on base. We could have picked you up some food.'

'How was the job?' Cooper pushed his chopsticks out of their paper packet. 'I'm dead jealous. I've been waiting for a coastguard callout since I started working here and there we were stuck in a multi-vehicle pile-up on the motorway.'

'It was awesome.' It was Maggie who answered Cooper. 'I think it might have been one of the most exciting callouts I've ever had.'

Joe swallowed hard. Was she referring to that wild boat ride? The experience of treating a patient in a very unusual location…?

Or could she be referring to what had happened when they'd arrived back on base?

Maybe Maggie would also be disappointed if they never got to do that again.

'How come you're still here?' Jack asked. 'We heard the ambulance being dispatched to meet the coast-guards' boat ages ago.'

'We got pretty cold and wet,' Joe told them. 'Maggie had borderline hypothermia. We both needed a hot shower and a change of clothes.'

'Skin-to-skin contact might have been quicker,' Jack said around a mouthful of noodles.

Cooper laughed. 'And a lot more fun.'

Maggie sat down at the table with them. 'I'll remind you of that when you and Jack get sent out into the elements.'

'Hey...' Cooper was still grinning. 'I'm a happily married man.'

'And we're just good friends,' Jack added. 'Don't listen to those rumours.'

Maggie was laughing now, too. The atmosphere felt perfectly normal and that was the moment that Maggie finally caught Joe's gaze.

She looked happy, he realised. Sure, there was a question in her eyes but it was probably exactly the same question that was becoming a chant somewhere in the back of his own head.

Was it going to happen again?

'It can't happen again.'

Maggie needed to say it before Joe did. Because it might feel like less of a disappointment if it was her own decision?

But...*oh*...

She'd never had sex like that. Ever. She'd suspected

that Joe might be good at it—he'd had plenty of practice over the years, after all—but she'd never expected
that he could be *that* good.

The insanity had begun to recede rapidly in the wake
of that extraordinary encounter, however. Even as Maggie had stood there in the steam, trying to catch her
breath, she'd been increasingly aware of the enormity
of what they'd just done and was reminding herself, in a
flash of clarity, of all the reasons why she'd known she
had to ignore the attraction she'd developed towards Joe.

It could destroy their friendship.

It could harm their working relationship.

In a moment of panic, Maggie had done the only
thing she could think of that might lessen that enormity, and she'd cracked a joke about him demonstrating
another one of his hidden talents. It wasn't enough, of
course. She knew they needed to talk about it and that
it had to happen fast and not be left to get more awkward to deal with, like that baby daddy conversation
had become. But Cooper and Jack had arrived back on
base as she'd headed upstairs and it seemed to take for
ever until they got another callout and she was left in
the staffroom alone with Joe.

He was staring at her now that she had opened what
could be the most awkward conversation they'd ever
had. She'd expected him to look relieved at her statement or possibly embarrassed at being reminded of what
they'd done but it wasn't easy to interpret what she could
see in those dark eyes. Wariness, she decided. He was
waiting to see what she was going to say next. Whether
it might be going to start with a 'but'.

'It shouldn't have happened in the first place.' She lowered her voice even more. 'And I think it was my fault.'

It was definitely her fault. Joe had tried to talk her out of it, hadn't he? She'd practically insisted. Told him to shut up and kiss her again.

'Sorry,' she added.

'Excuse me?' Joe's eyes had narrowed. 'Are you suggesting I've got no self-control? If I'd wanted to stop, Maggie Lewis, I could have stopped. Okay?'

Maggie blinked. 'Okay…'

He'd wanted it? As much as she had? Well, well…

'I'm not saying it was a good idea,' Joe continued. 'But we're both adults. We both made that choice and we can both deal with it.'

Maggie nodded. 'But it can't happen again.'

'No.'

'We can still be friends, right?'

'Of course.'

'We can still go to the movies this weekend with Cooper and Fizz and Jack?'

'Sure.'

'And it won't be weird?'

'It might be a little bit weird,' Joe admitted. 'But we'll cope. And we're not going to talk about it again, okay? We're not even going to *think* about it at work.'

Maggie's nod emphasised her total agreement.

But then she caught Joe's gaze and a curious mix of apprehension and excitement tightened something deep inside her belly.

They both knew it was totally going to happen again.

'We did it again.' Joe pushed his hair back from his forehead as he let the rest of his breath out in a soft groan. 'When we said we wouldn't.'

'Yeah…but we had to find out, didn't we?'

'Find out what?'

'Whether it was going to be as good as the first time.'

'Yeah… I guess…'

'It was, wasn't it?'

'Oh, yeah… Possibly better…'

Joe was still wondering how that could actually be true. He was lying on his back, his eyes shut, still waiting for his heart rate to return to a normal level, still feeling the aftershocks of discovering that it wasn't some never-to-be-found-again alchemy of unusual elements that had made sex with Maggie so unbelievably awesome. It was simply the explosive combination of their personal chemistries.

This was a normal bed with no danger of being discovered, after a normal day off, although he couldn't currently remember the plot of the movie they'd gone to see with their friends. He'd been careful to use the usual level of protection he always used but none of that normality had diminished the excitement or satisfaction of that sex.

'Mmm…' Maggie sounded as if she was smiling. 'So what are we going to do now?'

'Don't know. It's still not a good idea, is it? We're friends. We work together.'

'It's not as though it's never happened before. Look at Cooper at Fizz.'

'That's completely different.'

'Why is it different?' He felt Maggie moving and turned his head to find she was propped up on one elbow.

'They got married.' Joe was aware of a beat of discomfort now. Was Maggie thinking that this new development in their relationship was leading somewhere? 'I don't want to marry you, Maggie.'

'Don't even go there,' Maggie agreed. 'I don't want to marry you, either. Believe me, I'll know who I want to marry—probably within a few minutes of meeting him. That's how it happened for my mum and dad. They took one look at each other and just *knew*. It certainly wasn't something I was thinking when I met you, mate.'

The relief was enough to make Joe smile into the darkness. 'You don't have to sound quite so adamant.'

'Hey… We both know we're on different planets when it comes to a life partner. You told me your life story. I totally get that you don't want kids.'

'And you do.' Joe nodded.

'Six of them,' Maggie said.

Joe shuddered. *'Really?'*

'Yep.'

'Why?'

'I grew up as an only child. Don't get me wrong, I had a great childhood and I love my mum and dad to bits, but the best weekends or holidays I ever had were when I got to tag along with a friend's family and their brothers and sisters.' Maggie flopped back onto her pillow with a sigh. 'Good times. Like picnics or parties. Once, it was a combination. My friend Suzie had a huge family and I got invited to her picnic birthday party. There were balloons tied to the trees and fairy bread and games like…oh…do you remember Bullrush?'

'The game of tag where everybody who gets tagged turns into a chaser?'

'That's the one.'

'It got banned at my school for being dangerous. Too many kids got injured.'

'The fun police are everywhere,' Maggie muttered. 'We got to climb trees in those days, too. And jump off rocks and just have fun and…' a poignant note crept into her voice '…it was just so much more fun in a big family.'

'Fun's good,' Joe murmured. He wanted to change the subject, however. He could imagine a small Maggie in a scene like that, running around or jumping off rocks, her blonde curls bouncing and her face glowing with the joy of it all. He couldn't remember anything really joyous about his own childhood and he certainly didn't want a reminder of the less than happy memories. It was in the past and best left there. Besides, that wasn't actually what they'd been talking about.

'So we're on the same page, then. This isn't something that's going anywhere?'

'No.'

It was Joe's turn to prop himself up on his elbow. 'No, we're not on the same page?'

Maggie grinned up at him. 'No, it's not going anywhere. We're both adults, Joe. We're both single. We're not doing anything wrong.'

'It could mess with our friendship.'

'Not if we're both on the same page and we're not expecting it to go anywhere. Maybe it shouldn't have started, but it did and you didn't exactly have to twist my arm to come home with you after the movie tonight, did you?'

'No.' In fact, whose idea had it been to keep the evening going after Cooper had declared that he and Fizz needed to head home straight after the movie because his pregnant wife needed her rest? Joe couldn't remember. Much like their encounter in the shower room at the base, it had been a mutual and pretty much simultaneous choice.

'And maybe it's not going to last long at all but while it's fun, is there anything wrong with enjoying it? Having some fun?' The tip of Maggie's tongue appeared as she ran it across her bottom lip. 'I don't know about you, but it's a very long time since I've had quite *this* much fun.'

'Mmm…' Joe's head had begun dipping the moment he'd seen that tip of her tongue. Any fears of ruining their friendship or working relationship were evaporating in the face of what Maggie seemed to be offering, which was a 'no strings, no expectations' enjoyment of the best sex ever. What man in his right mind was going to argue with that?

His lips were on Maggie's by the time she finished speaking so he only just managed a couple of extra words. 'Fun's good…'

Oh…thank *goodness*…

Maggie stayed where she was for a long minute, sitting on the toilet with her head in her hands as she breathed the longest sigh of relief ever.

The last few days hadn't been fun at all.

She'd been late with her period. She had been so absolutely sure that she had been in the safest possible part of her cycle that night in the shower room but then her period hadn't arrived and it was *always* on time. She'd actually been on the verge of a trip to the pharmacy to buy a pregnancy test kit. Well, to be honest, she should have done it days ago but she'd managed to maintain a state of almost complete denial.

She didn't need to go down that route now and the

wave of relief was overpowering. She even had an explanation for the unexpected blip in her regularity because that was often due to stress, wasn't it? And Maggie *had* been stressed about that falling out with Joe. Not as stressed as she'd been the last few days, mind you.

Maggie wasn't even going to try and imagine what it might have been like having to explain to Joe that she'd got her timing wrong enough for the consequences of that first time together to be disastrous. And an accidental pregnancy would have been a disaster, she had no doubts about that. Any thoughts of planned single parenthood had been banished for the moment in the wake of that conversation with Laura, but if she ever contemplated it again it would definitely be some anonymous sample from a bank. Involving anyone she knew would make things impossibly complicated.

Involving Joe would be the end of the world...

Her relief must have shown in her smile when she came out of the bathroom and ran to join Joe as he was getting into the chopper in response to their pager signalling a callout.

'You look like you've won the lottery,' Joe said.

'It's been too quiet today, that's all. I was getting bored.'

'This should do the trick then. If a local crew has called for urgent backup it could be a critical case.'

Maggie nodded as she clipped her harness together. With the kind of injuries that could be caused by being trampled by animals that weighed half a ton, this could be a challenging job.

Just the kind they both loved.

A 'hot' one.

It took only a few minutes' flying time to reach the farm on the hills behind one of the outer city suburbs.

'There's a mob of sheep down there.'

'We'll buzz them and come around again. That should persuade them to give us some room.' Andy the pilot and crewman Nick were both peering down at the intended landing site for the rescue helicopter.

'The horses might be more of a worry.' Maggie was also focussed on the ground below as sheep began to scatter to get away from the noisy machine overhead.

'You don't like horses?' Joe sounded surprised. 'Think of them as motorbikes with brains and you'll get on just fine.'

'Motorbikes don't club together and run you over. Where's the bunch of horses that trampled our patient?'

'They've been shifted to the next paddock,' Andy said. 'But there hasn't been time to round up the sheep. It's okay…looks like we've got plenty of room now. Let's have another go…'

The helicopter tilted as it turned and Maggie could see the horses now, well away from the cluster of people, some farm vehicles and an ambulance.

Joe had the doors open by the time the skids touched the grass. Maggie shoved her arms through the straps of the pack and they both crouched, exchanging a glance as they ran under the still turning rotors of the helicopter.

There was more than just the adrenaline rush of facing an unknown challenge together that was shared in that glance, though. On Maggie's part it had a lot to do with the relief she was feeling but she knew the message that Joe was conveying in that split second of eye contact and she could agree with it wholeheartedly—

an acknowledgement that what was going on in their personal lives at the moment was not interfering in any way with their working relationship. If anything, it was making it better.

They'd been a tight team already but something had definitely changed since they'd become so much closer out of work hours. They both knew their 'fling', or whatever it was, couldn't continue long term and the relief Maggie had felt with the arrival of her period today was an indication that it probably needed to end sooner rather than later because there was more at stake here than simply a physical relationship but…not just yet…

This new layer to her working relationship with Joe was amazing—a side effect of the recent change to their friendship? Was it the intimate knowledge of each other that had added a new depth to that friendship? Or was it that their friendship had made sex such a different experience, adding humour and tenderness into the mix?

Whatever it was, it was special but even the flash of a glance that had reminded her of the bond between them couldn't interfere with the professional focus Maggie knew they both had right now. If anything, for her, it made that focus sharper. She was working with the person she trusted more than anyone on the planet. Her best friend who was, temporarily, also her lover. She wanted to do the best job she possibly could, not only for her patient but so that Joe would be as proud to have her as his partner as she was to have him.

A man with a small girl in his arms and a taller boy pressed against his leg were standing beside the figure on the ground as Maggie and Joe ran towards them, their packs on their backs. His face, creased with worry, relaxed a little as they arrived.

'Thanks for coming, guys.'

'No worries,' Joe said.

'This is Caroline,' one of the ambulance officers introduced them, and then started his handover. 'She's thirty-six. Came out this afternoon to check on one of the horses and got trampled.'

'It wasn't their fault.' Caroline was conscious. She looked pale and as if she was in pain but being fully alert was a reassuring sign that her head injury was not too severe. 'I was trying to put a halter on Star and I accidently touched the electric fence behind me. She got a shock and bolted and that panicked all the others. I got knocked down and trodden on a few times.'

'She's got a head injury,' the ground crew paramedic said. 'Pupils are uneven. She's also complaining of sore ribs and an injury to her lower leg. No breathing problems so far and vital signs all good. She wasn't knocked out and GCS was fifteen when we arrived. She used her mobile phone to call her husband for help.'

'That's me,' the man with the children said. 'I'm Barry.'

'What's wrong with Mummy?' The little girl in his arms looked even more terrified than her older brother. 'Why can't she get up?'

'She's got sore bits, sweetheart.' It was Maggie who looked up to smile reassuringly at the child. 'That's why we need to look after her. Like Mummy looks after you when you've got sore bits.'

The child nodded. 'I felled over yesterday. Mummy put a plaster on my knee, see?'

'I do. It's a big plaster.'

'It was sore. But I didn't cry.'

'That was very brave.'

'I'm being brave, too, Lucy.' Caroline turned her head to smile up at her daughter. 'Just like you.'

'Were you lying on your back or your front when you fell?' Joe asked. He shone a small torch into each of her eyes. Uneven pupils could be a variant of normal so the way they reacted to light might be more of an indication of how serious the head injury could be. Both pupils were reactive to the light, which was another reassuring finding.

'My front.' Caroline closed her eyes and groaned as Joe began to check the swollen area of her scalp.

'She's had two point five milligrams of morphine.'

'What's your pain score now, Caroline? Out of ten, with zero being no pain and ten the worst you can think of?'

'About six…a bit better than it was before.'

'Where does it hurt the most?'

'My leg…and my head.'

'Maggie will top up that pain relief a bit for you. I'm just going to check your ear.' He turned to look in his pack for the otoscope, only to find Maggie was holding it out to him. 'Thanks, mate.'

She was already busy on her next task as he crouched low to shine the light of the otoscope into Caroline's ear and he knew that as soon as she'd given Caroline some more morphine Maggie would be assessing the leg that was causing so much pain.

Sure enough, as he registered the concerning patch of colour on his patient's eardrum that could indicate a collection of blood beneath, he could hear Maggie's calm voice.

'Push your foot against my hand... Okay, now pull up against it... Where does that hurt?'

They were both delving into their packs for supplies a minute or two later. Joe needed a bandage to hold a dressing in place on Caroline's scalp and Maggie was finding a splint for her lower leg.

'Haemotympanun,' Joe told Maggie quietly. 'But her neurological status seems stable.'

'I can't be sure if it's a fracture or muscle injury to her leg but it's swollen and painful enough to make me query compartment syndrome. Limb baselines are lower than they were when the first crew arrived.'

'We'd better get this show on the road, then.' Joe reached for his radio. 'Nick? Could you bring the stretcher, please?'

Maggie splinted Caroline's leg. As the ambulance crew helped Joe lift their patient and then secure her to the helicopter's stretcher, she turned to talk to Caroline's husband.

'We're going to take Caroline in to the emergency department of the Royal. She's going to need a scan to rule out a possible skull fracture and an orthopaedic specialist to deal with the leg injury.'

Lucy burst into tears. 'No...don't take my Mummy away.'

'It's okay, Luce,' Barry said. 'We'll go in the car. You'll see Mummy again very soon.'

'You will,' Maggie said. 'But would you like to give her a big kiss first? And tell her how brave she is?'

From the corner of his eye, as Joe did up one of the

strap buckles that would keep Caroline secure on the stretcher if they hit any turbulence, he could see Maggie hold out her arms and the little girl respond by reaching back. Maggie settled the child on one hip and then held out her hand again to the silent, scared-looking boy.

'I'll bet Mummy needs a kiss from you, too.'

'I do…' Caroline's voice wobbled but she managed to hold it together while she exchanged kisses and reassured her children. Then it was Barry's turn to lean over the stretcher and kiss his wife.

'We'll be there as soon as. Love you…'

Caroline just nodded, clearly unable to trust her voice as Joe and Nick began to carry her towards the helicopter. Joe looked back to see Maggie giving Lucy a cuddle before transferring her back into her father's arms. For just a moment he saw her as part of that family picture of a man and woman and two gorgeous kids.

Add in a few more kids and it was exactly what she wanted in her own life.

Exactly what he might have wanted in his life, if things had been different. And Maggie would have been the woman he might well have chosen to be the mother of those children.

But that was never going to happen and if he was a true friend he'd be encouraging her to get out there and find the partner—hopefully the love of her life—who would be able to give her what she wanted so much. He shouldn't be wasting her time by keeping her distracted with a relationship that was no more than a 'friends with benefits' one that really shouldn't have started in the first place.

He was still watching as Maggie began to run towards him to catch up. The sound of the rotors got louder as Andy readied the aircraft for take-off.

She looked different for some reason, he thought, turning back to direct the loading of the stretcher into the helicopter. Some kind of glow about her despite the lines of concern on her face that he knew were all about their patient and her family. Or was it just because he'd started to see her as so much more than simply his friend or colleague? Like the way he'd noticed different things about Maggie when he'd realised how attractive she was.

Maggie Lewis was just a stunning human being, that's what it was. And if he could have given her what she wanted, Joe would have been at the head of the queue. He knew perfectly well how easy it would be to fall in love with Maggie if he stepped past that roadblock. But he also knew that that wasn't going to happen, which meant he would never be in any queue of potential life partners.

It wasn't fair to hold Maggie back. They needed to stop what was happening between them before it went on too long.

Before it got too difficult to stop because it was so damn good?

Maggie pulled the door shut behind her, gave him a thumbs-up sign and settled herself in the seat at the head of Caroline's stretcher where she could both monitor her patient's condition and supply any needed reassurance.

Joe buckled himself into the seat at the side of the stretcher where he was in a good position to reach any equipment and provide any treatment needed on the short flight to the hospital.

He spared only the briefest of another thought concerning Maggie.

Yes, it had to stop.

But hopefully not just yet…

CHAPTER SIX

'WE'RE JUST GOOD FRIENDS.' But Joe's sideways glance at Maggie held a question. *Have you been talking to someone about us?*

Her subtle headshake served as both a reassuring response to Joe and a sign of impatience with Adam, the Aratika HEMS doctor on duty with Cooper today, who'd asked if there was something going on between Joe and Maggie.

'Looked like more than that when I saw you both out dancing in that bar last week,' he persisted.

Maggie shrugged. 'We're both single. We felt like a night out. It's no big deal.'

It wasn't a big deal. Yes, she and Joe saw each other once or twice a week and sometimes went out and always enjoyed great sex and, yes, it should have stopped by now after nearly two months but it was still fun and neither of them had anyone else waiting in the wings, so why not?

'Oh…beware…' Fizz turned from where she was reading notices on the board in the staffroom. 'That's how it started with me and Cooper. We were just good friends and look at me now…' She patted her protruding belly.

'How long now, Fizz?' Joe sounded like he was keen to change the subject.

'Three months. And I was three months along when I got married, which means… Hey, Coop. It's our three-month anniversary today. Where are you taking me to celebrate?'

'That's why I've snuck you on base for one of Shirley's Sunday roasts. Best meal in town.'

'Aww…' Shirley was stirring a large pot on the stovetop. 'You're a good boy, Cooper Sinclair. I knew you were going to be from the moment you arrived here. I'll be ready for you to carve this meat soon. I'm just finishing the gravy.'

'Can I help?' Maggie joined Shirley at the bench.

'You could drain those carrots and then put some butter and parsley on them.'

'It's no wonder I'm putting on weight, Shirley. Between your roast dinners and all those cakes and cookies, I've got no hope.' She might have to make a bit of an effort, in fact. Her uniform trousers had been noticeably tight when she'd put them on this morning.

'You just need to do a bit more dancing, then.' Shirley's glance implied that she knew exactly what was going on between Maggie and Joe and wasn't about to have any wool pulled over her eyes.

Maggie made a mumbled sound of agreement. She threw a knob of butter and the already chopped parsley on top of the carrots and put the lid of the pot back on.

'I'll put the plates in the warming drawer, shall I?'

'They're already in there.'

Shirley was a stickler for doing things the right way and that included warmed plates for her food. And despite the unspoken rule that places at the table for Sunday lunch were only for the crews on duty that day, nobody was going to complain about Cooper's wife being included. Fizz had had to give up her shifts on base while she was pregnant and everybody missed her company, especially Maggie.

She leaned her head against her friend's shoulder for a moment as Fizz came up and slung her arm over Maggie's shoulders.

'Glad you came,' she murmured. 'I don't get to see you that often these days.'

'You should come and visit, then. Instead of going out dancing with Joe.' Fizz's tone was teasing. She didn't think there was anything going on between them and why would she? Everybody knew that Maggie and Joe had worked together for years with nothing happening. What had changed to make Adam suspicious, not to mention Shirley being convinced? Was the new bond that had made them a closer team than ever somehow visible from the outside?

Fizz was sniffing appreciatively. 'I'm starving. That gravy smells divine, Shirley.'

'Secret ingredient.' Shirley nodded. 'And you should be starving. You're eating for two.'

'That doesn't excuse my current gluttony.' Fizz grinned. 'So what's the secret ingredient, then?'

'If I told you that, it wouldn't be a secret any more, now, would it?'

Maggie laughed along with Fizz but she took a deeper sniff, wondering if she could work out what the mysterious ingredient could be. Oddly, none of the aromas from the food smelled as nice as they usually did. There was a note in the mix that made her feel slightly queasy, in fact.

Fizz had her head much closer to the pot as she sniffed. 'Aha...could it be garlic?'

Shirley's chin came up. 'Not telling. Cooper? You want to come and carve this meat?' She opened the oven door with one hand, picking up her oven gloves with the other. 'Adam, why don't you make yourself useful and come and get these veggies out of the oven and onto the table? I'm too old to be lifting that heavy tray.'

The laughter was more general this time. Shirley might be in her seventies but she was ageless. A much-loved institution now and nobody wanted to think about her not being an honorary member of the staff. She'd been a part of Aratika for longer than Maggie had been, having started to supply the crews with her wonderful baking after her son's life had been saved by a helicopter crew many years ago. She'd started coming in to cook breakfast just after Maggie had been lucky enough to join the team five years ago and the Sunday lunch tradition had begun not long after that.

Adam pushed his chair back and came towards the kitchen area but Shirley was already pulling a tray from the oven—the muffin tin that had a dozen of her famous Yorkshire puddings in it. The heavier oven tray with the delicious array of roasted potatoes and other vegetables was on a lower rack.

'I'll need those oven gloves,' Adam said.

Shirley straightened, holding the muffin tin in her hands. Cooper was off to one side, sharpening the carving knife, and Maggie and Fizz were still standing by the sink when it happened. The muffin tray slid from Shirley's hand to crash on the floor, sending the Yorkshire puddings flying in all directions. At almost the same instant, Shirley crumpled, clutching at her chest. Adam caught her.

'Here…sit down, Shirley.'

Maggie was crouched in front of the older woman by the time Adam had lowered her to sit on the floor with her back against one of the kitchen cabinets.

'What's happening, Shirley? Have you got chest pain?'

Shirley nodded. 'Right here…' Her fist was pressed against the centre of her chest. 'Oh…it feels like I've got an elephant sitting on top of me. It's hard to breathe…'

'I'll grab a life pack…' Joe ran from the staffroom, Cooper on his heels.

'Do you have any medical conditions we should know about?' Fizz had her hand on Shirley's wrist. 'High blood pressure? Angina?'

Shirley nodded. 'I take pills for my blood pressure. I don't have angina. That's what my Stan had, before he died with his heart attack.' She had gone very pale now and Maggie could see beads of sweat on her forehead. 'Is that what this is? Am I having a heart attack?'

'That's what we're going to find out.'

Joe and Cooper were back with a life pack, a medical pack and an oxygen cylinder. They took cushions from one of the couches in the staffroom and made Shirley more comfortable, propping her up with an oxygen mask in place as they all tried to contribute to finding out what was happening and treating it by getting vital signs, including a twelve-lead ECG and putting an IV line in so they could give her some pain relief.

Don, the base manager, came into the room, closely followed by Andy. 'Can we do anything to help?' he asked.

'Maybe get a stretcher from the back of an ambulance. We'll be heading for the Royal pretty soon.'

'Chew this up for me, Shirley.' Fizz lifted the oxygen mask, ready to give Shirley the white tablet.

'What is it?'

'An aspirin. I'll get you a sip of water to wash it down.' Maggie found Joe and Cooper both still studying the ECG graph.

'It's not huge but there's definitely widespread ST segment elevation. And some T wave changes starting.'

'We need to get her into ED as quickly as possible,' Joe nodded. 'And up to the catheter laboratory if needed.'

'You and Maggie take one of the ambulances,' Don said. 'Adam and Cooper can cover any helicopter call-out for the moment. I'll call in some extra staff so you can stay with Shirley for a while.'

'I'm going, too,' Fizz said. 'I can stay as long as it takes.'

'But…' Shirley pulled down her mask so that they could hear her clearly. 'But you'll all miss your Sunday lunch…'

'We're thinking about all the Sunday lunches to come,' Fizz teased her gently. 'It's far more important to us to make sure you're going to be around for a long time yet.'

Joe drove the ambulance to the Royal and Maggie and Fizz stayed in the back, looking after Shirley and giving her the best reassurance that they could, knowing that it could contribute to keeping her safe from a potential cardiac arrest.

'Just relax,' Maggie told her. 'Keep your breathing nice and slow.'

'You're going to be well looked after,' Fizz added. 'They'll want to do another ECG in Emergency and they'll take some blood tests. It's quite likely that they'll take you up to the catheter laboratory after that.'

'Why?'

'Because that's where they can see exactly what's going on in the arteries in your heart and, if any of them are blocked, they can fix it. You'll come out as good as new. Better, even.'

Maggie could see the fear in Shirley's eyes so she squeezed her hand. 'Don't worry…we're not going to leave you by yourself.'

They stayed with Shirley for her initial tests and then waited for the results of the blood tests, which came back swiftly, and then waited again until the catheter laboratory staff on call for a Sunday could get back to the Royal and set up for angiography. They accompanied Shirley in the lift and Maggie even offered to put on a lead apron and stay with her in the laboratory but Shirley refused.

'I'm fine… Whatever they gave me to relax is working very well. I'd much rather you all went and found yourselves something to eat. You said you were starving, Fizz, and that was a long time ago now. You go and look after yourself and that bubba. Maggie and Joe can make sure that you do.'

So they went back to the staffroom in the emergency department to wait until Shirley's procedure was finished and they could see her settled into the coronary care unit. They bought packets of sandwiches from a vending machine and Fizz busied herself making hot drinks for them all.

Maggie took a sip of hers. 'Oh…' She screwed up

her nose. 'This coffee tastes really weird. Disgusting, even. Is it really stale or something?'

Joe tried his. 'Tastes perfectly okay to me,' he said. 'Nothing wrong with it.'

Fizz laughed. 'Maybe you're pregnant, Mags. Coffee was the first thing I went off. I can only drink tea now.'

It was a mistake to catch Joe's gaze but Maggie hadn't been able to stop it happening. She could see the way his eyes darkened, as if his pupils had dilated due to shock. She tried to send him a reassuring message. It wasn't true. It couldn't be. They'd been very careful ever since that first time and she'd had a period after that.

When was that, exactly? Maggie counted back in her head as she dragged her gaze away from Joe's. She started peeling the plastic cover off her pack of sandwiches. It was over a month ago so she must be due for her next period anytime. It was okay. She'd had a fright last time and it had been okay.

Fizz had been watching the interaction between them. 'Oh, my goodness,' she murmured into the silence that had fallen. 'So Adam was right?'

'It's not a thing,' Maggie said. 'We really are just good friends. And I'm *not* pregnant.'

She could feel Joe's gaze on her as she picked up her sandwich and took a bite. She could actually feel what he was thinking—that it really was time they stopped sleeping together when even the thought of something going wrong was a threat to their friendship and working relationship.

The mixture of bread, cheese and ham in her mouth suddenly felt like cardboard and it became a mission to swallow it.

'You don't like your sandwich?' Fizz asked. 'Want to swap with one of mine?'

Maggie shook her head. 'I might be coming down with something,' she muttered. 'I'll get a glass of water.'

She stood up but then sat down again, holding her head in her hands.

'What's going on?' Joe demanded.

'Felt a bit dizzy, that's all.'

'Could be low blood sugar,' Fizz said. 'Did you eat breakfast this morning?'

'No…but I don't usually eat breakfast, anyway.'

Joe had his fingers on her wrist. 'Could be low blood pressure. Her radial pulse is quite weak. And a bit rapid.'

'Come with me.' Fizz stood up and waited for Maggie to get up again. 'I'm going to check you out.'

'Good idea,' Joe said. 'Need a hand?'

'No. Finish your lunch.' Fizz glanced at her abandoned meal. 'We'll be back soon.'

She took Maggie into an empty cubicle. 'Get up on the bed,' she instructed. 'And tell me what's really going on.'

'I told you. I'm probably coming down with some bug.'

Fizz was wrapping the blood-pressure cuff around her arm. 'Symptoms?'

'Nothing much. I just feel a bit off and my skin feels odd. Like my clothes are uncomfortable.' Maggie used her free hand to undo the button on her trousers. 'That's better…' She lay back on the pillow and closed her eyes.

Fizz was silent as she slowly let the air out of the cuff and took her blood-pressure reading. 'Your BP's fine,' she told Maggie.

In the silence that followed, Maggie wondered if Fizz was finding the kit to test her blood sugar but then she opened her eyes to find that her friend hadn't actually moved from the side of the bed. And that she was staring at where she'd opened the button of her trousers. At the red marks her waistband had left on her skin. Her friend's voice was quiet when she spoke.

'You're quite sure you're not pregnant?'

Maggie swallowed hard. She still hadn't finished adding up the weeks in her head. 'I might be a little late,' she confessed. 'But I was late last month, too, and that was okay. I think it was just due to stress.'

'Normal period last time?'

'A bit light, I guess. Normal enough.'

'Are your breasts tender?'

'They always are a bit when I'm about to get my period.' Maggie pushed herself up. 'I *can't* be pregnant, Fizz. There was only one time when we weren't super-careful and that was ages ago and, as I said, I've had a period since then.'

'A late one. You do realise how common it is to have some bleeding in early pregnancy, don't you? Like, twenty five percent of women.'

'Don't say that,' Maggie muttered. Of course she realised. She'd been a midwife. Had the rush of relief of believing she wasn't pregnant conveniently washed away that particular bit of knowledge?

Fizz put her hand on Maggie's abdomen. 'Can I have a feel?'

'Sure.' Maggie lay down again just to buy herself some thinking time. Even if the unthinkable had happened and she was pregnant, surely Fizz wouldn't be able to feel anything.

'Hmm…'

'What?'

'I'm absolutely sure I can feel your uterus and that's not easy to do unless someone is getting close to twelve weeks along. That would fit with your weight gain as well. And thinking that your coffee tasted strange.'

Maggie shook her head. 'Nope. Can't be.'

Except that she was counting weeks in her head again. Back to the night of that coastguard job. If she *had* become pregnant then she would be…about ten or eleven weeks along now.

Oh… *God*…

'Is it Joe's?' Fizz asked quietly.

It was hard to speak through a suddenly dry mouth. 'Don't say anything,' she whispered.

'Of course not. Are you going to tell him?'

She didn't have a choice, did she? 'I need to figure out how to do that first,' she said. 'It'll be the last thing he wants to hear.'

'You're not looking too thrilled yourself.'

That was such an understatement that Maggie let out a huff of laughter. And then she found herself blinking back tears. 'What am I going to do, Fizz?'

'Get some irrefutable evidence, for starters. I'd eat my hat if I was wrong but stranger things have happened. You could pee in a cup and I'll test it for you here, if you like. Or take a blood test.'

Maggie shook her head. 'No. What if Joe comes in?' She was doing up the button on her trousers again. 'I'll do it tomorrow.'

She knew what the result would be. It all made perfect sense now. She'd just been looking the other way, even when she'd had reason to suspect it right from the start when her period was unusually late. But, no, she'd stuck her head in the sand and pretended everything was fine because she'd decided that it had to be that way. She'd glanced at the potential consequences and put them in the 'too hard' basket—and grabbed at what seemed to be a reprieve with both hands.

'You'll need to get a proper obstetric check-up as soon as possible. And an ultrasound. That'll give you a more accurate estimate of dates. Hey...' Fizz put her arms around Maggie. 'It'll be okay, hon.'

Reassurance might be a good thing when someone was having a heart attack, to keep the heart rate down and oxygen level up, but it didn't feel at all useful at the moment. Or believable.

It wasn't going to be okay.

Not at all.

'You should go home.'

'I'm fine. Fizz told you there was nothing wrong with me.'

'You've been weird all afternoon.'

Joe opened the fridge in the staffroom and looked at all the food that had been packed up and stored. It looked like nobody had had any appetite for Shirley's roast dinner after it had been interrupted in such a dramatic fashion. Cooper and Adam were out on what would be their last job for their shift and the night duty staff were due to arrive soon. Don was upstairs in his office and Maggie was sitting on one of the couches, her legs tucked up, staring into space, which was so unlike her it was disturbing. She never sat and did nothing like that. She talked to people or read something or busied herself in some way and she did it with an enthusiasm that made those around her think she was making the most of every minute of her life. It was one of the things Joe had always loved about Maggie—how good you felt in her company—how much brighter your day became.

He walked over to her now and perched on the arm at the other end of the sofa.

'Shirley's going to be fine, you know. She sailed through that angioplasty. She'll be home in a couple of days and probably here cooking breakfast by the end the of the week. Or another Sunday roast.'

Everybody loved Shirley's Sunday roasts but, for Joe, they were even more special because they felt like the kind of family ritual he'd never had as a child. Shirley was almost more of a mother to him than his own mother had ever been.

'I know that.' But Maggie's smile looked a little forced.

'So what's the matter?'

Maggie gaze slid away from his. Had he said something to upset her? Joe thought back to when things had started to get weird this afternoon. Maybe Maggie was coming down with something and it was just too early for Fizz to have picked it up when she'd had a look.

Or maybe it wasn't something *he'd* said.

'It was that coffee thing, wasn't it? That's when things got weird. When Fizz suggested you might be pregnant.'

Maggie still wasn't looking at him. In fact, she looked as if she was frozen now. Not even breathing. A shiver started at the back of Joe's neck and trickled all the way down his spine.

'You are…aren't you?'

Finally, slowly, Maggie turned her head and looked up to meet his gaze and the truth was blindingly obvious.

Joe swallowed hard. 'I don't understand. We've been so careful.'

'Except that first time.'

'*What?* How far along *are* you?'

'I'm not sure exactly. Fizz thinks it's close to twelve weeks. If it was that first night that would mean about eleven weeks.'

Joe closed his eyes, grappling with emotions that were rushing at him like tsunamis. Panic? Anger? He managed to keep his tone level.

'And how long have you known?'

'I still haven't done a test. It didn't even occur to me until Fizz was so sure but it makes sense. She reminded me that twenty five percent of women can have bleeding in early pregnancy that they might think is a normal period...' Her voice trailed away. 'When it isn't.'

Joe could hear the ice around his words. 'You told me it was safe. You *promised* me that it was safe.'

'I thought it was. I truly believed it was.'

'Really?' Joe was losing the battle to keep those overwhelming emotions at bay. He got to his feet, hoping that a bit of pacing might help. It didn't. He swung back to face her.

'I'm not sure I believe you, Maggie. It's a bit of a co-incidence, isn't it? You tell me how desperate you are to have a baby and then...' His brain was taking him back to that steamy night. He could hear echoes of words.

His words—*We can't do this*...

Maggie's words—*Why not? I want this, Joe*...

But what had she wanted so much? Sex with him or the possibility of becoming pregnant? Panic about what the future might hold could wait. Right now, this was about being betrayed. By the one person he would never have believed could do that.

'I *trusted* you...' His voice was loud now. He never shouted at anybody, ever, but this was getting alarmingly close.

Maggie was scrambling to her feet as well. 'I know. I'm sorry, Joe. This is as much of a shock to me as it is to you.'

'I don't think so. You *wanted* this. You were *planning* to be a single mother.'

'No...' Maggie's voice was raised now. 'I mean, I *thought* I wanted it but then I changed my mind. And even if I hadn't changed my mind, I wouldn't have wanted it to be like *this*.'

'What the hell is going on in here?'

They both turned to find Don Smith, Aratika's manager, at the foot of the staircase that led to the upstairs management office and control desk.

'We can all hear you yelling at each other.'

'It's private,' Joe snapped.

'Not any more.' Don was walking towards them, shaking his head. 'Are you pregnant, Maggie?'

'I think so...' Joe saw the moment the tears welled up in her eyes and one escaped to roll down her cheek. 'Yes... I'm sure I am. I haven't done an official test but it all adds up.'

He didn't like to see Maggie cry but there was nothing about any of this that Joe was liking. Quite the opposite. This might, in fact, qualify as being one of the worst days of his life.

Don glanced at Joe. 'You're the father, I take it?'

'Apparently.' It was a cruel thing to say. Maggie

would never cheat on anybody, even if it hadn't been a 'real' relationship.

Don was looking at Maggie now. 'And you're keeping the baby?'

He heard Maggie gasp. He was shocked himself that Don would even ask.

'You might think it's none of my business,' Don said, 'but it actually is. I want you to take a few days' leave, Maggie. You've got a lot to think about.'

'But—'

'You'll have to step down from active duty. We'll find you another position. If nothing else, I don't think you and Joe can work together again. Judging by the last ten minutes, patient care could be compromised by the issues between you two.' He held his hand up as Maggie opened her mouth to say something else. 'I don't want to know about your private lives but I'm not having it affect the operation of this rescue base.' He glanced at his watch. 'It's nearly changeover. Go home, both of you.' He was shaking his head as he headed back towards the stairs. 'I think we've all had enough of today.'

'He can't do that,' Maggie whispered. 'He practically just fired me...'

'He can. And he did.' Joe had never been this angry in his life. He walked away from Maggie before he found himself saying something he might later regret and he didn't stop moving until he'd left the building and wrenched his car door open.

'Hey, Joe!' One of the night shift crew was getting out of her car. 'You getting off early for good behaviour?'

'Something like that.' Joe actually managed to find a smile. 'Have a good one, Angie.'

He dropped into his driver's seat and slammed the door shut, backing out and taking off and deliberately ignoring what he could see in his peripheral vision.

Maggie, standing by her bike, her helmet in her hands, but she wasn't moving to put it on. She was watching him leave.

He didn't want to speak to her again right now. He didn't even want to look at her. He was having his life ripped apart and there was nothing at all he could do about it. He was being forced into becoming a father when it was the last thing he'd ever wanted to be. He was losing the colleague who'd always been his favourite person to work with. And he was losing someone he'd thought would be one of his best friends for life.

This was worse than betrayal.

Right now it felt like complete destruction.

There was only one place he could be that might help him deal with emotions that were trying to make his head explode. Instead of making the turn that would have taken him home to his apartment, Joe turned the other way. Towards a beach that he knew would provide a challenge. It was a good thing he kept his board and sail strapped to his roof rack most of the time. He must have known that, one day, it might feel like he needed the wind and the waves in order to stay sane.

It felt like it might actually save his life today.

CHAPTER SEVEN

SHE'D KNOWN IT could be the end of her world as she knew it.

But she hadn't realised it would feel quite *this* devastating.

On more than one occasion of being slowed down or stuck in city traffic as Maggie made her way home, she had to swipe at the tears streaking her cheeks beneath her visor.

This was her fault.

How *stupid* had she been?

Classic signs of pregnancy and she'd simply ignored them all. The tender breasts and weight gain. Today hadn't been the first time she'd thought food tasted or smell wrong, either. She'd even dismissed feeling nauseated last week as being due to a greasy takeaway the night before.

Blind. And stupid.

No wonder Joe thought she'd done this on purpose. Who wouldn't after hearing her banging on about being happy to become a single mother?

And no wonder he hated her right now. He was probably relieved that she wasn't going to be allowed to be on the front line of any emergency service while she was pregnant and, as from tomorrow, he would have a new partner as part of his crew.

Oh...help... Maggie swiped her face again and gave an enormous sniff. She'd betrayed her best friend and nobody was going to believe it was the last thing she would have done intentionally. She'd lost the job she loved so much as well. She'd probably have to go and help Danny with uniforms and supplies and restocking the kits. Or she'd be assigned to a research project and be stuck behind a desk collecting data and putting it into spreadsheets.

Fizz had had to give up being on the helicopters due to her pregnancy, too, but at least she was able to keep working in the emergency department for as long as she wanted. She also had the support of a loving partner who'd probably been thrilled when they'd discovered they had a baby on the way.

This was Joe's worst nightmare, wasn't it?

As Maggie turned up the road that led up the valley to her house, she was still thinking about Fizz. Or rather about her wedding night. About when Joe had opened up and told her why he would never want to bring a child into the world.

Kids get caught in the flak... They can grow up thinking that it's their fault. That, no matter how hard they try, they can never fix things...

Maggie could remember very clearly how much she'd wanted to cuddle that small, unhappy boy hidden beneath the surface of Joe's adult life.

The urge to put her arms around him and hold him now was even more powerful.

Because she cared. So much. She loved him.

Not just as her best friend and favourite workmate.

How broken she was feeling right now told Maggie that perhaps she didn't just love Joe in terms of friendship. Was she *in* love with him? Was that why the thought of not having him in her life from now on was ripping her apart so painfully?

Something else she'd been conveniently blind about, maybe. Had she really believed that they could just 'have fun' together and then go back to their old friendship with nothing fundamentally changed between them? And how had she been so absolutely sure that you couldn't fall in love with someone you'd known for so long? That you'd have at least some idea it was going to happen within the first few minutes of meeting them?

As blindsiding as this was, it certainly felt like the kind of heartbreak that came from the end of a relationship with someone she had been completely in love with. She'd told Joe that the 'real thing' had a basis of genuine friendship but that there had to be chemistry involved. Well, they'd found that chemistry, hadn't they? It had just been too easy to dismiss the alchemy as 'fun' because they both knew there could never be a future together. Maggie wanted a family. Joe didn't. End of story.

Walking inside made Maggie come face to face with another part of what would be her new reality in about six months' time. Single parenthood. Laura looked tired. Worried.

'What's up?' Maggie asked.

'Harry's not feeling well. I'll have to keep him home from school tomorrow if he's not better but I can't afford to miss my shift...' Laura took a second glance at Maggie. 'Sorry... I shouldn't just dump on you like that,

the moment you come through the door. You don't look
like you've had the best day yourself.'

'It's okay.' It was actually a relief to have someone
else to think about. 'What's the matter with Harry?'

'He's got a sore tummy and doesn't want to eat anything.'

'Any vomiting or diarrhoea?'

'Not yet.'

'Is he running a temperature?'

'I was just going to take it.'

'You do that,' Maggie said. 'I'll put the kettle on
and make us a cup of tea.' Wine would be preferable,
she thought, but that was off limits from now on. 'And
don't worry about tomorrow. I've got some time off so
I can look after Harry.'

'Really? I thought you'd only just started work for
this week.'

'It's a long story. I'll tell you later.' Maggie poked her
head around the kitchen door to wave at Harrison, who
was lying on the couch, watching a cartoon on televi-
sion. 'Hey, Harry...sorry you're not feeling well, buddy.'

His little face was pale beneath that thatch of dark
spiky hair but he managed a brave grin as he waved
back that melted Maggie's heart. He was such a cute
kid and a delight to live with but Maggie knew she got
to enjoy all the good bits and not have the responsibility of the other side of the coin, like childhood illnesses
or injuries or the financial stress of being the sole pro-
vider. The world of single parenthood.

How had she ever contemplated going into that world
voluntarily?

She could see just how terrifying it was going to be.
Where was she going to live? How was she going to be

able to afford everything she and the baby would need? How would she cope if the baby got really sick and she was all by herself?

Her future was not going to be anything like her fantasies of a big, happy family having picnics. She'd probably made it even less likely that she would ever find someone to share her life with. Look at Laura, who hadn't even been on a date in the last five years as far as Maggie knew.

Her flatmate came back into the kitchen with a thermometer in her hand. 'It's normal,' she said.

'That's good.'

'It's probably just a twenty-four-hour bug of some kind. Or maybe he'll bounce back by tomorrow morning. Oh...thanks...' Laura reached for the mug of tea Maggie had made and then sat down at the table. 'Now...tell me what's going on with you.'

'Hmm...' Maggie sat down beside her. 'You'd better brace yourself...'

It was easy to pick up speed in this much wind.

Easy to hit the wave at just the perfect angle and push down with your legs and then jump and grip with your toes to roll the windward edge of the board to catch the wind and to bend your arms and knees to fly even higher.

Not so easy to keep the tail of the board in the right place so you didn't spin out when you touched down again on the choppy surface but Joe had done this a million times.

It never got old.

And it never failed to clear anything else out of his head. He just couldn't think about anything other than how to keep upright and sailing. He couldn't be aware of anything other than the chill and splash of the water, the rush of wind and the adrenaline spike of every jump and successful landing. The burn of tired muscles had to kick in at some point, of course, but it was almost dark by the time Joe finally hauled his gear across the beach to the car park.

The things he didn't want to think about were already creeping back by the time he was tying his board and sail onto his roof rack and it didn't help that going windsurfing had reminded him of being on the beach, not so long ago, with young Harry—another fatherless little boy like he'd been himself. Another reminder of just why he'd never, ever wanted to be in this situation. Having consumed so much physical energy by the windsurfing session, the raw emotional edges had blurred more than a little. But he still felt betrayed.

He was still too angry to ever want to speak to Maggie again. Joe cast a sideways glance at the familiar buildings as he drove past the Aratika Rescue Base on his way back into the central city and his apartment block. It was just as well that Don was forcing her to stand down for a few days and was removing her from front-line duties. Joe was nowhere near ready to see her again.

She'd used him. She'd probably been planning it ever since that day they'd delivered the baby with the shoulder dystocia. When she'd been carrying the kid and said, '*I think I want one...*' She'd asked him to be the sperm donor but then had just gone and done it despite him telling him exactly why it could never happen.

A stop at a red traffic light on a big intersection was long enough to let his thoughts throw a curveball into his anger. Okay, it was a bit of a coincidence that the fertile time of her cycle had just happened to be on a day they'd had the kind of job that almost never happened and Maggie had been close enough to hypothermia to have difficulty getting out of her uniform. She couldn't have actually planned that.

So it hadn't been entirely her fault, had it?

He hadn't dealt with those unexpected feelings of attraction towards Maggie and made sure that nothing ever happened. Worse, on that night in the shower room, he could have walked out. He could have kept walking so that they'd never opened that Pandora's box of sex between them. Or he could have, at the very least, gone to his locker, found his wallet and taken out that condom he always carried, just in case.

He'd been stupid.

It was no excuse that he'd trusted Maggie and believed her when she'd said it was safe. He had to take at least part of the blame.

Maggie got the rest of the blame.

The only one that couldn't be blamed was the new being that existed because of what had happened that night.

The baby.

His baby.

History was repeating itself. Two people who were entirely unsuited to be in a relationship were now bound to each other for ever as the parents of a child. An accidental pregnancy that would produce an unwanted child, like he had been.

No…that wasn't entirely true. Maggie wanted this baby. She was never going to tell that child that they had ruined her life. But Joe had a sudden flash of what her face had looked like earlier with tears rolling down her face. Her body language when she'd been standing beside her bike watching him leave with those slumped shoulders and air of defeat. She might have thought that a baby was what she wanted but she certainly wasn't too happy about finding out she had one on the way, was she?

So perhaps she hadn't planned it at all.

But it didn't actually matter now because it had happened and everything had changed.

He'd lost a friend he'd thought he could trust above anyone else.

He'd lost his colleague. There'd be no more shared excitement about getting dispatched to a challenge that was 'hot' enough to be a thrill.

He'd lost the freedom that had gone with an unencumbered future as well. Joe had no idea just how he was going to face up to the kind of responsibility of being a father but he wasn't about to repeat history and be the kind of man his own father had been. His own child was not going to grow up feeling like they didn't have a father.

It was too much loss for one day, he decided as he parked in the basement car park of his downtown apartment block. Too much change.

But it wasn't quite over.

The letter he pulled from his box in the foyer didn't get opened until Joe had showered off the sea water and had a nice, cold beer in front of him, but any comfort he was trying to give himself evaporated as he read the notice from his landlord.

This apartment block had been deemed an earthquake risk and needed urgent strengthening work.

Joe had little more than a month to find himself somewhere else to live.

* * *

He wasn't coming.

It was already fifteen minutes after the scheduled time for Maggie's appointment at the antenatal clinic for her first ultrasound examination.

She hadn't seen or spoken to Joe since she'd been stood down from her duties at the Aratika Rescue Base nearly two days ago. It was becoming automatic to check her phone repeatedly to see whether she might have missed a reply to the text she'd sent yesterday. She'd informed him of the results of her first appointment with an obstetrician that had confirmed what they already knew, and where and when this appointment for the first ultrasound was happening.

A part of Maggie was also clinging to the admittedly very faint hope that, somehow, the chaos of what was happening in both their lives would begin to settle down to a point where it might still be possible to salvage some of their friendship. They had to be able to talk to each other, didn't they? To make decisions about the future?

Not that Maggie expected anything from Joe. She'd tried to make that clear when she'd finished the text she'd sent him yesterday.

I'm not telling you this because I expect you to be here. It's entirely your choice. It just feels wrong not to keep you in the loop.

'Margaret Lewis?' A technician came into the waiting area.

'That's me.' Maggie got to her feet, wincing a little at the discomfort her very full bladder was creating.

'I'm about to pop,' she told the technician. 'I hope I can last long enough.'

'You'll be fine.' The technician smiled. 'Most women forget about their bladders once they can see their babies. My name's Stella. Is your partner coming?'

'I...um... I'm not sure. He may have been held up.' Not that it felt accurate to refer to Joe as any kind of partner. She wasn't even working with him any more, let alone anything more personal. 'He's an air ambulance paramedic.'

'Oh, wow... That would be such an amazing job.'

'It is.'

And Maggie was missing being at work. Missing Joe. Grappling with the disturbing realisation that she'd fallen in love with someone who would only ever see her as a friend. Even though she had her flatmates around her at home, and Laura was being so sympathetic to her situation, Maggie was feeling very alone. Her mother had offered to travel to Wellington and come with her to this appointment but Maggie had declined the offer— just in case Joe decided he wanted to come. If he did, things would be tense enough without giving him the added pressure of being assessed by one of his child's grandparents.

'Okay...climb up on the bed here. We just need your tummy exposed. I'll tuck a towel over your clothes to protect them from the gel.'

'Ooh...that's cold...'

'It'll warm up in no time. Right...let's get started. I'll let you know what I'm doing as I go along. First up, I'm just going to check your ovaries and uterus and things like where the placenta is lying. Then we'll—' Stella broke off as there was a soft tap at the door. 'Yes?' she called.

The door opened a crack. 'They told me to come through,' a male voice said. 'Is that okay?'

Stella glanced at Maggie, who nodded, even though her heart had just skipped a beat. 'That's Joe,' she said. 'My...the baby's father.'

He came into the room. 'Sorry I'm late,' he told Maggie. 'I had trouble finding somewhere to park.'

His gaze slid away from hers, which made Maggie think that maybe the difficulty hadn't had anything to do with finding a parking space and that it had actually been deciding whether he was going to come at all. It didn't matter. He was here now and...and it felt right.

Better than that, even.

'Stand behind the bed,' Stella told Joe. 'Close to Maggie's shoulder. That way you can both see what's happening on the screen.'

It felt really good to have him in the room. Maggie had to close her eyes for a moment to force back the prickle of tears. She had to clench her fists to remind herself that this wasn't anything like any fantasy she might have had about seeing her baby for the first time. Having the man she loved beside her sharing images that were all about their future together as a family.

That nobody was going to be holding her hand as this little miracle unfolded...

He almost hadn't come.

Joe had started to answer Maggie's text on a dozen or more occasions but, every time, he had deleted his messages before they got sent. Any words he chose felt stilted and couldn't come anywhere near expressing what he wanted to say—probably because he didn't actually *know* what he wanted to say.

He was still angry at being put into a position he had been so determined to never be in. He still felt betrayed. But mixed into those feelings was that determination not to be the man his own father had been. He was going to do better and that meant being somehow involved with his child's life right from the start. Starting with this examination that had actually taken quite a lot of courage to face up to.

Things were about to get very real.

'So we use the crown-rump length for dating,' Stella the technician said, as Joc took a deep breath and focussed on the screen of the ultrasound machine. 'It's the most accurate method, giving us a date to within five to seven days, but it's less useful after twelve weeks because the baby's starting to curl up by that stage.'

The images on the screen were just a blur of smudged black and white to Joe but Stella was pausing the cursor and clicking to make a mark before moving confidently to another point to repeat the process.

'I see the date for your last period would put you at about eleven weeks, but you had an episode of bleeding when you would have expected your next period?'

'More or less,' Maggie said quietly. 'But definitely a bit late. And, looking back, I was worried and then I was so relieved that I didn't think about it any more. It wasn't…um…it wasn't exactly planned…'

Joe clenched his jaw. That was an understatement. The tone of Maggie's voice echoed in his head for long moments after she'd stopped speaking. She sounded so unlike herself.

So subdued. As if she was having as much trouble as

he was getting his head around this shocking development that was going to change his life for ever. Change both their lives but it was going to change Maggie's life far more than his because she was going to parent this child twenty-four seven. He would be a supportive but far more distant figure.

'These measurements confirm that,' Stella told them. 'I'd put baby at eleven weeks, four days. Almost twelve. You're pretty much through your first trimester.'

Yes... Joe could feel the remnants of those shock waves.

He hadn't been wrong to trust Maggie. She really had believed that they were safe.

In silence, he kept watching the screen, taking a professional interest in the images that Stella explained to them both. The view of the four chambers of the heart was fascinating and it was getting easier to identify structures as they glimpsed organs like the bladder and kidneys. The long bones of the legs and the movements of joints had his eyes glued to the screen and then Stella changed the angle of the transducer and pressed it a little more deeply onto Maggie's abdomen.

'Oh...nice,' Stella murmured. 'We don't always get such a good 3D mug shot.'

And there it was. Their baby's face in such astonishing detail it felt like he could reach out and touch this newly forming little person.

His child...

Stella was taking a screenshot. Joe could imagine Maggie keeping a copy of that photo. Showing it to their child in years to come.

This was the very first time we saw you...

Something very unexpected was happening for Joe

right now. He had come here prepared to put his hand
up to take responsibility and be part of his child's life.
What he hadn't anticipated at all was that he was going
to feel...so connected. So emotional. He was swallowing a rather large lump in his throat as Stella finished
up her examination and moved the transducer again.
They got a final, and poignant, glimpse of the baby.

The bottom of a single foot, with each tiny toe clearly
visible.

'Cute.' Stella smiled. 'Let's get a picture of that, too.'

And then it was over and Maggie was walking
through the corridors of the Royal's maternity suite's
outpatient department, holding an envelope that contained several black and white images.

Joe walked beside her. The silence between them
felt odd but not hostile.

'Can I buy you a coffee?' he asked.

He saw the flash of surprise in her eyes. Wariness,
even. But then Maggie gave a soft huff of laughter.
'Maybe a tea?'

'Oh, sorry... I forgot.'

'That's okay. You've had a lot on your mind.'

'Yeah...'

Instead of taking a table in the small café in the hospital's foyer, Joe bought their drinks in takeaway cups
and they went outside to a courtyard area away from
the main entrance, where there were plenty of bench
seats and a small garden with a fountain.

For a while, they sat side by side in silence. It was
Maggie that broke it.

'I really am sorry, Joe. This isn't your fault and I feel
really bad because I know how much you didn't want it.'

'It is partly my fault,' he said. 'It does take two to tango.'

His choice of words reminded him of dancing with Maggie. Of how solid their friendship had seemed, the night of Fizz and Cooper's wedding, when he'd told her stuff about his childhood he'd never told anyone else. It also reminded him of holding her in his arms when they hadn't been dancing and of how good the sex had been. No, not good. Totally, unbelievably amazing.

So what if they weren't in love or they'd never had any intention of being in a 'real' relationship? They had so many things in common, didn't they?

Including a baby now. Maggie had put down her cup to open the envelope and she'd pulled out one of the photos. The one of that tiny foot.

'It's so real now,' she said softly. 'I know it's not what we wanted and I know it's going to be tough but…you know what?'

Joe nodded slowly. He knew exactly what. 'You already love this baby.'

'Yeah…'

'I'm going to be here for you. For him…or her…' Joe gently touched the foot in the photograph with his fingertip. 'We can do this together. Like the "dream team".'

'You don't want that, Joe.'

'Actually, I think I do.' Joe turned to meet Maggie's gaze. 'I came here today because I was determined to be a better man than my father was but right now I can understand what he was trying to do and…maybe it would have worked if my mother had actually wanted me. If she had loved me from the moment she first saw me, like you do with this baby.'

Maggie was looking bewildered. 'Maybe what would have worked?'

'Their marriage. Being able to provide a happy home for their kid. For me.'

Her eyes widened. 'Are you saying what I think you're saying?'

Joe swallowed hard. And then he nodded. 'Yes. I want to be part of this baby's life. Part of your life. We could be a family, Maggie, and I think... I think we could make it work.'

She was staring at him and Joe could see that she had tears in her eyes. Happy tears? He took a deep breath and forced his lips into a smile.

'Marry me,' he said.

CHAPTER EIGHT

IT WAS ON the tip of her tongue to say yes.

How stupid was that?

Part of her didn't think so. The part that included her heart, which was squeezing itself so hard at the moment because when you were in love with someone, what you wanted to hear more than anything else was that they were prepared to commit to a lifetime together.

But the other part of Maggie that included her head was dismissing it in no uncertain terms and it was her head that directed her words.

'You've got to be kidding,' she said to Joe. 'You, of all people, should know that getting married just because you've got a baby on the way is a totally stupid thing to do. For everybody involved, but most especially for the baby.'

She could see the flash of agreement—or maybe it was relief—in his eyes but he was frowning as well. Was he as conflicted as Maggie felt?

'But this is different,' he said.

'How?'

'We're such good friends. We've known each other for years. We *like* each other...'

The squeeze on Maggie's heart tightened enough

to be painful. 'Like' was not a word she would use to describe how she felt about Joe. She couldn't tell him that, of course. About how much she was missing him already? About how wrong she'd been to think she would never want to be anything more than friends with him? How vulnerable would you make yourself by doing that? And how crushing would it be to get reminded that he could never feel that way about her. It was kind of like having to hide those first flickers of sexual attraction because revealing them might have damaged what they had in a special friendship.

Maggie's breath came out in a sigh. It was beyond damaged now, wasn't it? That old, safe friendship with no complications had been blown to smithereens.

'I love you, Maggie, you know that, don't you? We're best mates.'

'Yeah…' Maggie pressed her lips together to stop herself saying anything else.

Being prepared to commit to a lifetime together wasn't actually the thing you wanted to hear most of all when you were in love with someone, she realised. The top of that list would be the three little words Joe had just said to her. Except he had qualified them. Diluted them into something that wasn't enough.

Could never be enough.

Maggie could never marry anyone who hadn't fallen into the crazy, overwhelming space that she was in, preferably at exactly the same moment. The moment when they both just knew that this was 'it'. That they had found their person. You *fell* in love, everybody knew that. You weren't friends with someone for years and years and then just woke up one day and realised that you were head over heels in love, having somehow slipped sideways into that state without noticing it happening.

So maybe what Maggie was feeling for Joe was just something to do with pregnancy hormones. Or the ripple effect from the emotional bond she was developing with this baby she had been unknowingly carrying for so long already. Whatever. Her head was in a mess. So was her heart.

'I understand why you think it might be a good idea,' she said slowly. 'But you've actually been there, remember? You felt like your parents' miserable marriage was your fault.'

'Maybe ours wouldn't be miserable. We enjoy each other's company. We work together well. Hey…we're the—'

'Don't say it,' Maggie warned. 'Can you hear yourself? Saying that being friends and being able to work together as some kind of "dream team" is a good enough reason to get married? Don't you want more than that from someone you're going to hopefully spend the rest of your life with? Something like romance? Passion, even? Because I sure do.'

She slotted the photographs back into their envelope.

'I'm not going to shut you out, Joe,' she added. 'You're this baby's father and you can be as much a part of his or her life as you want to be, but I'm not going to marry you. I'm not going to marry anyone who isn't as much in love with me as I am with him.'

Oh, help…did that sound like a confession? No, it was just a general statement. Maggie wasn't even sure she could trust the notion that she *was* in love with Joe any more given that it could just be crazy hormones. It was Joe himself who'd said that hormones always wore off. He might have been talking about the kind of hormones involved with falling in love, but surely pregnancy hormones didn't last the whole nine months?

She needed time, anyway. She had barely started getting her head around the fact that she was going to become a mother. Sorting out how she really felt about Joe might need to go on the back burner, although the idea that they could salvage the foundation of their friendship was very welcome.

Joe seemed to be in agreement.

'Fair enough,' he said. 'And you're right. As usual…'

The smile didn't look as forced this time—the way it had when he'd proposed to her. It looked like a smile she'd seen on Joe's face countless times. A genuine, warm smile.

The smile she loved. How could she not smile right back?

It was so good to see a smile on Maggie's face again.

She'd looked so upset the last time he'd seen her, in that shocking confrontation when he had found out he was going to become a father. Today, in the dim light of the ultrasound room, she'd looked flat—as if she'd had the stuffing knocked out of her. And she'd looked so wary when he'd offered to buy her a coffee. Had she expected him to have another go at her?

Another unexpected thing had happened when he'd been looking at those images of the baby. Not just the feeling of being connected and close to tears and wanting to protect that tiny being. Maybe it had been the wash of how powerful those feelings were that had made any residual anger about all of this fade enough to seem insignificant.

He hadn't been betrayed. He believed Maggie had genuinely thought they were safe. And accidents happened. This could have happened with any of the women who'd been part of his life in the past and, if anything, he was lucky that it had happened with Maggie. Other women might have expected—demanded, even—the public commitment of marriage, but it was the last thing that Maggie wanted and she was right.

They'd known all along that they weren't meant to be life partners. Joe had to admit that the offer had been impulsive. He had personal experience of exactly what kind of fallout there could be from using an accidental pregnancy as a good reason to get married. He was relieved that Maggie had turned him down. It felt like a lot of pressure had just been lifted off his shoulders.

It wasn't unusual to co-parent these days without being in any kind of relationship with the other parent and if they were on friendly terms that had to be immeasurably easier. He and Maggie had been very good friends and this smile they were sharing now felt like the first step back to that friendship.

'I'd be bad husband material, anyway.' Joe's smile faded. 'I'm going to be homeless pretty soon if I don't get on with finding a new place to live.'

'What? What's happened to your apartment?'

'The building's being emptied. They've got to do some major strengthening. It's been identified as an earthquake risk.'

'We've got a spare room at the flat. We still haven't found a replacement for Cooper. If you get desperate, I'm sure everybody would be happy if you used the room. Until you found a place of your own.'

'Hmm…' Joe glanced sideways at Maggie. Those

last words had revealed that Maggie had made the offer before she'd really thought through any consequences.

It could be very awkward. The reminder of the physical relationship they hadn't actually officially ended would be there between them all the time. And, okay, it probably was over now but that wouldn't stop the memories, would it?

Those flashes of sensation—one of which Joe was experiencing right now—that reminded him of just how amazing sex with Maggie was. Oh, man…he felt guilty for even thinking about that when there were far more important things he should be facing. Like taking responsibility for the child he had fathered. Like finding himself somewhere to live.

'I think it's fate,' he told Maggie. 'I'm thirty-seven. I've been saving money for a long time without making a sensible investment. Maybe it's time I bought a real house. Something a bit more child-friendly than an apartment, anyway. With a garden, perhaps?'

Did Maggie realise that he was talking about something more than simply a house? It was difficult to try and explain something he didn't understand himself, though. Those feelings during that ultrasound. That he'd understood that Maggie already loved this baby because…he'd felt at least something similar to that himself. 'And a swing,' he added, his voice cracking just a little. 'For…when this kid comes to visit his dad, you know?'

Maggie was silent for a long moment. When she finally raised her gaze to meet Joe's he'd never seen an expression like that on her face before. It looked like total amazement, laced with…hope? Excitement? Except that there was something else there as well. Something that made him want to hug her and tell her that everything was going to be okay.

He'd seen Maggie's face glowing plenty of times but not like this. As if her normal confidence was nowhere to be found. As if she was stepping onto new ground and it was scary and she couldn't quite believe that someone was offering to keep her company.

Joe wanted to do more than keep Maggie company. He wanted to keep her safe.

It felt perfectly natural to put his arm around her shoulders and pull her sideways for a quick hug.

'We'll work this out,' he said. 'Together. You'll see.'

'So I don't have to be stuck in the basement with Danny, helping out with supplies all the time. I'm allowed to use one of the SUVs for first response if the base gets asked for assistance. I just have to wait for backup for any lifting.' Maggie sighed as she poured hot water over the tea bag in her mug in Aratika's staffroom. 'I told Don I'd be much happier on a bike. It's so much quicker to get through traffic that way.'

'Are you still riding your bike?' Cooper sounded surprised as he looked up from where he was peering over Joe's shoulder at the screen of his phone.

'Don't go there,' Joe warned. 'I tried suggesting that it might not be such a good idea last week and I got my head bitten off.'

'Oh, sorry... I wasn't thinking.' Cooper turned back to the phone. 'I got the same lecture from Fizz. Pregnancy is not an illness. Women can work until they go into labour if that's what they want to do. Aye...that one, mate.' He reached forward to point at the screen. 'It looks awesome.'

'My obstetrician says I can carry on with anything that I normally do.' Maggie kept her tone level. She had enough changing in her life right now without being pressured to give up her beloved bike just yet. 'That I'll know when it's time to stop because it's getting uncomfortable. Apart from the heavy lifting, of course.'

'And keeping out of the way of any aggressive patients,' Joe muttered. 'Or hazardous accident scenes.'

Cooper chuckled. 'You're getting onto thin ice. Maggie's sensible. You can trust her judgement.'

'True.' Joe looked up and Maggie couldn't help her breath catching as those warm hazel eyes captured her own gaze. Since they'd shared that appointment for the first ultrasound examination of their baby, they had been tentatively restoring their friendship, step by step—hopefully along with the trust that had been implicit.

Not the extra, physical side that had been added into that friendship, of course. How could they, when it was the reason they were both facing a very different future from the one they might have been expecting? But it was a good start. They could talk to each other at work, even though that currently seemed to consist of Maggie demanding every detail of the more interesting cases Joe had been deployed to, usually with one of the HEMS doctors like Tom or Adam as his crew partner.

He'd had a job yesterday where a hunter had fallen down a steep bank onto rocks in thick forest in the Rimutaka Ranges.

'Why couldn't you winch in to the scene? Was it too windy?'

'How far did you have to walk? Did you have any help to carry the gear?'

'You had to abseil down to the patient? Wow...how did that go?'

'What else did you find on the secondary survey? Did he have abdominal as well as chest injuries?'

'So how did you deal with the failed intubation attempt? Did you try more padding to adjust the positioning? How fast was the swelling obscuring what you could see?'

Joe understood how much Maggie was missing being on the front line and it was becoming their new normal—to have a debrief even though Maggie hadn't been to the job, the way they would have if they'd managed the case together.

'Yeah, I had to use padding to get the earlobe in line with the sternal notch but it was difficult. It was getting dark already and we were down a cliff in the middle of a forest. Maybe we should have considered a tracheostomy earlier. It was touch and go there for a while. What would you have done?'

Right now, the expression in Joe's eyes suggested that he would welcome her opinion on something else.

'So...come and see what you think of this house,' he said. 'It's up on the hill. Not far from where Cooper and Fizz live.'

'It's a great suburb.' Cooper nodded. 'There's a good crèche nearby and a primary school. We've got it all sussed.'

Maggie stepped forward to look at the images Joe was scrolling through on a real estate website. She had to resist the urge to lean close enough to be touching his shoulder or to let a stray curl of his hair brush her cheek.

These waves of longing had to be controlled until her wayward hormones had settled down and the swirls of confusion had cleared and she could totally believe that she wasn't in love with him. It was enough for now that Joe was no longer angry with her. That he believed she hadn't deliberately set out to get pregnant and that he was willing to become involved as a responsible parent.

Except it didn't feel like enough. The confused part of Maggie's head—and heart—was telling her that she wanted more. That she was fighting a losing battle by pretending it was something temporary that would wear off soon. And those messages were in conflict with others that were reminding her that Joe would definitely not want more. That the fragility of the new relationship they were forging would be very easy to damage and that new damage on top of the recent trauma would spell the end of any trust between them.

She focussed on the screen. The house being advertised for sale was an old weatherboard villa with a big veranda wrapping around two sides of the house and a room with a turret on the corner.

'It's gorgeous,' she said. 'Like a little castle. But it's *huge...*'

'It's divided into two flats,' Joe said. 'Which means I could rent half of it out which will help pay the mortgage.'

'The harbour view's amazing.'

'And the garden. Look at that.'

'Bit of work there,' Cooper warned. 'Do you really want to spend your days off mowing lawns and weeding gardens? When will you find time for your windsurfing?'

Maggie couldn't miss the slight hesitation before Joe spoke. 'Things change,' he said quietly. 'And sometimes the new things are worth giving up other stuff for.'

Was that a doubtful note she detected in his voice? Sad, even? No…it sounded more like Joe was getting used to the big changes to his life that were coming. That he was prepared to embrace them. Mind you, it was hard to imagine him giving up the freedom of skimming waves to be that domesticated.

'It's a lot different to your modern apartment,' she said. 'Old houses take a lot more housework. And maintenance.'

'Looks in pretty good nick to me. It's been rewired. And painted.'

'Photos can be very deceptive. You've learned that much in a couple of weeks' house-hunting, surely?'

Joe grunted. 'I'm running out of time. You know what?' He tapped the screen. 'I'm going to call the agent and set up a viewing. Come with me, Maggie.'

'Why?'

'Because you're good to talk about things with. Bounce ideas off. And I can trust your judgement, that's why.'

'Management of the case of a house instead of a patient? With an extensive debrief?'

Joe's smile told her she had hit the nail on the head. 'You up for it?'

'Sure.'

Maggie kept her tone light but that confusing swirl of messages and feelings ramped up a notch. She couldn't let Joe recognise the magnetic pull that made the prospect of spending time alone with him so compelling but she almost resented the sensible part of her brain that was warning her this might not be a good idea. That she could be putting roadblocks or, at the very least, diversions in the way of sorting out what her real feelings were and how she was going to deal with them. Surely spending more time with Joe was exactly what would help to sort the mess in her head and her heart?

'This definitely sounds like a project that needs the attention of the "dream team",' she added jokingly. 'Just let me know where and when.'

The house was beautiful.

With polished wooden floors, high ceilings with ornate plasterwork and rooms big enough to seem totally indulgent by modern standards, it was a glorious example of an early New Zealand villa.

And Maggie had fallen in love with it the moment she'd walked through the heavy, wooden front door with its stained-glass panels. Tall sash windows made every room light enough to see the patches of peeling paint on the ceilings and the deep scratches and marks from years of high-heeled shoes, dogs' nails and probably children's toys on the floorboards. The signs of a house that had been well lived in. A family home...

A big family home. The kind you could have fitted six children in before it had been divided into two apartments. The kind of home that Maggie could have imagined in those days of dreaming about a large family—right down to a dog or two.

'You could have a dog,' she found herself telling Joe. 'How cool would that be?'

He didn't look excited by the idea. 'It's not fair to keep a dog if you're working full time,' he said. 'I wouldn't want the responsibility.'

Maggie turned away to look at the view from the enormous bay window in this huge sitting room. It was similar to the view that Cooper and Fizz had from their small villa, with a lovely glimpse of Wellington Harbour in the distance. She could actually see a helicopter gaining height as it came from the direction of the Aratika Rescue Base. Who was on board? she wondered. And what kind of adrenaline rush would the challenge produce? Would it be what she and Joe might consider a 'hot' one? She missed the intensity of that work. She even missed the long days and the sometimes exhausting physical challenges. Joe was right, though. You couldn't do a job like that with its twelve-hour or more shifts and leave a dog at home alone.

But if a dog was a responsibility that Joe didn't want, how did he really feel about a child being in his near future? It was still too early to feel this baby moving inside her, but Maggie put her hand on her belly anyway— her fingers spread a little as if she needed to protect it.

'So this half of the house has the view. I have to say it's one of the best I've seen in a very long time.' The real estate agent had been enthusiastically drawing their attention to every detail of the house from the moment they'd entered. 'I imagine you'd choose this half to live in and rent the other half out? I've got an estimate of the kind of income you could expect to make from doing that, if you want to look at it, Joe?'

'Yes…thank you.' Joe went to stand beside the agent to look at the clipboard she was holding.

'It's lucky that both apartments are empty at the moment. You could get possession very fast if your offer was acceptable. I understand you're in a bit of a hurry?'

'Mmm…' Joe had flipped a page on the clipboard. 'So these are the floor plans? The second apartment looks smaller.'

'It still has two bedrooms and a good-sized sitting room that was originally another bedroom, I believe. Or maybe a library. You could easily knock through and take it back to its former glory as a large family home.' The agent sent a smile in Maggie's direction. 'How perfect would that be for when you guys want to start your family?'

'We're not a couple,' Maggie told her, surprising herself with a tone that was uncharacteristically rude. It wasn't that the agent needed to know. It was more like a stab of disappointment that had prompted her to say something. She and Joe might be having a baby together but they weren't starting any kind of 'real' family. It was more than disappointing. It felt heartbreaking enough to tell Maggie that her hormonal imbalance was nowhere near settling down. Good grief...there was something about the agent's words, or this house-viewing business, that almost had her on the verge of tears.

'We're just friends,' she added, trying to make her tone friendlier. 'I'm here to provide a feminine viewpoint, that's all.'

'Oh... I beg your pardon...' The agent's cheeks went pink. 'Well...how 'bout I leave you to have a look at the bedrooms and bathroom on this side and then I'll meet you in the other apartment? That'll give you a bit of time to talk about things.'

Maggie walked closer to the windows to stare down at the garden. There was a lovely patch of lawn before the slope merged into a grove of trees. She could see a path leading somewhere and an old tyre swing hanging from the large tree branch. She could also feel Joe moving towards her.

'Just friends?' he asked quietly.

Maggie swallowed hard. 'What would you call us, then?'

'I don't know.' Joe blew out a breath. 'Definitely friends, but there's something bigger now as well, don't you think? We're going to be parents together.'

'Not exactly together.'

'You know what I mean. We're both going to be the parents of the same baby. It feels…more than "just friends".'

'Yeah…' It was Maggie's turn to sigh. 'It's certainly more complicated than it used to be.'

The silence felt awkward.

'I *love* this house,' Maggie said brightly, to try and change the subject. 'It needs work but it feels like it would be a lovely place to live.'

'I love it, too.' Joe nodded. 'And…you know what? It could be perfect—for both of us.'

Startled, Maggie turned her head swiftly, her eyes widening as she looked up at Joe. 'What are you talking about?'

'It's just occurred to me that this could be the ideal solution.'

'Solution to what?'

'To being co-parents but not together.'

'I still have no idea what you're talking about.'

'This house has two sides. Part of the same house but separate. Imagine if I lived on one side and you lived on the other?'

Her mind jumped to that scenario with remarkable ease. She would see Joe every day. They would be a part of each other's lives. They could share meals together, maybe, and gardening chores. Almost like a real family.

She could actually see herself out there in a couple of years, harvesting some vegetables from the garden, and she could see Joe push that tyre swing with a toddler sitting inside it, shrieking with glee. In the periphery of that flash of fantasy, Maggie could even see the waving tail of a happy dog. A golden retriever, perhaps…

But there was something else, too. Someone else? Joe's latest girlfriend, probably. She would see him bringing new ones home. Ringing in the changes because they'd got too close and wanted more than he was prepared to give. He might tell her about it over a glass of wine in the evening — because she was his friend. A good friend. The mother of his child, in fact, but still only a friend.

She couldn't do it. Because it would be nothing like a real family. She would be close to Joe but there was a very real possibility that she would feel even lonelier than she did at the moment. Wanting to be with him. Wanting to touch and be touched by Joe. Maggie could feel herself welling up with that new twinge of longing. Oh, boy… There was still no sign of the effects of these new hormones wearing off. If anything, they were getting more powerful.

'You okay?' Joe's voice was concerned.

'Mmm…' Maggie fought for control, focussing on the view again.

'You hate the idea, don't you?'

'I…um…think it might make things too difficult.'

'I thought it would make things easier. As far as sharing the parenting, anyway.'

'I'm sure it would,' Maggie murmured. 'But…it might be *too* close, you know?'

'Not sure I do.' Joe was frowning. 'We've stopped

seeing each other like that, haven't we? It was a mistake to mess up our friendship with sex. And…you were very clear about not wanting to marry me and I agree that it needs more than a basis of friendship to make that kind of commitment, so…that's the end of that, isn't it?'

Maggie needed to agree with him. She tried to nod her head but it wasn't quite working. She did tilt her head up to start the movement but all that did was let her gaze snag on Joe's and she could see that he was thinking about exactly what she was thinking about.

'Oh… *Maggie*…'

His voice was a low rumble laced with desire. He lifted his hand to lay his palm gently against her cheek and Maggie felt her eyes drifting shut as she leaned into the touch. She couldn't see Joe's head slowly dipping but she could feel the heat of his skin becoming more intense as he closed the distance between their faces. And then she was aware of only the electric tingle as his lips covered hers, moving over them so slowly, so tenderly, it was utterly heartbreaking.

'Oh…don't mind me…'

The cheerful voice of the real estate agent felt like someone was throwing a bucket of cold water in their direction. They both jerked apart.

'I wondered what was taking you so long,' the agent continued. The knowing smile on her face suggested that she knew any earlier embarrassment had been misplaced. 'I see you are…um…pretty *good* friends.'

It was Maggie's cheeks that had gone pink this time. She couldn't meet the agent's gaze. She couldn't look at Joe, either.

'So…do you want to look at the other apartment?'

Maggie could feel Joe's gaze on her. Willing her to

look up again. Wanting to know whether she was interested in the opportunity this house could provide of living so closely together while they co-parented their child.

She forced herself to look up. To meet his gaze and shake her head just enough to relay the information that she couldn't do it. That the kiss they'd just shared had made things even more complicated and it wouldn't be a good idea for anybody involved here.

It seemed that he understood. Given the swift way his gaze slid away from Maggie's, it also seemed that he was either regretting that kiss or he was also feeling confused about how to define their relationship—or lack of it.

'I don't think we need to see the other apartment at the moment,' he told the agent.

'Oh…' She sounded disappointed. 'So you're not interested in the house, then?'

'On the contrary.'

Joe's voice was clipped. He was going into his efficient mode, Maggie realised, sounding like he did when he had a patient in critical condition and it was a race against time to save a life. He was in charge and he was going to make something happen.

'I love the house,' Joe added, seeming to grow an inch or two taller as he straightened his spine. 'I'll come back tomorrow and bring someone who can assess the condition of the place properly but I'll certainly be putting an offer in. As soon as possible.'

CHAPTER NINE

'I HEAR YOU'VE gone and bought a house, Joe.'

'Yep. The contract went unconditional yesterday. I take possession in a couple of weeks.'

Joe was restocking a drug roll, sliding ampoules into the row of tiny pockets. Fentanyl, ketamine, morphine... He itemised the drugs on the record sheet, signed his name against the entry and then handed the sheet to his partner for the additional signature. He was working with Tom Chapman today, the specialist consultant in the emergency department of the Royal who had begun working at Aratika when Fizz had had to give up her air rescue shifts.

'Exciting.' Tom nodded. 'From what Andy said, it sounds like a big place.'

'It's an old house. Divided into two apartments. Hey...you're not looking for somewhere new to live by any chance, are you?'

Tom laughed. 'No. And I like my little apartment. Easy to clean and maintain. Boring but very practical.' He shook his head, still grinning. 'Bit like me, really.'

Joe chuckled. He hadn't worked with Tom that often yet and knew nothing about his private life but he had always been impressed with this experienced doctor's ability to stay calm in any emergency and deal with it in a confident and highly skilled manner. Okay, he didn't smile that often and there was something very serious in his gaze a lot of the time but he had an absolute passion for his work and it was obvious that he cared very much for every patient he worked on.

'Hmm.' Joe continued gathering other supplies like the small, foil packages containing alcohol wipes, plastic packages with Luer plugs and a roll of tape, but he flicked Tom a sideways glance. 'You're not boring, mate, but you're probably a lot more sensible than me. I may well find I've bitten off more than I can chew, house-wise. Don't know what got into me.'

'You must have fallen in love with the place.'

'Nah...' Joe shook his head. 'I don't fall in love with women so it's not likely to happen with a house. It's a good investment, that's all.'

Except that a nice, practical little apartment like Tom had might have been an even better investment. Why had he made up his mind on the spot like that and then followed through with a second viewing and negotiating an agreed price? Because he had the thought lurking in the back of his mind that he might be able to persuade Maggie that the separate but close living arrangements could really work?

Or was it because it felt like a real home? A real family home. The kind where you could have a Sunday roast for lunch. He'd looked at that old swing in the tree in the garden and imagined what it would be like growing up in that house as a kid. A kid who felt wanted—the way he was determined that his child would always feel. The way he'd never felt himself, as a child. A kid with two parents, even, and it was a shock to realise that he could so easily see himself and Maggie as those loving parents. To imagine them loving each other as well as their child...

There were feelings being stirred that Joe had never wanted to revisit. Disturbing emotional currents that he had no idea how to deal with. It wasn't just to do with the baby, either. It had been a big mistake to kiss Maggie again. That had been lurking in the back of his mind for the last few weeks as well. Haunting his dreams and interfering with his focus too frequently to be acceptable. The softness of her lips. The warmth and smell and *taste* of her...

It was impossible to remember that kiss and not have his mind open a door that let his thoughts sneak off into the memories of what it had been like to kiss Maggie Lewis a lot more thoroughly. To feel the shape of her body beneath his hands and his lips. To be able to laugh, even, as sexual play led to the kind of release that had been a complete revelation for Joe.

He shouldn't be thinking about it at all but he couldn't really identify those feelings that were being stirred up and therefore had no idea how to fix his confusion. It didn't help that there was so much more he had to think about now that his future was moving in a direction he hadn't wanted to consider. The future that featured himself as a father.

It wasn't just that he was missing the sex. If that was all there was to it, it would have been easy enough in the last few weeks to have reconnected with an old girlfriend, perhaps, or find someone new. Instinct was still telling him, very firmly, that that kind of hook-up would not solve anything, no matter how good the sex might be. If anything, it would probably make it harder to sort out what was going on in his head, which was quite confusing enough already.

And maybe Maggie was feeling the same kind of confusion. Maybe that was why she seemed to have been deliberately avoiding spending any time alone with him ever since that house viewing. Was she missing him in anything like the same way he was missing her?

At least it was always possible to shut off any of those thoughts when he was actually involved in any kind of patient care but times like this, out of work hours or on station between missions, it seemed impossible to stop his thought processes getting hijacked. What he should be thinking about right now was making sure he had everything available in his kit that might be needed on the next critical case they were called to. He put more effort into focussing.

'Do we need any laryngeal mask airways?' Tom called, from the other side of the storage room.

'Yes. Grab a size four and five.' It was always good to have extras of the sizes they used the most often.

Tom handed him the airway devices. 'Anything else?'

'I think we're done. Let's see if we can get a coffee upstairs before we get another call.'

Both men paused as they walked past the windows that overlooked the helipad. Andy and Nick were still busy cleaning the chopper after the last mission they'd been on that had involved a fair bit of bodily fluids getting splashed around. Dark grey clouds were gathering in the sky above and a few raindrops pelted the windows and trickled down the glass.

'We're going to get some more accidents with this

weather front coming in,' Tom said. 'The wind was bad enough without adding in the rain.'

'We did good at the last one,' Joe reminded him. 'I didn't think we'd get her into ED alive. That was a nasty smash. Vans can be hard to control in a high wind.'

Tom nodded slowly. 'They're the best jobs,' he said quietly. 'When you know for sure that the time saved and what we can offer in the way of pre-hospital medicine is what really made the difference between life and death. That some police officer isn't on his way to knock on someone's door and deliver the news that life, as they know it, is over.'

Wow... Tom really could get serious at times. Joe couldn't think of anything to say as they carried on into the staffroom to be greeted by a cheerful voice.

'You boys are just in time. My banana cake got cool enough to ice while you were out. And I've put some whipped cream in the middle. Sit yourselves down for five minutes.'

'It's you who should be sitting down for five minutes, Shirley. You never stop.'

'I feel better than I have in years.' Shirley was beaming as she set plates with large wedges of cake on them in front of Joe and Tom. 'Twenty years younger, in fact. Have you seen Maggie anywhere? She loves my banana cake.'

'It's her day off,' Joe told her. 'I think she was going up the coast to visit her parents.'

'Is she going to move back home?' Shirley asked. 'When that baby arrives?'

'Not that I know of.'

Surely Maggie would have said something if she was considering moving out of the city? Her parents were a good ninety minutes' drive away. But then again, why would she say anything? They were friends, not life partners. Living in a different town didn't mean that they couldn't co-parent. It would just make it a lot more difficult. On the opposite end of the spectrum he had suggested with the idea that Maggie could live in the second apartment of that old house he'd just bought.

Shirley put mugs and a pot of coffee in front of the men. Her glance made Joe feel like she could see far more than he might be comfortable with.

'Has Maggie seen that new house of yours?'

Yep. Seemed like Shirley really was telepathic to some degree. 'She came with me.'

'It's got two apartments, I hear.'

Joe sighed. 'Yep. And, yes, before you ask, Shirley, I did suggest that Maggie move into one of them. She said she didn't want to. That things were complicated enough already.'

Shirley echoed his sigh and then tutted with disappointment as she went back towards a sink that was full of her baking and mixing dishes. She might have been muttering something about people not seeing things that were right under their noses but Joe pretended not to hear.

He stared at the slice of cake on his plate. 'I actually asked Maggie to marry me,' he confessed to Tom.

Good grief…why on earth had he said that to someone he didn't know that well? Because Tom was so calm and sensible that he might have some advice to offer? Maybe it was because he wasn't as close a friend yet as someone like Andy. Or Cooper, who was still bathing in the rosy glow of both marriage with someone he was very much in love with and the excitement of expecting his first child.

'She said no, I take it?'

'She thinks there's got to be more than friendship. That you've got to be in love.'

Tom ate a bite of cake slowly and then nodded. 'She's right.'

Joe tried to eat some cake in the silence that followed, punctuated only by Shirley banging cake tins in the background, but it was hard to swallow.

'I wouldn't know about that,' he said. 'Like I said, I've never been in love that I know of. With a house *or* a person.'

Because he'd never let himself get past those roadblocks?

'You'd know, if you were,' Tom told him.

'How?'

Tom shrugged. 'Everything's different. It's like the sun has just been turned on in your personal universe. Everything's so much brighter. Warmer.'

Joe stared at his colleague. There were certainly depths to this man that he had never recognised. 'You've been there?'

'Yeah…' Tom's smile was slow. Poignant. 'Past tense is right, unfortunately. I lost my wife and son in a car accident a few years ago now.'

'Oh… *God*… I'm so sorry. I had no idea.' Joe caught his breath. No wonder Tom felt so strongly about the kind of job they'd just been on when they'd saved the life of a young woman who'd crashed her car. No wonder he seemed so serious at times.

'It's okay.' Tom drained his coffee mug. 'You're not the only one with no idea. It's not something I talk about. It broke me but I've put my life back together. I know I couldn't do it again but I also know that you'll know when it happens to you. And that for a marriage to work, it needs to happen on both sides.'

And that was never going to happen. Maggie had made it clear right from the start that she would never feel like that about him. Joe wasn't in love with Maggie— he couldn't be—but he did miss her. He missed the easy friendship. He missed the sex, too, of course, but it didn't feel as if his personal universe had been plunged into darkness. It just felt different.

Emptier.

And because he wasn't in love with Maggie and she wasn't in love with him, Tom was in agreement that she'd been right in refusing to marry him. That meant she would probably be making the right choice if she chose to move away from the city to raise her child with the help of her parents.

Without him.

This new emptiness of his personal universe kicked up a notch or two. Joe reached for another forkful of his cake in the hope of filling a tiny portion of that emptiness but he didn't get the chance to sink his teeth into it. His pager sounded.

So did Tom's.

'Bike versus truck,' Tom announced. 'I knew we'd be in for a spate of accidents this afternoon.'

Andy already had the rotors going by the time the two men had picked up their kits and helmets and were climbing aboard.

'Got cleaned up in the nick of time,' he said. 'Buckle up, it's getting a bit wild out there and we're heading into the worst of it, up the coast.'

It was a ten-minute ride, buffeted by wind. Things seemed noisier than usual and their information was coming in by crackled sound bites. A motorbike had skidded on the newly wet tarmac and had been clipped by a truck on a corner. One person was unhurt, another was reported as Status Two, which meant that they were unstable and potentially seriously injured. Visibility was less than perfect with rain streaking the Perspex and landing on a section of the road that the police and fire service had cleared for them took all of Andy's skill along with the backup of the medical crew watching out for hazards.

'Clear this side,' Tom confirmed.

'Tail clear,' Joe added.

Droplets of water on Joe's helmet visor were intensifying the colours of the flashing lights of emergency vehicles as he strode, ahead of Tom, to the centre of the accident scene. Red and blue flashes from a police car and an ambulance. He could see that the cab of the truck was empty so the driver had got out. That was probably him sitting in the back of the ambulance with a policewoman beside him.

Joe could also see the wheels of the motorbike, which was lying on its side just in front of a cluster of crouching people that was obscuring his view of their patient.

'Air Rescue,' he called. 'Let me through...'

People shifted. Joe could see the feet of their patient poking out from beneath a blanket. A paramedic was focussed on whatever she was hearing through her stethoscope and another was pulling an oxygen mask from its packaging. Two fire officers were holding up a tarpaulin both to keep rain off the injured person and shield them from curious stares from onlookers. From the corner of his eye, as he stepped forward, Joe was taking in the damage to the motorbike as an indication of how serious this accident had been.

It still looked largely intact, which was a good sign but no guarantee that the rider might have escaped a critical injury. The only damage Joe could see was that a handlebar was bent and the paintwork was pretty scratched. Sky-blue paintwork, he registered. Unusual.

The same as Maggie's motorbike.

He took another step forward, aware of the chill running down his spine, and then he stopped so abruptly that Tom bumped into the kit on his back.

'No...' Joe could feel the blood draining from his head as he took in the pale face with that cloud of blonde curls surrounding it. Her eyes were closed. Was she even alive? He was frozen into immobility. How could he deal with this when he couldn't even think of the most basic thing he needed to do? When all he wanted to do was crouch down beside Maggie and take her into his arms?

'I've got this.' Tom stepped past him. 'Stay here for a moment, Joe.'

Tom knew who it was. He might not have worked at the Aratika Rescue Base for that long but he'd known Maggie well before that, from taking her patient handovers in the emergency department. He also knew what everyone else knew about Joe's relationship with Maggie and about her pregnancy.

So he knew it wasn't just one patient they had to worry about. It was two.

Maggie...and their baby...

Tom dropped his backpack and crouched beside the paramedic with the stethoscope.

'Accident wasn't high speed from what witnesses have told us,' a young paramedic told him. 'Sounds like she just hit a patch of oil in the road and the wheel slid out from under her. Her name's Maggie Lewis. She's thirty-five years old.'

'I know Maggie,' Tom said. He gripped her shoulder. 'Maggie? Can you hear me?'

Her eyes fluttered open. From where he was, still near her feet, Joe could see how anxious she looked. And how rapidly she was breathing.

'Vital signs?' Tom queried calmly.

'Blood pressure is one hundred over sixty,' the paramedic said. 'Respirations twenty-four. Heart rate is one twenty and her oxygen saturation is…' she looked over at the monitor '…ninety-two percent. That's down from a few minutes ago.'

'T-Tom…' Maggie pulled the oxygen mask away from her face, her voice hoarse. 'Can't…breathe…'

It was the sound of her voice that broke those frozen few seconds for Joe. He was moving now. Close enough for Maggie to see him. Close enough for him to see the very real fear in her eyes.

'J-Joe… I'm…'

'I know.' He put his hand on her cheek for a moment, before replacing the oxygen mask. 'We've got this. You're going to be fine.'

She had to be. That was all there was to it.

'She's got a chest injury on the left side,' the paramedic was saying now. 'Probably broken ribs. She's refused any pain relief because she's pregnant. About seventeen weeks, she said.'

Tom fitted the earpieces of his stethoscope, placing the disc on Maggie's chest. Joe was watching the con-

densation on the inside of her mask that showed the rate
of her breathing efforts increasing. She was also looking more distressed, her head rolling from side to side.

'I think she's got reduced air entry on the left side.'
The paramedic was frowning. 'It's hard to tell with all
the noise here, though.'

Joe felt like he was having trouble breathing himself.
That his own lungs were being squeezed.

'Absent breath sounds, left side,' Tom said quietly.
'And we've got some subcutaneous emphysema happening.' He touched an area of skin where there were
bubbles of air marring the smoothness.

'Needle decompression?' The paramedic was turning towards her kit. 'I've got the gear.'

But Tom was looking at Maggie. Reaching to shake
her shoulder. 'Maggie? Can you hear me? Open your
eyes...'

Joe felt the moment she lost consciousness and knew
that Tom had felt it as well. A few seconds later and
she stopped breathing. The men exchanged a single
glance. The air escaping into Maggie's chest from her
lung, probably due to an injury from a fractured rib,
had reached a critical level. Her lung had collapsed and
the pressure was building. It was pushing her heart towards the other side of her chest and the major veins
leading into her heart would be getting blocked. The
level of oxygen in her bloodstream would be dropping
dramatically. A respiratory arrest would be followed
by a cardiac arrest very soon if they didn't move fast.

'Simple thoracostomy,' Tom said, already opening
his pack to remove the roll he needed. 'Rather than
needle decompression. You agree, Joe?'

Joe could only nod. He still felt as if he couldn't

breathe. How could he, if Maggie wasn't breathing? The tension wasn't just in Maggie's chest. It was pressing down on Joe, so hard it felt like something might explode.

Thank goodness Tom, with all his experience and skill, was here to provide a more definitive treatment to this life-threatening situation. He was moving swiftly but calmly. Joe helped position Maggie's arm, lifting and turning it to put her hand under her head. He kept his own hand there as well, covering hers. Just needing to be in contact with her skin. Touching her.

You can't do this, he told her silently. *You are not going to die...*

He watched as Tom cleaned the skin over Maggie's ribs, made a cut with a scalpel and then opened the muscle with some forceps before inserting his gloved finger to make sure he had reached the chest cavity. As he pulled his finger out, he nodded with satisfaction.

Joe felt the movement through his hand and straight into his own chest. He was dragging in a huge breath at the same time as Maggie pulled in one of her own. And then another. The miraculous effect of the pressure being released had her eyelids fluttering again within seconds. Joe had never been happier to see those dark blue eyes so close to his own.

'It's okay,' he told her. 'You're going to be okay. We've got you...'

They had her into the helicopter a short time later.

'I've got her helmet.' Joe climbed in after Tom. 'There's no significant damage and the ground crew said she wasn't knocked out. Her GSC was fifteen on arrival.'

'I think she's been lucky.' Tom nodded. 'We'll be able

to check her thoroughly once we've got her into Emergency. Buckle up, Joe. I'll sit by her head. I want to keep a close eye on her in case she starts tensioning again.'

It was too noisy to try and talk to Maggie and Tom was taking excellent care of her so there was nothing for Joe to do but fasten his harness and go along for the ride.

He was still worried about Maggie. Of course he was. Worried about the baby as well, now that the terrifying threat of losing Maggie was receding. It was enough to give him a painful lump in his throat, thinking about how real that threat had been for a minute or two.

Thinking about what it might have been like to lose Maggie.

What was it Tom had said? That you'd know you were in love with someone because it was like the sun had been turned on in your personal universe. He'd just experienced the opposite of that, Joe realised. He'd recognised how dark his personal universe would be if Maggie disappeared from it. How much light and warmth he could lose.

He knew.

He'd known all along, hadn't he? He'd just been afraid to put it into words, let alone admit it aloud. The warmth and light had always been there but he'd thought it was no more than friendship because it was something so different from anything he'd experienced in his romantic liaisons. Now he could see it very clearly for what it actually was.

He loved Maggie.

He was *in love* with Maggie.

He could see her living in that beautiful house with him. As his life partner. His wife. The mother of his child. No…make that children…

Joe still had that lump in his throat as he walked beside Maggie's stretcher as they took her down to the emergency department from the helipad. He stood behind Tom in the elevator and it was then that he remembered something else that Tom had said earlier today—that he would know when he'd fallen in love, but that for a marriage to work it had to happen on both sides.

When the stretcher disappeared ahead of him through the doors of the main resuscitation area, Joe was remembering something else that had been said. Not by Tom. This was an echo of Maggie's voice he could hear in the back of his mind now. When they'd been lying in his bed, having ignored their decision not to let it happen a second time. Basking in the aftermath of the best sex ever. He could still hear how adamant she'd been in agreeing with him that marriage was not something he had any wish to consider.

'Believe, me,' she'd said to him. *'I'll know who I want to marry—probably within a few minutes of meeting him... It certainly wasn't something I was thinking when I met you, mate...'*

'Joe?'

He could hear Maggie's real voice now. Calling for him.

'I'm here.' He pushed his way through the team that had already been in the resuscitation area, waiting to receive Maggie.

The way she took hold of his hand and squeezed it so tightly gave Joe a weird prickle behind his eyes to go with that lump in his throat that wouldn't go away. It also gave him a flash of something like hope. Hope that perhaps he was important enough for Maggie to want to keep him in her life, even if she would never be in love with him or want to marry him.

'Somebody got that foetal monitor?' The consultant leading the resuscitation team was looking around the room as soon as they'd dealt with the first tasks of reviewing all Maggie's vital signs and then placing a tube to secure the drainage of air from her chest. 'Let's get it on.'

That request changed everything. It didn't matter how Joe felt about Maggie right now. Or how she felt about him. Even the relief that Maggie was breathing well and all her vital signs were within normal ranges got shunted into the background. There was only one important thing to know in this moment.

That their baby had survived this accident.

The realisation of how he felt about Maggie had opened floodgates that had been locked shut for what seemed like his whole life. It wasn't just Maggie that Joe was experiencing such powerful feelings for, was it? It felt like the life of his child was hanging in the balance. His son. Or his daughter. A child that he needed to protect. And that he wanted to be able to love.

'It's on its way from Maternity,' someone said. 'Shouldn't be long.'

'We've got a Doppler here,' Tom reminded them. 'I'll find it.'

Other members of the medical team were still monitoring Maggie's oxygen levels, heart rhythm, blood pressure and other vital signs. They were also doing an even more thorough secondary survey to make sure they hadn't missed any other significant injuries but, as Tom had thought, it seemed that the only real damage had been done when her ribs had been caught by the handlebar of her bike. Tom and Joe would normally have handed over the care of their patient and gone back to the helipad but there was no way Joe could leave and Tom had morphed from being a HEMS doctor back into his usual role of emergency medicine consultant.

He had the Doppler unit in one hand and the small probe in the other. Maggie's clothes had already been cut away and Joe could see that her bump was just starting to show and that made that lump in his throat get so big it was hard to breathe around its edges.

Maggie's grip on his hand, as Tom moved the probe over her belly, was so tight it was hurting but Joe was barely aware of the pain. He was holding Maggie's frightened gaze so he saw the emotion that flooded into her face when the sound of the baby's heartbeat was caught and magnified for all to hear. The rapid, blurred, underwater thump of the sound was well within normal limits. Fast, regular and strong. The most reassuring drumbeat ever.

'You'll need electronic monitoring for a while,' Tom told them. 'At least twenty-four hours, I reckon. But that's a healthy heart rate and you're not bleeding. For now, it looks as if baby's been cushioned well enough to escape harm. Let's concentrate on getting you sorted out, Maggie.'

Joe was still listening to the heartbeat that was the background to Tom's speech. Still struggling to draw in a normal breath. Maggie seemed to be having the same difficulty and her eyes were filling with tears as she broke that eye contact with Joe and turned her head away. She sucked in a breath that was more like a sob, which made her cry out in pain and wrench her hand free of Joe's.

'No X-rays,' the consultant in charge of Maggie was saying. 'But they're ready for her in CT.' He caught Joe's concerned glance. 'We're just doing a scan of her chest, not her abdomen. Don't worry. We're not draining any blood so it looks like a simple pneumothorax but we need to assess the underlying damage and make sure that surgery isn't needed.'

Joe leaned closer to Maggie. 'Want me to come with you?'

She shook her head—a slow side-to-side roll that made a tear trickle down the side of her nose. 'It's okay... I'll be okay. You need to get back to work. I'll text you later, Joe. I'll let you know what's happening.'

Maggie closed her eyes as she was wheeled from the room.

He knew that Maggie would be okay without him because she was surrounded by a great team who were completely focussed on her wellbeing. But he wanted her to need him. As much as he needed her.

Joe had never felt more alone in his life.

CHAPTER TEN

How lonely was this?

The only light in this private room in the Royal's maternity wing was coming from the screen of the foetal monitor beside Maggie's bed. The steady blipping sound had been turned down so as not to disturb her sleep but she could still hear it clearly and, even in the early hours of the next morning, she was listening just as intently as she had when they'd first checked for her baby's heartbeat in the resuscitation area. The monitor would also record any contractions if the worst happened and the accident triggered premature labour, but Maggie couldn't feel anything happening in her belly other than the weight of the transducers strapped to her skin by the two wide belts.

The loneliness felt like punishment. One that she was convinced that she probably deserved. Telling Joe not to come with her to that scan—to go back to work, even, as if nothing major had happened—had been so hard when all she'd wanted to do was cling to his hand for every minute of that ordeal. To have him hold her and repeat the reassurances that all the doctors had given her that the news was good. She didn't need surgery. Her baby seemed to be fine. Her chest drain could come out within a day or two and she could go home and re-cuperate with nothing more than sore ribs for a while. She had been very lucky.

But Maggie wasn't feeling lucky right now.

She wanted Joe to be here. She wanted to tell him how sorry she was. For derailing his life, even though it had been completely accidental. For not being pru-dent enough to have stopped riding her motorbike as soon as she knew she was pregnant. When he'd arrived at the accident scene, he'd looked more shocked than she'd ever seen him look and that had been almost as frightening as not being able to breathe properly, as well as the fear that something terrible could have hap-pened to the baby.

And she'd seen tears in his eyes when he'd heard the healthy beat of the baby's heart on the Doppler. It would have been understandable if there'd been an element of relief in the idea that the disruption she'd caused in Joe's life might have vanished but what she had seen in his face in that moment was something she would never have expected.

He'd looked as if their growing baby was the most precious thing in the world.

As if *she* was just as important.

It would have been so easy to believe that look. To trust it. But the rational part of Maggie's brain had or-dered her not to. Had spelled out how much harder it would be—when the drama of this event was over—to get back to normal. The normal that she and her baby's father were no more than friends. That they could never be more than friends.

She'd already been struggling, in the wake of that kiss the day she'd gone with him to view the house that he'd bought shortly after that. That had been a physical longing doing its utmost to pull her in and she'd managed to deal with it by staying away from Joe as much as possible since then. To actually believe that he cared so much would not be nearly as easy to escape from. It would be in her head, and her heart, every second of every minute.

That was how she'd found the courage to tell him not to come with her. That she would be okay.

But she wasn't okay.

Maggie was trying hard not to cry because any sharp intake of breath gave her a stabbing pain in her ribs so she concentrated very hard on keeping her breathing regular and careful. She didn't seem to be able to do anything about the tears rolling slowly down her face, however.

'I'm sorry, Joe,' she whispered aloud into her empty room.

She would tell him again, as soon as they had any time alone together.

It seemed impossible to get any time alone with Maggie over the next week.

Everybody knew that they were no more than just good friends, so it probably didn't occur to anyone that they might want time alone together. In the few days that Maggie was kept under observation in hospital, Joe always had Cooper or Jack or even Andy and Nick going with him to visit her. Or there would be staff members from the Royal dropping in. People like Tom. Or Fizz, who took every opportunity to spend her breaks with Maggie.

'To be honest, it's starting to get harder to stay on

my feet all day.' Fizz was looking very comfortable in the only armchair in Maggie's room, the day after the chest drain had been removed. 'You'll find out in a few months. Thank goodness...' Her smile said that she knew exactly how scary the accident had been for her friend.

Joe wasn't included in that smile. Were people uncomfortable to assume that he was just as invested in this unborn baby's welfare? That it was Maggie that needed the support because she was the one who'd always wanted children?

It was a can of worms that Joe was not about to open. 'How are the ribs?' he asked.

'It only hurts if I laugh,' Maggie told him. 'Don't make me laugh.'

It occurred to Joe that it was a long time since he'd actually heard Maggie laugh properly. Or laughed himself, come to think of it. How sad was that? He shrugged, a smile tilting one side of his mouth.

'When have I ever made you laugh? Serious workmates, that's what we are.'

Fizz snorted. 'Yeah...right...'

Maggie said nothing. She wasn't even smiling as she caught his gaze. Was she remembering what was racing through the back of Joe's mind? There'd always been so much laughter between them. The banter that always provided a chuckle of amusement or two. Jokes that came from nowhere. Tears that came with laughter when they'd discovered just how hot that new variety of chilli sauce was. The way Maggie laughed when she was just excited about life, like the time they'd been bounced around in rough seas on that outing with the coastguard. The laughter that came from pure fun and sheer enjoyment that he'd never, ever expected to be part of a sexual relationship.

Yes…maybe they were thinking about the same thing. Maybe that was why they both turned away from each other at the same moment.

'I get to go home tomorrow,' Maggie said brightly. 'And Don's going to give me a desk job so I can probably go back to work in a week or so. How good is that?'

After she was discharged home, she had her flatmates looking after her and usually had Laura's son, Harrison, cuddled up on the couch with her. The famous taco nights, which had been largely abandoned after Cooper had moved out, got reinstated but Maggie had apparently gone off chilli.

'It's giving me indigestion now,' she admitted. 'I don't think the baby likes it. Oh…' Her eyes widened. 'Just talking about it was enough to make him kick.' She grinned at Fizz. 'I haven't got used to feeling him move yet. It's so weird…'

'Can I feel?' Fizz went to sit beside Maggie on the couch, her hand out to touch Maggie's belly, but Harrison was there first.

'*I* want to feel,' he said. 'And how do you know it's a boy, anyway?'

'We don't,' Maggie admitted. 'Not yet.' She looked up, catching Joe's gaze, and he felt included in that 'we'. There was a softness in her gaze that made him feel more than simply included. As if he was welcome?

He so wanted to be included in the excited quest to feel the baby move but he couldn't ask. Not with the crowd of other people around. That needed to be a private moment. He wanted to be alone with Maggie. To feel his baby moving. To tell her how things had changed in the way he felt about becoming a father now. Maybe even to tell her how things had changed in the way he felt about her because…because he could almost believe, in this moment, that things had changed for her as well.

That something was different.

Something huge…

But how, and when, could he arrange to get that time with Maggie?

'You all packed up yet?' Cooper carried an oven tray with warmed taco shells past Joe. 'It's this weekend that we're all coming to help you shift, isn't it?'

'Yep. I'm good to go. I've hired a van to shift the bigger stuff.'

'I'll be there,' Jack promised.

'I won't be lifting too much,' Fizz said. 'But I'll provide the food.'

'I could help with that,' Maggie offered.

There was a general sound of disagreement. 'It's not as if you haven't already seen the place, Mags,' Fizz reminded her. 'And we know you. You wouldn't be able to stop yourself carting boxes around or something or shoving a couch because it's in the wrong place. You're under doctor's orders to rest, okay?'

'Wait till the housewarming party,' Cooper added. 'You'll be right as rain by then.'

That was it, Joe decided. Once the chaos of the move was over and Maggie had had more time to rest and recuperate, he could invite her to a housewarming party.

A very private one.

This was strange.

Maggie couldn't see any vehicles she recognised

parked in the street outside Joe's house. She checked
the text message on her phone again.

Spur-of-the-moment housewarming party tonight.
7p.m. Hope you can make it.

She'd texted back to ask what she could bring.

Just yourself.

He'd added a smiley face to his reply that had made
Maggie smile as well. A beat of excitement made her
realise how much she was looking forward to seeing
him. She'd felt left out of the moving process and that
had been days and days ago.

It was a bit after seven p.m. because she'd waited
for Laura and Harrison or Jack to get home so that she
could get a ride with them but they were late so in the
end she'd grabbed a taxi. And now she was standing
on the road on a warm, early summer evening and it
looked very much as if she might be the first of Joe's
friends to arrive for this impromptu party.

Maggie hadn't seen the house since the day of the
first viewing and she'd forgotten how gorgeous it was.
Magical, almost, with that romantic turret. Late afternoon sun was kissing the faded wooden floor of the
veranda and the front door was open a little, as if she
was expected. And welcome…

She climbed the steps to the veranda and pushed the
heavy door open a little further.

'Joe?'

There was no answer, so Maggie kept walking down
the wide hallway of this side of the house that contained

the larger of the two apartments. It didn't look like Joe
had got very far with his unpacking yet, because there
were stacks of boxes in one of the rooms she passed
and nothing more than a bed in another room. The big
sitting room with its amazing harbour view needed far
more furniture than the small couch in the corner and
the kitchen benches were covered with crockery and
cutlery that needed to be tidied away in a cupboard
somewhere.

Maggie shook her head. Why was Joe having a
housewarming party when he wasn't anywhere near
settled into his new home? And where was he, anyway?
The kitchen door was also open so she walked towards
that and looked out into the garden. Joe was there, tying
a bunch of balloons to the post of a grapevine-covered
pergola that shaded the terraced area adjacent to the
house. There were tartan picnic rugs on the grassy area
beyond the terrace and more balloons tied to the surrounding trees.

Much closer, there was a rustic wooden table that
must have been left by the previous owners and Maggie blinked at the plate of food that was taking centre
stage. Small triangles of white bread that had been buttered and sprinkled with brightly coloured hundreds
and thousands.

Fairy bread?

What sort of strange housewarming party was this?
It looked far more like a child's birthday party.

And then it hit her. She remembered telling Joe about
her friend Suzie's birthday party, when she'd been explaining why she wanted to have lots of babies. She'd
said that there had been balloons tied to trees and fairy

bread and chasing games and everything was so much
more fun because she'd been part of a big family.

Joe was re-creating that childhood memory but Maggie couldn't understand why. Or maybe she could, but
it was too much to hope for. Too much to trust. Maybe
that was what kept her standing there silently, simply
absorbing what had been created. For *her*. Feeling her
heart expanding with love for this man who'd gone to
so much effort on her behalf. And, as if he could feel
that love coming towards him, Joe turned and his face
lit up with that slow smile that just kept on growing.

'You're here,' he said unnecessarily, walking towards
Maggie.

'I am.' Her smile wobbled. 'I heard there was fairy
bread.'

Joe was getting closer. Close enough for Maggie to
see the way his eyes were crinkled at the corners with
his smile and how much warmth was coming from his
gaze.

'Am I the first one here?' she asked.

'You're the only one here,' Joe told her. 'I didn't invite anyone else.'

He was right in front of her now. Looking at her
like…like he had that day of the house viewing, when
they'd both realised they still wanted each other so
much, even though they'd agreed that their friendship
was not enough of a foundation for anything more.
Looking like he had during that rush of pure relief when
they'd heard the healthy beat of their baby's heart and
she'd felt like she was the most precious thing in the
world for Joe. Looking as if the only thing in the world
he wanted to do was to kiss her senseless.

'Oh… *Joe*…' This was just overwhelming. There

were hopes and dreams and fear and a bubble of sheer joy all trying to mingle deep inside her.

Maggie burst into tears.

'Oh, *no*...' Joe put his arms around her instantly. 'I thought you'd like this. Here...' He led her to the bench seat beside the big wooden table. 'Sit down. Are you all right?'

Maggie tried to nod.

He hadn't let go of her hand yet. 'And the baby? What did the doctor say today? Is everything okay?'

Maggie nodded again. 'She's confident that it's all good.' It was much easier to talk about something clinical than venture onto personal emotional territory that was a complete minefield, so Maggie took a deep breath and wiped the tears from her cheeks. 'Sorry about that...it's just these pesky pregnancy hormones.'

'Doubt it,' Joe said. 'I'm not pregnant and I was worried sick about you *and* the baby after that accident.'

'I'm fine,' Maggie told him. 'But... I'm still worried about the baby. What if...what if lack of oxygen has caused brain damage or something?'

'You weren't without oxygen for that long.'

'But I was in respiratory arrest. I *stopped* breathing.'

'So did I.' Joe picked up Maggie's other hand as well. 'And I was holding my breath until you started breathing again.'

She could believe that. It was something she'd done when she'd been learning to intubate a patient. Holding her breath once they stopped breathing to be confident that she'd secured an airway in plenty of time to prevent damaging oxygen deprivation.

'It wasn't long enough to do any damage,' Joe added. He was holding her gaze and Maggie could see the golden brown of his hazel eyes darken with some strong emotion. She could feel that emotion in his hands holding hers. A faint thrum of energy that ran up her arms and straight into her chest to squeeze her heart.

'It was just long enough for me to realise that I don't want to live without you,' Joe said softly. 'That I love you.'

Maggie tried to smile but her lips were trembling. 'I know,' she said. 'We're mates. Best mates.'

Joe's eyes darkened even more. 'No. I'm trying to tell you that I *love* you, Maggie. I'm *in* love with you.' He sucked in a breath. 'And I know that you might not want to hear that. And that you can never feel like that about me because you would have known if that was possible a very long time ago but…but I had to tell you. It's been doing my head in.'

The squeezing sensation around Maggie's heart had become a tingle that was going in the opposite direction now. All the way out to the tips of her fingers and her toes.

'I was wrong,' she whispered. 'I love you, too, Joe.'

'Like "in love" kind of love?'

'Exactly like "in love" kind of love.'

For a long, long moment they were silent then. Simply holding each other's gaze. Sinking into the moment of realisation that this was real. That they both felt the same way about each other. Joe leaned towards Maggie but it wasn't to kiss her. He leaned his forehead against hers in a gentle touch that made it feel as if their thoughts were mingling and it felt closer—more intimate—than any purely physical touch.

It was Joe who broke that astonishingly intense silence.

'Are you sure?' he asked very quietly. 'I mean, you

said you'd know if you were ever going to feel like that about someone. That you'd know within the first few minutes of meeting someone.'

'I did say that,' Maggie admitted. 'And I believed it. I thought falling in love was exactly that. Like tripping over something and falling fast. I didn't believe that it could happen slowly. Like a long slide.'

'But…when you knew…that was like falling, wasn't it?' Joe lifted his head. A smile was tugging at one corner of his mouth. 'That's how it felt to me. Like I was falling. Or maybe flying… Terrifying but…the most exciting thing ever, too.'

'I felt like my heart was being torn into little pieces. Because it was only when I thought I'd lost you that I realised what I was really losing. You were so angry with me, I thought I'd lost you for ever.'

'It was the same for me. When you stopped breathing and I couldn't breathe and I could see how dark the world would be for me if you weren't in it any more.'

'I told myself it was just pregnancy hormones and it would wear off,' Maggie said. 'But it's not wearing off and I don't think it ever will. I think it was there all along and I was just too blind to see it.'

Joe's smile was poignant. 'We couldn't see it because we were so convinced we were completely wrong for each other.'

'Maybe it was there right from the start.' Maggie was smiling, too. 'I think I fell in "like" with you that very first day we worked together. When we knocked over that bottle of chilli sauce.'

'And I fell in "lust" with you because talking about making a baby made me see you in a totally different way.'

Maggie laughed. 'And everybody should know that

mixing "like" and "lust" is the recipe for falling in love, right? Basic chemistry.'

'So…' The glint in Joe's eyes told Maggie that she was about to get kissed very thoroughly and there was a tenderness in that gaze that made her catch her breath. 'Is this it? The "real thing"?'

'Oh, yes…' Maggie had to blink back tears of sheer joy that sprang into her eyes. 'This is most definitely the "real thing". And I know because…'

'Because you're a *sage-femme*.' Joe's smile had become a grin. 'A wise woman.'

'Don't ever forget that.' Maggie grinned back up at Joe. 'Now, stop talking. Start kissing…'

EPILOGUE

'STOP *TALKING*... Oh, my God... I can't believe I let myself get into this. Never again. Never *ever* again...'

'You're almost there, babe. One more push...'

Maggie dragged in the biggest breath she could as she felt another contraction begin and then screwed her eyes tightly shut as she began pushing. She could do this. Joe had her back.

Literally. He was on the bed with her, supporting her back with his body, holding tight to both her hands. It felt like they were both taking part in bringing their baby into the world. And, a matter of minutes later, there she was.

Their daughter.

Skin to skin with her mother as Maggie cradled her against her breasts. Blinking dark, dark eyes at her father as he reached out with a single, gentle finger to touch the whorls of dark hair on her head.

'Welcome to the world, sweetheart,' he whispered. 'You have no idea how happy your mummy and daddy are to finally meet you.'

Joe's voice was thick with emotion. Maggie had tears on her cheeks. They were barely aware of the activity of their obstetrician and midwife, who left as soon as they could to give this new little family time together to bond.

'Isn't she perfect?'

'The most perfect baby in the world.'

'Of course she is. Oh…look. She's looking for food already.'

'Takes after her dad.' Joe grinned.

Maggie adjusted the position of the baby and helped her latch onto her breast. 'I think you're right. She's got dark hair. And her eyes look almost black.'

'That can all change. She might end up being as blue-eyed and blonde-haired and as gorgeous as her mum.'

Maggie's smile was misty. 'All parents think their baby is the most perfect in the world but I happen to know that our daughter *is*.'

'And Fizz and Cooper think their little Harley is.'

'He can be the most perfect boy. For now, anyway.'

'Until we have a son, you mean?' Joe's eyebrows shot up. 'Didn't I hear you say "never *ever* again" not so long ago?'

'Did I?' Maggie shook her head. 'I don't remember that.'

'We need more photos.' Joe reached for his phone. 'Oh, I forgot. Fizz and Cooper are hanging out in Emergency and told me to text when we were ready for a quick visit. Are we ready—to let the world in again?'

'We'll have to soon. The grandparents are on their way into town and this little one has an appointment with the paediatrician to get checked. Yes…tell the gang that they're welcome to pop in.'

Laura arrived with Cooper and Fizz, who had three-month-old baby Harley snug against her chest in a sling.

'I can only stay for a second,' Laura said. 'Harry's school called and I need to go and pick him up. He's been sick. *Again*... Oh...' Her face creased as she looked at the sleeping baby in Joe's arms. 'She's *adorable*. Have you decided on her name?'

'Not yet.'

'We can help,' Fizz offered. 'We're good at names.'

Maggie grinned. 'Says the woman who named her son after my motorbike.'

'I have to run.' Laura leaned over the bed to give Maggie a hug. 'You're looking amazing. Congratulations. Life will never be the same but it will be so much better...'

'This is true.' Fizz nodded. 'You're going to love your maternity leave.'

'I think most of it will be spent finishing our project of knocking the extra walls out in the house.'

'Give me a shout when you need any help.' Laura was on her way to the door.

'Thanks, Laura. I hope Harry's okay.'

'I'm taking him straight to the doctor. I might even bring him in here and get Tom to have a look.'

'Good idea,' Joe agreed. 'I'd trust Tom to check out my kid any day.'

Cooper shook his head as Laura slipped out of the room. 'You can't keep calling her "my kid", you know. She needs a name.'

'You could go all celebrity and name her after a piece of fruit?' Fizz suggested. 'Apricot, maybe? Or Plum?'

'No, no...' Cooper was grinning broadly. 'What about one of those philosophical ones that were on our shortlist? Journey? Or Travel.'

The rumble of laughter in the room was enough to make the baby stir in her father's arms. Joe caught Maggie's gaze.

'Bella's top of my list,' he said quietly.

'She *is* beautiful,' Maggie agreed. 'I think that's the one, Joe.'

'Hang on,' Cooper said. 'We haven't tried other motorbike names yet. What about Suzuki? Or Yamaha?' He put his arm around his wife. 'You know, we might have been a bit selfish to use Harley, don't you think? It was Maggie's bike, after all.'

'Not any more,' Maggie reminded them. 'I've got a nice, much safer little car now.'

'But you loved that bike,' Fizz said. 'Won't you miss it?'

A squeak from Bella prompted Joe to nestle her back into Maggie's arms.

'I think she's hungry again.'

He was being so gentle in moving the baby. Maggie could feel the love in that touch when his hands were between their newborn's soft skin and her own skin. For that moment they were all connected by a physical touch. And more…as Maggie caught and held Joe's gaze for a heartbeat and then another, she could feel how much love he had to give. To her. To their firstborn. To their future.

The question Fizz had asked was still hanging in the air. Would she miss her beloved motorbike?

'I'm not going to miss it,' she told Fizz. 'Not a bit.'

Because safety had just become a whole lot more important to Maggie. She had so much to live for now. So much love to give back.

For Joe.

For Bella.

For her family…

* * * * *

THE SURGEON'S
SURPRISE BABY

TINA BECKETT

MILLS & BOON

To my husband:
thank you for my chickens!

PROLOGUE

"WELL, I'M NO longer your boss."

Luca Venezio stared at her as if she'd lost her mind. No longer his boss? Was that all she had to say to him? The obvious relief in her voice told him that she'd been anxious to wield that particular ax. Only she'd just done it in a room full of his colleagues, who had suffered a similar fate. He'd stayed behind after the others had all filed out dejectedly.

She was perched on her desk, looking just as gorgeous as she had a year ago, when he'd first stepped into her neurology department. It had taken him a while, but he'd finally convinced her to look past her reservations about engaging in a workplace relationship and see what they could be like together.

And it had been good. So very good.

He took a step closer. "Is that all you have to say to me, Elyse?"

Her head tilted as if she truly couldn't understand what the problem was. Was this an American thing that he hadn't yet grasped? Just when he thought he was understanding this culture, the woman in front of him threw something into the mix that had him reeling.

Italy was suddenly beckoning him home. But he wasn't leaving without a fight.

She slid from her desk and stood in front of him. "Don't you see? This could be a good thing."

No. He didn't see it. No matter how he looked at it.

She drove him insane. With want. With need. And now was no different.

"Do you want me gone, is that it?"

She took his hands in hers, before her hands slid up his forearms. "Are we talking about from the hospital? Or from my life?"

It was one and the same to Luca. It felt like they'd been trapped in a game of tug-of-war ever since their first date. The harder he pulled her toward him, the more she seemed to resist letting him get close to her, and he didn't understand why. They were in a relationship, only nothing was easy. Except the sex.

And that had been mind-blowing. Maybe part of that was the uncertainty of it all. Maybe it had lent an air of desperation to their lovemaking.

Her green eyes stared into his, and the crazy thing was, he could swear he saw a hint of lust in there, even though she'd just fired him. Had she gotten off on delivering that death blow to all those people?

No. That wasn't the Elyse he'd known these past few months.

"What is it you want from me, Elyse?"

"Don't you know?"

He didn't. Not at all, but he was tired of playing guessing games with her. He cupped her face, trying to make sense of it all, but the swirling in his head gave him no time to think. No time to ask any questions. Instead, the refuge they'd sought after each fight opened its door and whispered in his ear, promising it would all be okay.

He no longer believed it. But his blood was stirring in his veins, sending waves of heat through him. Even as her lips tilted up, telling him what she wanted, he was already there, the kiss scorching hot, just as it always was. His tongue met hers, his hands going under her ass and sitting her back on her desk. The sound of her shoes hitting the floor one at a time and her hands going to his waist and tugging him forward between her legs answered his earlier question about what she wanted.

Hell. There was no question as to that. *Grazie a Dio* he'd locked the door behind him, thinking that what he'd had to say to her he wanted said in private. Right now, though, the last thing he wanted to do was talk.

And he was so hot. So ready. Just as he always was for her.

The desk was wide, the middle bare of anything.

Made for sex.

He grabbed hold of her wrists and tugged her hands away so that he could take a step back to unzip.

The sight of Elyse licking her lips was his undoing.

He came back to her, reaching under her skirt to yank her boy shorts down, tossing them away. Then he eased her down until her back was flat against her desk, her breasts jutting upward, the outline of her nipples plainly visible beneath the thin white blouse.

"Do you want me?" His hands palmed the smooth skin of her hips and tugged her to the very edge of the desk.

She bit her lip, her legs twining around his until he was pressed tight against her, his hard flesh finding a wet heat that destroyed any hopes of prolonging this.

He drove home, her sharp cry ending on a moan, her hips moving as if to seat him even deeper.

"*Dio*, Elyse…" His eyes closed, trying to grasp at any shred of control and finding nothing there.

His thumb moved from her hip to her center, hoping to help things along, but the second he touched her, she exploded around him, her gasped "Yes," sending him over the edge. Bracing his hands on the desk, he plunged home again and again, his body spasming so hard his vision went white for a brief instant. Still he thrust, unwilling for the moment to end.

Because that's exactly what it would do. What it needed to do.

His movements slowed, reality slowly filtering back in.

Hell. As good as this was, it had solved nothing.

Nothing.

The job had been the thing that had held him there, made him keep trying, even as she burned hot and then cold.

But now she'd killed the job. And in doing that, the relationship. What they said about goodbye sex was evidently true.

He didn't try to kiss her, just moved away, zipping himself back in, even as she sat up on the desk.

"What's wrong?"

Was she really asking him that? Everything was wrong. But he was about to make it right.

"Did you put my name on that list of people to be fired?"

She frowned, coming off the desk, retrieving her undergarment, turning away from him as she slid them over her legs. She didn't answer as, with her back still turned, she pushed her feet into her shoes, black high-heeled pumps that he had always found so sexy.

By the time she finally turned around, his last shred of patience had disappeared and he no longer needed a response. "You know what? It doesn't matter. You've been pushing me away ever since I got here, so I'm finally giving you your wish. I'm leaving. Going back to Italy. You actually did me a favor in firing me, so thank you."

He put a hand on the doorknob, half thinking she would call his name and tell him it was all a big mistake. Tell him that she didn't want him to go. He tensed, knowing that even if she did he was no longer willing to go on as they had been. Maybe he'd revisit that decision in a week...in a month. But right now, he needed time to think things through.

Except there was no sound from behind him as he opened the door. As he stepped through it. As he closed it.

Maybe that was all the thinking he needed to do.

So he started walking. And kept on walking until he was away from the hospital and on his way out of her life.

CHAPTER ONE

"I'M FINALLY GIVING you your wish."

Elyse Tenner hesitated, those words ringing in her ears just as fresh and sharp today as they'd done a little over a year ago.

Luca leaving hadn't been what she'd wanted. But it had evidently been what he'd wanted.

The entry door to the upscale clinic—complete with ornate scrollwork carved into the stone around it—was right in front of her. But she couldn't make herself open it.

Not yet.

It had been easier to find him than she'd thought. And yet it was the hardest thing she'd ever done in her life. Well, almost. A part of her whispered she should get back on that plane…he would never be any the wiser. And yet she couldn't, not now. The weight of the baby on her hip reminded her exactly why she'd come here.

She needed him to know. Needed to see his face. Get this whole thing off her conscience. And then she'd be done.

"Scusi."

The unfamiliar word reminded her that she was far from home.

"Sorry," she murmured, stepping aside to let the man pass. Unfortunately, he then held the door for her, forcing her to make a quick decision. Leave? Or stay?

Then she was through the door, the black marble floor as cold and hard as the words she'd said to a group of people at work thirteen months ago.

The man didn't rush off like she expected him to do, but said something else to her in Italian. She shook her head to indicate she didn't understand, shifting Annalisa a bit higher on her hip.

"English?" he asked.

"Yes, do you speak it?"

"Yes, can I help you find something?" He glanced at the baby and then back at her. "Are you a patient?"

"No, I'm looking for…"

Her eyes skated to the wall across from her, where pictures of staff members were displayed along with their accreditation. And there he was: Hair as black as night. His eyes that were just as dark. But unlike the chilly floors beneath her feet, his had always been warm, flashing with humor. The eyes in the picture, however, were somber, the laugh lines that had once surrounded them barely noticeable.

Elyse swallowed. Had she done that to him?

Of course she had. But her back had been up against a wall. She'd had a choice to make. It had obviously been the wrong one.

She'd chosen the coward's way out. Just as she'd done nine months earlier. But she was here to make amends, if she could. Not in their relationship. That was certainly gone. Destroyed by her pride, her stupidity, and her fear of history repeating itself. But she could at least set one thing right. What he did with that information was up to him.

"You're looking for...?"

The man in front of her reminded her of her reason for coming.

What if he wasn't here yet? It was still early.

Oh, he was here. He worked notoriously long hours. "I'm actually looking for an...old friend. He used to work at the same hospital that I did in the States."

"Luca?"

Relief swamped her. "Yes. Do you know where I can find him?"

He glanced at her, a slight frown marring his handsome face. "Refresh my *memoria*. Which hospital?"

"Atlanta Central Medical Center."

"Ah, I see." Something about the way he said it made her wonder exactly what Luca had said about his exit from the hospital. It didn't matter. Nothing he could have said would be worse than the truth. Although she hadn't orchestrated the layoffs, perhaps she also hadn't fought them as hard as she could have. At the time, a tiny part of her had wondered whether, if she and Luca weren't working together, it might be a way to repair some of the rifts that had been growing between them. Rifts she knew she had caused. But scars from a previous relationship had made her extremely wary of workplace romances.

And Luca hadn't been able to see how their dating could complicate their jobs, even after they'd erupted in a fierce argument during a meeting, disagreeing over the diagnosis of a patient and causing the whole room to stare at them. Kind of like this man was doing now.

"I'm sorry," he said, as if realizing his gaffe. "Come. I'll take you to Luca."

"Thank you. I'm Elyse Tenner, by the way." She shifted Anna yet again. She'd gotten her directions wrong, leaving the bus a few stops too early, and the heat was taking its toll on her. So much for going in looking cool and unruffled.

"Nice to meet you. I'm Lorenzo Giorgino. I work with Luca here at the clinic. I'm one of the neurosurgeons." He held out his arms. "Why don't you let me take her? You look tired."

Yet another blow to her confidence. But he was right. She was exhausted, both physically and emotionally. Between jet lag and the long walk, she could use a place to sit down.

She hesitated for a moment, then he said, "I promise not to break her. I have two...*nipoti*. What's your word for it? Nieces?"

Smiling, she held Anna out to him. She should have brought her baby sling, but she hadn't been able to think straight since the plane had touched down. Nerves. Fear.

Hadn't Luca told her he was in no hurry to have children? He had. More than once, in fact. She swallowed hard, even as this doctor's hands cradled the baby like an old pro, speaking to her in Italian.

He glanced at Elyse, just a hint of speculation in his eyes. "Ready?"

Not at all, but she wasn't going to make her confessions to anyone other than Luca himself. So she lied.

"I am. Lead the way." In handing Anna over, the die had been cast and her decision made. She was going to walk into Luca's office with her head held high and tell him that Anna was his daughter, and then hope that, in doing so, she'd made the right decision.

Luca stared at the EEG readings in front of him. Taken from a six-year-old boy, they showed the typical running waves of a Rolandic seizure. Benign. Filippo would more than likely outgrow them. Great news for his parents, who were worried out of their minds. It was always a relief to have a case where there was no threat to life. Just a temporary bump in the road.

Kind of like his time in the US had been. One big bump in the road, followed by a wave of smaller ones that still set him back on his ass at odd moments. But he thought it was getting better. His mind dwelt on her less. Or maybe it was just that he kept himself so busy that he didn't have time to think about her.

Kind of like he was doing now?

"Porca miseria!"

A second or two after the words left his mouth, there was a knock on the door to his office. Great. He hadn't mean to swear quite that loudly.

"Yes?"

Lorenzo appeared in the doorway, holding a baby.

Shock stilled his thoughts. "Everything okay?"

"Someone is here to see you."

It was obviously not the baby, so he raised his brows in question.

"She said she worked with you in Atlanta."

A section of his heart jolted before settling back into rhythm. He'd worked with a lot of people at Atlanta Central.

"Does this person have a name?"

"I'd probably better let her tell you herself." Lorenzo switched to English.

This time the jolt was stronger. Lasted longer. Surely it wasn't... But the look on his friend's face told him all he needed to know.

He hadn't dated since he'd returned to Italy and didn't see himself doing so anytime in the near future. And those plans to revisit his decision to leave Atlanta permanently? Put off over and over until it was far too late to do anything about it.

He hadn't been able to stomach going back to his hospital in Rome either. His parents and two sisters lived there, and he hadn't felt like answering a million questions. Oh, there'd still been the worried texts and phone calls about why he'd suddenly returned to Italy, but since they hadn't been able to see his face, he was pretty sure he'd put their fears to rest. As far as they knew, he'd simply decided to practice in his own country. A short tenable statement. One he'd stuck to no matter how hard it was to force those words past his lips.

He ignored the churning in his stomach. "Okay, where is she?"

Instead of answering, Lorenzo pushed the door farther open and came into the room, revealing the woman who'd driven him out of the States and back to Italy.

Hell!

Chaotic memories gathered around, all of them pointing at the figure in front of them. He swallowed hard in an effort to push them back.

"Elyse? What are you doing here?" There was a slight accusation in his tone that he couldn't suppress. A defense mechanism, another way to hold back the wall of emotion.

Dio. He'd fallen for this woman, once upon a time, and then she'd gone and stabbed him in the back in the worst possible way. Better to let her know up front that he hadn't forgotten.

But why was she in Italy?

When she didn't answer, Lorenzo turned and handed her the baby. Shock flared up his spine. He looked from one to the other as a sudden horrible thought came to him. Did the two of them know each other? Was that why she'd made sure he was fired?

No. Of course not. Lorenzo had never been out of Italy as far as he knew. There was no way the two of them could have met.

"I'll go so you can talk." Lorenzo glanced at Elyse. "It was very nice meeting you."

"Thank you. You as well."

Then he backed out of the room and closed the door behind him with a quiet click.

Something in Luca's brain had frozen in place, the gears all stuck for several long seconds. His ass was also still firmly in his chair, something his mother would have frowned about.

But the memories were still doing their work, each one stabbing his heart and sticking there, like darts on a dartboard.

She ventured closer to the desk. "Luca?"

Somehow he dislodged his tongue, making a careful sidestep around the biggest question in his head while he puzzled through it. "How's your mother?"

He glanced at the baby. Elyse didn't have any siblings, so that wasn't a niece she was holding. Had she adopted a child after he'd left?

"She's still hanging in there. The Parkinson's progression has remained slower than average."

They'd tried an experimental treatment a few years back that had helped tremendously, even if it hadn't rolled back the clock.

"Good." Of course she hadn't traveled all this way just to report on her mother's condition. That left one question: Why was Elyse Tenner standing in the middle of his office, holding a baby? He nodded toward the seat in front of the desk. "Would you like a coffee?"

She sank into one of the chairs with what looked like relief. "I would love one, thank you."

"When did you arrive?" He got up and measured grounds into his coffee press and turned on the kettle to heat the water. The mindless task gave his fuzzy brain time to work through a few of the more obvious items: yes, she was really here, and he was pretty sure she wouldn't be if he'd simply left his toothbrush at her place. So it had to be something important. Important enough to travel across the ocean to see him.

His eyes went to the baby again before rejecting the thought outright. She would have told him before now.

"My flight arrived this morning."

"You have a hotel?"

And if she didn't? There was always his place. His thoughts ventured into dangerous territory.

Not happening, Luca.

He carried the pot with its water and coffee to the desk and set it down before retrieving two cups off the sideboard.

"Yes, I stopped at the hotel first, before coming here."

He poured the coffees and reached into the small

fridge beside his desk, hiding his disappointment by concentrating on the mundane task before him. She'd always taken her coffee like he did, with a splash of milk. He added some to both, stirring a time or two before pushing one across toward her.

He studied her face. It was pale and drawn, her cheekbones a little more pronounced than they'd been a year earlier. "So what brings you to Italy?"

There was a marked hesitation before she answered. "You, actually. I need to tell you something."

That jolt he'd experienced earlier turned into an earthquake, pushing all other thoughts from his head except for the one staring him in the face.

"You do?"

"Yes." Elyse slowly turned the baby to face him. "This is Annalisa." Her eyes closed, and her throat moved a time or two before she went on. "She's your— she's *our* daughter, Luca."

A hundred emotions marched across that gorgeous face over the course of the next few seconds, ranging from confusion to shock before finally settling on anger. His hands came together, fingers twining tightly, the knuckles going white. "My what?"

The words were dangerously soft.

He'd heard what she'd said. He just didn't believe it. And Elyse wondered for the thousandth time if it wouldn't have been better just to leave well enough alone. To raise Anna on her own and let Luca stay in the dark about his part in her existence. But she owned it to Annalisa and, if she was honest, to Luca himself, to own up to the circumstances behind their daughter's birth. If he rejected her claim outright, then at least she'd tried.

She probably should have tracked him down during her pregnancy, but it had been a difficult time. She'd been so caught up in grief over his leaving that she hadn't realized she was pregnant until she'd missed her third period. A test had revealed the worst. And she knew exactly when it had happened. That day in her office. The day he'd left the States forever.

She had been going to call and tell him, but each time she'd picked up the phone, she'd gotten cold feet, afraid that hearing his voice would undo any tiny bits of healing that had taken place. She'd kept telling herself she'd do it tomorrow. Except a month of tomorrows had gone by, and then things had suddenly started to go wrong with her pregnancy. She'd been placed on bed rest. Her parents had come to the house to help her. Her mom had been a trouper, despite her own medical issues.

Elyse wasn't even sure the baby would survive at that point, so she'd elected to keep the news to herself in case the worse happened.

And now she couldn't…would never be able to…

Annalisa was the only chance she would ever have to do this right. She swallowed back her fear.

"It's true, Luca. She's yours. I thought you should know." She settled the baby against her shoulder once again.

He swore. At least she thought it was a swear word, from his tone of voice.

God, she'd been right. He didn't want Anna.

She'd been wrong to come. Wrong to tell him.

"You *kept* this from me? All this time? You come waltzing into my office with Lorenzo, who is holding a baby that I think is his niece?" He drew an audible breath. "Only he hands the baby to you. And now you tell me she's *mine*?"

Her chin went up in confusion. "It isn't like it was easy. You left, and you had no intention of coming back, isn't that right?"

"Yes."

"And didn't you insist more than once that you didn't want children?"

That had him sitting back in his chair, his eyes going to Anna. "I did, but that was—"

"I didn't think you'd even *want* to know."

"You didn't think I'd… *Mio Dio*. Well, you were wrong. And my statement about kids, if I remember right, included the phrase 'not right now.' The word 'never' was not mentioned. Ever."

How was she supposed to know that? There were men who would be just as happy to never father a child and who wouldn't want to know even if they did.

But as she'd taken that choice away from him, he had every right to be angry with her.

"I'm sorry. Things were tenuous at the time." She didn't go into the particulars of the precarious pregnancy or the fact that she would never give birth to another child. Anna might be his concern, but the other stuff? Not so much, since they were no longer a couple.

And that fact hurt more than it should have, especially after all this time.

"Tenuous." His brows drew together. "*Tenuous?* You let a colleague of mine hold my child before I get a chance to, and that's all you can say?"

Yep, she was right. He was mad. Livid, even, and she couldn't blame him. She held Anna close against the tirade.

He noticed it, and his eyes closed. "Dammit, I'm sorry."

The sudden ache in her chest made her reach out and touch the edge of his desk with fingers that trembled.

"No, *I'm* sorry, Luca. It just never seemed like the right time and I couldn't... I didn't want to tell you over the phone." She didn't want to admit how afraid she'd been to hear his voice. And after Annalisa's birth she'd had a recovery period that most new mothers didn't have to worry about. It had delayed any travel plans she might have made. So here they were. In the present.

"When?"

She withdrew her hand. What was he asking? When Anna was born? When she was conceived? That was the kicker. They'd had sex in the aftermath of the announced downsizing, when there had been anger on both sides. Their coming together had been volatile and passionate. But the erotic coupling had solved nothing and only after her missed periods had she remembered that they hadn't used protection.

In the end, the layoffs that she'd hoped would save their relationship—by removing the work dynamics that had bothered her so much—had done the opposite. She hadn't wanted anyone to think she played favorites, and Luca had never asked for special treatment.

But memories of a former boyfriend's behavior had loitered in the background, ready to pounce, warning her of what had happened in the past. Of what could happen again if she weren't careful. Kyle had also been a colleague. He had asked—and expected—her to make allowances for things at work, most of them small and unimportant. But with each instance she'd gotten more and more uncomfortable with the relationship. Just as she'd been ready to break things off, he'd asked her to overlook a mistake he'd made with a patient. She hadn't, and he'd been fired.

She told herself she'd never put herself in that position ever again. Except then Luca had come along and all those warnings had been in vain.

Remembering his question, she decided on the simplest answer possible. If he wanted to do the math, he could. "Anna is four months old."

"Four months." He placed his hands flat on the desk. "I want to spend time with her. Did you come by yourself?"

He didn't ask if she was sure Anna was his. A lump formed in her throat.

"And I want you to spend time with her. That's part of why I came. No, I didn't come alone. Peggy came with me. You remember my aunt?" If her mom had been well enough, Elyse would have asked her to come, but since she couldn't, this was the next best thing. She'd needed the moral support or she might have backed out entirely.

As many times as Luca had asked her out, she might have held firm to her resolve that there would be no more work relationships after Kyle. Until the day Luca had come out of one of the surgical suites after monitoring a patient's brain waves, white-faced, a grim look of defeat on his face. It had done her in. She'd walked over to him, laid a hand on his arm and asked him out.

He'd said yes. The rest was history. A history peppered with moments of beauty and the sting of pain.

But the way he made love...

The realization that her eyes were tracking over his broad shoulders made her bite her lip and force herself to look away.

God! The attraction was still there—still very real. Even if the fairy tale had crashed to dust around her feet.

But from that rubble had come her baby girl. She would go through every bit of that pain all over again if she was the end result.

"After all this time, why come at all? You could have let things be. Never told me at all," Luca pressed.

The very things she'd told herself as she'd booked her flight.

"It was the right thing to do." Her hand went to Anna's head, rocking her subconsciously, still shielding her.

He looked at the baby for a second and walked over to the window, staring out, hands thrust in his pockets, shoulders hunched. "*La cosa giusta?* The right thing would have been to tell me long before she was born."

"Would it have changed things?"

He swung back around to face her. "I don't know. I wasn't given that choice, was I?"

"No." Maybe she needed to tell him at least a little of the circumstances. "When I said things were tenuous, I meant it. The doctors weren't sure Anna was going to make it for a while. And I didn't see any reason to say anything if…"

All the color drained out of his face, and he walked back to the desk. "*Dio.* What happened? Is she okay?"

She rushed to put his mind at ease. "She's fine. Now. I had placenta previa. It didn't resolve and there were a couple of incidents of bleeding, heavy enough to cause worry." And in the end it had been life-threatening to both of them when it had ruptured. "I wasn't going to do anything that might put her at even more risk."

"And telling me would have done that?" He dragged a hand through his hair.

"I was talking more about physical stress but, yes. Inside I think I was afraid of jinxing the pregnancy. As if telling you might cause everything to fall apart, and I'd lose her. I didn't see any reason for us both to grieve if she didn't survive."

Not that she'd been sure he would. Because she'd convinced herself that he'd be horrified to have fathered a child in the first place.

"And after she was born? Why wait four months?"

She wasn't quite ready to share more than she already had.

"Does it really matter? I'm here now."

He crouched in front of her and touched the baby's arm with his index finger. "I can hardly believe she's mine."

"She is." She wasn't sure if he was questioning Anna's parentage, but either way she understood. Here came a woman who shows up over a year after they break up, claiming he'd fathered her child. "We can do a paternity test, if you want."

"No, I know she's mine." He looked up into her face. "Can I see her?"

She realized Anna was sound asleep, but the baby was still facing away from him.

A tiny flutter of relief mixed with fear went through her midsection. While she hadn't thought Luca would reject his own daughter outright once he knew she existed, she hadn't been sure what his actual reaction would be.

She carefully turned the baby, cradling her in her arms so that he could see her tiny face. A muscle worked in his jaw and he stroked her hair. "How long are you here?"

"I have a little time left of my medical leave. I want you to get to know her. But…" she hesitated "…I want to have some ground rules in place. Come to an agreement first."

His fingers stilled. "The only agreement we need is that we have a child." There was a hard edge to his voice that told her he wasn't going to let her call all the shots here. And she wasn't trying to.

"I know that, Luca. I'm hoping we can—"

"A daughter. My daughter." The anger had melted away and in his voice was a sense of awe. "Annalisa."

A dangerous prickling behind her eyes made her sit up, teeth coming together in a way that forced it back. "Yes."

His head came up. "I have a few ground rules of my own. First we are going to figure out our schedules and come up with a plan."

His fingers flipped pages on his phone for a moment, probably looking at his caseload. "I have some free time right now, in fact. So I can drive you back to your hotel, and then we'll sit down and talk about any concerns you might have. But I want to make one thing perfectly clear. I *will* be a part of my daughter's life. No matter how much you might dislike me personally."

CHAPTER TWO

PEGGY SLIPPED OUT of the room as soon as the greetings were exchanged. She promised to be back in an hour.

A prearranged signal to keep Elyse from enduring his company?

His gut tightened in anger, even as his eyes soaked in the sight of his daughter. Now that the shock was wearing off, he could finally look beyond his own emotions and see Anna for who she was.

Unlike her *mamma*'s silky blond locks, which had always driven him to distraction, the baby's hair was black and thick and stuck up around her head at odd angles that made him smile. A red satin bow gathered one of the bunches onto the very top of her head, where it did a tiny loop-the-loop. As dark as her hair was, her skin was Elyse's through and through. It was as pale as the sand on the beaches of Sardinia. When she grew up, she'd probably blush just like her *mamma* too.

Cieli, he'd loved the way Elyse's cheeks had bloomed to life when he'd whispered to her at night. Realizing his gaze had moved from the baby to the green eyes of the woman holding her, he gave a half smile when color swooped into her face. Right on cue. Some things never changed.

And neither did his reaction to them.

Elyse cleared her throat and looked away, jiggling the baby in her arms. "So her full name is Annalisa Marie."

Maybe coming back to her hotel hadn't been such a good idea after all. But he'd wanted this discussion to happen in a more private setting. He didn't want Lorenzo or anyone walking in on them and asking questions before he had some answers.

"Marie. After your mother?"

Her attention turned back to him. "Yes."

He liked the nod to a woman he had come to admire in the few times they'd met, but there was also the sense of lost time...lost opportunities. He hadn't even been able to help choose his own child's name. Hadn't been there to see the first time she'd rolled over—if she had yet—and whatever other milestones four-month-olds normally achieved. "You gave her an Italian name."

"It was only right. She's half-Italian." She smiled, although there was an uncertainty to it. Had she honestly thought he wouldn't want his own child? Just because of some offhand comment he'd made? His reasons for saying it had had more to do with not scaring Elyse off—he hadn't wanted her to think he was rushing her to deepen their relationship. He did want kids. Just hadn't needed them right that second.

And now he had one. He was already in love, after only knowing her for an hour.

"Do you want to hold her?"

The question made him stop. Did he? His jaw tightened. Another thing he'd missed: holding her at birth.

He could worry about that later, though. Right now, he needed to concentrate on what was in front of him, not what was out of his control, as difficult as that might be.

And, yes, he wanted to hold her. He held out his arms and Elyse carefully placed their daughter in them. Looping an arm beneath her legs to support her, he held the baby against his chest, her baby scent tickling his nose. A sense of awe went through him.

He glanced at Elyse, who had taken a step back and stood watching them, arms wrapped tight around her midsection. There was a look on her face that he couldn't decipher. Despite the bitterness and chaos of their breakup thirteen months ago, he and Elyse had at least done something right. They'd made this tiny creature. Murmuring to her in Italian, so her *mamma* wouldn't understand, he turned and walked toward the hotel's window and looked out over the city.

"You don't know me yet, Annalisa, but I promise you will." Was that even realistic? How long was Elyse planning to be in Italy? She'd said she had a little medical leave left but hadn't specified how much.

When would she be back?

Bile washed up his throat when he thought of going months or a year between visits. But how could it be any different than that? Atlanta and Florence might as well be on separate planets.

He looked through the window at the city below. "This is part of your heritage, Anna. I want you to see Italy. To grow up speaking its language." He was going to make that happen, somehow.

A sound behind him made him look back. Elyse had moved to the front door, as if ready to push him out of his daughter's future before he'd even planted himself into her present. What he'd said was the truth, though. He was going to be a part of her life.

He could start by making sure they were all under the same roof for the duration of her stay. "You should come stay at the house, instead of at the hotel. I have some spare bedrooms. Your aunt will come as well, of course."

"I don't know." She bit her lip. "It might be better if we stayed here at the hotel."

"Why?"

He was already booked solid with appointments at the hospital for the next month. He couldn't just blow them all off and take a vacation. Especially not a couple of the patients who were set to undergo treatment in the coming days.

He crossed the room. "You've had Annalisa to yourself for four months. I'd like you to be there when I get home. When I get up."

Hell, was he talking about wanting Anna there? Or Elyse? He'd better make it clear. "I want as much time with her as possible. And there's a kitchen and more room to spread out than you have here. It'll make it easier on everyone."

"I don't..."

He shifted the baby into one arm, tilting Elyse's face with the crook of his index finger. "Say yes. It would mean a lot to me."

Something flickered through her green eyes before she said, "Are you sure? It'll be for a whole month."

A month. Said as if it were an eternity, when really it was only a millisecond. But at least now he knew how long he had with his baby. "A month is nothing."

The weight of his daughter in his arms felt right.

Good. He didn't want to give that up. Not in a month. Not in a year. Not in a lifetime.

With her head still tilted, they stared at each other.

"Is it?" Her words came out breathy, lips still slightly parted.

Damn. His midsection tightened in warning. A warning he ignored, leaning closer even as she seemed to stretch up toward him.

Annalisa chose that moment to squirm, and fidget, giving a soft cry. The spell was broken, and he stepped back.

"Sorry," she said. "She's getting hungry." The breathiness was gone, replaced by a wariness he didn't like.

He handed the baby over, watching as Elyse went to the bed and sat, unbuttoning her blouse and helping the baby latch on.

The fact that she did it right in front of him made the tenseness in his chest release its hold.

He'd been her lover, for God's sake. Why should he be surprised?

What did surprise him was that she'd come to Italy at all. Did she really care about him getting to know his daughter? Or was she simply assuaging any future guilt she might feel if Annalisa asked questions about who her father was?

Did it matter?

Yes, it did. Because her motivation behind this trip would set the tone for their future encounters. If she was just looking for the occasional photo op to show that she'd made the effort, she was going to be sorely disappointed. He wanted—no, he *intended*—to have an actual relationship with Anna. He would not be content with being the type of absentee father who did nothing more than send an occasional gift at birthdays or Christmas.

Adorable snuffling sounds came from the bed, where the baby still nursed. Suddenly he couldn't bear to watch anymore, looking on from the outside.

"I'm going down to get a drink. Do you want anything?"

Elyse looked up, the slight smile that had been on her lips fading. "A water, if it's not too much trouble?"

"No trouble at all."

A few steps later, he was opening the door, tossing one last look over his shoulder as he exited. But not before his eyes met hers and he saw the one thing he'd never wanted to see in them: fear. What was she afraid of? That he might try to take Annalisa away from her? He would never do that. But he also wasn't going to simply step back and pretend his child didn't exist.

The elevator ride gave him the little bit of space and time he needed. It unclogged the lump in his throat and eased the ache in his chest. At least for the moment.

She'd agreed to come to the house. That was something. She hadn't refused outright.

There was no sign of Peggy in the empty lobby where he asked for a coffee and Elyse's water. It made sense. The Peggy he'd known in the States was kind and considerate. She might make it a point to stay away for more than an hour, if she thought they needed the time to work out stuff with the baby.

Luca had juggled some of his calendar, but he still had appointments this afternoon, so he wouldn't be able to stay long as it was.

Dammit. He could just clear his calendar for the rest of the day—or a week, for that matter—but it wasn't fair

to the clinic's patients. And even shuffling the cases to
other neurophysiologists in the area would be a challenge. He was sure everyone else was just as slammed
as he was. This was tourist season and a busy one for
most of the doctors and clinicians in the city.

So what did he do?

All he could do. Make sure he used his time with
Elyse and Annalisa wisely and hope that he could find
a compromise that would suit all of them. She'd agreed
to move into his house. They'd start with that.

Why had she agreed to stay at his home?

The expression on his face when he'd looked at her,
that's why. The raw emotions that had streamed through
her. The way he'd gripped his daughter tightly as if
afraid to let her go. None of that fit with the man who'd
said with such confidence that he didn't want children.

It was one of the million and one excuses she'd told
herself every time she'd picked up the phone to call him
and then set it back down again. She hadn't been sure
how Luca would react to the news that he'd fathered a
daughter, which was why she'd finally decided to come
to Italy and look him in the eye. If he'd shown any hint
of horror or rejection at the news, Elyse would have
been devastated. She would have turned back around
and caught the first flight out of Italy to save her daughter the pain of having a father who didn't want her.

But he hadn't rejected her, had insisted he wanted
to be a part of her life. The distance between Italy and
her homeland was going to make that extremely hard.

If he were still in Atlanta, it would have been so
much easier.

Would it have been?

It wasn't like she'd could have hidden the weight gain from him. He'd have known. Plus the added stress of having him right there might have made an already difficult pregnancy worse.

And knowing Anna was going to be her only child?

None of this was easy, and having him stand there as she'd nursed had driven that point home. It was a relief to have him leave. It gave her enough time to finish up, since Annalisa was barely hanging on, her long dark lashes fluttering as she got sleepy.

Moving the baby to the crook of her arm, she quickly closed herself back up before lifting the baby to her chest and gently rubbing her back until she burped. And a good burp it was too. Elyse chuckled and got up to put the baby in the portable crib she'd brought on the flight with her.

Anna shifted in her sleep, raising small fists that slowly floated back down until they were at her sides.

Wow. She could stare at her daughter all day long. There were times she found herself forgetting what she was supposed to be doing because of it. Once she started back at the hospital, that would all change and life would become chaotic once again.

One month. That's all she had left.

She didn't want to think about how long it would be until Luca could see Anna again. Elyse would be able to follow the minuscule day-to-day developments of their daughter's personality and physical growth.

He would miss out on so much.

But she didn't know how to make it better.

Maybe he could move back to the States.

And do what? Her hospital's neurology department was still operating on a skeleton crew and they weren't looking to expand that area. But there were other hospitals and other clinics. Surely he could find a place at one of those, just like she'd thought he would do all those months ago.

Why would he, though? She'd been awestruck at the little bit of Florence she'd seen as she'd come in. The city was gorgeous, with true old-world charm that couldn't be matched. The Florence Cathedral and its domed roof was one of the most beautiful buildings she'd seen in her life. She needed to make a point to get a closer look at it. Then there was the Pitti Palace and so many other historic sites that she wanted to explore. Maybe while Luca was at the hospital, working, she, Peg and the baby could do some sightseeing.

After seeing where he came from, she couldn't imagine him wanting to move back to Atlanta. But maybe the baby would change that.

Did she want it to? It was hard seeing him again. The punch to her senses had been just as jolting as the first time she'd laid eyes on him. And when he'd tipped up her face... God. For a second, she had been sure he was going to kiss her. Had wanted him to so badly.

How much worse would that be if they lived a half-hour apart? Or maybe even closer than that? Or saw each other every day? She was obviously not as over him as she'd thought.

There was a quiet knock at the door and then Luca came in, holding a coffee in one hand and a water in the other. Suddenly she was wishing she'd asked for one of those instead of the water. "Thank you," she said as she took the bottle, her eyes still on his cup.

He must have noticed her wistful gaze because he said, "Did you want coffee?"

"No. It's okay. I'll just have water." She uncapped her bottle and took a quick slug, the cold liquid making her stomach clench as it hit. She couldn't repress the slight grimace. She drank water because it was good for her, but it had never been her favorite beverage.

"Are you sure you don't want some? It has milk. Just like you like."

Something about that sent a rush of moisture to her eyes. She wasn't even sure why. He'd given her coffee in his office too. It had to be the stress of the trip and everything that went with it. Before she could stop herself, she blurted out, "Could I? Just a sip."

"You're the one who introduced me to milk in my coffee." He smiled and handed her the cup, the heat of it in her hands a welcome change from the incessant blowing of the air conditioner. She took a tiny sip.

Oh! That was good. Rich and dark and full of flavor. She took a second sip and then a third before finally forcing herself to hand the cup back.

"Are you sure you don't want more?"

"Positive. But that was delicious."

He smiled. "Italian. Hard to beat."

Yes, it was. And not just the coffee. She'd missed him. Missed the good times. The lovemaking. The laughter. But she didn't miss what had come toward the end. That huge fight during the meeting about the patient's diagnosis had caused a major rift between them. Add that to her growing uneasiness about their relationship, her fear that she would repeat the mistakes she'd made with Kyle. And then the final blow of the downsizing. She hadn't even been able to warn Luca about it before it happened due to that same fear of showing him preferential treatment.

It was easier with him gone. She kept telling herself that, even though easier didn't necessarily mean better. It was just less complicated.

Less complicated? Was she kidding? They had a baby now. She shook that thought away, washing the coffee down with another sip of water, as if that would take care of the predicament she found herself in. If she'd had an abortion she wouldn't be here right now.

And yet... Her eyes went to the baby's crib. There's no way she'd give any of this up, even if she could.

"Remind me to buy some Italian roast coffee before I go back to the States."

"It won't be the same as drinking it here."

No, it wouldn't. Life itself wasn't the same since he'd left. But he'd made it pretty obvious back then that he wasn't interested in working things out.

Maybe they'd been similar in all the wrong ways. They were both neurologists, even if their respective specialties had subtle differences to them. Elyse treated patients, and while Luca dealt with patients as well, his side was more involved in testing, interpreting and diagnosing. But the two subspecialties overlapped. A lot. And there had been times she'd been certain of a diagnosis and had spoken her mind. Luca had never challenged her.

Until that one difficult case, when he'd done so during a staff meeting. If he'd been a nurse, a tech, or even another doctor, it might have been a nonissue. She could have listened and then made a decision based on the evidence at hand. That would have been that. But because it was Luca, she'd found herself wanting to defer to him. Not because she thought he was necessarily right but because of their relationship. And she knew herself well enough to know it would happen again. Why? Because she'd been there once before with Kyle.

If she and Luca had worked at different hospitals, those murky situations wouldn't have arisen in the first place. They could have...

She sighed, cutting herself off. All the might-haves in the world wouldn't change the reality of what was. Or the fact that he'd clearly found it easy to leave Atlanta—and her—behind.

Luca sat in one of the two club chairs in the room, backed by a wall that was thickly textured, like those in many of the buildings she'd seen. Elyse perched on the edge of one of the two beds. Thank goodness the maid service had already been and tidied up. It might have made an already awkward situation even more unbearable.

Elyse decided to tackle the elephant in the room. "So where do we go from here, Luca?"

"I don't know." He glanced at the crib, where the baby was currently sleeping. "Right now, I'm wishing I had more than a month with her."

"I know. I wish you did too. But my maternity leave is going to end. I don't see how I can extend it." She didn't add that she hadn't been sure of his reaction.

The fact that he was sitting here saying he wanted more time with Anna created an entirely different problem.

She went on. "If you have any ideas—other than my leaving her behind—I'm open to suggestions." She hadn't meant it as a jab at the past, but the quick tightening of his lips said he'd taken it as one.

"I would never ask you to leave her."

"I know that."

His elbows landed on his knees, hands dangling between his strong thighs. Thighs that she'd once…

Nope. No going down that path, Elyse. That's what had gotten her in trouble in the first place.

Luca had captured her attention from the moment he'd walked onto her floor at the hospital. Only she had just gotten out of a difficult relationship with Kyle a year earlier and hadn't been anxious to repeat the experience. She'd resisted going out with him, feeling proud of herself, until he'd walked out of that surgical suite that day looking like a beaten man. He'd touched her heart, and the rest was history. She'd told herself the attraction would eventually burn itself out. It hadn't.

Even now, she knew she still wanted him.

He looked up. "I think we're overlooking the obvious solution."

Her heart leaped in her chest. Was he saying he wanted to get back together?

And if he did?

She swallowed. He lived here, and she lived in Atlanta. Besides, the damage had been done. He'd never forgive her for firing him. He'd made that pretty clear when he'd left.

"I guess I'm still overlooking it, because I don't see an obvious solution at all."

"We could get married."

Her mouth, which had been open to make a completely different suggestion, snapped shut again. Surely she hadn't heard him correctly?

"I'm sorry?" Maybe he *was* saying he wanted to get back together. But marriage? Um, no. Not a possibility.

She hurried to send the conversation in a completely

different direction. "Maybe you could just move back to the States? We could work out an agreement for visitation."

Why had she said that? Maybe because that was the only obvious thing her brain could catch hold of. They could work at different hospitals and be aloofly friendly. Like those famous divorced couples who managed to get along for the sake of their kids.

"That's not quite what I had in mind."

"I can't marry you. We don't even like each other anymore." She forced out the words, even though they were a lie. She did like him. A little too much, in fact.

"You can't marry me? Or you won't?" Luca got up from his chair and went over to stand by the crib. He leaned over, fingers sliding over the baby's forehead, pushing back some dark locks of hair. Then he twirled the tiny ponytail in a way that made her stomach clench. Watching him with their baby girl set up an ache she couldn't banish.

It wasn't something she was likely to see every day as Annalisa grew up. But she couldn't marry him. Aside from the fact that he didn't love her—he'd as much as said so by not challenging her comment that they didn't even like each other—she couldn't have any more children. She had barely had time to grieve over that fact herself, much less tell anyone else.

Lord, she shouldn't have come here.

"Both. Getting married just because of Anna would be wrong. And not fair to either of us."

He turned to face her with a frown. "Is there someone else?"

"What? No, of course not." She gave a nervous laugh. "I've just had a baby. There's no time for romance."

"But there would be if the timing were better?"

"That's not what I'm saying."

"Well, I can't move back to the States right now. Not with my caseload."

Disappointment winged through her even though she knew he was right. He couldn't just pick up and leave at a moment's notice. "It was just a suggestion."

He looked up, his gaze holding hers in a way that made her swallow. "You're currently on maternity leave. No patients or boyfriends waiting in the wings, right?"

Something began unfurling inside of her. Something she hadn't thought about. Something she hadn't even wanted to think about. Was he going to ask her to marry him again? If so, would she be able to resist?

"No, but the no-patients thing is only for a month, and then I have to be back."

"What if you didn't?"

"Sorry?"

"What if you didn't go? Instead of me moving to the States, what if you stayed here—in Italy—instead?"

CHAPTER THREE

PEG ARRIVED BEFORE Elyse could give him an answer to the staying-in-Italy question.

But the look of horror on his ex's face said that marriage was off the table. For good. He wasn't even sure why he'd asked that. It had just come to him as the easiest solution as he'd stood over his daughter's crib. But Elyse had made it clear that the chances of a marriage between them working were just about nil: they didn't even like each other. He could only assume she was speaking for herself.

Although he hadn't liked her very much either when she'd kicked him and the others out of their jobs. But after arriving back in Italy, he'd been the one doing the kicking…and it was his own behind. He should have stayed and finished that last fateful conversation—even if it had only been to gain closure. But he'd been so hurt and utterly furious that he couldn't have found the words in English to express any of it.

"Everything okay?" Peg looked from one to the other, a worried expression on her face.

Her niece gave her a smile that didn't quite reach her eyes. "Great."

It wasn't great. It was frustrating. He felt totally impotent to change things right now. But he was going to. Was going to fight, if necessary, to be involved in his daughter's life. Elyse marrying him would have made sure that happened. Maybe she was right to refuse. Kids were pretty intuitive nowadays. Annalisa would have eventually seen right through the sham, setting them up for a messy divorce down the road.

So no tying the knot. But surely they could live in the same vicinity. Or at least the same country. If she could put off going back to work for three months or maybe even six, he might be able to swing moving back to the US. Even if that prospect didn't thrill him like it once had.

Only with Elyse explaining to Peggy that they were going to be staying at his house, the chance to talk about things was gone. For now. He'd just have to pull her aside or sit them down when they didn't have an audience and hash it out.

And afterward? If she agreed to stay in Italy? She would have to remain in his house for the duration, because she wouldn't be able to afford a villa or even an apartment without working.

Luca wasn't at all sure how he felt about that. Especially after the way he'd reacted to her a few minutes ago.

He scribbled down the address and handed it to Elyse. "Just ask a cab to take you to this address. I'll let my housekeeper know to get a couple of rooms ready."

"Housekeeper?"

The way she said the word made him uneasy. "Emilia. She doesn't live there. Just comes during the week to clean the place up. Today happens to be one of those days. She won't mind. And she normally fixes a couple of meals and puts them in the fridge for me. There's a ton of food, so don't worry about cooking."

"That was part of the reason you wanted us to stay at your place, though, because you had a kitchen we could use."

He smiled. She'd caught him. "I said you could use it, but I didn't say you had to cook in it."

"No, you didn't."

But her voice said she was beginning to have some misgivings, so maybe it was time to make himself scarce before she changed her mind. She'd already turned down his proposal of marriage, he didn't want her backing out of anything else. "I would go with you, but I have a patient scheduled in half an hour."

Peg spoke up. "We'll be fine. And thank you for letting us stay in your house. It will be a lot more comfortable for the baby than the hotel...won't it, Elyse?"

"Yes. Thank you."

The prodding and the reluctance of Elyse's response made his smile widen. He had an odd ally in Peggy, but if it got him closer to his goal—having his daughter within reach—it was worth it.

"I should be home before dinner. Just rest. The recovery time for jet lag is one day per hour of time difference."

"In that case, we'll be well recovered by the time..."

She let the sentence trail away, and he wasn't sure if that was a good thing or a bad thing. Was she thinking about staying longer than a month? Or warning him that she would soon be leaving?

He was sure she and Peggy were going to have quite a discussion once he walked out of that door. Going over to the crib one last time, he murmured to Annalisa, telling her he would see her in a few hours. And hopefully his time with her would be measured in years, rather than just a few short weeks.

"Mary Landers, aged forty-three, a tourist from the US who has been having seizures over the last two weeks. She's in the MRI machine right now. The team could use a second look."

The receptionist at the front desk had already alerted him of that fact when he'd arrived. But his favorite nurse always liked to chat for a minute. His scheduled patient had already been advised that he'd be a few minutes late.

"I'll head up there now. Anything else I should know?"

With her silvery hair and friendly personality, he and Thirza had hit it off immediately. He could count on her to give him additional information on patients if he needed it, rather than having to look things up in the system. The fact that she had an eidetic memory was a great asset for the clinic.

"She got a workup at one of the neighboring hospitals and they suspected a brain tumor because of the cluster of symptoms that came with the seizures, but their scan didn't turn up anything concrete. They've added contrast to the one done here, hoping to get a better view of the way the vessels are laid out."

"Do you remember the cluster of symptoms?"

She brandished a slip of paper and a smile. "Of course. I wrote them down for you."

"Grazie."

He was glad of the work. It would take his mind off the fact that he would once again be living with Elyse.

Only temporarily, though, and he'd decided that was a good thing. Elyse was right. Marriage would have been a mistake.

Going up the stairs, because waiting for the elevator had never been his style, he exited through the door on the third floor and went to the imaging section. Once there, he used his passkey to get into the observation area.

"Luca, glad to see you. We still have about ten minutes before the scan is finished."

"Where's Lorenzo?"

"He's in surgery. He'll be down as soon as he finishes up."

The city of Florence was a tourist magnet, and they treated people of many nationalities. It helped that several of the doctors at the clinic spoke English with varying degrees of fluency. Faster communication meant faster treatment.

He glanced down at the paper in his hand: Seizures, double vision in the left eye, tremor on that same side, muscle weakness. He could see why the other clinic had initially thought she had a brain tumor. They did present with similar symptoms.

"Hey! Stop!" One of the techs was staring down at the patient. "She's seizing!"

The whole room went into action. They retracted the sliding table from the imager, while multiple staff members rushed into the room. Thank God they didn't allow family to observe the procedures.

A few minutes later, after administering an injection of lorazepam, they were able to stabilize her. She slowly regained consciousness, totally unaware of what had happened. She remembered a momentary sense of confusion just before the seizure hit.

Luca frowned. "How close were we to getting those scans finished?"

"About seven minutes."

"Before putting her back in the tube, let me look at what you have. Maybe we won't have to finish it."

Going back into the control room, they scrolled through the scans, the contrast agent helping to visualize blood vessels.

Dannazione! Everything looked pretty normal.

Wait.

"Can we replay those last images?"

The tech backed the slides up and slowly went through them again.

"There." He tapped a pen to the screen where a small, hyper-dense lesion nestled in the left ventricle. "See that?"

"I do. And I can understand how the other hospital missed it. Cavernoma?"

"It looks that way."

A cavernous malformation wasn't like an arteriovenous malformation, where the high pressure in the vessels put the patient at risk of a stroke or brain bleed. Cavernomas were normally asymptomatic, in fact. But since this patient had presented with both seizures and neurological deficits, the cavernoma was probably the cause and would have to be treated.

The problem was, the ventricles were deep in the brain and traditional microsurgery in those areas didn't always go well.

Elyse would love to sit in on this case.

Maybe she could. And it might be a way to coax her

into staying longer. There was no reason she couldn't observe or weigh in with an opinion, was there? As long as she wasn't actually treating the patient, it should be fine.

"What do you think Dr. Giorgino will want to do?"

"I think he'll want to do a combined approach. Ventriculoscopy followed by microsurgery."

"Tricky," said the tech.

"Yes, but by getting an actual look at it, rather than just an MRI image, there's a better chance of success. I saw one of them done when I was in the States." It had actually been one of Elyse's patients. She'd performed the surgery and successfully removed the cavernoma. As far as he knew, the patient's symptoms had completely subsided afterward. "I actually know someone who's done a resection of one of these. I'll put her in contact with Lorenzo."

Again.

Lorenzo Giorgino—the good-looking man who'd held Anna in his office—was one of the top neurosurgeons in Italy. And he actually welcomed outside advice, unlike some specialists. Hopefully Elyse would be willing to help. She could even consult over the phone if she didn't want to actually come in to the clinic.

A little whisper at the back of his brain questioned whether that was a good idea. He'd had a visceral reaction when he'd found out the baby in Lorenzo's arms was actually his own daughter.

But they were all grown-ups. He could handle it.

Luca let the team know they'd found the problem and didn't need to put the patient through another round in the MRI machine. It would be up to Lorenzo and some other specialists to recommend treatment to control her symptoms until a surgery date could be set. The sooner the better.

As soon as that was resolved, he moved on to see the rest of his patients, putting Elyse, Lorenzo and everyone else out of his mind.

"Of course I'll help. I'd love to look at the scans."

Elyse was surprised that Luca had asked her to consult on a case after what had happened in Atlanta.

But this was Italy, not Atlanta. She was no longer the one in charge of his department. She was on Luca's turf now.

"I remembered the cavernoma case you had. The patient had a really good outcome, if I remember right."

"Yes, she's had no more problems since. It was in the right lateral ventricle rather than the left, but the procedure would be the same. You have a neurosurgeon who can perform it?"

She and Peg had moved into the house that afternoon. Her aunt loved it. She'd taken Annalisa into the garden to explore while Elyse had curled up on the couch with a magazine, which was where Luca had found her.

Even his housekeeper had left for the day. And meeting her had turned out to be a lot less awkward than Elyse had expected it to be. She wasn't sure if the woman knew the exact circumstances surrounding her sudden arrival, but it had to be pretty obvious. A woman shows up at her boss's door with a baby in tow... it didn't take a genius to figure it out. Emilia had eyed her daughter with interest, but the kindness behind the glance had prevented Elyse from bristling.

"We do. It's actually the doctor who brought you up

to my office yesterday. I don't know how many, if any, of these he's done, but he's an excellent surgeon. One of the best."

"If he's careful and really pays attention to where he is at any given second, he should be fine."

"Which is why I wondered if you'd speak with him and compare notes. He's a good guy, I'm sure he'd be amenable."

"He seemed nice. I'll need to talk to Peg and see if she's okay with me going, but it sounds fascinating. And much better than lying around your pool all day, nice though that is."

He smiled, coming over to sit on one of the chairs flanking the couch. "You could always treat this like a vacation. Where's Annalisa, anyway?"

"She's in the garden with Peg. She should be in any moment. Whatever your housekeeper left in the oven smells divine, by the way. I could get a little too used to this." Then realizing he could take that as agreement to his marriage proposal, she added, "At least for this month. I haven't decided on moving to Italy, though, Luca. I'm not sure I'm ready to leave my job. I don't even know what I would do here."

"It wouldn't be forever. Could you at least ask for your leave of absence to be extended? Just long enough for us to think things through properly. I don't want either of us to feel rushed and then later be unhappy with the decisions made."

He'd done that exact thing once. Only there was no hint that he was unhappy with that decision.

He was right. A month was a very short time to come up with a plan for a lifetime.

"I don't know if they'll let me. I have a contract that

spells things out." What if they decided to let her go just like they had Luca and the rest of them?

Well, her former colleagues had all bounced back, from what she'd heard from various sources. Surely she would too, if it came to that. She was pretty sure any of the larger hospitals in Atlanta would welcome her on board. She just wasn't sure she would welcome them. She'd been at Atlanta Central Medical Center ever since she'd graduated from med school. She didn't know any-place else.

That fact may have led her to make her own rash decisions. Like staying on at the hospital instead of walking out with her team in protest at the firings. Everything had happened so fast she'd had no time to digest what it really meant to her.

She set aside the magazine she had been looking through when Luca leaned forward. "Will you at least try? Ask them and see if it's a possibility? If it's not, and you're not willing to quit, then we have some things that need to be done quickly. Like getting my name added to her birth certificate."

A zip of shock went through her. Oh, Lord, she hadn't even thought about that. Hadn't thought about much other than informing him that he had a daughter. And now when she thought about it, that had been a pretty cold-blooded way to go about it. This was his child and yet in her head she'd made it into a mere formality, like a business letter: *We would like to inform you that...*

Annalisa was anything but business-oriented. She was a living, breathing human being who had a mother...*and* a father. To make it about anything else would be criminal. Maybe marrying him wouldn't have been as big a stretch as she'd made it out to be. It would make officially naming him as Anna's father easier.

Her heart cramped. But to marry him for anything other than love... She couldn't do it.

She wasn't sure how to add him to Annalisa's birth certificate, or if they could even do it from Italy. He was right. She needed to at least ask the hospital for more time off. If they said no, her decision was made. But if they said yes...then she had some decisions of her own to make. And quickly.

"I'll call the hospital tomorrow morning and get the lay of the land."

"The lay of...?"

"Sorry. It means see if they're agreeable to an extension."

His English was so good it was easy to forget that it wasn't his native tongue. Some of the expressions didn't make much sense when you dissected them. That was another thing. He spoke excellent English, but her Italian was limited to what she'd learned from Luca and some of that made her blush. Not exactly the kind of talk that occurred around the dinner table. In fact, she could feel her face heat at the memory of some of those desperate phrases muttered in the heat of passion.

She hurried to ask, "Lorenzo speaks English pretty well, if I remember right."

"Yes. Most of the staff have some understanding of English. Anything you or they don't understand, I can translate."

"Thank you. If Atlanta does give me additional time off, I think I'd like to take a language course, if I can have Annalisa there with me."

"If you can't, I'm sure Emilia would love to watch

her. Or I could set up a portable crib at the clinic and have her there. With me."

She opened her mouth to argue with him, but then snapped it shut when she remembered she'd already had four months to get to know her daughter. He'd had under a day to adjust to the fact that he was a father. Guilt pressed hard against her chest, making it difficult to breathe.

She uncurled her legs and leaned forward to take one of his hands.

"I'm really sorry, Luca. I should have found a way to get word to you. I just didn't know if she was even going to—"

"You're here now. Let's just leave it at that." Something in his eyes flashed, though, making her wonder if he was really that quick to forgive her.

She let go of his hand, stung by the coolness of his voice. Especially after the way the slide of her palm against his had awakened nerve endings that had gone into hibernation. It had been a long, cold season and there was no end in sight.

Who could blame him if he hated her? She hadn't been that quick to forgive herself. But how much worse would it have been if Anna had gone looking for her father once she reached adulthood and he'd found out about it then? Now, that would have been unforgivable. And both Annalisa and Luca would have missed out on some precious memories.

In the end, she'd done the right thing. Even if it wasn't the easy thing.

"Okay." The whispered word took a while to get out. "I don't know what else to say."

"I know this has been hard on you as well." His gaze softened. "I'm glad you came. Really glad."

With his black hair and dark eyes, he'd been the epitome of tall, dark and mysterious. And with the difference in cultures, his body language wasn't as easy to pick up on as American men's were. Maybe that's why she'd been so drawn to him, even as she'd tried so hard to keep her distance. Unlike her, though, he'd let his feelings come through loud and clear from the very beginning, making her sizzle inside.

That had been wildly attractive. Looking back, it had only been a matter of time before she gave in. Only she'd never expected to be the one doing the asking. But she had. It had seemed inevitable at the time, though.

Luca knew what he wanted and set out to get it. Not something she was used to in the men she'd known. Not even Kyle had been so driven. Getting swept off her feet had been a heady experience.

She just had to be careful that she didn't let his charm affect her all over again or influence her in certain areas of her life. Like talking her into a sham marriage. For a second or two, the word "yes" had teetered on the tip of her tongue. But down that road lay craziness. Even if it had been for *their* daughter. A fact she had to remind herself of several times a day. She was no longer calling all the shots when it came to making decisions about Anna.

Before she could think of anything else to say, he stood and reached down his hand. "You must be hungry. And tired."

From her position her eyes had to skim up his body to get to his face. Heat flared as her glance swept over parts she'd once known in all their glory.

If it had been anyone else, she might have thought he was standing over her to intimidate her, to make himself look bigger and stronger, but she knew that wasn't how he operated. And other countries didn't have the same bubble of personal space that Americans did. At least, that's what she'd learned from Luca. He tended to stand close. To kiss close. To love close.

Elyse closed her eyes for a second before forcing herself to nod in the hope that he'd take a step backward, so she could stand as well. He must have read her mind, because he did just that, the hand he'd held down toward her dragged through his hair instead. He took a second step back. She climbed to her feet, only to discover that he was still well within her personal space. And with the couch behind her, she had nowhere to go.

His finger lifted to touch her cheek in a way that sent a shiver over her. "We're going to figure this out, Elyse. I promise."

Figure what out? How to kill the emotions swirling inside her that just would not die? Because his touch and the low rasp of his voice were doing just the opposite.

"I hope so."

Just then she heard the back door open and Peg's voice as she chattered to Annalisa.

"Perfect timing all around," he said, moving away from her.

"Yes, it is." Elyse smoothed her shirt down over her skirt with trembling hands, anxious to hide the turmoil whipping through her. She'd hoped all of those odd pangs of need for him would go away with time. And they had faded somewhat, but his presence had evidently popped a trapped bubble of longing, because a stream of it was hitting her system hard. So hard it was difficult to concentrate on anything but the way he looked, his scent, the way she'd once felt in his arms.

Staying at his house, for a week much less a month, was such a big mistake. She hurried over to Peg and lifted Annalisa out of her arms, hugging the baby to her.

Luca came over and chose that moment to kiss his daughter on the cheek, and when he looked up, they were inches apart, his lips heartbreakingly close. And there it was again. That quivery sensation she'd had a minute ago. Then he pulled back, with a smile that was full of hidden knowledge.

He knew exactly what he did to her.

"I'll go get check on dinner," he murmured, and then he was gone.

Her aunt glanced at her, eyes wide. Elyse wasn't the only one who'd noticed the disruption in the space/time continuum.

"Oh, my," she said, "I think I'll go help him. Annalisa is probably hungry for her dinner as well. She was getting a little fussy outside. Looks like I picked the wrong moment to come in."

"Oh, no, Peg. You picked the perfect time, believe me."

"I'm not so sure…"

But Anna *was* fussy again, starting to shift and snort. The precursor to a complete meltdown. The baby wasn't the only one close to a meltdown. She could feel one coming on herself. She threw her aunt a grateful smile. "Thanks, I'll feed her and put her down for a nap, so we can eat in peace."

Peace? Ha! Not much hope of that. Not as long as Luca was around.

Well, she was going to have to figure out how to deal with him before she did something completely stupid. Like fall for him all over again.

CHAPTER FOUR

"I DON'T KNOW, Elyse, we were counting on having you back on time. Isn't there any way you can keep to your original schedule?"

Not the words Elyse was hoping to hear this early in the morning. She'd dragged herself out of bed, nursed the baby, stuffed her feet into flip-flops and made her way out of the bedroom. Annalisa had gone back to sleep as soon as she was full.

As it was so early, she'd decided to get the thing she dreaded most out of the way. She called the hospital and reached the administrator. He was not overly accommodating, which was normal. She should be happy he was being difficult, that she would have an excuse to leave when her month was over but, oddly enough, she wasn't.

She couldn't blame him. It had been several months already. Her complicated pregnancy had meant not working as many hours as she'd used to. And then she'd been put on complete bed rest. No more patients, no more going into work. At all.

"I'll do my best. I'll let you know in a few days what I've decided." She thanked him and hung up the phone.

The longer she was here, the more complicated things promised to get with Luca. Surely whatever they had to work out could be done in a month. And he'd talked about maybe moving back to the States once his patient load was redistributed, in about six months' time.

Elyse swallowed. In six months Annalisa would be crawling and doing all kinds of other things. And Luca would miss all of it.

How was that fair? But how was staying here for six months fair to her? She would probably have to quit her job, put her career on hold in order to stay. And then there was her mom. Where would she be in six months? Yes, she had her younger sister Peg, her husband and a multitude of friends she could call on. But she only had one daughter: Elyse. And she would only ever have one grandchild.

There was no good solution. Something she'd told herself all day yesterday. They were going to have to come up with some kind of plan, though. And she knew that "plan" needed to include having Anna's father in her life.

That little act of fertilizing an egg had bound them together for life in some way, shape or form. That had been the easy part. The fun part. She shivered; yes, it had been a lot of fun.

Oh, there was fun in raising a child too, but it was definitely life-altering, in more ways than one. Luca would find out the reality of that soon enough. Like giving up months of a career that had taken years to build. He'd told her he couldn't move back to the States because of his patient load and had asked her to move to Italy instead. The problem was, he'd already practiced medicine in Atlanta, so he could take up where he'd left off with his career, whereas she...

TINA BECKETT 57

She would have to give up everything she'd worked for. Scrabble up the ladder all over again.

Wasn't Anna worth it? Absolutely. But if there was a better solution, she wanted to find it. And that meant some give-and-take on both their parts.

That would be something else they'd have to talk about. She didn't want to scare him, but she also didn't want him to just sit back and be content with coming over and kissing his daughter's cheek periodically. Annalisa's view of men was being formed with each interaction. It was up to both of them to make sure those interactions were meaningful and healthy.

She glanced down the hallway. Peggy was awake, evidently. Her bedroom door was open and when she made her way over there, there was no sign of her. Anna was still sound asleep. She padded to the kitchen, where she found her aunt chatting with Emilia, who was poised to crack an egg on the edge of a bowl.

"Good, you're awake. We were just talking about how you like your eggs." Peggy turned her head and mouthed, Oh, my God.

Elyse forced back a laugh. Her aunt wasn't used to having things done for her. She preferred to wait on people, not the other way around. "You don't have to cook for us, Emilia. We know how to make eggs." She said the words in rapid English before pulling herself up short and slowing way down. "I'm sorry. Did you understand?"

"Yes. I like cook," Emilia replied with a smile.

Hoping Peggy wouldn't jump in and try to take over, she pronounced each word carefully. "Thank you. And I like eggs...scrambled?" She made a stirring motion with her hand, hoping to get across the meaning.

"Why are you talking like that?" Peg asked.

"What do you mean?"

She laughed. "One of Emilia's kids is studying English in the States. She understands quite a bit, she just doesn't like to speak it because she's afraid of making mistakes."

The housekeeper nodded as if in agreement.

Well, Emilia wasn't the only one afraid of making mistakes. Elyse was too. And not just with regard to the language. She was afraid of making a terrible mistake with her daughter or with Luca. One she'd have a hard time recovering from.

Don't hurt either one of them, Elyse.

The thought came unbidden and was unwelcome. She wouldn't if she could help it. Right now she was doing the best she could with what she had.

While Emilia cooked their breakfast, Peg motioned her into the other room. "You're going to the hospital to consult on a case this morning?"

Luca must have told her.

"Exactly how long have you been up?"

"Long enough to sit and have a chat with him." She squeezed her niece's hand. "He wants a relationship with her, honey. You need to give him a chance."

She frowned. "That's why we came here. To tell him about her."

"That's not what I mean, and you know it. He told me he asked you to stay in Italy, but that you weren't sure."

"Did he also tell you he asked me to marry him?"

"He what?" Her eyes went round with surprise. "What did you say?"

Elyse grimaced. "What do you think I said? No,

of course. It was an impulsive suggestion. He didn't mean it."

"Are you sure?"

"Very sure. And as for staying, I just don't know how that would work. My administrator basically said he wants me back at the end of a month."

"Are you going to go? This is Anna's future we're talking about."

Elyse looked off into the distance for a moment. "I know. He hurt me, Peg."

"Are you so sure that was a one-way street? He lost his job, and you were the one who told him. You don't think that hurt *him*?"

"I had no choice about him losing his job. And I felt it was better coming from me than from a hospital bureaucrat."

"I'm not saying what you did was wrong. But it still had to sting."

She shrugged. "He left. Packed up his bags and was gone soon after the announcement."

"And you're afraid he'll do the same to Annalisa? He won't, you know he won't." Peg tilted her head. "Anna is a part of him. They'll always have that connection, no matter what his relationship with you is like."

Something burned behind her eyes. What Peggy said was true. That even if Elyse meant nothing to him, he would always love their daughter.

"You're right as usual."

"I'm going to go back to the hotel, if it's all right with you. It'll be harder for you two to work things out, if I'm hanging around. Unless you need my help with Annalisa. And my vacation is only for a week."

Elyse's eyes widened. "Please don't abandon me."

"I'm not. But you and Luca need this time together—even if it's only related to your daughter. I'm going back to do some sightseeing." She held up a hand. "Don't worry, I'll text you if I run into problems. And if you need a babysitter during the week, I'll be around. After that, you're on your own. And you'll be fine. You all will."

Elyse wasn't so sure about that.

She slung her arm around her aunt's shoulder and squeezed. "I wish I had your certainty, but I do understand." Of course Peggy wouldn't want to be in the room if she and Luca ended up having a huge argument about arrangements. They did need to hammer this out. Without an audience. Even though she hated the thought of being in the house alone with him.

Because of him? Or because she didn't trust herself?

She didn't dare answer that question.

"Thanks for coming with me to Italy. Are you sure you don't want company on your sightseeing tour?"

"I'm positive. I hear there's a romantic gondola tour down the Arno River. Maybe I'll meet a hunky Italian and get lucky."

"Aunt Peggy!"

"Don't you 'Aunt Peggy' me. You're no stranger to the birds and bees or you wouldn't have that sweet little thing in the other room."

She couldn't argue with that.

"You don't even speak Italian."

"Some things you don't need words for. Don't worry. I'll check on you every night until I'm back home in the States."

Elyse smiled. Her aunt was only ten years older than she was, so she was more like a sister than a parental figure. Peggy's husband had been much older than his bride and had died almost five years ago, leaving Peggy a fortune. But it hadn't changed her in the least. She was still the same fun-loving person she'd always been. She'd even insisted on paying for the trip to Italy.

"Make sure you do. Do I need to set a curfew?"

Her aunt laughed. "I'd only break it." She kissed her niece on the cheek. "It's not every day I get to see Italy."

Emilia peered around the corner and motioned to them. Judging from the luscious smell coming from the kitchen, breakfast must be ready.

She guessed Anna would be coming with her to the hospital this morning. She smiled. Well, Luca might as well have his first official reality check about having a baby. He was going to find out it wasn't always convenient.

But Elyse wouldn't change it for the world.

Going into the kitchen, she found two plates already set with eggs, ham, thick slices of what looked like homemade toasted bread, and small pots of jam. "This looks delicious. Thank you so much, but aren't you going to eat?"

"Eat…no…" The woman frowned. "Ate six o'clock."

She must have eaten with Luca, then. Glancing at Peg, she said, "Were you here when Luca was eating?"

Peggy sat and dug into her eggs with gusto. "I came after he was done. Emilia offered to make me something then, but I wanted to wait for you."

"I'm sorry. You should have knocked on the door."

"I knew Annalisa would wake you soon enough. I wanted you to get as much sleep as you could."

"Well, I slept great, thank you."

"I'll pack while you're at the hospital so leave the baby with me."

So much for Luca getting his first taste of real fatherhood. "I can take her with me."

"You'll have her to yourself soon enough. I need a few more snuggles before I go, since it looks like I won't be seeing her for a month. That's going to be hard on everyone back home. Especially your mom."

"I know, but it'll fly by."

And if she decided to stay longer than a month?

There was no easy answer. Luca was Anna's father. Nothing was going to change that. And she realized she wouldn't want to, even if she could.

Luca saw her coming down the hall, those hips swinging to an internal tune that he used to know so well. He'd half wondered if she would skip out on him once she found out that Peggy was going back to the hotel.

Her aunt had told him this morning that she wanted to give them time and space to talk things through. He'd tried to insist that she wouldn't be in the way, but she'd turned out to be almost as stubborn as her niece was.

It must run in the family.

Well, it ran in his family too, so he couldn't fault her there.

And he needed to be realistic in his expectations. Elyse had made concessions in coming here, so he needed to make some too. He was going to turn some of his patients over to another neurologist, so he could spend time with his daughter. They could sightsee, or picnic...or whatever the hell Elyse wanted to do. He wasn't courting her, he insisted to himself. He was courting his daughter, hoping to make up for lost time.

At least he hoped that was all it was. Because every time he saw the woman…

He forced that thought back as she reached where he was standing. "Thanks for coming. I have the patient workup waiting in my office. Lorenzo will meet us there in about fifteen minutes to go over everything. Surgery is scheduled for tomorrow."

"I was surprised that you had your own office."

"Yes, didn't you in Atlanta?"

She smiled. "*Touché.* Yes, I did. Sorry."

"It's fine. Anyway, I thought we could discuss the procedure and then see the patient herself. She's American and will probably be happy to see someone from her homeland besides her husband."

"I'm good with that." She sighed. "This is one of those times that I wished I'd paid more attention in Spanish class."

"Spanish?"

"It might help me at least a little bit. I mean, I know I won't need it with this patient, but what if you want me to weigh in on others?"

"Spanish is closer to Portuguese than Italian, although there are some similarities." He smiled. "I can teach you some. I'd really like Annalisa to learn Italian."

Elyse frowned, and he cocked his head. "Is that a problem?"

"No… I just…" The tip of her tongue scrubbed at her upper lip for a second before retreating, but not before the act made something in his gut tighten. He remembered that gesture and a thousand other ones. They were all there in his memory as fresh as the day he'd put them there.

Dio. Would they ever fade?

He hoped not.

Licking her lips normally meant she was going to say something she thought he wouldn't want to hear.

"What is it?"

"My administrator really wants me back at the end of my leave, so I only have this month. Unless I quit my job."

He wanted his parents and sister to meet the baby, but they lived in Rome, almost three hundred kilometers from Florence. They could make the trip there and back by train in a day, but he'd hoped to be able to spend a week or so in Rome to make proper introductions. They still could. It would just have to be carefully arranged.

He needed to call his parents first and let them know they had their first granddaughter. They would be thrilled, even though his folks were a bit old-fashioned about some things.

"We'll figure something out."

"I hope so."

"Is Peggy at the house with Anna?"

"Yes. Did she tell you, she's going back to the hotel and will be returning to Atlanta as planned?"

"Yes. She told me she was going to talk to you about it."

"She did. I'm not sure how I feel about it, but she doesn't want to be in the way. I guess in case we have bitter arguments about Annalisa."

"And will we?"

She looked at him as if needing to consider something. "I really don't want to fight over her. We're both adults, Luca. I'm assuming we both have our daughter's best interests at heart."

Said as if she wasn't sure that he did. That stung.

Made him wonder if she'd ever completely trusted him. With anything. Including her heart.

The end of their relationship said she probably hadn't.

"You assumed correctly. Don't ever doubt it." His answer was sharper than he'd intended it to be and made him realize they were still standing in the middle of the hallway. "Why don't we talk more about Anna after our meeting with Lorenzo?"

"Yes, of course." She looked relieved.

"Elevator or stairs?"

"Stairs, if we can. Especially after that huge breakfast Emilia insisted on fixing us."

He smiled. Emilia had worked for his parents for years, helping them throw elaborate parties, so she did tend to go overboard where guests were concerned. Not that he entertained much outside work. He'd never actually brought a woman to the apartment. Hopefully Emilia wouldn't get any funny ideas. "She thinks everything can be solved by a good meal."

If only it were that simple.

They took the stairs to the third floor, where all of the offices were. Coming out into the main foyer, where leather chairs sat in a large circle on the marble floor, he headed to the far corner, where his office was.

"Why are there so many pictures on the walls? I noticed them downstairs in the entryway as well."

As he saw them every day, they had become so much background noise, but looking at the long line of images he could see how it might look to an outsider. The hospital in Atlanta had been sterile and efficient. But Florence was a city with a rich cultural history as far as art went. "Hospitals have started putting up pictures of nature as a way of enhancing the healing process."

Arched brows went up and she scanned the wall, the bottom half of which was painted blue, whereas a buttery cream covered the upper half. A handrail had been placed along the break in colors, the artwork providing another visual delineation between the two. "Interesting. Do all hospitals in Italy do this?"

"Probably not all of them. It's a relatively new concept. The Clinica Neurologica di Firenze adopted it about five years ago."

"Firenze?"

It was easy to forget, even with all the tourists, that the name of the hospital meant nothing to a non-Italian speaker. "Sorry, it's the way we say Florence."

He smiled, remembering the way she would puzzle through an Italian phrase, trying to make sense of it, when they had been together. She'd loved him speaking Italian while they made love, the little sounds she'd made sending him spinning into space more than once. Long before he'd been ready.

He swallowed. Not something he wanted to remember.

Unlocking his office, he motioned her inside. "What time do you need to get back to relieve Peggy?"

"I think I have a few hours. I'm still nursing, but more in the morning and at night, since I was getting ready to go back to work. I've been supplementing with bottles for the last couple of weeks."

"Okay, sounds good."

There was a knock on the door and Lorenzo opened the door a crack and said, *"C'è stato um cambiamento di piani."*

Luca motioned him inside, answering him in English. "A change of plans? What kind of change?" He inserted, "Sorry. Lorenzo, you remember Elyse?"

"Yes. Of course." He took her hand and smiled at her. "But you must call me Enzo."

Her cheeks flushed a deep red. "Okay."

What the hell? Luca's eyes narrowed, centering squarely on his friend. "You mentioned that something had changed."

"Yes, Mary Landers has had two seizures in the last two hours. I've moved surgery up from tomorrow to today. In two hours, to be exact. I have to prepare in a few minutes, but I would like to run by you the method I'm planning on using, Elyse, if you don't mind."

"Of course not. Can we go over the chart together?"

Luca pulled the chart he had and handed it to Lorenzo. Soon the pair were going over things, heads bent close as they studied and discussed the findings. He didn't like the way they looked together, her blond locks contrasting with Lorenzo's close-cut black hair. Elyse spoke in quick, concise statements, explaining her case and how it was similar to and different from the one at hand. "My patient didn't have back-to-back seizures like this one, but they're similar. And going in with a ventriculoscopy followed by microsurgery is the same method I would choose if she were my patient."

Lorenzo looked at her and said, "Perfect. *Grazie*. Will you be observing?"

"If possible."

"Yes. There's a microphone in the observation room. If something strikes you during the surgery, feel free to mention it. Also, it might help the patient if you went in and spoke with her beforehand."

"I will. Thanks."

He took her hand again and gave it a squeeze. "See you soon."

Luca frowned. What was with his friend? And since when did he ask anyone to call him Enzo?

But before he could even formulate a response, Lorenzo was out the door.

"Are you sure you have time to observe? It will probably last several hours."

"Peggy has enough supplies for quite a while. I'll give her a quick call though and check." She glanced at him. "Are you scrubbing in as well?"

"They have another neurophysiologist who will be monitoring the patient's readings, but I'll be available to interpret a scan if they need it during the ventriculoscopy."

He remembered the first time he'd heard mention of a burr hole and realized that drilling through the skull was a practice that hadn't entirely faded out with time. It still had its place, and this was one of them.

"I wish embolization techniques worked for these types of malformations, but they don't."

He'd always liked talking about work with her. She was intelligent and thoughtful. Not hurried, not intimidated, even though neurology was still a male-dominated field. She wasn't in it to show anyone up. But she wasn't afraid to push back over a diagnosis either, which he'd witnessed firsthand. The death of a patient had changed things between them. She'd stopped discussing cases with him, had become distant and moody. It had continued until the layoff occurred.

He'd never been able to figure out exactly what had happened between them.

"No, it would be wonderful if it was a relatively easy

fix, but with the type of procedure Lorenzo is going to do, he'll have to enlarge the burr hole to double its size and go in manually."

"Hopefully the seizures are caused by the cavernoma and not something else," she said.

"Testing has pretty much ruled out anything else." He paused. "Are you ready to go see her?"

"Yes. And thank you for asking me to come."

"You're welcome."

He put the computer to sleep and they both stood, trying to exit the same side of the desk. They bumped shoulders and she gave a husky laugh as they tried to maneuver and ended up doing a little dance that still put them in each other's path.

"Well, this isn't working." He tried to wait for her to move away first, but she didn't. When he looked at her, her glance was on his face. There was an intensity there that made his head swim.

Suddenly he was on a different plane—transported back through time and space.

Her teeth went to her bottom lip and clamped down, eyes shifting to his chest.

A blaze of heat went through him. Was she checking him out? His brain thought she was and that was enough for certain parts of his body to stir.

"Elyse?"

She didn't answer, but her brows went up, so he knew she'd heard him. She looked like she was waiting for him to do something. He had no idea what, because the only thing he could think of doing right now was kissing her.

Unless…that's exactly what she was waiting for.

That was enough for him.

His hands went to her shoulders and he stood there for several long seconds.

Then he kissed her.

CHAPTER FIVE

THE SECOND HIS lips touched hers, her eyes slammed shut, and she was trapped in a warm sea of familiarity. One she'd blocked from her thoughts until this very moment. His mouth was firm, just like it had been, his taste exactly the same. dark roasted coffee and everything that went along with being Luca.

"Dio." He came up long enough to mutter that single oath before kissing her again.

The word made her whole body liquefy. She could remember long strings of Italian that would help drive her to the very brink of ecstasy and then hold her there until he was ready to send her over the edge. And then he would start all over. A slow, wonderful torture that she never wanted to end.

Her arms went around his neck, and she pressed herself against him, needing to get closer even as he edged her back until her bottom was against the back of the chair. She struggled to balance herself on it, even as she wanted to turn and lean over it, inviting an exploration of a different type.

Lord, she was in trouble. Big trouble, but she didn't want to stop. Didn't want to do anything that would change the course of where this might be headed.

She'd missed him so very much.

His hand went to her breast, palm pressing against her tight nipple with a caress that sent a shock wave through her. And something else.

A warning tingle. Oh, no!

It was the signal that her body had felt the stimulation and completely mistaken the reason for it.

Her hands went to his shoulders and pushed, terrified she would end up with two wet circles on the front of her blue blouse.

As soon as his mouth came off hers, and he took a step back, she crossed her arms over her chest and applied pressure, hoping it didn't look as obvious as it felt. It worked. The tide began to recede.

In the meantime, Luca dragged a hand through his hair that she could swear shook a little. "*Dio*, Elyse. Sorry. I didn't call you to my office for that." His accent was suddenly thicker than normal.

She knew he hadn't. If he'd been interested in sex, there was always the house.

A house they would now be spending a lot of time in…largely alone.

She almost groaned aloud. If something like this happened when they accidentally bumped into each other, what would happen when it wasn't an accident?

Ha! She wasn't about to find out. She would have to keep their daughter between them as much as possible. Surely he wouldn't kiss her while she was holding Anna.

If she was embarrassed now, what would she be like if there were no clothes, no way to hide what was happening?

It was a natural process. Nothing to be ashamed of. She used her breasts to nourish her baby.

But they were also sexual. And right now it was hard to separate one from the other. She wasn't sure she even wanted to. She'd just assumed she wouldn't have sex again until after Anna was weaned, since there were no prospects hovering on the horizon. Not even a blip on the radar.

The breakup between her and Luca had been too traumatic. And with the shared reality of a baby, it was still too raw. Anna connected Luca to her in a very tangible way. That connection was now permanent, like it or not.

He was looking at her, waiting for some kind of response to his apology.

"It was both of us, not just you. I think our emotions— you finding out you have a child and me finding out that you want to be a part of her life—got the better of us."

Did she really believe that? Not for one second. It had been the past coming back to haunt her that had caused it.

"Yes, that must be it." The words were half muttered as if he hadn't really meant her to hear them.

He was staring at her chest, and she realized her arms were still tightly crossed over it. Now that the tingling had stopped she could let the pressure off. She unfolded them and allowed them drop to her sides. There was no way she was going to tell him why she'd been doing that, but hopefully he hadn't seen it as a self-protective gesture. It had been, but not in the way he might think.

She smiled. "Florence is a very romantic city. I'll have to watch my step from here on out."

"No. No, you won't."

The way he said it gave her pause. Was he saying he

wasn't going to have a problem staying away from her? Well, that was good. Wasn't it?

Yes, it was. "Well, now that we've settled that, shall we actually go see the patient? Preferably before they prep her for surgery? I'd like to see how she is."

"Of course. The surgical unit is on the first floor, so it's back down the stairs for us. Or would you rather—?"

"The stairs are fine." She needed to keep moving. At least for now. The hope was that it would keep her from thinking too much.

A few minutes later, they were in Mrs. Landers's room, and she chatted with Elyse in English. The woman seemed relieved to have another native speaker, although she had her husband, and most of the staff spoke English. Maybe it was just knowing that Elyse was in the medical profession that made her feel more at ease. "The procedure should help you feel a lot better."

"Will it clear up my double vision?"

"That's the hope. As well as the seizures and your other problems." She glanced back at Luca for confirmation.

He inclined his head. "You might not notice a huge difference right away, but once the inflammation from the malformation is gone, things should settle down."

"I hope so. Todd wanted me to go back to the States to have the procedure, but I just wanted to get it over with. And we read that this center is one of the best in Europe." She reached for her husband's hand.

"We do quite a few procedures on blood vessel problems. Cavernomas are fairly rare but, even so, they're well studied."

A nurse came in. "It is almost time. Are you ready?"

Her English wasn't quite as fluent as some of the others', but it was enough to elicit a smile from their patient.

"More than ready." She squeezed her husband's hand and he leaned down to kiss her on the forehead.

"Love you."

"You'll be here when I get out?"

"I'm not going anywhere, sweetheart. Ever."

The words brought a lump to Elyse's throat. She resisted the urge to look over her shoulder to see what Luca's expression was—or if there was even any reaction at all.

Would he have been like this in the delivery room as she'd had Anna?

It was too late now. She'd never know. The lump turned to an ache that wouldn't go away.

Mary was wheeled from the room and Todd followed her, giving them a nod of his head.

She forced herself to speak. "Do we need to help him find the waiting room?"

"One of the nurses will show him where to go. He can walk with Mary as far as the doors of the surgical suite. It's kind of a ritual. Most loved ones accompany their family members."

"I don't blame them. I would too." She'd had no one but her mom and dad when they'd had to do the C-section for Annalisa. Luca had been long gone.

Not a helpful thought.

She was curious, though. "Did you come to Florence as soon as you left the States?"

She wasn't sure why she asked that, but once the words were out, there was no way to retract them.

"No, I spent some time in Rome with my folks first." He motioned for her to walk down a corridor.

"By the way, I would like them to meet Annalisa, if you'd be willing."

That caught her up short for a second or two. She hadn't even thought about that.

"Yes. Of course. I can't imagine there *not* being time, even if I'm only here for a month."

They came to a set of double doors with red lettering that she took to mean authorized personnel only beyond that point. "Do I need a visitor's pass or anything?"

"As long as you're with me, you'll be fine."

Would she? She could remember a time when that hadn't been the case, when being with him had been anything but fine. That had been right before he'd left for parts unknown, and she'd never seen him again.

Until now.

She swallowed. He wanted his parents to meet Annalisa. Of course he did. She was their granddaughter. "How far is Rome?"

"It's about an hour and a half by train. Double that by car."

She remembered his patient load. "You'll be able to get time off work?"

"I should be able to move things around."

Luca led the way to a set of doors each with a number and the words "Sala Operatoria." Operating Suite, maybe? It was amazing how she could kind of decipher certain terms. But that was only if she was standing there studying them. Hearing someone speak was an entirely different matter. Even the word for Florence sounded nothing like the English word. It looked like the word for fire or something.

"In here."

He motioned to a room marked "Sala di Osservazione."

She went through and saw a tiered bank of about fifteen seats. There were already three people in there on the far side of the room chatting in low voices. Judging by their white lab coats, she assumed they were either still in medical school or were first-year residents. It didn't look like an entire class, since none of them had that "professor" look to them.

There was also a microphone hanging front and center, just as Enzo had told her there would be.

Luca found them seats in the front row toward the middle, and she sat, looking at the room below with interest. "Will they pipe sound in here? I know Enzo said we could make comments."

"Yes, *Enzo* did."

Why had he emphasized his colleague's name like that?

Before she could attempt to figure it out, he went on, "There's a microphone hanging above the operating table, just like in the States, and everything in the room is recorded. Surgeons are encouraged to relay what they are doing. All of it will go on record, unless there's an emergency, then everyone focuses on the patient's welfare above all else."

She had turned her head toward him to focus on what he was saying, only she kept finding her gaze dropping to the movement of his lips. Lips that had been on hers a few moments earlier. Not good. That kiss had done a number on her. She needed to forget it. Chalk it up to the rekindling of old emotions.

Only she'd thought those were all dead.

She jerked her attention back to the front, hoping he hadn't noticed. Maybe it was the lack of closure that was messing with her equilibrium. There'd been no time for closure. She'd received word that his job as well as several others were being done away with. She'd announced the news. They'd had frantic sex. And he'd left. Just like that. It had been a whirlwind breakup.

Nothing clean about it.

Her thoughts were interrupted when they wheeled the patient into the room. Enzo entered already scrubbed and ready and was bent over the patient.

"He's talking to her about what's going to happen. He likes to look his patients in the eye before beginning and asking if they have any questions."

"That's a little different than how I do it, but I like it." Elyse normally didn't come in until the patient was already sedated and surgery was ready to begin. But she did stay with them until they came out from under anesthesia and also visited them in Recovery—when they were more likely to remember her.

The surgeon then moved away, and his team gathered around him, except for one of the nurses and the anesthesiologist, who began administering the sedation drugs.

"It looks kind of like a football huddle."

"That is basically what it is. They're getting any last-minute information, and Lorenzo is making sure they know which instruments he plans to use and the order he'll need them." He glanced at her. "They're surgical nurses so they tend to be intuitive, and most of them know what to expect, but it still helps to be reminded."

Yes, it did. Just like she'd reminded herself a few minutes ago that their relationship wasn't just under general anesthesia. It had flatlined and was gone, not surviving what life had thrown at it. She shouldn't go looking for it to wake up and recover, like Mrs. Landers would hopefully do.

Soon the patient was sedated, and the area of her head where the surgery would take place was clipped, shaved and had a sterile drape placed over it.

"He'll do the trepanning first." It's what they had talked about. It would result in the burr hole being drilled to a larger diameter, but the smaller hole gave the endoscope a solid surface on which to rest as it was guided through the delicate tissue.

"Yes. He'll want a precise location and size before actually going in to remove it," Luca replied.

Even though there would be a record of those things on the MRI scans, nothing replaced having a physical look at it.

"I'm surprised you're not down there in the mix." She looked over at the monitor and saw a man to the left of the patient, checking the tracings. A neurophysiologist. Just like Luca. He would be monitoring the patient's brain function during surgery.

"It was a last-minute change in plans, remember? The surgery was supposed to be tomorrow. I told him I'd be available for a second opinion, if needed."

"You were supposed to be in the operating room tomorrow? What happened? Why aren't you in there now?"

He looked at her, eyes meeting hers. "You happened. Anna happened. I need to free up my time. I'll be doing more of that in the coming weeks."

She swallowed then laid her hand on his arm, squeezing lightly. "I'm so sorry, Luca. Our coming here has totally disrupted your life."

Anna had disrupted hers as well, but she wouldn't trade it for the world.

"Not disrupted. I would call it more...*deviare*."

Her head cocked to the side, trying to figure out what the word meant. Devi...something. Deviate, maybe? From what?

"I think the word in English is to re-road?"

"Ah, reroute?" Okay, that was much better than deviated. Because to deviate from one's planned path was...

Exactly what she'd done. But it wasn't horrible. She'd adapted, and she was happy. Happier than she'd ever been, in fact. The only part that made her truly sad was knowing she couldn't have any more children like her daughter.

"Yes, reroute. But I am glad you came. Glad you told me the truth."

Even though she was more than four months late. More than that, if you counted the pregnancy itself. And she hadn't told him the entire truth, but the rest of her story didn't matter. It didn't affect him. Just her.

She glanced down when the sound of the cranial drill engaged. She remembered practicing how to stop precisely when the skull wall was breached so as not to damage the grey matter below. Newer technology was arriving and there were now drills that came with measured stops that took some of the thinking out of it.

Within seconds, they'd reached their goal, the hole swabbed, and the endoscope fed through. A screen on the far wall went live—she was pretty sure that was for the benefit of those in the observation room. Enzo looked through the overhead surgical microscope as the tube made its way toward the ventricle in question. With each step, he relayed to the listening device what he was doing and what he saw, with Luca translating close to her ear so as not to disturb the others in the room.

The tickle of his warm breath hitting her skin was intimate. Almost unbearably so. But she didn't want him to stop. In fact, she propped her chin on the back of her hand and let herself enjoy listening to the sound of his voice.

"Approaching lateral ventricle. Entering space." There was a pause while Enzo readjusted his instruments and probably took stock of what was appearing on the screen. "Malformation is approximately three centimeters in diameter, causing a slight deformity of the left side."

The voice in her ear stopped when the voice on the loudspeaker halted, but the reactions happening inside her head kept right on going, setting up a weird tingle that made her shiver. She'd told herself to enjoy it, but she was starting to like it a little too much.

There was a period of silence that went on for about thirty seconds. It was almost as if the room had gone into a state of suspended animation, with everyone waiting for Dr. Giorgino's verdict.

As much as she wanted Luca to continue, maybe she'd be better off wishing the surgery ended quickly. Before she did something stupid. Like she had during that kiss.

Enzo lifted his head and spoke. And so did Luca.

"We should be able to dissect it with minimal damage."

The words made her swallow, but it engendered a very different reaction from others in the room. Muscles that were tense went slack with relief.

The surgeon then called out orders as the burr hole

was enlarged enough for the instruments he would use. She understood none of it.

"Do you want me to keep translating?"

"If something important happens, I'd like to know, but I'm familiar enough with the surgery to understand what's happening on the screen. Thank you, though. I did want to know what his verdict was."

She forced a smile, telling herself she was relieved that his lips were no longer at her ear. But there was also a sense of loss that she was no longer allowed those kinds of privileges.

He sat back in his chair, and Elyse thought she saw a hint of relief in his own eyes. Maybe she wasn't the only one affected by their proximity.

They'd been very good together in bed. He had taken her places she'd never been before. Her relationship with Kyle had paled beside him. She somehow doubted anyone else would move her the way Luca had, even though their time together hadn't been all that long. Just four months.

She'd never met his parents, although he'd met hers. Then again, her parents lived within an hour's drive of the hospital, while his lived on a different continent.

And yet he wanted them to meet Annalisa. He'd never said whether or not he'd told them about living with her in the States. She'd never asked, because she'd thought they had plenty of time for all of that.

Only they hadn't.

Elyse forced herself to settle in to watch the rest of the procedure, noting the similarities and differences between what was done in this center compared to what she would have done back home. She made a mental note to herself to research a couple of items to see if anyone was using the techniques she was seeing here. Maybe she could learn a thing or two.

Had Luca carried any techniques back from the States with him? She was curious.

"Did you change the way you do things at all after you came back? Or is neurophysiology basically the same here as it is in Atlanta?"

"Why do you ask?" The look on his face was of genuine puzzlement.

"I don't know. I'm just curious. I've seen a couple of things that I'm going to look into. The order in which Enzo clamped off those blood vessels is a little different. Not in a bad way. I liked what I saw on the screen."

"Ahh, I see. Yes, I think there are things that I probably changed. Things I learned or saw during my time at your hospital that I have applied here."

Your hospital. A sting of pain went through her.

It had been his at one time too. Until she'd severed his connection to it.

Actually, she hadn't severed it. The administration had, and there'd been nothing she could do about it.

You could have quit too. It might have saved your relationship with Luca.

Doubtful. He'd asked her if she had put his name on the list of people to be fired. She hadn't. But at the time she'd been glad it was there, thinking that if she was no longer his boss, maybe some of her conflicted emotions about dating someone she worked so closely with would dissipate. Her reaction had probably been a knee-jerk one, and not entirely rational, but it had been very real. To her, anyway.

He was extremely talented, she'd thought. He could have worked anywhere in Atlanta.

He hadn't wanted to do that, though. Neither had he seemed interested in salvaging what they'd had.

How much of that had been her doing? Probably a lot. And she owed him an apology.

Keeping her voice low, she said, "Luca, I'm sorry for the way things at the hospital unfolded. I know it wasn't easy. For any of you." She hesitated, but needed to get the rest of it out. "I didn't put your name on that list. I had no idea who was on it until it was handed to me. But I should have found a way to warn you before I told everyone else. At the time, though, I was worried about that being seen as playing favorites."

"Playing favorites. We were living together at the time, no?" His jaw tightened. "It doesn't matter. It's... how do you say it? Water under the bridge. It's over."

Yes, it was. And so were they. The anguish of that day still washed over her at times. Except now they had a baby. Someone who could make her smile, make her glad that that period of her life had happened, despite the way it had ended.

Needing to pull herself together, she took her phone out of her pocket and checked it for text messages. There were none. Peggy knew her well enough to call or text if anything happened, even if it wasn't a big deal.

"Everything okay?" he murmured.

"Yes, just making sure Peggy wasn't trying to get a hold of me for anything."

"What time do you want to get home?"

The words confused her for a second, then she realized he was talking about his house, not her place back in Atlanta. "If the surgery won't run too long, I'm fine staying until the end."

They were still speaking in hushed tones, but Luca

hadn't tried to lean in close to her again, for which she was thankful.

Ears were now off-limits.

Although she wasn't sure how she was going to break that to him if he decided to translate for her again, or if she even wanted him to.

Because she had a strange feeling that if he leaned in and started whispering again, she would sit there and pay rapt attention. Not to the words. But to the way he made her feel.

Not good, Elyse.

But how exactly was she going to stop her reaction? It was almost as elemental as the tingling in her breasts had been during that kiss.

The man coaxed feelings from her that she neither wanted nor needed.

No, scratch that. She didn't need them, but she did want them.

Wanted them enough to kiss him, as she'd already proved.

So how was she going to fix that and prevent it from happening again?

Simple, she needed to avoid situations where her self-control was at risk.

Ha! You mean something like living under the same roof as the man? A stone's throw from his bedroom?

She sighed. Yes. Exactly like that.

Only now that she'd gotten herself into that situation, she had no idea how to get herself back out of it.

CHAPTER SIX

ANNA CHORTLED WHEN Luca bit into his toast.

He cocked his head, trying to figure out what was so funny about it.

"She laughs at odd things. It's like she's trying to figure out her world."

Elyse had evidently noted his confusion and tried to explain what was behind it.

Watching the baby on her lap, he forked up a bite of egg, giving an exaggerated *"mmm…"* of pleasure, and the laugh got louder, turned infectious enough that Elyse started giggling along with her.

"Who knew eating could be so amusing?"

"She's only doing it to you."

To prove her point, Elyse picked up her toast and bit off a piece of it, chewing with exaggerated movements of her jaw. Anna didn't even spare her mom a glance. She just kept staring at Luca.

He tapped his finger on the very end of the baby's nose. "Glad you find your…father…so funny."

Why had he hesitated over saying that? Was it because he still didn't quite believe a child so perfect and beautiful could possibly be his? Elyse had already offered to have a DNA test done but, like he'd told her, he didn't need one. The baby was his. He felt it in his bones. There were things about her coloring, how different her hair was from her mother's, that made him sure that Annalisa was from his family.

Except for the dimple in the baby's cheek, which she definitely got from her *mamma*. Elyse had a dimple on the very same side of her face. He could remember touching it when she smiled, fascinated by the way it puckered inward. It was hellishly attractive. And when he saw Elyse in his dreams, she always had that secret dimple.

He dreamed about her.

He could finally admit it to himself, if not to her. But he hadn't quite figured out how to deal with those dreams. And when he had been translating for Lorenzo a couple of days ago, it had come back to him that he'd muttered in her ear in one such dream, saying all the things he wanted to do to her. He'd woken up hard, needing her so badly. Only she hadn't been there. It had all been in his head.

Well, not all of it. It had been elsewhere too.

When his body had begun to react to those memories as he'd translated for the surgeon, he'd decided he needed to stop it. He'd backed off, needing to get himself under control. He'd thanked his lucky stars when she'd told him she didn't need him to translate for her anymore.

"I called my parents yesterday."

She stopped playing with Anna's fingers. "You did? What did they say?"

There was a nervousness to her voice that he didn't like. "I didn't exactly tell them. Not yet. I thought maybe it would be better just to let them see her and then explain it."

"I don't know... It was easier with my parents. Although they were upset that you'd left. I told them it was my fault, but they didn't quite believe me, I don't think."

"I was hurt. And angry. And things hadn't been going well between us for a while. I thought this was maybe your way of pushing me out of the picture."

She frowned. "I would have told you, if that were the case."

"So you think things were actually good?"

"I didn't say that."

He set down his fork. "You don't have to. We were over before you ever read out that list of names, and you know it."

"I guess we were."

She didn't look happy about that. Then again, she hadn't looked happy at the time either. She'd just looked...guilty.

He'd caught that same expression on her face a couple of times since she'd arrived in Italy, but he wasn't sure what that was about. At first he'd thought it was about her possible involvement in getting him fired. But she'd already made her big confession about that.

And yet even this morning she'd glanced at him and then looked away quickly.

Was she hiding something? Something other than her part in the layoffs?

He couldn't imagine what it might be. Or how it would even have anything to do with him, at this point. If Anna was his, that was the only thing that was important.

"You're okay with Mamma and Papà meeting her? And you, of course."

"I guess so. It's bound to be a shock, though. What if they hate me? I had convinced myself that because you didn't want children, you wouldn't want her either. I decided I'd come, do what I thought was right and then turn around and go home. I didn't stop to think who else might be impacted by the delay."

"I love her. How could I not? What I said back then about not wanting kids was…a moment of stupidity." She wasn't the only one who hadn't stopped to think about the impact of his behavior—or his words. He could see why she'd been afraid to tell him about Anna. "I'll just accentuate the positives when I tell them."

Her brows went up, and she shifted Anna to the other side of her lap. "Which are?"

"The fact that they have a healthy, happy grandchild. And…" What were the positives other than that? It was hard to list them when she said it in that tone of voice. "And they will fall in love with Anna as soon as they meet her."

"I hope so." She took another bite of her toast, chewing for a long time.

She was worried. So was he, for that matter. But what he'd said was true. Once they got over their surprise, they would welcome both Elyse and Annalisa with open arms. His mom would probably even try her hand at matchmaking—which he needed to shoot down right away and firmly explain that he and Elyse were no longer together, neither would they change their minds.

Was he so sure about that? He'd been positive that Elyse would forever reject his requests for a date. Then one day—out of the blue—she'd taken his hand and asked him instead. But that didn't mean she was suddenly going turn the tables and ask him to marry her.

If she'd accepted his proposal, would they be making an engagement announcement to his parents instead of just a birth announcement?

But she hadn't. And they weren't.

"It will be fine." He wasn't sure if he was trying to convince himself or her. "How is Peggy doing?"

Elyse smiled. "She's doing great, from what her texts and social media accounts say. She is taking full advantage of her newfound freedom. She's even been out on a date, which I did not approve of, by the way."

"You don't want her falling for an Italian?"

She laughed. "Since I fell for one once, that's not the issue. It's the fact that she's not going to be here long enough to start up anything meaningful."

"And encounters must always be meaningful?" He wondered if she would remember the first time they'd slept together. He had waited for that first date for so very long and when it had happened…it had been impulsive and wild, and she'd hooked him from the moment he'd caught his breath.

She looked away, those cheeks of hers turning a shade of pink that made his insides shift.

She did remember.

"At least we were living in the same country at the time," she said.

"So you wouldn't have given me the time of day if I'd been a tourist in your country?"

She wrinkled her nose at him. "Probably not. And since I was department head, I really shouldn't have done so even then." Her face went serious. "Those dynamics are never a good idea. I think we proved that."

He touched Annalisa's hand, the thought bothering

him somehow. "And yet if we hadn't gotten together, Annalisa wouldn't exist. Wasn't she worth it?"

Her teeth came down on her lip. There was a pause. One that was long enough to turn uncomfortable. Then she said huskily, "Yes. She was worth it. I'd do it all over again, even knowing what I know now."

"So would I."

She gave a sigh. "Hopefully your parents will feel the same way. That having a grandchild is okay even without having daughter-in-law attached. Someday, I'm sure you'll meet a wonderful Italian girl and settle down. Maybe you'll even change your mind about wanting kids sooner rather than later."

"I think I already have. Quite some time ago, actually. Things just didn't work out quite the way I thought they would."

"You did? I—I didn't realize."

Why had she said it that way? Was she hoping he already had someone so that she was free to pursue whoever she wanted? Would she get married and allow his daughter to become someone else's?

"I already have a child. Don't ever forget that."

She caught his hand. "I didn't mean it like that, Luca. I just meant that Annalisa isn't the only grandchild they're likely to have. And you're probably not going to be single the rest of your life."

He didn't see himself getting involved with anyone else for the foreseeable future, and he wasn't sure why. He'd immersed himself in work for so long, he wasn't sure he knew how to stop. At least he'd thought that until Elyse had come back into his life. And now suddenly he was rearranging everything in his life for her.

No, not everything. And it was for Anna, not for Elyse.

Only the hand holding his said that wasn't entirely true.

"For now, I'll leave it to my sisters to give them grandchildren. If they ever meet someone, that is."

He hadn't thought about what might happen if Elyse met someone else and they had a baby together. Would her husband or boyfriend insist she cut off contact with him? Deny him access to Anna?

That thought made him feel physically ill.

"I know we talked about it before, but I'd still like to draw up an agreement."

As soon as he saw her face, he realized it was the wrong thing to say. She let go of him and drew Annalisa closer to her. "What kind of agreement?"

He could have said a custody agreement, but he knew that would be met with swift resistance. Besides, she'd come to Italy in good faith, trying to do the right thing. She'd said so herself. And if he thought about it, Elyse was not the type of person to let herself be railroaded into anything.

He chose his words carefully. "About visitation."

The wariness didn't fade from her eyes. If anything, it grew. "You think we need something formal in writing? I wasn't planning on keeping her from you."

His intent hadn't been to make her angry, but something was going on with her that he really didn't understand.

"You talked about me meeting someone else, and it made me think about the reverse. That you might meet someone who wouldn't want me involved in your life or Annalisa's."

Her grip on the baby loosened. "Would *you* do that, if you had a child and started dating someone else: prevent the other parent from seeing him or her?"

"No. I wouldn't." There was no hesitation in his answer because it was the truth.

"Well, I wouldn't let someone do that to you either, Luca. I would never keep her from you unless I thought it was for her own good."

Her own good? How would that ever be the case?

It wouldn't. So stop being so sensitive to every little thing.

That was going to be hard. Because, like it or not, Elyse was only here for a little while. A month was nothing, in the greater scheme of things. And where Elyse went, Annalisa went.

"When you say 'for her own good' I'm not sure what that means."

She raised her brows and then grinned. "Well, let's see... If you were in an Italian prison on a life sentence for murder, I might hesitate before bringing her to see you."

He laughed. "Since I don't see that happening, I would have to have been wrongly convicted."

He'd been trying to lighten the mood, just like she had, but it must have fallen short because her smile faded. "What if you married someone who was unkind to Anna?"

Another hint that she had no intention of getting back together with him? It shouldn't sting, but it did.

"I will make sure that never happens." Not only because there were no current prospects but because he would never do anything to harm his daughter.

"How can you be so sure? Sometimes people aren't exactly who they seem on the surface."

He leaned closer, making sure she heard every word he said. "You seem determined to set me up with some unknown—but evidently unhinged—person. Why is that?"

"What? I'm not. I'm just setting up a hypothetical situation."

"Let's turn it around. What if you date a series of commitment-phobes and make Anna think relationships never last?" Lorenzo's knowing smile popped into his head. That man wouldn't know a serious relationship if it bit him on the ass. What if Elyse decided she liked that kind of man? After all, she seemed to have moved on with her life without a backward glance at him.

"I wouldn't. I won't. But I understand what you're saying. Let's just agree that we'll both try to do whatever's in her best interests."

The tense muscles along his shoulders eased their grip. "Agreed. Speaking of things that are in Annalisa's best interests, we've already talked about going to see my parents. Would you be okay with it being in the next couple of days? I know it's short notice, but I've checked my work schedule, and I think I can spare three or four days to spend with them."

"This soon?"

"Is that a problem?"

"No, I think I just expected us to have time to figure things out before jumping in at the deep end."

"If we wait until we iron out every tiny detail, Anna will be eighteen."

He'd decided that waiting for a break in his schedule wasn't going to happen if he didn't make it happen. This was the first step in doing that.

"You're right, of course. Let me check with Peggy, so she doesn't think I just abandoned her."

He'd forgotten about her aunt. "Does she need you to stay close by?"

"Are you kidding? She's pretty independent. I just meant that if she got into some kind of difficult situation, I'd want her to know how to reach me and that I'd be a few hours away. Oh! What should I take for a gift?"

"For my parents? No need to get them anything."

Annalisa started to squirm, a cry rising from her tiny chest. "I want to take something. I know they'd get a gift for me, wouldn't they?"

He held out his arms for the fussing baby. "Annalisa will be the only gift they need. They'll be thrilled to meet her and spend some time with her."

"I'm going to be stubborn on this one. Can you point me in the direction of a store that might have something they would like?"

He sighed. She wasn't going to take no for an answer. "Here in Italy flowers and wine are traditional gifts for a hostess, although I hope you'll think of my mother as more than just a hostess. She's Annalisa's grandmother."

"I know that. Really, I do. Any particular type of flowers?"

"Just not carnations. I know you use a lot of those in the States, but here they are primarily used for mourning and funerals."

"Okay." Her eyes widened. "Thanks for telling me that, because I almost certainly would have brought the wrong thing."

"I'll leave a couple of hours early on Friday and we

can get something before boarding the train. There are shops not far from the station."

Annalisa wiggled and gave another—angrier-sounding—cry. At which point Luca smelled something that wasn't quite right. In fact, it smelled a little bit like…

Poop.

No wonder she was fussy.

"Do you have a diaper bag nearby?"

"Why?" She glanced at the baby and then up at him. "Oh…she…"

"I do believe she's filled her diaper."

"I'll take her." She stood and reached her arms out for the baby, waiting until she was back in her possession before continuing. "I need to feed her, anyway, so I might as well change her too. We can go over Diapering for Beginners at another time."

He smiled, liking the fact that she was willing to let him take on some of Anna's care. Elyse had talked about her aunt being independent. Well, it must be a family trait, because that independent streak reached to the furthest branches on that particular family tree. "I'll look forward to it."

"Hmm." She rocked the baby back and forth. "Wait until you have one that shoots halfway up her back. You may change your mind."

"I won't. I promise." He nodded at his phone, which was on the counter. "I'll get the dishes cleaned up and then go to the hospital for a couple of hours. Maybe afterward we can do a little bit of sightseeing in town, if you and Anna are up for it."

"We will be, if you're sure you have the time."

"I'm learning to make time for what's important."

The smile she gave him reached her eyes, crinkling them at the corners. "Thank you, Luca. For everything."

She showed him how to strap the baby into the car seat she'd brought, unexpectedly nervous about spending time with him. Which was ridiculous. She'd spent loads of time with him when he'd lived in Atlanta. But this was different. That had been on her turf. And now she wasn't. She also had Annalisa to worry about as well. What if the baby was so fussy that she got on his nerves?

No, Luca was one of the most patient men she'd ever known. The only time she'd seen him truly irritated was when an insurance agency had tried to tell him that the procedure he'd wanted to do on a patient was experimental and wouldn't be covered. He'd hit the roof, going to the hospital administrator and demanding he help the company change their minds. Instead, the administrator had needed to sit Luca down and explain the way things worked in their health care system.

After a series of appeals and a peer-to-peer call between the insurance agency's doctor and Luca, they'd gotten it ironed out and the patient had gotten the surgery, which had ended up saving her life. From then on he'd been firm and insistent, but had followed the rules. In fact, Luca had been able to finagle more insurance coverage for patients than her, and she always tried her hardest.

It was in his voice. That deep mellow baritone that still made her knees go weak. It worked its magic on everyone. Except for hospital bean counters who were only worried about the profit margins and sometimes didn't see the faces behind their decisions. Like when they downsized her department. Now she was seriously overworked. So was everyone who was left in Neurology. In fact, Elyse wasn't taking new patients at all. She didn't have the time.

"There—is that right?" He fiddled with the straps to the car seat even after she'd assured him it was perfect.

"You're a careful driver, Luca, which helps."

He said maybe he'd changed his mind about having kids. When had that happened? When he'd seen his daughter for the first time? Her eyes closed, a lump forming in her throat. She was glad that he might want more. Wasn't she?

Thank God she hadn't accepted his marriage proposal only to find out he did indeed want more children.

He leaned over and kissed Annalisa's forehead, turning the lump in Elyse's throat into a boulder. "I will be even more careful than usual."

They got in, and he waited for her to buckle in as well. She gave an inward eye roll, swallowing down her earlier emotions and moving to a neutral subject. "How is Mrs. Landers?"

"I checked in on her yesterday. She's recovering nicely. They're hoping she can go home in a few more days. They want to make sure there's no more seizure activity first."

"Will they do physical therapy with her to help strengthen some of the affected muscles?"

"Yes, there is a rehab facility right next to the neural science clinic. And she'll be followed up by Lorenzo for a couple of months. Any scans will come through me, so I'll be able to see how she's doing as well."

In a couple of months Elyse would be long gone. She wasn't sure how she felt about that anymore.

Then they were on their way into the center of the city, where the famous Florence Cathedral could be seen.

"Why do you call the cathedral the *Duomo*?"

"It means dome, which is why most of the residents just use that, rather than its formal name, which is Cattedrale di Santa Maria del Fiore."

"Wow that's a mouthful. I can see how the Dome would be easier." Not only was it a mouthful but hearing Luca speak his native tongue still turned her insides to mush.

How was that even possible?

Within fifteen minutes they had found a paid parking area for the car. "Most of these are done with tour guides. We can join one of the groups, or we can do our own thing, whichever you prefer."

"I'm sure you know just about as much as the guides, so could we do it on our own, just in case Annalisa decides to give us trouble." She got out of the car and unstrapped the baby from the seat.

"I'll carry her."

"Are you sure? She gets heavy pretty quickly. I have a sling."

"She's as light as a feather. And, yes, I'm sure. Just show me how to put it on."

She helped Luca get fitted with the sling, surprised he would let himself be seen with something like that. But she had to admit he looked beyond sexy whenever he held Anna. Women were going to envy her. Little did they know they had nothing to fear.

He was available. But not today. Her chin went up. Today he was all hers.

She snugged Anna into the curve of the carrier. The poor thing blinked up at them as if trying to figure out what kind of trick this was.

It wasn't a trick, and Elyse had to admit she felt a trickle of jealousy. She used to love lying against the man's chest when they were in bed. And now they had a baby.

Before she could stop herself, she took her phone and snapped a picture of him.

"What are you doing?"

She had no idea. Just knew she wanted something to remember this moment by when she got back to the States. "She'll want pictures of you together."

It was a lie, but there was no way she was going to tell him the true reason. That there was something heartbreakingly beautiful about seeing him and Anna together.

He smiled. "As long as you don't plan to use it as blackmail material."

"Ha! No."

He settled the baby a little closer to his midsection, curving his left arm around her body. "We'll have to walk quite a bit as the streets near the center don't allow cars."

Another pang went through her. They'd done a lot of walking when they had been together in Atlanta. Only then they'd held hands as they'd strolled, having eyes only for each other. Sometimes those walks had even been cut short by a single look from him that had had them both hurrying back to her apartment.

There would be no holding hands today. Or hurrying home. Elyse gripped her hands together as if her life depended on it.

Maybe it did. Or at the very least her sanity.

She hadn't been able to get that kiss in his office out of her mind. It replayed itself time and time again, ending in that moment when her body had mistaken the signals for something else.

She hadn't explained it to him then, and she wasn't about to attempt an explanation now. Besides, it was better just to let him think that she'd come to her senses. And she had. Just not for the reasons he'd thought.

Despite all of that, it was exhilarating being with him, especially since there'd been a time when she'd thought she'd never lay eyes on him again.

It probably would have been better if she hadn't. His presence threatened to rip apart her defenses, leaving her wondering exactly what lay behind them. She had a feeling she knew. She just didn't want to face it.

She could get through a month, surely.

And meeting his parents? Would she get through that too? What if they tried to send little hints her way that she should marry their son? No. He wouldn't have told them about the proposal, surely.

"You doing okay?" He moved next to her, shoulder brushing over hers as he walked beside her. The brief contact and the concern in his voice left her with a longing that made her ache. He sounded like a concerned husband.

Only he wasn't.

And the sight of him carrying their child?

Oh, God. It looked natural, earthy, his white shirt rolled up over tanned forearms. Italians didn't dress down as much as Americans did, and seeing him in his own environment helped her understand so much about him. Like the fact that he hadn't been trying to impress people with his clothing choices when he'd been in Atlanta. It was just the way he was. His khaki slacks had a fresh-pressed look to them. Probably Emilia's doing, or maybe he took his clothes to a cleaner. But he was lean and devastatingly handsome with his sunglasses pushed on top of his head. Elyse had opted to slide hers down onto her nose, not so much to protect herself from the sun as to provide an additional barrier between them. Or maybe it was to keep him from reading her thoughts.

Evidently, Luca needed no such protection. He was confident and completely unmoved by her. Or was he? There had been moments when she'd been sure that—

"All roads lead to the Duomo."

"Excuse me?"

He grinned at her. "No. I mean literally. All the streets in this area empty out at the cathedral."

"Oh." She hadn't been so much confused by his words as that they'd echoed her thoughts. Because at the time they'd been together all her roads had led to Luca.

And he likely knew it. He had women throwing themselves at him all the time. There were several at the hospital who had given him sideways glances, probably wondering how someone like her had landed someone like Luca.

She couldn't have given them an answer, because she had no idea why he'd chosen her.

And their last act as a couple had been to make Annalisa.

The huge cathedral suddenly loomed in front of them, jerking her thoughts to a standstill.

It was huge. Magnificent.

She touched his arm, wishing she could loop hers through it, just like in days past. "I can't believe I'm standing here looking at something so incredibly gorgeous."

"Neither can I." The low words made her glance over at him. Then she swallowed. And swallowed again, unable to figure out how to keep breathing in and out.

Luca wasn't looking at the church. Or Anna. Or the surrounding area. His gaze was fixed wholly on her.

CHAPTER SEVEN

LUCA'S ARMS CRADLED the baby's body in an effort to keep from reaching out to Elyse. He'd dreamed of bringing her to his home country one day, of showing her the sights, and here they were. But it wasn't quite the way he'd envisioned it. Because in his fantasies they'd had a huge Italian wedding first, with all his family in attendance. And all hers.

Only life and egos and what he'd seen as deception on Elyse's part had changed everything.

But it hadn't been.

She'd said she hadn't been a part of the decision-making process regarding the layoffs. So this whole time he'd been operating under a faulty assumption. He suddenly looked at her through eyes that weren't quite so cynical—weren't quite so unforgiving.

But did it change anything, really? The events leading up to the firing hadn't changed. And at the time they hadn't been able to see their way through them.

And now?

"Scusami. Una foto?"

He jerked back to reality, realizing someone was trying to take a picture and he and Elyse were in the way. Staring at each other like star-crossed lovers.

"Mi dispiace."

They moved out of the line of fire and headed toward the cathedral itself. He could try to say he'd been looking at something in the distance and not at her, but it would be a lie. And he couldn't bring himself to force out the words. So he just kept walking.

Annalisa chose that moment to wake up, blinking eyes coming up to meet his.

Elyse was there immediately, leaning over to look at her. "I'm here, sweetheart."

His chest contracted. For the last four months, Elyse's face had been the first and last thing his daughter had seen each day. It was as if he hadn't existed.

And whose fault was that? If he hadn't stormed off after they'd had sex that last time —if he'd swallowed his damned Latin pride and come back and demanded she answer his questions about the layoffs and why she was pushing him away—he might have been able to experience his daughter's birth. Her first smile. And she might see him as a parent figure instead of just some random face in the crowd.

Elyse unbuckled their daughter and swung her up into her arms.

She glanced at him, as if realizing something was wrong. "I'm sorry. Why don't you hold her without the sling? She needs to get to know you."

It was as if she'd read his mind. And if the baby started crying?

Well, it was something they would have to work through if he wanted to be a part of her life. And he did. Objectively, it might be easier just to turn away and pretend none of this had ever happened, but he couldn't.

Not only because he wanted to do the right thing but also because he already loved her.

In only four days.

It was unreal, but it was true.

He held his arms out and Elyse placed the baby in them for the umpteenth time. And it was magic. All over again. This was his child. His daughter.

He talked to her in Italian, just muttering things in a long stream of consciousness way that probably wouldn't make any sense to anyone. But he didn't care. There were emotions bottled up inside him that needed an outlet and it was better if Elyse didn't understand the words.

He bounced Anna gently, moving a little distance away. She was listening.

Whether it was five minutes or fifteen, he wasn't sure, but he finally walked back to Elyse, just as Anna started to squirm. "It's okay. Mamma is right here."

"And so is Daddy."

He wished she would stop smiling. Stop seeming soft and approachable again, unlike those last days when her demeanor had been cool and sharp.

There was a part of him that said he wasn't as over her as he'd thought he was. As he'd hoped he was.

He shut those thoughts down as the line started to move, and they had to put Annalisa back in the sling. Then they were finally inside the famed Florence Cathedral.

He wasn't disappointed by her reaction. Elyse gasped when she caught sight of the mosaic floors that were laid out in a grid, each section boasting a new pattern. He tried to see them through her eyes, although it was hard, since patterned streets, sidewalks and the like were such an ordinary part of life in Europe.

These were magnificent, however. And they were spotless.

He rocked Annalisa so Elyse could enjoy the sights without interruption. And she did, even as they moved along with the crowds. The tour groups were instructed not to linger so that everyone got a chance to see it. And even though their party was small enough that they weren't required to join one of the groups, he could tell Elyse was trying to be considerate of those behind them. Keeping his voice hushed as was the custom inside, he said, "It's beautiful at night with the lights. Maybe after our meal we can come back and look."

"I'd love that."

"Do you want to climb to the cupola?"

She glanced at Annalisa. "I don't think so. Not with her. I'm just happy to have been able to see the inside. The floors and ceilings are beyond anything I could have imagined."

The wave of tourists washed them back toward the exit, the crowd pinching together as it neared the doorway.

There was a sudden staccato burst of sound up ahead and then a scream of pain. Everyone froze for a second, then someone behind Luca shoved his shoulder and forced his way past. Someone else did the same. The crowd came to life, and what had been a steady procession became a frenzied rush as more and more people struggled to get to the exit.

Luca hadn't thought it sounded like gunfire, although in this day and age he couldn't rule it out.

He grabbed Elyse's hand when it looked like they

might be separated, keeping his arm curled around Anna to keep her from being crushed against those in front of him. "Stay close!"

She did, letting go of his hand and wrapping one arm around his waist and gripping his sleeve with the other. They got to the doorway and Luca got a glimpse of something he recognized. A walker. Flattened as if it had been folded and lying on the floor. And next to it...

Oh, hell. He braced himself and stopped, using his body to force those behind him to flow around. Elyse saw it at the same time he did.

Blood. And gray hair.

"God! We have to help her."

"Take Anna and go. I'll see if I can at least keep them off her until help comes. Tell anyone you see who looks official what's happened."

It wasn't easy, but they managed to get the baby out of the sling, and Elyse took her, doing her best to maintain her footing as she was swept through the doors along with the stream of tourists. He didn't dare kneel to check the victim; instead, he turned to face those still coming toward him, making himself as big as possible and shouting at those who would have shoved him aside, first in Italian and then in English. "Go around! There's an injured woman."

It worked. He kept shouting for what seemed like an hour, but was probably five minutes before the crowd thinned, slowed and then dissipated. He saw a set of barricades about twenty yards away, holding the people back.

He swiftly knelt to tend to the woman, a nun, her head covering pulled away. Blood came from a split lip and there was also a large gash on her forehead, the blood from which had formed a small puddle on the mosaic. She'd probably lost her footing and been trampled. A security guard hurried over and with him was Elyse.

"Thank you," he said to her. "Are you and the baby okay?"

"We're fine. They've called for a rescue squad."

She must have found someone who spoke English.

He felt for a pulse. It was strong but quicker than he'd like. "She's breathing, but probably has a concussion at the very least."

"Pupils?"

He smiled up at her. "You read my mind." He opened the woman's eyes one at a time and checked the pupillary reflexes as Elyse knelt on the mosaic floor next to him, still holding the baby.

"They're both reactive. A very good sign." He then ran his hands over her arms and legs, palpating for breaks.

"There."

"What is it?"

The bone in her left leg was pressed against the skin but hadn't pushed through.

He didn't pull away the clothing, just said, "Her femur is broken. It won't take much to become an open fracture. We can't move her until the squad gets here."

"I agree."

Switching to Italian, he explained the situation to the guard. Not to mention there was no way of knowing if there were spinal or internal injuries.

Two other nuns approached. One of them put a hand over her mouth, turning her face toward the other in shock.

"It's Sister Maria. She fell behind our group. We're visiting from Rome. We had no idea she was hurt."

Elyse stood, putting her hand on the stricken nun's shoulder. "Help is coming."

The guard asked how many were in their party.

The one who'd spoken up answered. "There are two more sisters outside. They're waiting to see if we could find Maria. Will she be all right?"

Maria's eyes flickered and then opened, and she moaned, even as she tried to shift, one hand trying to reach her leg.

Luca pressed gently against her shoulder. "Lie still. You've been hurt. I'm Dr. Venezio and this is Dr. Tenner. We're going to stay with you until help arrives. Does anything hurt besides your leg?"

The woman closed her eyes for a minute, maybe taking stock of the different parts of her body. "My head. The fingers of my hand." She raised it to show digits that were swollen and purple.

He winced. How many shoes had trodden on that frail hand? Thank God Elyse had made it out with the baby. The same thing might have happened to her. Gently taking the nun's hand, he felt it, stopping when she gasped. He reassured her and then turned to Elyse.

"They'll need to get an X-ray to be sure, I can't feel past the edema."

Elyse nodded. "Could be crush injuries. They'll need to watch for compartment syndrome."

"I agree."

He'd forgotten how well they worked together. Most times, anyway. He glanced at Anna, surprised to see she was silently taking it all in.

A team pushing a stretcher hurried toward them. Luca quickly went through who they were and what they knew about the patient. "Trampling incident. She has a fractured left femur, which needs to be splinted. She'll probably also need her spine stabilized and a neck brace. Vitals are good, but she's complaining of pain in her head and her hand is pretty swollen, there may be a bleeder in there."

One of the techs was trying to get everything down while the other one gathered the necessary equipment from his bag. With Luca guiding the process with some input from Elyse, they soon had Maria loaded while someone went to find the other nuns, who were waiting outside, to let them know what had happened.

And then they were gone, leaving Luca to stand and reach down a hand to help Elyse up, as she was still holding Anna. They went outside before the barricades were taken down and watched to make sure there were no other incidents.

"Well, that wasn't how I expected the tour to end," he said.

"I'm just glad no one else was hurt. Trampling incidents can be horrific. She's lucky she's alive."

"Yes, she is." Something made him drape his arm around her shoulders and give her a quick squeeze. Maybe just thankfulness that it hadn't been her or Anna who'd been injured, even though he was sorry that anyone had been caught in that. All he could assume was that the walker had toppled over, hitting the hard floor a couple of times. The sound of it could have made people jump to the worst possible conclusion and panic, especially when combined with the screaming. As a result, an innocent woman had been badly hurt.

Elyse laid her head on his shoulder, sending warmth washing through his chest. He tightened his grip.

Never in his wildest dreams about her had he pictured this scenario.

But he liked it. A little too much.

"You're still wearing Anna's baby sling, you know. I think you got a couple of sideways looks from those guards."

"Let them look. I'm proud to wear it."

"Are you?" She glanced up at him for a moment and there was something in those big eyes of hers that made him wish for impossible things.

He didn't think she'd want to know what he'd really like to do. What being with her right now was making him think. And adding that smile *à la* Elyse? It was deadlier than any aphrodisiac known to man. No little blue pills needed.

"I am."

Standing outside the cathedral once more, he glanced at his watch. Five thirty. It was still early by Italian standards, but maybe they could get into a restaurant without the normal crush of people. He actually knew of a place closer to the clinic that a lot of the staff went to. It would also give them a chance to swing by the house before they ate and change their clothes. He let go of her and held his arms out for the baby. "Are you hungry? I thought we might go out to eat early."

"That sounds wonderful."

When they got back to the house, Emilia was still there and insisted on staying to watch the baby while they went out and had an uninterrupted meal.

"Do not hurry back. I not hold baby since…my babies…" She held her hands to show how little they'd been, then reached out for Anna.

It was hard to say no when she so obviously enjoyed

cuddling Annalisa in her arms. She dropped into one of Luca's recliners, which had a rocking feature.

He pulled Elyse aside. "She'll be fine, I promise. And Emilia will call my cell if there are any problems."

"I trust her. And I need to buy more diapers, since I'm close to running out of the supply I brought with me. Can we stop by a grocery store?"

"Yes. Of course. I should have thought of that."

"Some things don't cross your mind until it becomes a necessity."

He puzzled through the words. Was she only talking about diapers? Or was there another meaning behind the words.

Regardless, it was true. He'd just instituted a new rule of no touching when it came to Elyse, born out of necessity. Having his arm around her outside the Duomo had made him realize how dangerous it was to touch her, even when it started out innocently enough.

They said goodbye to Emilia and headed out in the car.

"Should we bring something back for her?"

"She'll have already prepared a meal and put it in the fridge. There is usually a lot of leftover food. I normally send some of it home with her, so she knows to eat what she wants."

"Oh, no. I didn't realize she was cooking something for us tonight."

"We'll eat it tomorrow. It's fine."

"If you're sure. How long has she been with you?"

"She is actually one of my parents' housekeepers. She's been with them for more years than I can remember. When I came back to Italy, she volunteered to come and make sure I didn't starve—my mom's words."

"I guarantee you won't. Not with the way she cooks." She paused, then added, "What happens if you leave again?"

Was she talking about her suggestion that he move back to the States? He loved his work at the clinic—felt like he was doing a lot of good where he was.

But he also loved his daughter. Wouldn't he move heaven and earth for the chance to be with her?

Yes, he would.

"If I left, she would probably opt to go back to my parents." His mother and father were wealthy, his father managing his own shipping company. "She's part of the family. They love her."

She laughed. "Your parents sound like great people. I'm still a little nervous about meeting them, though. Especially under these circumstances."

He could understand that. He was still a little worried about their reaction himself. But probably not for the same reasons she was.

"You'll like them. And they'll love you."

"As much as they love Emilia?" She smiled as she said it.

"More."

She blew out a breath. "Did you tell them after we talked last time?"

He knew she was referring to Anna. "Not yet. I've been thinking through my approach."

"If we just show up with her in tow, that conversation might prove to be a little more difficult."

She was right. He couldn't just spring it on them and pray for the best. Especially not if Elyse was in the room. His parents needed time to digest the information and plan how they were going to approach it before they got there. "I'll do it tonight."

"Good." She looked relieved, getting out of the car and surveying their surroundings. "This is lovely."

"It's close to the clinic and pretty popular."

"I can see why."

They went in and the scents of garlic and mozzarella tickled his nose, making his mouth water. The hum of voices and laughter only added to it. He'd been right to come to Florence. He'd loved the city from the moment he'd set foot into it. There were complaints about the tourists from some quarters, but having lived in another country for over a year he felt a kinship with them that killed a little of the homesickness he'd felt for Atlanta. Even now when he heard a Southern accent from the States, it brought back memories. Good memories of warm food and even warmer people, even if he never had gotten the hang of drinking iced tea.

And if he moved back to the States, he would have to leave his new city behind.

"Luca! *Qui!*" He turned his head and saw Lorenzo motioning them over.

"Dammit." He groaned aloud. "Did I say this was a good idea?"

"Embarrassed to be seen with me?"

There was something in her face that said she really believed he might be.

"What? *Dio*, no. I'd hoped to have a little time alone with you after sharing you with the clinic." He hurried to add, "To discuss our future. With Annalisa." He was making a mess out of this whole thing.

Then again, he'd made a mess out of his relationship with her as well. They might as well join Lorenzo and the other two surgeons at the table. What happened to this being an early time to eat for Italians?

A waitress came up to them, and he motioned to the trio at the table. "Could we get another chair?"

She brought one and everyone adjusted their places to accommodate them. Even with the moves, Luca found himself squeezed in next to Elyse, knees touching. There was no way to avoid it. When he glanced at Lorenzo, who was on the other side of her, he wondered if her knees were touching his as well. The idea made him subconsciously press a bit closer, an impulse he neither liked nor welcomed.

Giorgino introduced her to the other two doctors, not waiting for Luca to translate. Drs. Fasone and Bergamini each stood to shake her hand.

He told the other two in Italian that Elyse was a surgeon in the US.

Dr. Fasone cocked his head. "What do you specialize in?"

"I'm a neurosurgeon."

Fasone smiled. "Working at a neuro-clinic, you can be fairly sure that many of us are as well."

Coming here had been a huge mistake. The only married man in the party was Dr. Bergamini.

Why did he even care? He and Elyse were no longer together. It shouldn't matter if she set her sights on someone else.

Well, Lorenzo was a serial dater, out with a new woman almost every week. And Fasone was…well, he was just a nice guy. Someone exactly like Elyse might fall for. He'd certainly be a stable influence on Anna. But that didn't make Luca like it any better.

He was suddenly conscious that his knee was clamped to hers. Unconsciously claiming her for his own?

Dannazione. He needed to get himself together.

He did that by remaining silent while they exchanged stories, with Lorenzo telling the other two doctors about the cavernoma surgery and Elyse's part in it. "It is sometimes good to have an outside perspective, yes?"

Lorenzo smiled at her in a way that made Luca tense. The server came over and took his and Elyse's orders.

"I'll have whatever you're having," she murmured to Luca. The urge to shoot the other surgeon a look of triumph came and went. He was being childish. She wasn't going to fall for Lorenzo's charm.

He ordered two plates of ravioli with salads on the side, then paused for a second, turning to her. "Salads here come with anchovies. Do you want yours without?"

She blinked. "I've never tried them, but if that's how the salad comes, that's how I'd like mine."

A sliver of pride went through him. Not so much for his homeland but for the fact that Elyse was willing to eat what was common in his culture. "I hope you like it more than I did your sweet tea."

"Didn't I tell you? That's what I'd like to drink with my meal."

This time he laughed. "We have enough tourists that some of the restaurants do serve it. This one, I'm not so sure."

"I was joking. I'll have a sparkling mineral water."

He frowned. "No wine?" In the States she drank wine and Italy was known for its wide array of good ones.

"Not tonight." She gave him a pointed look, and then

he realized she couldn't, because of Anna. How stupid could he be? It was too bad. He'd hoped to introduce her to Chianti—produced in the town that bore its name—which was only around fifty miles from here.

"Do they have sparkling water?"

"Yes." He turned to the server. *"Acqua frizzante e un chiante."*

Once the server left, he glanced at the men. "You've already ordered?"

"Right before you came in," Lorenzo responded, turning to Elyse once more. "You like the food *dall'Italia*?"

"I love it." This time her knee nudged Luca's twice. She'd sensed the hint of flirtation in Lorenzo's manner and was reassuring him. It was an old game they'd played many times before. If another man so much as looked at her, or if he thought someone was trying to come on to her, she would touch him. Or nudge his knee under the table. Or lay her hand on his thigh to reassure him that she wanted to be there with him. Only him.

That wasn't the case here, but it still helped his muscles release some of their tension. She was telling him she wasn't going to respond to the other man's subtle advances. Luca had never been outwardly jealous, but she'd always been able to sense when he became uneasy.

Drinks were soon poured, and Lorenzo gave a toast in Italian, which Luca translated. "To interesting cases and even more interesting conversation." This time, though, Luca sent the other man a slight frown, which resulted in raised brows on Lorenzo's part. But he helped steer the conversation back to neutral territory,

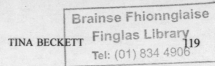
with the other surgeons asking about procedures in the States and comparing them to Italian medicine.

"What was your most disappointing case?" Fasone asked.

This time Luca did tense. He was pretty sure that would be the case that he and Elyse had disagreed on so vehemently and in which they had both been wrong. A simple blood test had ruled it to be something else entirely, but the diagnosis had come too late.

"Well, we had a patient who came in suffering from massive headaches that weren't responding to over-the-counter pain meds. The symptoms led me to suspect a tumor and Luca disagreed, thinking she had a blood clot. An MRI showed we were both wrong. But almost as soon as we wheeled her out of the imaging room, she threw a clot and had a massive stroke. She had polycythemia vera."

Luca added. "Her bone marrow was producing too many blood cells. But they were platelets, not the red blood cells normally found in the condition. It was a rarer form of the disease."

Fasone grimaced. "That's tough. It doesn't sound like you had much hope of saving the patient even if you had diagnosed it from the beginning, though."

"No, she waited too long to come in. She'd been experiencing symptoms for several years and there was already evidence of a couple of previous transient ischemic attacks."

"I'm surprised you two are still talking," Giorgino said with a smile. "Those are the kinds of disagreements that can ruin friendships."

He didn't know the half of it, but Luca forced a shrug.

"We were both wrong. So I guess there was no gloating to be done."

Elyse added in a soft voice, "No, there wasn't."

But the disruption of a staff meeting followed by a two-hour argument over whose hypothesis they should follow had damaged their relationship. Not long afterward, the ax had fallen in the form of jobs disappearing.

She'd said she was sorry for that. And he believed her. But did it change anything? In some ways, maybe it did.

Their salads and antipasto came, and the conversation turned to food without him having to force the issue, which he was more than ready to do. If the subject of their breakup was going to be rehashed, he certainly didn't want it to be in front of an audience.

Elyse speared a piece of lettuce and added one of the slivers of anchovies. He waited while she put the bite in her mouth. Her eyes widened.

"Verdict?"

"It's salty. And quite strong. But I like it." She tilted her head and looked at the other surgeons. "So your turn. What were your most disappointing cases?"

They each shared a case that had turned out badly. One had been human error, but the others had all been just the difficulty of coming up with a speedy diagnosis when things were already heading south. So he and Elyse weren't the only ones who'd lost patients. And the PV case wasn't his only difficult one, but it had been the most dramatic. And the one with the most personal repercussions.

Was there anything he could have done differently?

He wasn't sure. If Elyse hadn't already started to subtly withdraw from him, it might not have become the volcano it had. But she had. In tiny increments he hadn't understood but which had become pronounced after the death of the patient.

Maybe it had been the fact that he and Elyse had worked too closely together. The emotions of their relationship had gotten in the way of how they'd dealt with that patient—he could see that now. It had also got in the way of how they'd responded to each other in the midst of that crisis. Sharp words had cut more deeply. Anger had seemed ten times more significant than it should have.

Her knee had shifted away from his when talking about the PV patient, but as the others had shared their defeats, she'd relaxed once again.

Her blond hair shimmered in the dimly lit restaurant. And with her expressive face, hands moving as she discussed disease processes, he could see why Lorenzo— or any man, for that matter—would be attracted to her. She had it all. Brains, beauty and an innate kindness that was rare. A man would be a fool not to be drawn to her.

Luca found himself staring at her, loving the way she smiled. And frowned. The sound of her voice. The way she listened intently as she tried to find her way around accents and unfamiliar words.

He pushed his plate away, just as she turned to him. "Do we need to check in with Emilia?"

"Maybe. I'm finished if you are."

"I am."

Luca motioned for the check and paid their bill.

She smiled at the table as they stood. "Thank you for entertaining me. I'm sure there are things you would have preferred to talk about other than medicine."

Bergamini, who'd been the quietest of the bunch, said, "It's always interesting to observe how we deal with difficult diagnoses." He fixed Luca with a stare. "Sometimes we get it right. And sometimes we don't. When that happens, we need to learn from our mistakes. And try not to repeat them."

The man wasn't talking about their cases. No wonder he hadn't said much. He'd been "observing" but it had had nothing to do with medicine and everything to do with relationships. It stood to reason. He'd been married a long time, so he'd obviously figured out how to get it right.

Well, contrary to the man's opinion, Luca *had* learned from his mistakes. He may not have gotten everything right, but he'd come out on the other side with some new ways of dealing with issues.

Mostly that meant not getting involved with the opposite sex. But was that because of the breakup? Or because he was still hung up on the mother of his child?

Soon they were out of the restaurant, the cool air showing the first hints of autumn. By the time Elyse left Italy, temperatures would be dropping at night and staying cooler during the day.

She glanced at him. "Hey. That case we had. It was a hard call. I'm sorry I was so hateful during that."

"You weren't hateful. Just…passionate." He hesitated. "And just so you know, I wasn't aware there was a possibility of a pregnancy that last night or I wouldn't have left, I hope you know that."

He tried to figure out how to express himself. "Our relationship had become like the PV patient: producing an unhealthy amount of tension with no way to drain it off."

Treating polycythemia vera often meant drawing off excess blood in a phlebotomy session. It lowered the red blood cell count, lowering the risk of a heart attack or stroke.

She sighed. "Maybe it's true what they say about business and pleasure. They need to be kept separate."

"With us, there was no way of doing that. We were already involved and both in the same line of work." He smiled. "And that's what drew us together in the first place."

"Really? That's funny, because I was only interested in your…looks."

That made him laugh, since that word had always been her euphemism for something else. "You were, were you?"

She tossed her hair over her shoulder and glanced back at him. "You were always pretty damned good in…the looks department."

The joking faded away, at least on his part. She still thought that? Even after all that had happened? Well, hadn't he just thought about how gorgeous she was a few minutes ago?

The attraction was still there on both sides. "I was staring at you back in the restaurant, thinking about how heartbreakingly beautiful you are and how I didn't want Lorenzo Giorgino anywhere near you."

She stopped in her tracks and turned to look at him. "Enzo doesn't appeal to me at all. Oh, he's nice enough, and he's certainly good-looking, but I have a feeling he has a serial case of wandering eyes."

Ah, so she had seen through him. "He tends to date a lot of different women. And I don't like it that he has you calling him Enzo."

"You don't?" She smiled. "Well, you don't have to worry. My sights were always set on a completely different Italian."

Those words hung between them, and Luca moved a few steps closer, stopping right in front of her. "They were?"

"Yes." The whispered word slid through his senses like silk, winding around them and holding them hostage.

He swallowed. "Do I know this Italian?"

"I would hope so." Her palm went to the back of his head, fingers sliding beneath the hair at his nape, sending a shudder through him.

"Because...it's you, Luca."

CHAPTER EIGHT

His KISS TOOK her by storm, the awareness that had been bubbling just beneath the surface finally blowing the lid from the pan.

She loved the feel of his mouth on hers.

She always had. She'd ached for him since the day she'd landed in Italy. Long before that, actually.

She wanted him.

Desperately.

She was no longer his boss; there was no need to worry about consequences or what would happen tomorrow. They'd be dealing with each other for the rest of their lives. Wouldn't it be better if they were on good terms?

She shut down the center of her brain that sent out a warning that good terms and sex were not necessarily one and the same.

The kiss deepened, his tongue playing with the seam of her mouth.

God, she wanted to let him in. She pulled back, glancing pointedly at the door to the restaurant. They were still within twenty yards of it. She didn't want Lorenzo or any of the others seeing them. If this was going to happen, she wanted it to be in a place where it was just her…and him. "Let's go somewhere else."

"We can't go home."

Home. Did he even realize he'd said that as if it were her home too? She forced herself not to analyze that too closely. Especially since the word had been said against her lips in a way that pushed her closer to a line she recognized all too well.

"Hotel?"

"They'll be filled with tourists." He stared into her eyes. "How adventurous are you?"

"If you mean sex on a zip line, probably not that adventurous." She smiled. "We could always go back to your office."

"Mmm…" He smiled. "We've done the office bit once before. I was thinking of somewhere a little more intimate. Where we're guaranteed our privacy."

"Sounds promising." She slid her thumb over his lips. "So where is this mysterious place?"

"My car."

A ripple of excitement went through her. Luca always had brought a hint of danger to his lovemaking, going as far as sliding his hand under her dress once in an empty elevator. He hadn't taken her over the edge but had gotten her so desperate that she'd attacked him as soon as they were back in her apartment.

"And I know the perfect parking place. Are you up for it?"

"Yes." She trusted him not to put her in a position where she would be embarrassed.

He drove a few miles, his hand high on her thigh, reminding her of that encounter in the elevator. But this time he didn't venture any farther. Somehow that heightened her anticipation. Made her want him that much more. Fifteen minutes later, they pulled up in front of a gated house. No lights were on. "Are they home?"

"No, but it doesn't matter. We're not going inside. Reach into the glove box. There's a remote."

She quickly handed it over and watched as he pushed the button, sending the gates sliding in opposite directions.

"It's a friend's," he said. "I'm watching it for him."

"No cameras?"

"No."

"Ah...so this is what you meant."

"Yes. No one's around." He followed the driveway around to the side, where they were concealed from the nearby houses by a natural screen of vegetation. "The neighbors all know my car, and that I'll be popping in periodically to check on things."

"This probably isn't what your friend had in mind."

He turned off the engine and leaned over to kiss her. "Oh, I plan to check on things."

Lord, those "things" were starting to heat up. The thought of having sex in a car was suddenly the only thing she wanted to do. It was a first. One of many she'd had with this man.

But... She needed to do something before they reached the point of no return. Give him time to back out. Placing her hands on either side of his face, she held him a few inches away from her. "I have to tell you something. The last time we kissed, well... Something happened. Something you need to know about."

He gave her a wolfish grin. "Don't worry. It made some things happen to me as well."

"No, this was…embarrassing. My…um, breasts started tingling. Like when I get ready to nurse Anna."

His eyes widened. "That's why you pulled away?"

She nodded.

"*Dio*. I thought…" He closed his eyes and pressed his forehead to hers. "Never mind. It doesn't matter."

"Are you sure?"

Instead of answering, he leaned over and undid her seat belt, hands going to the bottom of her T-shirt and tugging it over her head. Her bra soon followed. "All I want to think about right now is you. And me. And what we're about to do."

Then he let himself out of the car.

"What are you doing?"

He opened her door and took her hand.

"I thought you said we weren't going inside."

"We're not, but it's a beautiful night. And I want to see you in the moonlight."

She stepped out of the car, trusting him when he closed the door and turned her around. He gathered her hair in his hand and leaned over to kiss her neck. "We're not going any farther than the hood of the car, where we're not cramped, and I can do this." His arms came around her and palmed her breasts, the sweet friction on her nipples making her moan.

"*Dio*. I love the sounds you make. Love what they do to me."

His hands slid over her torso and rounded her hips. Then his fingers walked down the backs of her thighs, the flow of cool air hitting her legs as he scrunched the fabric of her long gauzy skirt in his hands, his teeth still skimming the sides of her neck. It was heady and naughty, and she was frantic with need.

He'd always been good at this.

How she'd missed it. Missed him.

She gasped when he bent her over the hood of the car, which was still warm from the drive over. He braced his hands on either side of her, his hips pressed tight against her bottom.

Giving a shaky laugh, she said, "I don't think the nuns would approve of my attire right now."

"Maybe not, but I approve *con tutto il mio cuore*."

He played with the elastic of her boy-shorts. "I have missed your ridiculous choice of undergarments."

But it was said in a way that was the opposite of ridiculous. Evidently she wasn't the only one who'd missed things. She loved it when he mixed Italian with English. The more caught up he got, the more he reverted to the language of his heart. And it tugged at hers, turning her insides to mush.

Then those shorts were being pushed down. "Step out of them."

Gladly. And when his leg came between hers and urged them apart, she swallowed, spreading for him.

She would be lucky if she lasted until he was inside her. His wallet landed on the car next to her. Just when she was trying to figure out what he was doing, she heard the ripping of foil packaging.

Oh, God, she was so desperate for him, she hadn't even thought of protection—or the fact that she no longer needed it. An arrow ripped through her heart and came out the other side. The pain was short-lived, though, because right now nothing was more important than being with him.

The slow snick of a zipper made her heart pound.

So close.

There was a momentary pause as she imagined him rolling the condom down his length. Then he was back, and one hand slid under her rib cage, finding her nipple without hesitation, pulling hard and strong in rhythmic strokes.

"Ahh…" The sound came out as a long breath of air.

"You make my loins want to explode."

The odd wording would have made her giggle under normal circumstances, but right now she had never felt less like laughing in her life. Her body wound hard and tight with the continued stimulation. She'd never felt anything like this in her life.

She should ask him to slow down, but she didn't want to. Wasn't even sure she was capable of speech right now.

And that spring inside her was slowly twisting, getting closer and closer to the breaking point. She pushed her hips back, finding him briefly only to have him slide back out of reach.

"No!"

"What do you want, *cara*?" he squeezed her nipple and held it tight.

She pressed her lips together to keep from crying out, but the words spilled past the barrier. "I want you inside me. Please."

"Yes! *Dio*." His initial thrust was hard and fast, filling her completely.

A second later, she went off, her body contracting crazily around him.

He grabbed her hips and stabbed into her with an intensity that made her breathless and weak.

Then he gave a hoarse shout, before going completely still, straining inside her for several long seconds.

Then he slowly relaxed, curving his body over hers and staying right where he was.

He was still for what seemed like an eternity but was probably only minutes.

"Hell, Ellie, that was…"

"I know." His use of that pet name brought tears to her eyes. Ever since she'd arrived, he'd called her Elyse. Until now.

What had happened to them? How had life become such a damned struggle? But that was then. This was now. So what was holding them back from being together?

He eased out of her and turned her around to face him. He leaned down and gently kissed her, even as he crumpled the empty foil from the condom. That act made the tears that had been teetering on the edge of her lashes overflow their banks.

That. That's what was holding her back.

Stopping, he looked at her. "What's wrong?"

She gave him a shaky smile. "Hormones." It was a lie. But it was all she had.

"You're sure?"

"It's just been a while. I'm good. Just weepy in general." About the fact that they would never again produce a beautiful baby like Anna. That suddenly seemed like the biggest tragedy imaginable.

He nodded as if knowing he needed to give her a little space. Handing her the discarded pieces of clothing, he turned to give her privacy, zipping himself back into his khakis. Hurrying to get dressed, she dried her eyes, grateful to him. And very glad that this had happened here rather than at his place or, worse, at his parents' house. If it had to happen, better for it to be on neutral ground. Ground that she would never see again.

"Thank you," she said.

"For what?"

She wasn't sure. The gift of being with him one more time, maybe? "For not being weirded out by my crazy emotions."

"I have never been, how did you say…'weirded out' by anything to do with you." He tipped her chin up. "We are good?"

"Yes. We are." Good, but still not back together. There were no words of undying love. Which she was glad of, right? That would only create complications further down the road that neither of them wanted. His life was here now. And hers was back in the States. Anna was the only thing linking them.

At least for now.

Once their daughter was old enough to travel on her own, they wouldn't need to ever see each other again.

No. She'd already thought this through. There was always Anna's wedding and, later, hopefully grand-children.

She frowned. Why was she trying to find excuses to see him?

Probably because there was still a part of her that cared about him. That probably always would.

Not a good thing.

Because she was discovering that looking at some-thing through the eyes of passion was a whole lot dif-ferent than seeing it in the cold light of satiation. And as reality crept up over the horizon and shone down on them, Elyse wondered what this would look like to her tomorrow. The next day. And on the day she actually left Italy—and returned home to Atlanta.

Luca threw a bucket of water over the hood of his car, removing any evidence of what had happened last night. Not that they'd left any marks that he could find. Only the ones burned into his skull.

What the hell had he been thinking?

He didn't know.

They'd wanted each other, there was no doubt about that. But he'd wanted women long before he'd known Elyse and had not acted on that desire. He'd never been one for casual sex that went nowhere. And as it stood right now, his relationship with Elyse would do just that: go nowhere. And tomorrow they were to leave for their trip to Rome.

Elyse had brought Annalisa out for breakfast, but would barely look at him, which was why he'd gone out to wash his vehicle down, thinking maybe the physical act would help him erase the thoughts clogging up his head. He rubbed the hood dry, trying to blot out the heady memories of having her in his arms.

Impossible. They were engraved on his nerve endings and written on his heart. But he was going to have to figure out how to live with those memories or find a way to bury them.

Elyse came into the garage unexpectedly and glanced at the car before looking back at him. "Could I talk to you for a minute?"

He threw the rag into the bucket and faced her. "Okay."

"I'm not quite sure how to say this."

His sense of foreboding grew. "I find the best way is to just say it."

"About the trip tomorrow…"

"Yes?" Was she going to back out?

"I don't want to share a bedroom with you when we get there."

He sagged against the fender of the car, laughing. "Is that all?"

"I'm not sure why that's funny, but yes."

He glanced up to see a hint of anger in her face.

"No need to worry. My mother wouldn't let us share a room, even if we wanted to. She's *multo* old-school about things. In fact, she attends Mass every Saturday."

Her eyes widened. "Is that what that whole marriage thing was about?"

"Marriage thing?"

"When you asked if it would be easier if we were married?"

This time the anger was on his side. "You think I'd ask you to marry me as a way to appease Mamma? I would never do such a thing."

"I'm sorry, I just thought—"

"Listen. She would be disappointed if we married for anything other than love. I was wrong to have suggested it."

Her shoulders relaxed. "I'm glad. Because I would be disappointed in myself if I let myself be talked into marriage just to give my child a mother and a father."

He stiffened. "She has a mother and a father. Even without the piece of paper."

And that had not been at all why he'd asked her. Although for the life of him he still wasn't sure what his reasons had been.

"That's not what I meant."

"Then what did you mean?" The words came out sounding stilted and formal, which wasn't how he'd meant them to, but her words stung. She didn't have to convince him that she no longer loved him. It had been obvious that day in the hospital staffroom, when she'd read that list of names and tossed him from her life. And it was obvious now.

"I was talking about sharing the same last name. Anna doesn't care about any of that."

"No. You're probably right." He went on so that she didn't think he was overly bothered by the conversation. "I'm going to be heading to the clinic in about a half hour. Do you want to come with me, or would you rather stay here?"

She didn't answer for a few seconds. Then she said, "Could I come and bring Anna with me? I can put a cot in your office and lay her down for a nap. I really would like to see more of what the clinic does."

He smiled, a few of his muscles uncoiling. At least she hadn't come out here to say that she'd booked a flight out of Italy. He'd call his parents and make his explanations seeing as he'd been too distracted by Elyse to phone them last night. Everything was still on track.

At least he hoped it was. Time would tell if it would stay that way.

"How soon do you need me to be ready?"

"I have rounds in around an hour, so…thirty minutes?"

"Sounds good, I'll gather Anna's things."

His gaze skimmed her figure against his volition. If she noticed she gave no indication of it. "If you just put everything in the living room, I'll load it into the car."

"Thanks. Are you sure you don't mind us coming with you?"

"I'd be disappointed if you didn't."

Keep your enemies close, wasn't that how the saying went?

Only he really hoped Elyse was no longer his enemy. Because by the end of her time here he hoped they could at least be friends.

She was ready in thirty minutes, just as she'd said. But unlike the mountain of things he expected to see on the living-room floor, there was only a collapsible crib and a diaper bag packed with supplies. He glanced at it. "Are you sure you don't want to leave her with Emilia again for a few hours?"

She gave him a sideways glance and said, "No, I think I'd like her with me this time."

Was she afraid he'd try to sweep everything off his desk and take her there like he had on her desk in Atlanta? Or the hood of his car?

He'd learned his lesson and wasn't likely to repeat either of those mistakes. Only he wasn't sure the latter *had* been a mistake. There was such a thing as closure. Something he hadn't quite gotten before he'd left Atlanta. Maybe their encounter had been the formal goodbye he'd needed.

He didn't like that idea. At all.

"We can set up the baby cam in my office or use the camera on my laptop to observe her."

"I thought the same thing, so I have the baby monitor in the diaper bag."

"Great. My office door can be locked, but I'd rather be able to check on her from time to time."

"It's just like leaving her to sleep in her room at home. The monitor will alert us to any peeps she might make."

With that settled, he picked up the portable crib and the diaper bag and loaded them into the car while she picked Anna up from the baby blanket she'd spread on the floor.

Emilia came over to kiss the baby on the cheek. "You leave?"

"I'm taking them to the clinic with me. But don't forget that Elyse and I are going to Rome in the morning," Luca said.

"I no forget. But I miss Annalisa."

He smiled. He was sure his housekeeper would probably miss the baby more than she would him.

"We'll only be there a week."

Elyse shifted and looked away. Maybe "only a week" to her seemed like an eternity. But, for his parents, it would fly by, and he wouldn't be able to tell them when they'd be able to see their granddaughter again.

No, he was sure Elyse would want to work out some kind of schedule. But if he only saw Annalisa once a year, that added up to just eighteen times before she was an adult. The pain that idea caused him was so deep he wasn't sure it would ever go away.

That brought him back to the question he'd asked himself over and over again. If he'd known Elyse was pregnant, would he have still left America?

His response was the same as it had been last time. No. He wouldn't have left.

But she hadn't known at the time, and he *had* left, so asking those types of questions caused nothing but torment.

He needed to concentrate on the here and now and figure out a plan for the future. Or he would be left with nothing to look forward to, except recriminations—aimed solely at himself.

CHAPTER NINE

MARY LANDERS HAD had no seizures in the last two days. Elyse gave her hand a quick squeeze. "I'm so glad you're doing well. I hear they're releasing you today."

"Yes, they are. We're going to wait a couple of weeks and then we'll head back to the States. School starts soon, and we don't want our daughter to miss any of it."

Annalisa was sound asleep back in Luca's office. In fact, he'd stayed behind to watch her, not quite comfortable with leaving her alone, despite the baby monitor. She wondered if that was the real explanation or if he simply couldn't get his fill of his daughter.

If so, she knew the feeling.

She couldn't quite get her fill of him. And she was pretty sure she never would. She'd proved that by having sex with him on his car.

Her heart had cracked in two over him once before, and the way she was going, it could very well break all over again.

"What grade is your daughter going to be in?"

"Fifth. Bella starts at a new school, so we want to make sure we're back."

The couple only had the one child. Mary had shared that they'd tried to get pregnant again but couldn't. And adoption took so long they'd opted not to go in that route, especially since her husband was in the military, and they might change locations before the process could be completed.

She understood completely. It was something she hadn't told Luca, even after he'd used a condom the other day. In the beginning, she'd kept it to herself because she hadn't thought it was any of his business.

And now?

She wasn't so sure. When she'd gone out to the garage and looked at the car, it had been on the tip of her tongue to tell him. But she'd chickened out.

What would be accomplished by telling him?

"Is she excited?"

"She misses her friends, but since we moved locations and not just schools, it makes it easier. Military kids learn early to cultivate relationships where you find them, because you never know when life will drag you somewhere else entirely."

"I can certainly understand that."

Elyse had a lot in common with those families. Life had changed drastically for her in the space of thirteen months. Her relationship with Luca had ended. Then had come the pregnancy and the resulting hysterectomy.

That was about as drastic as it got without someone dying.

On the positive side, she still had her ovaries, so she hadn't been thrown into premature menopause in the midst of everything else.

A hot flash might be a little difficult to explain, and since Luca hadn't taken her skirt off he hadn't even seen her hysterectomy scar, not that he would have surmised that she'd had her uterus removed from that scar alone.

Didn't she owe it to him to tell him? She didn't know. Everything was just a tangle of confusion right now.

"Elyse, could I see you for a moment?"

She whirled around, expecting Luca to be standing in the doorway, leaning sexily against the doorjamb, but no one was there.

"I think it came out of your pocket," Mary said in response to her obvious confusion.

"My...oh, the baby monitor." Luckily it had a two-way speaker feature. She pulled the receiver from her pocket and used it like a walkie-talkie. "What's up, Luca?"

"Anna's hungry. Or something." She suddenly heard the sound of Annalisa crying over the speaker. Luca must have aimed it at the baby, or maybe he was holding her.

"I'll be there in just a minute. Thanks." She dropped the device back in her pocket, a sense of amusement going through her at the tinge of panic that had colored Luca's voice. She remembered feeling that very same fear the first time Anna had cried, when all of the doubts she'd repressed during her pregnancy had come roaring back. What if she wasn't enough for her baby? What if she couldn't get her to stop crying? Or, worse, what if she couldn't tell the difference between something simple and something serious?

So far, she'd dealt with each crying session as it came and had learned the difference between distress and simple hunger. Despite her difficult pregnancy, Anna had become a relatively healthy baby.

So far, anyway.

She went over and gave Mary's arm a gentle squeeze.

"If I'm not here when they release you, take it easy and have a safe flight back."

"Thank you for everything."

She actually hadn't done anything, except to consult with Enzo and give the family some encouragement. But she could imagine how grateful she'd be for a visitor from her homeland if the situation was reversed.

"You and your doctors did all the work. I was only here in case they needed translation work, but Luca could have done that on his own, anyway."

"Luca?"

Ugh, she'd used his first name rather than his title. "Dr. Venezio."

"Oh, yes, of course. He did speak great English. Is Anna your baby?"

"Yes, she is."

"With Dr. Venezio?"

Suddenly she realized that the patient had added everything up and come to the right conclusion.

Mary was leaving soon, though, so it didn't really matter if she knew.

"Yes, he's her father."

"I thought so. There was something there between you. A couple of looks…"

Her brows went up in surprise. "You were a pretty sick lady when you came in here. I'm surprised you had time to notice anything besides what you were going through."

"I think there was a need to know everything I could about my doctors before I underwent surgery."

"Dr. Giorgino performed your surgery."

"Yes, but Dr. Venezio played a pretty big role in diagnosing it."

"That's true." She paused, then finished the story for her. "Luca and I broke up before I realized I was pregnant."

Mary blinked. "That must be hard, especially working with him." She reached out a hand and Elyse took it. "I hope everything turns out for the best for both of us. This is my husband's last tour of duty and then he plans to use his engineering degree to go into architecture. So let me know if you want a house designed. He's pretty good."

"I will. And thank you." She leaned down and gave the woman a quick hug. "Take care of yourself."

"You too."

And then Elyse left and walked toward the elevators to see what was going on with Luca and her daughter.

When she entered the office, it looked like a tornado had hit. There were three diapers strewn on the floor and Luca was standing in the middle of the room with a big wet mark running down his shirt. "I thought you said she was hungry."

"I thought she was too, but I tried to change her diaper first, like you told me."

"And?"

"We never exactly finished Diapering for Beginners."

Her eyes widened as she realized what the wet spot was. Annalisa had peed on him. She hurried to take the baby. "Oh, Luca, I'm so sorry. I was saying goodbye to Mrs. Landers and lost track of time. I thought the diapers were self-explanatory."

"They are. But trying to hold her and get the diaper situated were harder than I expected."

"It's okay. I remember how hard it was that first

time." She dragged the baby blanket over to the discarded diaper, laid her daughter down on top of the barrier and quickly strapped her into it. She glanced around. "Where are her shorts?"

"In the crib. That's where I tried to change her first, then when I couldn't figure it out, I put her on the desk to see if I could get it right."

He hadn't. "At least you tried." She picked up the shorts and stuck one of Annalisa's legs into it and then the other.

The baby stopped crying. Immediately.

Luca dropped into his office chair looking like he'd just been through a particularly difficult surgery. "I'm sorry. I wouldn't have interrupted you if I'd realized."

"It's okay. We were done, anyway." She hesitated, but then decided to come clean just in case Mary let it slip before she left. "Mary guessed that Annalisa was ours."

He frowned. "So?"

"I wasn't sure if you'd want anyone here to know."

"Since Lorenzo was holding her when you two walked into my office, I'm pretty sure someone already does. Besides, I'm not ashamed of her. Or of you. Better to admit everything than to have some twisted version of events travel down the gossip chain."

Admit everything. Something she hadn't exactly done.

Maybe she should take his advice and admit everything.

She touched his hand. "Hey, I think I should—"

There was a knock at the door, and Lorenzo stuck his head in, eyes taking in the scene. "Sorry, am I interrupting something?"

"No." Luca stepped closer to the door. "Did you need something?"

The other man frowned but only hesitated a fraction of a second. "I sent a note asking for a read on a patient this morning, did you get a chance to do it?"

"What time did you send it?"

"Eight this morning."

That would have been around the time she had gone out to the garage and seen him wiping down his car.

The memory of him bending her over that hood sent heat scorching through her.

Luca glanced at her, head tilting before saying, "I can look now, if you're okay with waiting."

"Yes. I have a consult in about fifteen minutes. The patient is adult. Worsening symptoms since yesterday."

Luca went to his computer, the keys clicking as he looked for whatever it was the surgeon wanted him to see. "Elyse? Care to throw your opinion in as well?"

She went around the desk to find him looking at a series of MRI slides. "Oh, wow."

The images showed a series of lesions in different parts of the brain. "MS?" she asked.

Giorgino nodded. "This is what I thought too."

It looked like a typical case, but there was something…

Luca shook his head. "I don't think so. They're on the basal ganglia. Nothing on the brain stem, like you'd expect with MS." He stared at the images. "Maybe acute disseminated encephalomyelitis?"

"ADEM?" she said. "Yes, it could be."

Similar in many aspects to MS, ADEM often came on after an illness. But it was seen mostly in children, not adults. "How old is she?"

"Fifty-four," said Lorenzo.

"Was she sick recently? Have any type of vaccine?"

The surgeon came around to look at the screen as Luca scrolled back through the medical history. "Nothing."

"Is there someone here with her? A relative, maybe?"

"Suo marito."

Giorgino explained that her very worried husband was down in the waiting area. Calling down to the lobby and asking them to relay the question, they soon had their answer.

"She came down with the shingles virus about a month ago."

Elyse bit her tongue to keep from playing devil's advocate. She hated to be wrong, but in this case she had to admit that Luca probably was correct in his diagnosis. Plus the fact that looking at the scans a little closer, the lesions were more perivenous as opposed to the way multiple sclerosis normally presented. At least this time they hadn't argued about it. Although she might have presented her theory more vehemently if they had been on her home turf, which made her wonder why she hadn't here. Maybe because they weren't as close as they once had been.

Or maybe she'd learned a thing or two since then. If that was the case, something good had come of their last few arguments. Something besides Annalisa.

"Standard treatment, then," she said, "consists of high doses of dexamethasone or methylprednisone to lower inflammation, wouldn't you say?"

Luca and Giorgino suddenly began speaking in rapid Italian that she couldn't keep up with. The surgeon's glance went to her once then back to Luca.

Did they disagree with her treatment plan? Or was the surgeon asking about what she meant to Luca?

No, of course he wasn't. She was being paranoid. They had to be talking about treatment options.

Then Giorgino was gone with a wave and a quick word of thanks.

"Everything okay?"

Luca clicked off the computer screen. "Yes, he went to initiate treatment. He said to tell you thank you."

"That was a pretty long thank you. Besides, you came up with the diagnosis first."

He grinned. "Yes, but I'm not nearly as cute as you are."

"You're a funny guy."

Through it all, Anna had remained quiet as if she knew that they were doing something important. Now that they were done, though, she gurgled, then jammed her hands into her mouth.

"I thought you said she wasn't hungry."

"She shouldn't be. Not yet. And now that the Great Diaper Crisis is over, she should be fine."

"Diaper crisis?"

"Um, you still have a little wet stain on your shirt." A sudden thought made her laugh. "No wonder Enzo looked at us kind of weird. Probably thought something kinky was going on in here."

"Good thing he didn't see us yesterday, then." The sardonic note in his voice stopped her in her tracks.

She guessed what they'd done was a little beyond what they'd experimented with in the past. But it had been incredibly exciting, and she was finding she didn't regret it nearly as much as she should have. "Yes. Good thing."

The moment of telling him she couldn't have kids had come and gone.

"Is the department in Atlanta still downsized?"

The question came out of the blue, taking her by surprise. Was he thinking about her suggestion of moving back to the States? "Yes, unfortunately."

"Why did you stay, then? Afterward?"

"I couldn't leave the patients without anyone there. I know they would have replaced me, but I felt an obligation to them. I still do."

"Even if the hospital works you to death in the process? With those kinds of cutbacks, there's no way you can do justice to the patients that come in."

He was voicing exactly what she'd been thinking. Her voice went very soft. "I know that. But I have to try, while attempting to turn the boat back in the other direction. Sooner or later, they're either going to have to close our trauma center or hire more staff. Because lots of times those trauma cases involve neurological issues."

"Agreed." He touched her hair. "Anna needs you healthy and well. Not a...a wrung-out towel that has nothing left for herself."

"A wrung-out towel?" Is that how he saw her? Not very flattering.

"It doesn't quite come across the same way in English."

"I think I understand what you're trying to say. But since I haven't worked since I had her, I don't know how it's going to be yet. The hospital is using a borrowed surgeon from a sister hospital until I come back online."

"Online. Like a computer program?"

She knew he was trying to help, and she shouldn't

be offended, but she didn't like the inference that she would give Annalisa any less than all she had.

And if she really did become a wrung-out towel, like he'd said?

"You have your life together, no bumps in the road, I suppose."

His brows went up. "There have been some very big bumps, especially recently, but as you can see I am making time for both of you."

"As will I when I go back to work."

He nodded. "Very good, then. Let's talk about something else. Like our trip to Rome."

They spent the next twenty minutes discussing their game plan for that first actual meeting. And when they were done, Elyse wasn't sure whether tomorrow was going to be a celebration. Or a wake.

But they would all find out, very soon.

CHAPTER TEN

HIS MOTHER'S GREETING over the phone was filled with warm excitement. "Everything is ready here. I have the ingredients for your favorite meal, ready to prepare. Are you bringing Emilia with you?"

"Not this time, Mamma, but I am bringing someone with me."

"Una fidanzata?"

He cringed at the word fiancée. How exactly did one explain that someone was the mother of your child but not attached to you in any way, shape or form? You didn't.

"Are you sitting down?"

"Don't tell me. You really have chosen someone?"

His mother had been on his case to find a wife for the last several years. Even in medical school she'd asked about girls, despite the fact that the last thing he'd had time for was finding that special someone.

Until he'd met Elyse.

"No. But there was a girl. For a while. In Atlanta. We broke up, but I've since found out that there was… is…a…" He cleared his throat. "A baby involved."

"I don't understand, Lucan. A baby involved in what?"

"She has a child, and that baby is mine."

There was silence over the phone, then he heard her shrieking for his father to come into the room.

Luca held the phone away from his ear to avoid hearing loss.

Dio. He'd known she'd be shocked. Dismayed, maybe. But ultimately he'd thought she'd be happy.

His father must have arrived because he heard rapid-fire voices, but he couldn't make out what they were saying. Then his father came on.

"Luca, what the hell is going on? Mamma says you have a child?"

"Is she okay?"

"She's sobbing."

Damn. She was taking this a lot harder than he'd thought she would. He was glad now that he'd gone into his bedroom to make the call and doubly glad he hadn't waited to tell her upon their arrival in Rome. "I'm sorry, Papà. I only found out myself recently."

"Sorry?" He paused and shouted something to someone, evidently his mother. "I can't hear over her wailing. Why are you sorry?"

"Well… Mamma is crying."

A gust of laughter blew through the line. "She's not crying because she's sad. She's happy. Ecstatic. She was sure this day would never come."

"I'm not married to the baby's mother—and I don't plan on ever getting married to her." That sent a shaft of pain right through his chest. Because at one time he had fantasized about Elyse walking down that aisle. He'd had the ring in a little box in his drawer for a month. He'd held on to it, waiting for the right moment to come. It never had. And now it was stuffed in his sock drawer somewhere, since he'd never had time to return the ring before he'd left for Italy.

"Is she a good girl?"

He blinked at that. "She's a grown woman, Papà, and if you mean is she nice, then, yes, she's very nice. It just didn't work out between us. She flew to Florence to tell me a week ago."

"How old is the baby?"

"Four months, and she's a girl. Annalisa Marie Tenner."

He waited while his dad relayed the information. "Why doesn't she have your last name?"

"Because I wasn't there when she was born. And maybe Elyse wasn't sure what to do about that fact."

He'd assumed she hadn't wanted to give Annalisa his last name because she hadn't been sure how he would react to the news. Or maybe there had been a period of time when she wasn't sure if she would even tell him.

But that was something he could do nothing about at the moment. Maybe later, once they'd come to some sort of understanding and things weren't quite so emotional.

Strike two for having sex with her on the hood of his car. It had muddied the waters and made it hard for him to do anything but think about those last memorable seconds. Because he badly wanted to do it all over again.

And there was no way he could. He needed to keep his head about him, especially now that his parents knew. He didn't want to give them false hope.

Again, his dad stopped to relay the information. "Papà, just put Mamma back on the phone, please."

A minute later, she came on the line, speaking so fast that he could barely understand her. Something about wanting to have a huge party to introduce the baby to the extended family.

Dio! That hadn't been on his radar at all. "Let me talk to Elyse first. She might not want that kind of attention."

"Elyse? This is the mother?"

"Yes. And I'm not sure she's up to one of your parties."

"Of course she is. This is our first grandchild. Everyone must know."

He was pretty sure everyone already did with the way she'd carried on a few moments earlier. "We're only going to be at the house for a week. There won't be time to put anything together."

"Yes, there will. I'll make it work. It can be on your last day at the house." She paused her tirade. "But only a week? How will we get to know either of them in that time?"

He hadn't talked to Elyse about spending more time than that, although she was slated to be in Italy for a month. But he'd been hoping to get to know his daughter a little bit better without his mother hovering over his every move. "She won't be here that long. She's only in Italy for a month and she's been here nearly a week already."

"A month? Spend the rest of the time with us, then."

"No, Mamma, I can't. I have to work. I've already taken a week off as it is."

"We barely see you." The complaint was one his mother always made.

"That's not true. You saw me less than six weeks ago."

"Why don't you come back to Rome and work?"

They'd been over this same argument time and time

again. Priscilla believed all her children should be gathered around her. And his sisters were. They had both settled less than ten kilometers from their birthplace. After his breakup, though, Luca hadn't been able to bear the thought of moving back to Rome. His mom was far too intuitive. Between her and his sisters, they would have yanked every last detail from him.

It looked like they might get that chance after all.

"I told you. This clinic specializes in neurology. They're doing great work."

"There are clinics here in Rome as well."

"I'm already here, Mamma. I can't just uproot myself." He paused, not letting his voice run ahead of his mind. He decided to steer her back to one of her original subjects just to save himself. "About the party. Nothing too big. Promise me."

Elyse was going to kill him for throwing her to the sharks, so to speak.

"It will just be family. Maybe fifty people."

"No. That's too big."

"But your aunts, uncles and cousins will be offended if they're not all invited."

"I don't think I even have that many cousins and aunts."

"Oh, at least that many. I can think of a hundred off the top of my head."

Okay, so now fifty was sounding a whole lot better. "Let's not invite all of Rome, Mamma. And I really need to ask Elyse if it's okay. If she says no, we'll have to skip it."

"Ask, then. I'll wait."

"She's probably already asleep. I'll ask her in the morning before we leave and call you then."

He doubted that Elyse was asleep at nine o'clock, but the last thing he wanted to do was knock on her bedroom door and have her answer in pajamas. Or worse.

"Do you promise? Call me early. I have a lot of work to do as far as planning goes."

This time he gave an audible sigh. "Nothing too extravagant. Please, Mamma."

"Of course not. You know me."

Yes, he did, which was why he'd said it. But it really didn't matter. She was going to do whatever she wanted to, and his sisters were probably going to be cheering her on the whole way. Not the way he'd wanted to introduce Elyse to his family. Priscilla had a kind of frenetic energy that others tended to feed off. Either that or they were horrified by it.

She was in her element when planning *festas*. He could remember all the huge Christmas and Easter bashes that she'd hosted. "Just a few family members" quickly became "the" place to be on holidays. Distant relatives finagled invitations just to come and see what his mother had cooked up for that particular celebration. Time to hammer his point home.

"Keep the guest list small. Elyse doesn't speak Italian, so she's going to feel totally out of place as it is."

"I will enlist your father's help. I will tell him to rein me in if I'm getting too...what was the word? *Stravagante*."

She said it with such a flourish he had to laugh. "You're impossible, but *ti amo*, Mamma. Don't do anything until I call you in the morning."

"I won't, I promise. I love you too, *mio figlio*."

He hung up the phone and sat on his bed for a minute. Should he ask Elyse tonight?

No, because, again, that would entail him knocking on her bedroom door. Which was probably why his subconscious was pushing for him to do just that.

Well, it could keep pushing all it wanted. This time he wasn't listening.

"She wants to do what?"

Elyse was horrified. Luca's mother wanted to throw a party—for Annalisa—and she knew nobody. Suddenly she wondered if coming to Italy had been a mistake, if everything she was doing here was just going to make things worse. She glanced in the back seat, where Annalisa was sleeping, hoping beyond hope she was doing the right thing.

"It will keep her busy and stop her from asking too many personal questions."

She could just imagine what some of those questions might be. A party didn't sound too bad when you looked at the other possibility. She relaxed in her seat. "I don't even speak Italian."

"I'll translate for you. It's only for relatives, and she's excited about meeting Annalisa. That's what you were worried about, right?"

True. Luca had said his mother was old-fashioned. It would have been worse if she'd wanted to hide Annalisa away and never speak of her to anyone outside Luca's immediate family. But the last time he'd translated for her, she'd been a royal wreck. She'd have to be careful about letting that happen again.

"Yes. Tell her okay. I just don't want to embarrass anyone."

"Elyse, you could never embarrass a soul."

She shivered the way she always did when he said

her name. His accent combined with that low graveled voice gave the word an exotic sound that got to her. Every single time.

"Oh, believe me, I could. I embarrass myself all the time. In lots of different ways."

He took his hand off the stick shift and touched her knee. "You're an excellent surgeon. And caring and compassionate with your patients."

A smile came up from deep inside her. "Right back at you."

He tilted his head, and she realized he wasn't sure what she meant. His English vocabulary was so extensive that she sometimes forgot there were still things that confused him. "It means that I think you're also an excellent doctor and caring and compassionate with your patients."

He grinned. "In that case, I thank you."

"Your mom knows we're not together?"

His hand went back to the gear stick and she immediately regretted voicing the words. He'd already said he would let his mom know that they had broken up. "Yes, she does."

"Sorry. I just wanted to make sure I wasn't supposed to play your doting wife."

He laughed. "Would you? Play a doting wife, if I asked you to?"

He's joking, Elyse. He doesn't mean anything by it.

"Of course I would." She batted her eyelashes at him in a theatrical sort of way. "Think your mother would believe us?"

"Probably not." He took a turn that put them on the ramp to a highway. "She always knew when I was lying before I even opened my mouth."

"Well, I guess we shouldn't lie about our relationship then, should we?" Which made Elyse a little nervous, since she was no longer certain what was truth and what wasn't. She'd told herself she was over him for so long that she'd come to believe it. But was it the truth? There were moments when the past came blazing through in all its glory and she was sure she'd been wrong about everything. Like after they made love the other day. It had taken everything she had to reason herself out of it.

If Luca asked her today to stay in Italy, stay with him, would she?

He didn't love her.

But what if he did? something inside her whispered. What if he did?

"So no lies, right?"

The words made her jerk around to look at him. "What?"

"Where were you?"

"Oh, sorry, I was thinking about what to wear to the party."

One of his brows went up and stayed up, but he didn't challenge her words.

No lies? Ha! She was starting out on the right foot with that one.

If his mom was as intuitive as Luca said she was, she was going to have to watch her step before the woman decided she and her son were actually meant for each other. "Go ahead and call her."

"Thank you. She promised it would be a small affair." He pushed a button on his dashboard and she heard a woman's voice answer in Italian. Luca answered in kind and a rapid-fire conversation took place, none of which Elyse understood. But she heard Luca placing emphasis on certain words and his mother answering.

Priscilla—wasn't that her name?—had a melodic voice that Elyse instinctively liked. There was a strength to it, but not the kind that forced its will on anyone.

Within five minutes it was over, and Luca pushed another button. "She said to say thank you and tell you that she loves you already."

Her heart clenched.

"She sounded sweet on the phone, even if I couldn't understand her."

"My sisters are a lot like her."

"Tell me about them." That seemed like a safe enough topic.

"Well, Isabella is a lawyer. She's very smart and intuitive about people."

Another person who would be able to see right through her. She was starting to get this horrible sense of foreboding about this whole visit. "And the other one?"

"Sarita is the baby. She is studying to be a psychologist. She's in her final year of studies."

A lawyer and a psychologist walk into a bar...and try to figure out the biggest lie of them all: that she no longer loved their brother.

Because she suddenly realized she did. She still loved him, after all this time.

God. How had this happened?

So much for thinking her feelings for him were dead. Obviously that wasn't the case.

Fake it. Fake it good, Elyse.

"So do Sarita and Isabella live in Rome?" Maybe

they would only arrive for the party and then head right back out.

"They both do, so you'll get to spend some time with them."

Well, at least he'd mistaken the reason she'd asked. "That will be great. Do they speak English?" Maybe if they couldn't understand her, they wouldn't read between the lines.

"Yes, they both are pretty fluent, unlike my parents, so they can help translate as well."

That was the last thing she wanted. Would her body language immediately give her away?

"Great." Time to switch her thoughts to the road in front of them to keep herself from keeling over in shock. Or start to worry that every little thing she said would make him guess the truth. She swallowed, trying to shake the fear away.

"The signs on the highway look so bizarre to me. Did the ones in the States seem strange to you when you were there?" Thank heavens her voice didn't come out as shaky as she felt inside.

"What?"

"Everything being in another language."

He glanced at her. "A little. The worst was getting used to miles instead of kilometers and Fahrenheit instead of Celsius."

"I can see how that would be strange." She licked her lips and reached for another neutral topic. "Italy is gorgeous. I love everything about it."

There was a pause. "Everything?"

Had he seen through her already? If she kept on like this, she was doomed.

She tried to deflect one question with another. "Did you love everything about Atlanta?"

"Pretty much. Maybe not the traffic, even though we have that here as well."

She ran out of questions, so she sat there and leaned her head against the headrest. Anna was sound asleep in the back, so she focused on the sound of the tires against the roadway, instead of the realization that had shaken her to the core.

Random bits of thought swirled around like the leaves caught in a stiff breeze. She might be able to reach out and catch one of them, but she was too afraid of what she might find written on it. So she let them go on their way, closing her eyes and blocking out everything except for that constant background hum, her limbs slowly relaxing. Gradually getting heavier and heavier.

The swirling stopped, and one leaf drifted downward, settling in the corner of her mind. And on it was a single terrifying word.

Love.

Elyse had seemed distracted ever since they'd arrived at his parents' house. It was understandable, but he was sure there was something else underneath it. That feeling that she'd kept something hidden from him ever since her arrival in Italy.

Well, he hadn't spilled his every thought to her either.

He'd translated the introductions, and she'd responded politely when they made small talk, but he couldn't shake the feeling that something was wrong.

So far the only genuine smile he'd seen on her face had happened when his mother had lifted Anna into her arms and squeezed the baby to her chest, eyes closed, tears pouring down her cheeks. At that moment Elyse had glanced his way and smiled, putting her hand over her trembling lips.

That had been genuine. But it had also been short-lived.

Priscilla, who'd installed herself in an ornate rocking chair, looked up. "Would you show Elyse to her room and carry her bags up? I'll hold the baby."

She wasn't likely to let go of Anna anytime soon. And that was fine with him. It was better than the alternative, which was for her to have given Elyse a much cooler reception.

But she had been warm...effusively warm. His dad had beamed as well. He hadn't had a chance to hold Annalisa yet, but he'd only left his wife's side long enough to bring a pitcher of water and some fruit juice, setting the offerings on a sideboard with some glasses. He wasn't as openly emotional as his wife, but he too was deeply moved by seeing his grandchild for the first time.

He glanced at Elyse. "Are you okay with that?" He wasn't going to assume anything. Not anymore. Especially with the mood she was in.

"I am. But I can get my bags."

He picked them up before she could make a move. "I've got them. Care to follow me?"

Leading the way up the stairwell, he glanced back and saw her hand reach for the banister and grip it tight.

Hell, she was shaking.

"They love her." If that's what she was worried about, he wanted to set her mind at ease. "I told you they would. She's their granddaughter. Even if she wasn't, they would still love her."

"She's yours. I swear."

He reached the landing and turned around quickly, which made her pause a couple of steps from the top. "Have I ever implied that I thought she wasn't mine?"

"No, but I could understand how—"

"I know she's mine. I don't need a test to tell me that. I never did. I *know* you. Know I was the only one you were involved with, even if we weren't always getting along very well." He set the bags down and went to her, cupping her elbows. "She has your eyes, but I definitely see a melding of the two of us when I look at her."

"So do I." She wrapped her arms around his midsection and laid her head on his chest. The move left him glued in his spot.

"I wish…" She sighed. "I guess it doesn't matter what I wish. It is what it is, and we just have to do the best we can."

He rested his chin on her hair, closing his eyes. He'd missed these moments.

Suddenly her arms dropped back to her sides and he felt that slow withdrawal that had happened so many times toward the end of their relationship, when he'd been left wondering what had gone wrong.

Dammit. Turning, he started back up the stairs.

They stopped at the end of a long hall of closed doors. This door in front of them was also shut tight. "This is yours. Mine is right across the hallway."

She gave a quick laugh. "I would have thought they'd have put us as far apart as possible. Maybe even on different floors."

"No, it would have been you who did that." He couldn't resist throwing out a reference to a distance that was so much more than physical.

"What do you mean?"

He wasn't touching that question, because he might say something he regretted. "You're the one who insisted on separate bedrooms."

"I know." She muttered something under her breath before pushing open the door. Her breath came out in a whoosh of sound. "Luca, it's beautiful."

The room was big, as were all the bedrooms. And directly across from them was a huge four-poster bed carved from mahogany.

"I'm glad you like it."

He set her bags on the floor just inside the door. He nodded over at a matching tall dresser. "The drawers will be empty. Feel free to unpack."

"Will your mom be okay with Annalisa for a while?"

"Of course. I'm sure she's hoping we'll be a while."

He realized how that sounded when something flashed in her eyes, and she was suddenly back from wherever she'd gone, wholly present, wholly accessible.

Unsure how long this reprieve was going to last, his gaze trailed over her features before settling on her lips.

She'd fallen for him at one time.

And what about now?

If he kissed her, would she kiss him back?

Would they slam the door and fall onto that tall bed and make love?

If he stood here much longer, he was going to do exactly that. So it was time to leave. And fast.

Before he put his thoughts to the test and gave his mother a false sense of hope. Because even if he would have liked another chance to work things out, it was doubtful that Elyse would. Despite that one episode on the hood of his car.

"Do you want anything before I go?" His lips tightened when those words were as blundered as the last ones.

"No. Nothing, thanks. I'll be down in a few minutes."

He took that as a dismissal and was through the door in an instant, closing it behind him before he said something he'd regret. Something that could never be erased.

Heading back the way he had come, he threw one last glance at the dark wooden surface of the door and wondered if she knew.

Wondered if she realized that as he'd stood there wishing he could kiss her, he'd almost muttered the phrase he'd held back that night in Atlanta.

He loved her. Had never stopped loving her.

And, hell, if it wasn't going to be his undoing.

Because there was nothing he could do—no deity he could implore—that could erase what was now burned onto his very soul.

CHAPTER ELEVEN

THE PARTY HAD been organized for tonight, the penultimate night of their stay, which was both good and bad. It was good in that she'd barely seen Luca the evening before except for dinner. Elyse wondered if he was making himself scarce on purpose, which would be good for her. Except she didn't seem to feel that way.

This morning, though, he'd met her for breakfast and said he'd show her around the grounds. "If you need some privacy, there's a small *terrazza* a little way from the house, which is where I used to go as a kid. I built a fort there for just that reason, in fact."

"Wow, is it still there?" Somehow she couldn't imagine Luca needing to get away from anyone. He was self-assured and confident. She was pretty sure he hadn't suddenly gained those characteristics the second he'd become an adult.

"The *terrazza*. Yes, it's still there. The fort? No, it's long gone. It was made out of a collection of cardboard boxes. It even had different rooms."

"I somehow can't imagine you making a play fort."

He tilted his head. "Why not? Don't most kids?"

"Yes, I made my share in the house. Blankets over

the dining-room table. I didn't quite get as ambitious as you did. I just wanted to have a secret place to read."

"So did I."

That was another thing that surprised her. She'd pictured him playing soccer and doing sports, not being a kid with his nose stuck in a book. "You liked to read?"

"Loved it. Especially adventure stories. I loved danger."

Now, *that* she could see. Maybe the danger in those books had infused itself into his being, because she couldn't imagine a man more dangerous to her senses than Luca was.

Before she could think of an answer that was as far from that thought as she could get, Priscilla swept into the room and said something, which Luca translated as a greeting. Then she and her son had a quick argument, and his mom gave him a frown and looked at Elyse and said something in Italian. When Luca didn't explain, she said in broken English. "Please say her."

Luca sighed. "She wants to know if she can take Annalisa into town and get her a new dress. I told her she has all the clothes she can possibly use, but Mamma wants her to have something that's from her. For the party." He looked in her eyes. "If you don't want her to, I'll explain that."

"Heavens. Of course she wants Annalisa to have something new for the party. It's fine. I have a bottle ready in the fridge for her."

When he relayed that back to Priscilla, she smiled, setting off a dizzying array of crinkles beside her eyes that really brought out the beauty in her face. Luca looked like her. So did Annalisa, if she was honest.

* * *

An hour later the two were out the door, leaving Elyse almost alone in the house with Luca, since his father had gone to work for the day.

The housekeeper was there, but she was busy with the caterers and other professionals who were getting things ready for the party that night. Luca had promised her it would be a small affair but, seeing the crew in action, somehow she didn't believe him. Who hired caterers for dinner with the family? And something about the way Luca had said "party" when he'd first talked to her about it made her think it wasn't going to be as simple as he made it out to be. All she could do was smile and hope for the best.

"Do you want to go for a walk? I can show you the actual garden where treasures were smuggled and dragons were slain."

That made her laugh. "Well, when you put it that way, how could I refuse?"

He led her down a mown path, the splash of flowers on either side of them looking wild and free. The funny thing was, those flowers had probably been carefully tended to do exactly what the gardener wanted.

"So where was this magnificent fort?"

"Right here."

The flowers had given way to an open cobblestoned area that had a couple of benches. Off to the side was a crystal clear pond that bubbled with fish and water plants. "Your parents let you have a cardboard village in the middle of all of this beauty? How long was it here?"

"A couple of years on and off. My sisters tended to tear it down almost as fast as I could build it. This is where they brought their friends, and they certainly didn't want their brother messing things up for them."

She could picture that scene happening. Since she was an only child, she hadn't had any of the competition that faced siblings. "They probably brought their boyfriends here later. It's the perfect place."

"Yes. It is. And they did."

She didn't want to ask, but she couldn't help it. "And you. Did you bring your girlfriends here?"

"Hmm... I can remember a time or two."

"A time or two? I bet you had them swarming over you."

He motioned her to a bench and then sat next to her. "No. No swarming. I've never been one to play around."

"No. You never were." Memories of them colored so many parts of her brain that she was pretty sure he'd traveled along most of her synapses.

He turned toward her. "Thank you."

"For what?"

"I don't know, exactly. Annalisa. The crazy times we had. Something beautiful came from what I'd always seen as scorched earth."

"Oh, Luca. I feel the same way. If we'd never gotten together...never had that fight in my office...she wouldn't be here."

His fingers touched her face. "We built our own fort and hid away in it for a while, didn't we?"

"Yes, we did."

Dark eyes stared into hers. "Is it completely gone?"

She could lie. Or she could tell the truth.

Hadn't they agreed not to lie to each other?

"No," she whispered. "It's not."

He exhaled heavily. "I so needed to hear that." His

palms skimmed her jawline. "Because I don't think it is either."

Then his mouth was on hers in a kiss that tested the whole scorched-earth theory, because it was still as beautiful and wild as those flowers they'd passed on their way here.

He stood and held his hand out to her, and there was no hesitation when she answered his invitation. Two minutes later they were in her room in that big bed, where he undressed her. Slowly. Carefully.

So different from the car experience, where things had been removed in frantic haste, but this was no less fulfilling. They explored each other, relearning curves and planes, seeking out subtle changes that had taken place over those lost months. He found her scar, but even as she stiffened, he shushed her.

"It's beautiful. This is where my Anna came into the world."

He made her feel cherished and cared about. And maybe even…loved?

Did he love her?

She swallowed. *Did he?*

Ask. Do it.

She couldn't make the words form on her lips, so she decided to show him instead, in the hope that he would whisper the words she longed to hear.

Instead, he climbed off the bed and pulled his wallet from his trousers and laid it on the bed. She closed her eyes, knowing exactly what that represented.

It didn't matter. She could tell him later. Once she knew for sure how he felt. Maybe he wouldn't need more kids. Maybe he'd be okay with just one. Just their Anna.

He went into the attached bathroom and when he returned he didn't have a stitch of clothes on. But he did have a small towel.

The question was almost lost when he climbed on the bed and straddled her. Then she found it. "What is the towel for?"

"I'm glad you asked." His smile was wicked. "Because I'm about to show you."

He draped the towel over her chest, covering both breasts. At first she thought he was worried about her modesty, until he gripped either end of the towel and slowly drew it back and forth over her. The thick terry teased the nipples underneath, creating a kaleidoscope of sensation that soon had her writhing on the bed.

"Ah... Luca, I'm not sure..." The words ended on a moan when he increased the downward pressure as he continued to seesaw the towel, over her, driving her wild.

Her hips bucked under him, but his weight on her upper thighs kept her from getting any kind of satisfaction. He leaned down next to her ear. *"Ti voglio così tanto bene."*

Was he saying he loved her?

Didn't know. Didn't care.

The towel stopped, making her eyes open.

"Don't worry, Ellie. I'm not done yet. Not by a long shot."

Picking up his wallet, he opened it, started to draw out a condom.

She stopped him with a hand on his. "We don't need one."

That was as close as she could get to the truth. She

could explain it all later, but right now she just wanted to feel him. All of him.

"*Dio. Cara.* Yes. I want that too. You don't know how much." He leaned down and took her mouth in a kiss that sent pretty little lights spinning behind her eyes.

Then the weight came off her thighs, freeing her for a second or two, before he gripped her hips and turned them so that she was where he had been. On top. Positioned in the perfect spot.

She went still for several seconds, poised on the very edge of heaven and not quite sure how she'd gotten there, or what she'd done to deserve it.

"Do it." His hands tightened on her hips, but he didn't try to yank her down. "Please."

Instead of taking him in a hurry, she eased down, feeling each silky inch of him as she took him in.

He muttered those words that meant nothing and yet told her everything she wanted to hear as she rocked her hips, retracing her path up and then sliding back to the bottom.

There was something unhurried and yet desperately rushed in her movements, and she couldn't quite choose one or the other. Until one hand covered her breast and the other tangled in her hair, pulling her toward his mouth. The combination of the friction of his palm and his tongue over hers made the decision for her. Her movements quickened, and she suddenly didn't care about anything other than how he was making her feel.

Up and down. Empty and full. She couldn't get enough. And when his fingers slid out of her hair and worked their magic elsewhere, she lost it, pushing down hard and then pumping to an internal rhythm. She climaxed, crying out against his mouth, even as he flipped her onto her back and drove into her again and again until he lost himself inside her.

There were several moments when she felt suspended in space. Untethered. Floating free.

Loved.

He hadn't questioned her decision about the condom. Had seemed to embrace it.

That had to mean something. Didn't it?

A single worry reappeared, joined by a second. Then a third.

She opened her eyes to find him watching her. She searched for something to say. "How long before your mom gets back?"

Groaning, he kissed her cheek. "I have no idea, but…"

She laughed. "You don't want to be caught necking in the back seat?"

"But we're not in a back seat. We're in bed."

God, she loved him. Loved these little differences that gave their world color and dimension. "It means we don't want to be caught together. In bed."

His nose nuzzled her ear. "I don't want to go."

"I don't want you to go either. But eventually someone is going to come looking for us. And when they do, I'd rather be fully clothed. And in our separate rooms."

He rolled off her, drawing her into his arms. "Okay. I'll go. But only because I don't want Mamma's party guests to go home with any salacious tales."

"Salacious?" That was suddenly her new favorite word.

"Yes. Of what we were making in this room." He got out of bed and leaned over her. "And just so you know, I do want more."

And then he was gone, leaving her with a tingle in her belly that wouldn't quit.

He wanted more.

Just the thought made her want to go find him and snatch him back to the room or to their fort or whatever they wanted to call it. As long as they were together.

With a joy she hadn't felt in a long time—one that was different from the day-to-day happiness that Anna gave her—she got up to shower and dress for the party.

CHAPTER TWELVE

HE HELD HER hand for most of the evening, trying to give her a boost of confidence while people spoke Italian all around them. Although he wasn't sure if the hand holding was for her...or for him. Those moments in the bedroom had been beyond anything he could have imagined, and they hadn't had a chance to talk about it.

She hadn't wanted to use a condom. Surely that meant she wanted a fresh start together? And more children. He'd made sure she knew he was in favor of that by whispering that he too wanted more.

She loved him, he was sure of it. Even if she hadn't said the words.

Then again, neither had he. But he would. Very soon.

He expected his mother to say something about all of this hand-holding, but she seemed oblivious. Everyone's attention was riveted on Annalisa, who was taking everything in her stride much better than she should have as she was passed from person to person.

"Are you okay?" Hell, he hoped he wasn't just imagining things.

She turned to him with a smile. "I am. For the first time in over a year." She nodded toward Anna. "She looks adorable in that dress your mom found."

"She has a knack for finding the perfect gift."

Anna was wearing a mint-green dress, complete with tulle around the full skirt and a satin bodice. She looked like a princess from a movie. She even had a tiny glittering tiara perched on her head. Luca had no idea how they'd kept her from knocking it off. But she hadn't. She was smiling and cooing and generally being the most beautiful thing he could imagine.

Other than Elyse.

While she wasn't wearing mint green to match her daughter, she did have on a black dress that ended just above the knee, her shoulders bare and tempting, her hair swept up into some kind of fancy knot with strands that wound their way down the sides of her face and tickled her nape. And she had on these high heels that made him think of things that were better off left unthought.

"Oh, I almost forgot! I brought that wine for your mom. We were going to get the flowers here, remember?"

"We can do that first thing tomorrow morning."

She licked her lips. "So your mom would definitely be scandalized if we shared a room?"

Two days ago he wouldn't have been able to envision a scenario where that kind of a question would come up. Or even thought. But he liked it…wanted things to keep moving in this direction.

"Ellie, I'm surprised at you." He gave her a grin. "In the best possible way. But yes. She probably would, although if I happen to have a nightmare involving the two of us kissing, and sneak into your room for comfort…"

She giggled. "A nightmare? Really? Should I be insulted?"

"Perhaps nightmare was a poor choice of word."

"I should think so." But she said it with a smile. And Elyse seemed…happy. He couldn't remember seeing her this way since…well, when there had still been some good in their relationship.

Her eyes trailed their daughter as she was handed over to yet another family member.

"Do you want me to bring her to you?"

"No, she looks happy."

"And how about you?"

Her brows went up and she leaned her head on his shoulder for a second. "What do you think?"

He noticed his mother was finally staring at them, and he had a fleeting thought that maybe they shouldn't be putting on a display of affection in front of everyone until they worked out the rest of their differences, but he wasn't about to push her away.

It was okay. Elyse was relaxed, and if she didn't care about his mother mentally putting rings on their fingers, then he shouldn't worry about it either. But he did have second thoughts about sneaking to her room tonight. If he was serious about doing this thing, then he wanted to do it right, not rush her into anything. His own prideful determination had messed up their relationship once before. He wasn't about to let that happen again.

Hopefully, if things went well, there would be many, many more moments like these. Slow, easy moments that led to something strong and lasting. And if it meant him moving back to America to get there, then so be it.

Elyse's arm flapped around on the bed beside her for a minute. Empty. A flicker of disappointment was quickly extinguished.

So what if he hadn't come to her room as he'd suggested he might? It had been a long evening. He had probably been exhausted. Just as she had been.

Cracking open her eyes and stretching, she couldn't stop a smile from forming. She'd been hoping to talk to him about the reality of her situation and why they hadn't needed to use that condom, something she hadn't been able to say when they had been making love.

He cared about her. She'd felt it brewing under the surface yesterday. His words had seemed to confirm that fact, but she wanted him to go into this relationship—if he even wanted one—with his eyes wide open. This time there would be no holding back or letting things fester and foment.

He'd held her hand last night. In front of his mom, his relatives and everyone. That meant something.

She glanced at her watch. It was barely seven o'clock and it was their last full day here. Climbing out of bed, she jumped in the shower, lathering up in record time. Maybe she could still catch him and have that talk before breakfast, if he hadn't already gone downstairs. Or maybe when they went to buy those flowers he'd talked about as a thank-you present for his mom for hosting her. There was still time. She was sure of it.

With her hair damp, and her face washed clean, she found the bottle of Chianti and dropped it into the red silk wine bag they'd bought to go with the flowers and put it on the mahogany dresser. She ran her fingers over the ornate lines that looked so at home in this room. Her glance snagged on the crib, where Annalisa was still fast asleep. Last night had worn her out. Her daughter didn't normally stay awake that late, but it had been a special night, and she'd fallen asleep in her grandmother's arms, bringing a lump to Elyse's throat and an ache to her heart. Suddenly a week with them seemed like no time at all.

You need to find Luca. Maybe you can work something out.

She went across the hall and softly tapped on his door, hoping that if the rest of the household was still asleep she wouldn't wake them. When there was no answer, she knocked a little louder. "Luca?"

Still no answer. She pursed her lips to the side. He could be in the shower. Or he could already be downstairs. She went back over and peeked in her room. Anna was still out. She'd nursed right before going to bed last night, so she could zip downstairs, find Luca and ask him if they could talk.

Tiptoeing down the treads, she stopped when she heard voices coming from the kitchen. One of them was Luca's. He was talking to a woman and sounded...concerned. Or something. Since he was speaking in rapid Italian she wasn't sure if she was reading him right. She started to turn and go back up the stairs but then the housekeeper appeared in the doorway and smiled at her, motioning her forward.

Ugh. But she was going to have to face him sometime. Except all the hopeful thoughts she'd had moments earlier were now faltering. Who was he talking to?

She forced herself to breeze through the door with a smile, hoping it didn't look like she'd been skulking in the doorway. Luca and his mother saw her at the same time, and the conversation immediately went silent.

They'd been talking about her. She swallowed. Maybe his mother had seen them last night and decided she didn't want her son taking up with someone from a different culture.

No. Things like that didn't happen anymore, did they?

She forced herself to speak, even though her throat felt packed with sawdust. "Good morning. How is everyone?"

Luca came over to her with a smile, throwing another glance toward his mom. He gave a quick shake of his head.

He didn't want her telling Elyse what they'd been discussing.

The sawdust turned to glass. Was it about Annalisa? Were they plotting how they were going to get her to spend more time in Italy?

You're being ridiculous. And paranoid.

His mom came over and took her hands, holding them up and kissing one. She winked at her son then turned her attention back to Elyse.

"Mamma…" Luca's voice was full of warning.

"Pssht."

Her response made Elyse's eyebrows go up. When they came back down they were contracted into a frown. "What's going on?"

Priscilla gave her hands a gentle squeeze. "You give Luca more babies?"

Babies?

The pain that stabbed her insides was sudden and intense, like the scars from her surgery when they had been new and raw. "Wh-what?"

Suddenly Luca's words from last night took on a whole new meaning.

Just so you know, I do want more.

Was that what he'd meant? He hadn't just been talking about making love?

God. Hadn't he mentioned changing his mind about

having children? She could have sworn the word
"maybe" had been in there, though.

Had he talked to his mother about it before discussing it properly with her?

Luca came over and touched his mom's arm, saying
something that made her let go of Elyse's hands and
turn toward him. "She love…" the woman tilted her
head as if trying to find the right words. "She love you."

His mom's gaze swung back to her.

She expected Elyse to respond? What could she say,
when this went to the very heart of her fears?

Of course Luca would want more children. And she'd
fostered that expectation by saying they didn't need to
use a condom. No wonder he'd seemed so happy about
it. He'd thought they were on the same page.

Oh, how wrong he was.

He and his mom had been talking about children
and families. And they had left her completely out of
the conversation.

What would happen if he knew she couldn't have
any more?

That wasn't something she was going to discuss in
front of anyone else. And suddenly she didn't want to
discuss it with Luca either. Not now. Maybe not ever.

Hurt and regret streamed through her system. If he
hadn't left and had been beside her during her pregnancy, he would have known exactly what she'd gone
through. The heartbreak of finding out she could never
have another child.

But he knew none of it. And she hadn't told him
when she'd had the chance, allowing things to become
twisted beyond repair. Just like they had in Atlanta.

"Ellie, are you okay?"

The room was blinking in and out of focus, and she realized tears were very near. She could answer his mom's questions truthfully, if she chose to: Yes, she loved her son. And, no, she wouldn't be having any more of his babies.

"I'm fine." She forced a smile, desperately needing to escape. "We'll have to sit down and talk about that. But I think Annalisa is about ready to get up."

"I'll come up with you," Luca said.

"No." She snatched a quick breath. "I'll bring her down in a few minutes, once I've fed her."

His mom came over, her smile gone. "You cross…" she pointed at herself "…me?"

Elyse's heart did the very thing she'd feared. It snapped in a few more places.

She leaned over and kissed her cheek. "No, I'm not cross. I love you." She hoped the woman would understand those simple words, because she did. She loved Priscilla, Carlos, Isabella and Sarita and most of all, Luca. She'd fallen in love with his whole family while getting to know them this week. But she couldn't stay here any longer.

The smile came back even as Elyse's tears floated closer to the surface. She was going to leave. She had to. The thought of telling Luca the truth was suddenly the last thing she wanted to do. He deserved to have those babies. Italian babies. Babies that were part of a large and happy family. She'd seen evidence of that wider family last night. They loved each other, had laughed and conversed. Even if he loved her, she didn't want to keep him from what someone else could give him.

He would get over her. He had once before. Quite easily, in fact.

She knew exactly what she was going to do. She was going to make sure Priscilla had some quality time with Annalisa today, and then her aunt was suddenly going to call her and ask her to return to the States. Her ticket back home wasn't for a couple more weeks, but surely she could find a flight out of Italy sooner?

And then she was going to try to forget this trip had ever happened. She would make sure Luca and his family were able to see Annalisa, but as far as rekindling a dead romance, she was going to let those smoldering ashes grow cold, once and for all.

CHAPTER THIRTEEN

SHE MADE IT to the airport.

God, she couldn't believe she'd gotten out of the house without Luca cornering her. Sporting dark glasses to keep anyone from seeing the state of her eyes, she went to the desk to ask about getting on the first flight she could find. Anywhere in the United States would work. She could worry about getting back to Atlanta once she was there.

She should have told him about the hysterectomy from the very beginning, but her stupid pride had kept telling her it was none of his business.

Well, she'd made it his business when she'd had sex with him. But to try to clear it up now?

No way. He'd said he wanted more children. He might be able to unsay it, but he couldn't un-want it.

"I need a flight to the United States. The first one you have available, please." Peg, who'd never intended on staying for the entire month, had flown home almost three weeks ago, and Elyse missed her desperately right now. Anna was in her baby sling and Elyse had one suitcase with her. She'd left everything else behind. Not that he'd try to come after her.

Except he might. She had his daughter. This wasn't like last time, when he had been the one who'd left.

The woman behind the desk leaned closer. "Are you okay? Do you need help?"

Yes. She needed a ticket. Then she realized the agent thought she was in some kind of trouble.

Of course, you dummy. You didn't give her a destination other than the whole country.

She was eventually going to have to get back in touch with Luca and work out arrangements for visitation. But she could do that with a long-distance phone call––the longer the distance the better.

"I'm fine, sorry." She reached in the front pocket of the diaper bag and pulled out her original ticket and handed it to the woman. "I need to get home sooner than I expected, that's all. Are there any flights to somewhere in Georgia or, if not, one of the neighboring states?"

The ticket agent looked relieved. "Let me see what I can do." She did some clicking of keys, her mouth twisting one way and then another as she seemed to mentally shoot down each option. "Wait. I think I can get you to Atlanta, actually. The flight leaves in two hours. You'll have a few hours' layover in Miami, if that's okay."

"Yes, that's perfect. Thank you so much." She tried to smile but was well aware that it didn't quite come out the way she'd hoped. "How much for the ticket?"

The price was steep. Very steep. But it was worth it. "I'll take it."

She took out her wallet, only to have a voice behind her say in English, "The lady isn't going anywhere."

Elyse froze. No. It couldn't be.

She whirled around.

Luca! How had he…?

How had he gotten here so fast? Unless he'd left Rome at around the same time she had.

She could hear the ticket agent asking her again if she was okay. She wasn't. Not at all. But unless she wanted the authorities called and Luca hauled away for something he didn't do, she needed to allay the woman's fears. She took a deep breath and faced her once again. This time there was a phone in the agent's hand. "Would you like me to call someone?"

"No, I'm sorry. He's the baby's father." Then realizing that sounded off as well, she explained. "We're both her parents. Everything is okay."

She got out of line, hoping that she hadn't just sunk their chances of talking this through without getting arrested.

Walking a few feet away, she half hoped he wouldn't follow her. But of course he did.

He stared down at her, then his hand went to his baby's dark head, sifting through the wispy strands. Anna looked up at him, her face breaking into a toothless grin.

Guilt clawed at the edges of her heart. This was wrong. She shouldn't have left without talking to him first, should have realized he would figure out where she was.

This time when the tears came she didn't try to stop them. "You shouldn't have come."

"Yes. I should have. I'm prepared to go back to the States with you if necessary until you tell me why we can't be together." He removed her sunglasses and lifted her chin. "Don't shut me out, Ellie. You did it in Atlanta too, and it tore me apart. Talk to me. Is it something I did or said?"

"No, you didn't do anything. I— It's…" She swallowed hard. "Why are you here, Luca?"

"Isn't it obvious? I love you."

Oh, God, she was right. But it was too late.

She shook her head, the tears coming faster. "It's not going to be enough."

"Why? If you're talking about the layoff, it doesn't matter anymore. We'll work at different hospitals." He used his thumbs to brush away her tears.

"It…" She closed her eyes and tried again. "You want more children, and I can't have them."

He frowned. "What?"

This was where he would hear what she had to say and walk away.

Or would he?

There was only one way to find out.

"The reason I didn't come to Italy with Anna before now was that when she was born there were complications. I had to have a hysterectomy. I can't carry any more children." Ever.

"But the condom… *Dio*. You said we didn't *need* it, not that you didn't want me to use one."

"You misunderstood. And I misunderstood when you said you wanted more. I thought you were talking about more…" she lowered her voice "…sex. But you actually meant you wanted more children."

She sucked down a breath. "And then your mom told me to have more of your babies and—"

"One minute." He appeared to be working through something. "First of all—how do you say it? My *madre* isn't the boss of me. Not since I turned eighteen."

"I know, but—"

"I am not finished." He pressed his forehead to hers.

"I did say I wanted more children, but it was in response to what I thought you wanted when we were in bed. Would I like more children? Yes, maybe in the future. But there are other ways of expanding our family and plenty of time to work it out. For now, you and Anna are enough. You will *always* be enough."

It couldn't be this easy. Could it?

"It's not fair to you."

"No." He plucked her old ticket from her hand. "This is what isn't fair. You leaving without telling me."

"You did it to me once."

His eyes closed. "And I was wrong. What I felt when I realized you were gone… *Dio*. I put you through hell, didn't I?"

"I think we put each other through hell."

"No more. The only question I have is this. Do you love me?"

She licked her lips. One last hurdle. *Do it, Elyse.*

"Yes, I love you. But what about your job? My job?"

"Those are things we can work out. Together." He slid his arm behind her nape and pulled her cheek to his. "When I realized you weren't in your room and that most of your belongings were gone, I couldn't believe it. My hands shook, and my gut twisted inside me.

"I made a mistake by leaving Atlanta last year. I told myself a hundred times I should go back and talk things out with you, but my pride wouldn't let me. And the longer it went on, the less likely it seemed that you would want me back. But this time—this time—I wasn't going to repeat that mistake. I am ready to move heaven and earth to make this work." He took a deep breath. "I just needed that 'yes' to my question about you loving me."

He kissed her forehead and then his daughter's.

"Whether we're here or in the States, the only thing that matters is that we're together. Our little family."

"I want that too."

His finger traced down the side of her face. "Anna is going to need both of us. And when the time comes, we'll add more."

Before she could react, he smiled. "I've always wanted to help children who are in difficult situations. What do you think?"

"Adopt?" She said the word softly, not quite believing that he was saying the very thing she had thought of doing.

"Yes. Would you like that?"

She closed her eyes and sucked down a deep breath, believing at last. "Yes. I would love that."

"So...there's only one more question. Will you marry me? My *mamma*, she's old-fashioned, remember? And she's very good at throwing big parties. Or a big wedding."

Somehow she didn't think this had anything to do with his mom's prowess as a hostess.

"Well, we wouldn't want to disappoint your mom, would we?"

"So your answer is yes?"

"It's definitely yes."

With that, his lips came down on hers with a promise of things to come. Of promises kept. Of futures realized.

And this time she was not going to second-guess herself. Or him. She was just going to love him. And let herself be loved.

There was nothing more important than that.

EPILOGUE

THEY'D TIED THE KNOT. Not because of Annalisa or anyone's parents, but for them. And true to form, Priscilla had put on the wedding of the century, even though they would have been just as happy standing before a justice of the peace. Elyse had talked Luca into letting his mom have her way. It made her happy.

And Luca had chosen Enzo as his best man, despite those earlier fears. It gave Elyse confidence that he trusted their love was strong enough to withstand any storm.

Her parents and Peggy had flown in from the States to celebrate, and Peggy had pulled her aside to whisper, "I knew it wasn't finished between you two. If Anna hadn't pulled you together again, he would have come back for you."

Luca had admitted as much in the breathless moments after the ceremony was over and they were ensconced in their swanky hotel room. "I already knew I'd messed up. My conscience wasn't going to leave me alone. It might have taken as much as another year, but I would have flown back to Atlanta and confronted you."

She'd shivered at the confirmation of her aunt's words. For her part, Elyse told him why she'd withdrawn back then as he held her tight and kissed her on the temple. "I'd had a bad office romance, and I was determined not to do it again. But then you came along, and I felt like I was making some of the same old mistakes."

"But we won't. I promise you that."

Promises were made and kept. She'd promised to talk to him instead of withdrawing emotionally, and he'd promised to call her on it if she didn't.

She'd torn her plane ticket up and called the hospital administrator and officially resigned, deciding to spend six months in Italy immersing herself in the language and culture. How could she not? Hadn't Luca done the same in America? Her Italian still wasn't the best, but she'd learned what some of those naughty words meant, and they made her blush even harder. She still had another month of language school, and then they would decide where to go from there.

Right now, none of that mattered.

Luca came up behind her on the veranda and looped his arms around her waist. "Everything okay?"

Turning to face him, she leaned back on the railing. "Just counting my blessings."

"You were up late last night and early this morning too."

"Thanks to you." She tipped her face up to look into those dark eyes she loved so much. "You know you're very sexy in the morning." She reached up to run her fingers along the stubble lining his jaw. He had on an old faded T-shirt and pajama bottoms and his tanned feet were bare. Sexy didn't begin to describe her husband.

"And you're evading my question."

She laughed. "You didn't ask a question. But I heard what you were asking. No regrets. I'm happy. Anna loves you desperately. I love you desperately. I'm just enjoying the moments we have to ourselves. Now that she's older, we don't get many of them."

So far they hadn't talked any more about expanding their little family. Adoptions in Italy had stringent requirements and they'd need to be married for three years before going through the process. And there was always surrogacy, if they decided to harvest her eggs. They had time. For once, Elyse was in no hurry to get things done.

"Emilia likes eating with her. You should give yourself a break every once in a while."

"I've had a long break. And I appreciate all her help. I just don't want to miss anything," she said.

"I know what you mean."

She wrapped her arms around his neck. "I'm so grateful for second chances."

"So am I." He leaned down and brushed his cheek against hers, before murmuring. "I love *second* chances. And maybe even third chances. Very, very much."

Since they'd made love only an hour earlier, he surely couldn't mean…

Something stirred against her. A sensation she knew all too well. "You're kidding."

"Does it feel like I'm kidding?"

The man was insatiable. And she loved it. They had a lot of time to make up for.

"Well, then, what are you waiting for?"

He swung her up in his arms. "Is that an invitation, *Dottore Venezio*?"

Dr. Venezio.

Oh, how she loved hearing him call her that. And, yes, she loved second chances. Would never tire of them.

"It is indeed, *Dottore Venezio*."

Then he was striding back through the French doors that led to their bedroom. Their own private sanctuary, where nothing was taken for granted, and where every kiss, every touch, every sigh centered around the most powerful word of all time: love.

* * * * *

COMING SOON!

We really hope you enjoyed reading this book. If you're looking for more romance, be sure to head to the shops when new books are available on

Thursday 27th June

MILLS & BOON

Coming next month

THE ARMY DOC'S BABY SECRET
Charlotte Hawkes

Tia had no idea how she got home. One moment she was leaving the lifeboat station, shifting her car into gear and hurtling out of the car park. The next, she was pulling into her father's driveway, blinking away the tears that threatened to spill out over her cheeks the entire eight-minute drive. And as she hurried up to the house her heart lifted at the sight of Seth's face peering out of the window, and his elated grin as he blew her frantic kisses.

She couldn't get her key in the door fast enough as she heard him racing down the hallway, already babbling to her about his day with Grampy. What was it about the prospect of a squeezing hug from her son that promised to settle her churning stomach and the turmoil of the past few hours better than any antacid ever would?

The door was barely open before Seth was dragging her inside, a finger painting in one hand and a sticky piece of toast in the other.

Reaching out, she began to close the front door when a foot wedged itself in the way.

A big, biker-booted foot.

She almost tipped backwards in her haste to stand up. Instinct making her send her curious son to his grandfather and closing the living room door behind them.

She hadn't even noticed him following her, let alone heard his bike. Yet there it was, parked right on the driveway as though he had every right to be there.

And Zeke, looming and furious, in the doorway. His eyes locked onto the closed door as she gripped the handle as though that could somehow delay the inevitable.

'What the hell, Tia?'

'Zeke…'

She should have told him. Back there in the lifeboat station. It was why she'd come back to Delburn Bay the moment she'd discovered Zeke was in Westlake.

Waiting for the right moment had been a mistake, because there was never going to be the perfect opportunity for giving a person that kind of news. And in delaying, she'd only made things ten times worse. A hundred times.

'I have a son?'

Continue reading
THE ARMY DOC'S BABY SECRET
Charlotte Hawkes

Available next month
www.millsandboon.co.uk

LET'S TALK
Romance

For exclusive extracts, competitions
and special offers, find us online:

 facebook.com/millsandboon

@MillsandBoon

@MillsandBoonUK

Get in touch on 01413 063232

For all the latest titles coming soon, visit
millsandboon.co.uk/nextmonth